Raymond L.

The Forgotten
The Confederation and The
Empire at War

A Forgotten Empire Novel

(The Forgotten Empire: The Confederation and The Empire at War, Book 5)

By
Raymond L. Weil
USA Today Best Selling Author

And

Julie Weil Thomas

The Forgotten Empire: The Confederation and The Empire at War

Books in the Forgotten Empire Series

The Forgotten Empire: Banishment (Book 1)
The Forgotten Empire: Earth Ascendant (Book 2)
The Forgotten Empire: The Battle for Earth (Book 3)
The Forgotten Empire: The War for the Empire (Book 4)
The Forgotten Empire: The Confederation and The Empire at War (Book 5)
The Forgotten Empire: War in the Confederation (Book 6)
The Forgotten Empire: The Fall of the Confederation (Book 7)

Website: http://raymondlweil.com/

Copyright © August 2021 by Raymond L. Weil Publications
All Rights Reserved
Cover Design by Humblenations.com
ISBN: 9798468653319
Imprint: Independently published

Raymond L. Weil

This book is a work of fiction. Names, characters, places, and incidents are either products of the author's imagination or used fictitiously. Any resemblance to actual events, locales, or persons, living or dead, is purely coincidental. All rights reserved. No part of this publication can be reproduced or transmitted in any form or by any means without permission in writing from the author.

DEDICATION

This book is dedicated to my dad, Raymond. Without him and his amazingly creative mind, none of us would have the pleasure of escaping to worlds and galaxies that only he could create. These characters and storylines allow all of us, and especially myself, to feel as if he's still right here with us showing us these new worlds and new possibilities.

My dad was not only a creative storyteller, but an amazing dad. From teaching us a good work ethic out on the farm to how to put together a great science fair project. Also, teaching us about teamwork and perseverance through coaching both my brother's soccer teams growing up as well as mine. He taught us how to be great parents, and how to have a long lasting marriage. How to be a great friend, how to laugh, and a lot about how to chase our dreams.

Dad never gave up on his dream of being an author, and look at the legacy that gave all of us. A place to escape, even if only for a little bit, from the things that trouble us. Worlds where anything is possible. A legacy that will live on for as long as someone somewhere is reading his words and stories.

The number of fans who have reached out to us to say how his writing has touched them and allowed them to escape their troubles has really inspired and touched our hearts. We thank you all, the fans, for allowing his legacy to live on through all of you.

I will do my best as I continue his storylines for as long as the fans are interested in reading them. Thank you for the opportunity to honor my dad and his legacy in that way.

The Forgotten Empire:
The Confederation and The Empire at War

Chapter One

An emergency meeting of the Great Council of the Confederation had been called by all the member races—except the Morag. Morag Councilor Damora was greatly aggravated, yet he would attend this meeting, even though he was wanted back on Morag Prime for a special meeting of the Morag High Council to discuss the disaster that had occurred in attacking the Human Empire. He was still in shock after being informed by High Councilor Addonis of the extent of the defeat.

The Morag fleets were decimated, and none of the objectives of the attack were achieved. It was the greatest single defeat in Morag history. Even more worrisome, the Druin and Zynth fleets had withdrawn shortly after Morag Admiral Norlan took over the minds of thirty Druin command crews and ordered them to death by suicide by flying their warships into the huge Human base on the inhabited moon of Gideon. This mistake by Admiral Norlan could create a deep and everlasting fissure in the council.

Stepping into the council chambers, Councilor Damora came to a sudden stop. Every one of the councilors for the other six races wore Lormallian telepathic nullifiers. "What is the meaning of this!" demanded Damora, his anger rising. "Nullifiers were not to be shared with other races!"

"We have decided the Morag can no longer be trusted," explained Lormallian Councilor Ardon Reull, pleased with how all the other races were now distrustful of the Morag. "You have lost the major portion of your fleet in attacking the Earth and now the Human Empire. As a result, I believe we can expect retaliatory raids soon, against our own worlds here in the Confederation."

Damora walked to his large chair and sat down, glaring at the other councilors with angry red eyes. "How dare you furnish nullifiers to other races. You agreed not to! Why have you broken your word?"

Ardon shrugged his shoulders. "You are the ones who are not trustworthy. By seizing the minds of thirty helpless Druin command crews, you murdered them, forcing them to commit suicide with their warships. What gives you the right to commit such a heinous crime against a fellow race of this council?"

Damora went silent for a moment. For the first time in thousands of years, the minds of the other councilors could not be influenced. "We are the most powerful of the seven races. The decisions we make in battle are not to be questioned. We do what is needed to keep this Confederation safe from outside influences, such as the Humans. I will remind all of you that we still have sufficient warships to crush any of your races if necessary."

Ardon's gaze focused sharply on Damora's. "But can you take on *all* of us? I have spoken to my government, and we are willing to furnish nullifiers to any of the other races represented by this council. Your days of mind control are over."

"How we conduct war is none of your business. We did what had to be done to defeat the Humans."

"But that failed," pointed out Ardon. "The Humans have demonstrated they are more powerful than you, and now, thanks to the new weapons they have developed, may be a threat to the entire Confederation. Your desire for war may have brought about the end to this Confederation."

Damora stood to his full height, his expression full of his growing anger. "The Humans are not more powerful than the Morag. The Humans are a weak race. It's only the defenses they have put around their worlds that challenge us. In a fleet-to-fleet battle, we would destroy them."

"I question that," replied Ardon. "I suspect, if the fleet numbers were equal, the Morag would easily be defeated by the Humans and their new weapons."

"You have created a threat to the entire Confederation," whistled the Zang councilor, his wings spread wide. "The Humans won't only come for you. Now they will come for all of us. It is your manipulations of our minds over the many centuries that has brought us to this point. Well, that time has come to an end. You will no longer manipulate us, and we will decide what to do, without you planting false ideas in our heads."

Klug, the Morphene councilor, stood. His constantly shifting form now resembled that of a pale humanoid. "The Morphene will no longer take part in this war. We now declare ourselves neutral and will notify the Humans of our decision. We greatly regret some of the atrocities we were forced to commit in the past, due to the manipulation of our minds by the Morag. Morag vessels, both warships and trading vessels, are now banned from our region of space."

Damora glared at the Morphene councilor, and then he looked over at Clun, the Druin councilor. "What about the Druins?"

"The Druins will stand by the Morag," said Councilor Clun reluctantly. "After all the Humans we have killed in the name of the Confederation, they will come after us as well." Clun paused and looked at Councilor Damora. "However, from now on, our crews will be protected by Lormallian nullifiers, so the Morag cannot control our minds. Our ships will no longer commit suicide, due to your mental manipulations."

"The Lamothians will stand by Morag as well," spoke the Lamothian councilor. "However, there is a condition. Any Humans we capture can and will be used in our feasts upon our worlds."

"You will bring the wrath of the Humans down upon you," warned Ardon. "They will not forgive you for what you have already done, and, by consuming more of their kind, their anger will only grow. They have already destroyed one of your worlds. Do you want the rest destroyed as well?"

The Lamothian councilor went silent and merely gazed at Damora.

"The Morag agree with the Lamothian condition," replied Damora. He then turned toward the Zynth. "What will the Zynth do?"

"We have not made a decision," replied Councilor Ralor Conn, as he dragged his sharp claws across the council table. "My government is still discussing our options. Councilor Damora, I should inform you that the leaders of the Zynth are now protected by Lormallian telepathic nullifiers to ensure Morag does not influence our minds. When my government has made a decision, you will be informed."

Damora looked at all the councilors, his gaze finally falling on Ardon. "I will leave now for a meeting with the Morag High Council. I should warn you that much of what you have done today will not go over well with them."

"So be it," replied Ardon. "We no longer fear you, and you cannot control our minds. This is a new day for the Confederation, and we will no longer be surrogates for the Morag."

Damora didn't say anything as he walked from the council chambers.

Ardon watched him go. "This council is now split between those of us opposed to what the Morag have forced us to do over the years and those who still support this evil race." Ardon looked at the Druins and the Lamothians. "The Humans will soon be coming for your worlds, and I don't believe you will stop them."

Ardon then switched his attention to the Zynth. "All the Morag wants is to use your race as cannon fodder in their war with the Human Empire. Make sure your government understands this. I no longer believe it is possible to defeat the Humans, particularly now that Earth is involved. We have seen them develop two new and terrible weapons. What will they develop next?"

The Zynth representative seemed to consider what Ardon had just said. "I will take your words back to my government. However, I fear the time for my people to change our ways is long past. We have embraced the ferocity of our past. For that reason, I feel certain my government will decide to join with the Morag."

Ardon nodded. The Zynth no longer controlled their own destiny. That destiny had been changed by the mental manipulations of the Morag. Ardon wondered how much harm the Morag had done to the other races. Every day Ardon became more familiar with what had been done to the Lormallian race.

However, for the Lormallians, it was not too late to return to a better life, away from cruelty and barbarism. Already changes were being implemented on all the Lormallian worlds.

One more thing Ardon had to do in the next few days. The Visth had contacted him to inform him that the Humans wanted to set up a meeting. The Visth had volunteered their world for that meeting and had also guaranteed his safety. Knowing the future of his people might very well depend on meeting with the Humans, Ardon had agreed. He also knew that, if the Morag ever found out, they would most likely kill him.

—

Admiral Cleemorl watched as Rear Admiral Barnes's supply fleet arrived in the Tantula System. The supply fleet consisted of ten dreadnoughts, forty battlecruisers, two mobile repair yards, twenty-eight supply ships, and twenty-three battlecarriers. The mobile repair yards were massive and the largest vessel ever built by any Human world.

"Why so many supply ships?" asked Colonel Jase Bidwell.

On one of the viewscreens, a large supply ship became visible, revealing a few missile ports and some energy beam turrets. "Many of them contain additional attack interceptors and parts for the interceptors. They also have extra rounds for the accelerator cannons, as well as missiles."

On another viewscreen, a pair of battlecarriers could be seen. "We sure could have used those battlecarriers earlier," said Colonel Bidwell. "Are Rear Admirals Barnes and Collison still going to attack the Confederation?" That was the original plan, before the Confederation launched their massive attack against the Empire.

Admiral Cleemorl nodded. "That's the plan. From what Rear Admiral Barnes told me, they will combine their fleets and concentrate on Morag shipyards, so they can't replace the ships they lost in the battles. The more they can reduce the size of the Morag fleet, the longer we'll have to get the Empire put back together and to repair the damage some of our worlds suffered."

Dylan looked at another viewscreen that showed Gideon. Hundreds of supply ships and other vessels from across the Hagen Star Cluster were at work on the large inhabited moon. The atmosphere was still a dark gray, with scattered static lightning. Dylan knew from the latest reports that nearly sixty-two million people had died on the moon during the attack. That was nearly 10 percent of the moon's population. At the moment, most of that population was living in massive underground bunkers.

"Admiral, we have a message from the *High Kingdom*," reported Lieutenant Trent Newsome. "They are ready to leave orbit, as soon as you give approval."

Dylan switched his gaze to another viewscreen, revealing the massive Imperial dreadnought that would be the home to Princess Krista Starguard for the next few months. She would be traveling to many of the more heavily populated worlds between the Hagen Star Cluster and the periphery of Human space, trying to get them to join the Empire. Krista would be traveling with a heavy escort. Dylan had assigned six additional dreadnoughts and thirty battlecruisers as a protective force. While he felt certain all the Confederation forces had pulled out of the Empire, he would not take any chances with the Princess's life.

"Inform Captain Barrow he can leave at his discretion."

"Captain Barrow says he will see you in a few months," replied Newsome.

Moments later, the massive dreadnought and its accompanying fleet vanished from the viewscreens, as the ships made the transition into hyperspace. Captain Barrow had orders to stay in contact with the *Themis* via hyperlight transmissions. Barrow was to send a message every four hours as to the fleet's location and the world or inhabited moon they planned on visiting.

Dylan had made arrangements for Rear Admiral Fulmar to stand by with a task force, in case Captain Barrow ran into any trouble.

"I understand the core worlds are sending out dozens of emissaries to speak to the governors and mayors of many other worlds," said Colonel Bidwell.

Dylan nodded. "Yes, the Princesses and the Imperial Council want to use the next few months to fully reform the Empire. If we can continue to build up our defenses and our fleets, we can make the Empire secure from future Confederation attacks."

At least that was what they were hoping. With a deep sigh, Dylan looked at another viewscreen, showing Tantula Five. Cheryl was out house shopping with the governor's wife, and they could be looking at anything from a quaint country home to a fancy mansion in the suburbs of the capital.

A few days later, above Golan Four, Vice Fleet Admiral Derrick Masters watched as Rear Admiral Collison's supply fleet dropped from hyperspace. The fleet had twelve dreadnoughts, twenty-three battlecruisers, two mobile repair yards, and eighteen supply ships.

"That will give Rear Admiral Collison thirty-five more warships to add to his fleet," commented Colonel Sheena Bryant.

Derrick nodded. "All of his supply ships are armed as well."

"How soon before all his damaged ships are repaired?" Collison's fleet was taking priority in repairs, as he still planned on attacking the Confederation. They were currently scattered in repair bays across the core worlds.

"Two more weeks," replied Derrick. "Some of his ships were hit pretty hard." Derrick's own flagship was still badly damaged and waiting for time in a repair bay. Ongoing repairs were being made, but some of the large holes in the outer hull would need some yard time to properly repair. Currently he wouldn't dare risk a hyperspace jump with his ship.

Derrick looked at the large tactical display. So far, nowhere in Human space had there been any signs of Confederation ships. Layla and the Imperial Council had emissaries out everywhere, trying to encourage more worlds to join the Empire. So far, they were having some success, and, if everything went as Layla hoped, the Empire would soon be the largest it had ever been.

-

Morag Admiral Voxx had his fleet in orbit around Morag Prime. Nearly half of the two thousand ships he had returned with would need some serious repair. Even two of the Conqueror class battleships that had survived the battle would need some yard time.

Admiral, you are being summoned to report to the High Council Chambers, reported First Officer Bale.

Admiral Voxx stood and looked at Bale. He knew what this might mean. *There is a chance you will soon be in charge of this fleet. Someone must take the blame for what happened in the Human Empire, and I am the only surviving admiral who was involved in the attack.*

You served the Morag well, replied Bale. *I'm sure the council will realize that.*

Let's hope so, replied Voxx, as he turned to leave the Command Center, fully expecting to be executed.

-

The High Council of the Morag was once more in session. This time some of the lower councilors, who did not normally attend the meetings, were present, filling out the council to its full fourteen members.

Head Councilor Addonis stood and looked at the other councilors with deep concern. *We may have doomed ourselves by attacking the Humans and particularly Earth.*

Impossible, responded Councilor Hiram. *We are the greatest military power in the known galaxy.*

Councilor Addonis looked over at Admiral Voxx. *Will you please give a detailed report of what happened to the fleets under the command of Fleet Admiral Colane, Fleet Admiral Torrant, and Admiral Norlan.*

Admiral Voxx was surprised at the request but did as asked. For well over an hour, he described the battles, the errors made, and the new weapons of the Humans. Several times he was stopped and asked to describe a particular aspect of the battles in even more detail.

The only reason I could save thirteen of the Conqueror class battleships is that they were more toward the center of the formation and not in the back with the rest. The Visth and their allies caused tremendous damage to the fleet because they attacked when the fleet was most vulnerable.

You identified over twenty-two different races involved in the attack with the Visth? asked Councilor Delann, showing considerable concern.

Admiral Voxx nodded. *Yes.*

We are losing control of many of the worlds outside of Confederation space, sent Councilor Hiram. *Can we send some fleet units to bring them back into the Confederation?*

Councilor Addonis shook his head. *We don't have the ships to send, without risking the security of our own worlds. At the moment, we have 4,238 modern Morag warships still available, plus those that returned with Admiral Voxx, and many of those need to be repaired. We also have 8,215 reserve vessels that we can use as well.*

It's still a sizable fleet, sent Councilor Dulant, who very seldom attended a meeting of the council, though he was a powerful telepath.

But one which we need to protect our worlds.

What about bringing more ships out of the reserve? asked Councilor Delann.

Councilor Addonis shook his head. *All that are left are very old, with weak weapons. They would be nearly useless in battle.*

Everyone looked at one another. No one had ever imagined the Morag being in this situation.

Do you think the Humans will attack us? asked Councilor Lomor.

Undoubtedly, answered Addonis. *The Earth Humans will definitely launch an attack after what we did to their Solar System. There is a possibility the two Earth fleets that showed up in the Empire at opportune times were actually sent to attack us but were forced to cancel their attack to help the Human Empire instead.*

There are some other issues this council needs to be made aware of, sent Councilor Damora. *The Great Council is splitting. We may only have a couple races who will still support us, the Druins and Lamothians. The other races are declaring their neutrality in this war against the Humans. The Zynth are undecided and will inform me later of their decision. Also all of the Great Council members wore the telepathic nullifiers developed by the Lormallians.*

This caused a stir among the High Council.

I thought they agreed not to provide any race—other than the Zang—with the nullifiers, sent Councilor Brant. *The Lormallians must be punished, if they have broken their word.*

How? asked Councilor Addonis. *We don't dare risk starting a war with other Confederation worlds right now. We must rebuild our fleet and keep the borders of our own space secure. Councilor Damora, it is essential that you return to the Great Council and ensure the Zynth stay with us. Also inform the Druins, the Lamothians, and the Zynth that the Morag High Council has made it illegal for any fleet admiral to control the minds of other races during a fleet battle. Other races' ships will not be used as suiciders.*

14

Damora nodded. *I will tell them, but they may not believe me. There is one more thing. I believe the Humans knew about our attack before we launched it.*

How! demanded Councilor Addonis, his eyes narrowing.

I believe the information came directly from the Great Council. We have intercepted a few messages between Lormallian Councilor Reull and the Visth. I believe Reull passed the information to the Visth, who in turn passed it on to the Humans. From what Admiral Voxx has told us, the races that attacked our fleets in the Golan Four System were also protected by nullifiers. It is obvious to me the Lormallians are trying to split the Great Council.

Councilor Addonis took a deep breath. *The time of the Great Council's usefulness may be coming to an end. I want secret talks held with the Druins, the Lamothians, and the Zynth, about forming a military alliance with us. That would give us four against three, and I doubt if the other three races would dare to anger us. It would at least guarantee there is no conflict within Confederation space between any of the seven races. At least not until we deem it is time.*

What about Lormallian Councilor Reull? asked Damora. *He is the cause of all of this confusion in the council.*

He must be eliminated, responded Councilor Dulant. *But it must be done in such a way that the Lormallians will not suspect we were behind his death.*

Councilor Damora shook his head. *They will suspect anyway, but I agree he needs to be terminated. He has become too much of a disruptive force in the council.*

Keep an eye on Councilor Reull, ordered Addonis. *If the opportunity provides itself, we will take him out.* Addonis then turned back to Admiral Voxx. *Admiral Voxx, effective immediately, you are hereby promoted to the rank of Fleet Admiral. You are now responsible for ensuring the safety of all of Morag space.*

Admiral Voxx was surprised but nodded his head. *Thank you, High Councilor. I will make the necessary arrangements. However, I should caution all of you. I believe, as soon as the Humans are able, they will attack us.*

Councilor Addonis nodded his head. *I agree with you. I don't believe the attack will come from the Empire, and they don't have the ships to attack both us and to defend their worlds. No, the attack will come from Earth, and they won't hesitate to bomb our worlds, if they can get to us. That is why we must continue to increase our defenses around all our worlds and inhabited moons. We must also increase ship construction to the maximum, and we must begin the construction of more shipyards.*

I would suggest we work hard on weapons development, suggested Councilor Delann. *The Humans have developed two new weapons, while we still rely on what we have always used. Surely our scientists can come up with something.*

Addonis went silent, and then he sent a message to all the councilors. *We recently sent a number of our best scientists to Bator Prime to search for potential weapons in the archives. They found nothing that would be new. I suspect, since the Lormallians control the archives, all such information has been removed or hidden.*

The archives are supposed to be available to all seven races, protested Councilor Brant.

They were, but we changed the rules when we began to use telepathy to control key members of the other races, sent Addonis. *I suspect we will find many things now blocked to us.*

What does this mean for our future? asked Councilor Lomor.

Nothing! answered Addonis. *Not if we take swift action now. It just delays everything a few years. We will build a fleet so powerful that no race or races will stand in our way. In time the entire Confederation will be under our power, as well as the Human Empire, Earth, and the races who have dared to leave our control.*

Addonis was confident the Morag would reign supreme in the end. There could be no other way.

Chapter Two

High Princess Layla Starguard was meeting with Chief Chancellor Stein, Fleet Admiral Marloo, and several other members of the Imperial Council in a conference room at the Imperial Palace on Golan Four.

"We lost nearly 47 percent of our active fleet units in the battles with the Morag," reported Admiral Marloo. "The Resistance fleet lost 32 percent of their active units, primarily because, in the Resistance fleet, a majority of their warships are smaller support vessels."

Layla nodded. She had called this meeting to better understand what the fleet needed and what the current assessment was of the danger from the Confederation. Layla also had a few other items she wanted to discuss. "Isn't it about time to join the Resistance ships in with the Imperial fleet? Many of the worlds that are producing Resistance vessels are already a part of the Empire."

"It won't be that easy," answered Chancellor Stein. "Many of those worlds, while a part of the Empire, are still fiercely independent."

Layla understood that. If it weren't for the Resistance, the new Empire could never have come into being. "I have no problem with that. The Resistance has done much to help build the Empire, but those days are now past. Every day we have new worlds asking for admittance. With every new world, we have more shipyards available to build warships. Already the Hagen Star Cluster, the Haven Nebula, the Vortex Worlds, the Lamina Stars, Vidon Seven, Helgoth, Xnea Two, Cleetus Three, Lydol Four, Bratol Three, Malor Two, Leonora Five, Macron Three—and of course the core worlds—have shipyards capable of building the ships we need."

"Some of the other worlds that have joined the Empire are in the process of building shipyards with our aid," added Chancellor Stein. "Soon we will have a massive ship-building capacity. Even some of the core worlds are adding new shipyards. No one wants to fall back under Confederation rule."

"All good news," said Layla. "We currently have 475 planets and inhabited moons in the Empire. By the end of three more months, I want that number to be over one thousand."

Everyone in the room looked at one another incredulously.

"One thousand?" asked Lindsay Littrel of Jalot Four, her eyes growing wide. "Are we ready for such an expansion of the Empire?"

"We need to get ready," replied Layla determinedly. "The House of Worlds is designed to handle the delegations of one thousand worlds. I've already ordered that it be expanded to handle twelve hundred."

"Twelve hundred," replied Chancellor Stein. "That would be larger than the original Empire."

"We have more inhabited moons with large populations," explained Layla. "Many of them are completely independent of their home systems or planets. They deserve the right to be represented in the House of Worlds."

Admiral Marloo leaned back, as he contemplated those numbers. "That would give us an unbelievable ship-building capacity."

"Those added worlds would have to be defended," added Governor Gregory Staley of Aquilla Three.

Layla nodded. "For the next few years, the entire Empire will be on a war footing, until the Confederation is no longer a threat. Already in the core worlds, we have an excess capacity to build defensive grid elements and even warships. We must continue to do so, until we consider the new Empire to be safe from attack."

"We must continue to research new weapons," added Admiral Marloo. "The Morag have seen our particle beam cannons, as well as Earth's accelerator cannons. It's only a matter of time before either they build defenses against those weapons or develop their own."

"Is that why Rear Admirals Collison and Barnes are going ahead with their planned attack on the Confederation?" asked Governor Alex Therron of Bratol Three.

"Part of it," replied Admiral Marloo. "The other reason is the Morag are at their weakest right now, after the losses they suffered in the recent attacks. Their worlds may be vulnerable, and, if we can destroy a number of their shipyards, we may buy considerable time to rebuild our fleets."

"How much time?" asked Governor Able Marsk of Lamora Seven.

Fleet Admiral Marloo let out a deep breath. "Maybe six months or more."

Layla was surprised at the time Marloo had mentioned. "How many warships could we have at the end of six months?"

"It depends on how many worlds we can get to join the Empire and how soon we can get their shipyards producing warships. At a conservative estimate, I would say our Imperial fleet could number six thousand or more."

Chief Chancellor Stein slowly nodded his head. "We need those six months. Can we afford to send any additional ships with the rear admirals, when they launch their attack?"

Fleet Admiral Marloo frowned. "Maybe a few. Our fleets have been hit pretty heavily. I'll speak to Vice Fleet Admiral Masters and Admiral Cleemorl and see what they think."

"One more thing I want to talk about," said Layla, as she looked at the people in attendance. "The Visth have informed me that Lormallian Councilor Ardon Reull has agreed to meet an Empire representative on the Visths' homeworld."

"What do we know about this Lormallian?" asked Governor Marsk.

Fleet Admiral Marloo was quick to answer. "Evidently he's the one who's responsible for the telepathic nullifiers. He's also been challenging the Morag at every opportunity in the Great Council—to the point that he is gravely concerned about his own life. He's extremely upset by what the Morag have forced his people to become. Already, due to his encouragement, the Lormallians are launching numerous reforms on their own worlds, as well as on the worlds they control. This might be an opportunity for us to drive an even larger wedge in the Confederation's Great Council."

"What about all the alien worlds that have joined with the Visth?" asked Governor Littrel. "I understand they have asked about joining the Empire."

"They have," replied Layla. "From the latest reports given to us by the Visth, nearly 347 worlds have broken off from the Confederation and seek admittance to the Empire. I believe Chancellor Stein can report on what we have been considering."

"I'd suggest that they form their own combined government, similar to ours, but there will be no monarchy, as these are dozens of different races. We would be willing to assist them in forming a new universal government. We would also be open to signing a mutual defense pact, as well as a lucrative trade agreement."

"Will they have consulates in the Empire?" asked Governor Littrel.

Layla nodded. "They will be allowed to have a delegation in the House of Worlds, so we can stay in better touch on developments, and they will have a method of making proposals to the House of Worlds or its individual members on trade."

"One more thing," added Fleet Admiral Marloo. "Many of those 347 worlds are already building warships to defend their planets. Give them six months of no interference from the Confederation, and they could easily have a fleet numbering around four thousand vessels or more. Keep in mind, like the Resistance, they do build a considerable number of smaller support ships."

"Can we send any ships to help protect them, until they're ready to defend themselves?" asked Governor Staley. "It seems to me that the more races we have who are willing to fight against the Confederation, the better off we'll be."

Fleet Admiral Marloo frowned but understood the necessity of allies. "Maybe in another month we could send a light task group. I don't believe we dare send more, not if we decide to send ships with the two Earth fleets to attack the Morag."

The meeting lasted for another few hours, with the group voting overwhelmingly to send a representative to meet Councilor Reull. They also agreed to help the Visth and the other alien races aligned with them in forming a new government similar to the House of Worlds.

Derrick was in a large shuttle, hovering near the site of the destroyed big shipyard. Already dozens of work shuttles and hundreds of construction robots busily cleared the site, preparing to start construction on the new shipyard, which would be even bigger. It would have both particle beam cannons and Earth's accelerator cannons built into it. It would be the largest shipyard ever built in the Empire, and it would have the firepower of a battlestation.

Shuttles moved large pieces of wreckage with their tractor beams, and their automated arms could grab and hold on to things. The wreckage would be taken to one of the space stations, where it would be melted down and recycled into beams, trusses, and metal plating.

Derrick watched as the shuttles moved carefully through the wreckage, while the pilots picked out the parts they wanted to remove. The work robots were already assembling the outer shell of the new shipyard. So far, only a few beams were in place.

"It's a start," commented Colonel Sheena Bryant, piloting the shuttle today, as she wanted the practice. Her hands flew almost effortlessly across the controls, as she moved the shuttle around the wreckage.

Derrick let out a deep sigh. "So much loss of life."

The space around Golan Four was full of the wreckage of numerous warships. It was full of bodies too, and several shuttles were assigned the duty of gathering those who had been killed for proper burial services. It was a gruesome job, but it had to be done.

"We have a lot of Morag wreckages as well," said Bryant. "I understand we found one of the big Morag battleships nearly intact."

"Yes, a lucky shot took out its power plant and opened up a large portion of its hull. The crew died rather quickly, and nearly 80 percent of the ship is still intact. We've already got people on board, searching it for anything that might be useful."

Derrick's gaze focused on a shuttle positioning a large piece of wreckage with one of its manipulator arms. Once the pilot was satisfied, he activated the shuttle's tractor beam, and the piece of wreckage followed the shuttle.

"Another twenty hours, and they'll have all the shipyard wreckage hauled over to the space station for smelting."

Derrick nodded. "Three months from now, the largest shipyard in the Empire will be here."

"Hard to believe," said Bryant. "We build things so fast nowadays."

"It'll only get faster, now that we're out from under the Confederation's influence." Derrick gazed out the shuttle's cockpit windows, which surrounded him, giving him a nearly unobstructed view of space and Golan Four.

In the distance, he saw an Imperial dreadnought and several battlecruisers orbiting the planet. He still had a sizable fleet in the Golan Four System, though much of it needed to spend some time in the repair bays. Derrick turned his attention to Golan Four.

The atmosphere of Golan Four was still a little gray from the antimatter warheads that had struck the planet. Massive storms were slamming into the coasts from the numerous antimatter hits to the oceans. Even the planet's weather control system could not contain the massive storms. Most of the coastal areas were covered in clouds and heavy rain.

Flooding was going on too, and energy shields were used to protect cities in danger from the storms. Some of those storms had winds in excess of three hundred mph. The meteorological people claimed the storms would continue for another two or three years, due to all the water vaporized in the antimatter strikes.

"It's really raining in Queen City," commented Bryant, as she gazed out the forward cockpit window. "My family lives nearby in a small mountain resort area, and they say they're seeing a lot of flooding in the lowlands."

Derrick nodded. "There'll be a lot of flooding in the lowlands near the oceans for the next few years." Derrick had no idea how many millions of tons of water had been vaporized in the Morag attack.

Colonel Bryant turned the shuttle and headed back toward the *Destiny*. "One of the shipyards contacted the *Destiny*, just before we came out here. They'll have a repair bay available for us the day after tomorrow."

"That's good," replied Derrick.

Derrick was anxious to get his flagship repaired. He had placed Rear Admiral Collison's ships as a priority for the shipyards, as Collison would soon be heading for the Confederation to attack the Morag shipyards. Once *Destiny* was in a repair bay, Derrick planned to go down to Golan Four to spend some time with Layla. For the last several weeks, he had been too busy taking care of his damaged ships and ensuring the system was secure. He was ready for some downtime, and seeing Layla again would go a long way to making him feel like he was home again.

The next day Layla met with Chancellor Stein. "Who should we send to meet with the Lormallian councilor?"

"He's actually a member of their government," replied Stein. "We need to send someone high enough up so he won't feel slighted. Keep in mind the person we send will be on the Visth homeworld as well, and we need to make a good impression."

Layla smiled. "I know just who to send. We'll send Andrew and Kala."

Chancellor Stein nodded his agreement. "I think that would be a good choice. We also need to send a military liaison as well."

Layla frowned. "That'll be more difficult."

"I may have an idea. What if we send Rear Admiral Carrie, an Earth Imperial representative, and General Gantts from the core worlds, to show Earth as our ally too?"

"Can we afford to send both of them?"

"Rear Admiral Anderson and his ships are due in tomorrow. They have been at Xnea Two, having their ships repaired. He's done quite well in the battles he's been involved in, and Admiral Masters needs another rear admiral."

Sadness covered Layla's eyes. She could still see the *Defiant*, smashing into the Morag flagship, all to protect Derrick's flagship. At that moment Rear Admiral Audrey Banora had died. Audrey had been one of Derrick's closest and longest friends. "Why don't you get with Fleet Admiral Marloo to make the military arrangements, and I'll speak to Andrew and Kala. The sooner we get this mission on the way, the better I'll feel about everything." Layla knew, if she could keep some of the Confederation races neutral, it could make a huge difference in the war.

-

One week later, Lormallian Councilor Ardon Reull was on his way to the Visth homeworld. He was in a special diplomatic vessel that Lormallian leaders often used to travel between various worlds of the Confederation. It was a small passenger liner, with half a dozen suites for diplomats. The ship had no armament, as it was a diplomatic vessel. However, it did have an extremely powerful energy shield for emergencies. In recent days Councilor Reull demanded that the ship be equipped with a more powerful fusion energy power plant. He wanted the strongest energy shield possible to protect him, as he was convinced the Morag wanted him dead.

-

The ship had taken a roundabout way to leave the Confederation to not be detected by the Morag. It was currently on a direct course for the Visth homeworld and should arrive in six more days, due to the extralong course they had chosen.

Captain Verdi Stord was in command of the ship and knew how important this mission was. All the members of his crew were required to wear the personal telepathic nullifiers at all times. In addition, the ship itself had the shipwide nullifiers installed. Captain Stord was taking no chances on any member of his crew falling under the mind control of the Morag.

-

Three days had passed, and Councilor Reull was in the Command Center, speaking to Captain Stord. They had dropped out of hyperspace to confirm their spatial coordinates, before continuing on to the Visth homeworld. "When we get back, I'll send you some computer files as to what our worlds were once like. You will be shocked to find out what the Morag have done to our civilization."

"I've heard of a few things," confessed Captain Stord. "I fear it will be very hard for our people to change from how we have led our lives for all these thousands of years."

"I agree," replied Ardon. "That is why the Ruling Triad has decided to implement these changes slowly. It may take several generations before we see major changes in our society."

"So long?"

Ardon nodded. "For some of us, it will be much quicker. However, for our population as a whole, it will only change with the education of our young people. Several curriculums in our school systems are being changed, and more will be as the years pass. In time, we will be the type of civilization our remote ancestors could only dream about."

At that moment, the sensor alarms sounded, and Captain Stord looked worriedly at the sensor officer. "What do we have?" Even though he had a horrible feeling as to what the sensor officer would say.

"Six Morag warships," reported the sensor officer. "Two battleships and four battlecruisers. We are already being targeted by their weapon systems."

"Raise energy shield," ordered Captain Stord. "Send out an emergency message, requesting aid."

"We're being jammed," reported the communications officer. "I can't get anything out."

The ship suddenly shook violently as a Morag antimatter missile detonated against the energy shield, nearly throwing Ardon to the deck. He quickly found a vacant seat and strapped himself in.

"I can't believe the Morag would attack a diplomatic ship," muttered the captain, as he tried to think of what to do. "Helm, how soon before the hyperdrive is recharged?" The drive had to be charged after every jump.

"Seven minutes," replied the helm officer.

On the viewscreen, the six Morag ships were rapidly closing the distance. They were now firing fusion energy beams at the ship's energy shield. "How is the shield doing?"

"Eighty-two percent and holding," replied the ship's first officer. "It might last another three or four minutes, but that'll be it."

"More contacts," reported the sensor officer excitedly. "It's our escorts."

Captain Stord smiled. Councilor Reull had said he fully expected the ship to be attacked. So, to be on the safe side, they had an escort force following ten minutes behind the ship.

In space on board the Lormallian battleship *Hammers Hand*, Admiral Mont Keld smiled as he saw the Morag warships. He had always wanted to take on a Morag ship, and now he had six of them in front of him. Admiral Keld had six battleships and fourteen battlecruisers in his task force. All protected by telepathic nullifiers. "Target those Morag ships and open fire!"

All the Lormallian warships opened fire with every weapon they had. Instantly the Morag energy shields were covered in weapons fire, as raw energy crawled across them. The attack was so sudden and so brutal that two of the Morag battlecruisers' energy shields failed, leaving their hulls open to attack. Fusion energy beams drilled into the hulls, opening up compartment after compartment. In just a matter of a few moments, the two Morag warships were riddled from fusion energy beam fire and were lifeless, just drifting dead hulks.

-

Morag Squadron Commander Zola was thrown from his command chair, as his shields took a tremendous strike of antimatter missiles. *Status!* he sent, as he stood and returned to his command chair. This time he buckled himself in.

It's a Lormallian fleet, replied the sensor officer. *I'm detecting six battleships and fourteen battlecruisers.*

The commander reached out with his mind to try to influence the command crews of those ships. His mental probe was stopped a good fifty meters from the hulls of the vessels. *Nullifiers. All ships switch your fire to the Lormallian warships.*

His mission was a failure. Even if he destroyed the diplomatic ship carrying Councilor Reull, the Lormallian fleet would know what he had done. No doubt it would result in war between the Morag and the Lormallians. The plan had been to destroy the diplomatic ship and let it be assumed it had just vanished somewhere in space. That could not happen now. He sent a brief message to his tactical officer. *While our other ships hold off the Lormallian warships, destroy that diplomatic ship in front of us.* He knew that time was rapidly running out.

-

Captain Stord was surprised by the renewed attack on his ship. However, he was fairly certain one Morag battleship would not bring down his ship's enhanced energy shield, at least not before the hyperdrive was charged. On the viewscreen, the battle in space was intense. The Lormallian escort ships continued to close, causing more damage to the Morag forces. Another battlecruiser blew apart, as an antimatter missile struck its hull. One of the battleships was split in two when an antimatter missile slammed into the center of the ship. Fusion energy beams then carved up the two pieces, making them lifeless.

"Two minutes until we can enter hyperspace," reported the helm officer.

-

Morag Squadron Commander Zola grew more frustrated with every passing minute. Only his battleship and one of his battlecruisers still survived. The rest had been destroyed by the Lormallian escort fleet. He had also just discovered that his own communications were being jammed. He knew, if he could just get a few thousand kilometers from the jamming signal, he could send a hyperlight message. He was about to order the helm to move his ship away, when a powerful force seemed to shove his ship sideways.

At the same time, he thought he heard a distant explosion. Using his telepathy, he checked the minds of his crew and discovered a massive hole in the side of the ship near engineering, and the sublight drive had been destroyed. The hyperdrive had also been heavily damaged.

Looking up at one of the viewscreens, he saw his remaining battlecruiser vanish in a massive fireball of antimatter energy. Leaning back in his command chair, he saw the diplomatic ship vanish as it entered hyperspace. His mission was a complete failure, and he knew he was about to die.

-

Lormallian Admiral Keld smiled to himself, as the full power of his fleet was turned against the lone surviving Morag battleship. It had already been heavily damaged, and its weapons fire had dropped dramatically. Keld watched one of the main viewscreens, as antimatter energy crawled over the battleship's shield, causing it to flare up brighter and brighter, until it suddenly collapsed.

Dozens of antimatter missiles slammed into the ship's hull, detonating in massive bursts of energy. When the energy cleared, the enemy battleship had been completely vaporized. Only a few wispy clouds of glowing plasma survived.

Checking his own fleet, he lost one battlecruiser, with two others lightly damaged. "Set a course and continue to follow our diplomatic ship. I want a seven-minute interval between us and them."

Admiral Keld would follow the ship all the way to the Visth homeworld. Once there, he would keep his fleet on the periphery of the system, until Councilor Reull was ready to return. While Admiral Keld doubted the Morag would attack again on the return trip, he would not take any risks with the councilor. Councilor Reull was just too important to the future of the Lormallian race.

Chapter Three

Andrew and Kala were on board the stealth destroyer *Starburst*. It had been designed to carry the Royal Family to safety in the case of an emergency. Since Princess Krista had the dreadnought *High Kingdom*, Andrew and Kala had decided to use the *Starburst* for their trip to the Visths' homeworld.

"What do you think the Lormallian councilor will have to say?" asked Kala, as she leaned back on a comfortable couch in the Royal Suite.

"It's hard telling," replied Andrew. "They only recently learned how the Morag have been controlling them. From what I understand, Councilor Reull talked the Lormallian Triad into siding with the Empire and the Earth Humans, rejecting the Confederation. The Zang and Morphene went along with them. From the reports we've managed to get, considerable friction exists in the Great Council between Councilor Reull and Morag Councilor Damora. So much so that the Lormallians sent a very powerful escort fleet to ensure Councilor Reull makes it to this meeting."

"Are we in any danger?"

Andrew smiled and sat down next to Kala, pulling her close. "Rear Admiral Carrie and General Gantts will make sure we stay safe. We have a substantial escort fleet as well."

"These negotiations will be important, won't they?"

Andrew nodded. "If we can keep some of the Confederation races out of the war, it greatly improves our chances of winning."

Kala let out a deep sigh. "Science is so much easier to deal with."

"Have you heard from your father recently?"

"He's moved to a new dig site in Africa. He says the clues he's uncovered in his previous digs all point to an area in the southern part of Egypt."

"I'm curious to see what he finds. I can't imagine what the connection can be between Earth and Golan Four."

Rear Admiral Carrie was on board her dreadnought, the *Exeter*. Currently she was in the Command Center, watching the tactical display. So far, they had encountered no hostile contacts, and they should arrive at their destination in another two days.

"Do you think it was wise for us to bring so many ships, considering how weak we are in fleet units at the moment?" asked Major Sullivan.

"It was a necessity," answered Rear Admiral Carrie. "We must keep Prince Andrew safe, and, if we can form a working alliance with these worlds, it will give us over 347 additional planets to help in the war against the Confederation. That alone makes it worth taking this risk." Carrie looked up at the tactical display, noting the friendly green icons of the fleet she had brought with her. She had four battlecarriers, eight dreadnoughts, and thirty-three battlecruisers. If it came to a battle, she was confident she had the ships needed to either protect the *Starburst* or to allow her to get safely away.

Stralon Karn, the Visth ambassador, paced nervously in his quarters. The Visth were a humanoid species, with a greenish tint to their skin and very large eyes. The hair on the top of their head was white and very thick. The Visth controlled eleven star systems and had been subjugated by the Confederation several thousand years in the past.

"We must ensure security is at a maximum," Karn said to Admiral Larr, who was in charge of all fleet units from the Visth worlds, as well as those allied with them.

"I believe we have a sufficient-size fleet stationed in the system to ensure security. Twenty-seven battlecruisers as well as 212 support ships. In addition, part of the Human task force assigned to help our worlds is here as well. It's provided four dreadnoughts and twelve battlecruisers."

Stralon Karn nodded. "Let's hope that's enough. This is a meeting the Morag won't want to see happen. They may have found out about it and will take steps to see that it does not occur. Barring any problems, Councilor Reull will be here late tomorrow and the Humans the following day."

"As soon as Councilor Reull arrives, I will increase our defensive readiness. After the Morag's defeats in the Human Empire, I doubt if they will attack, but we will be ready if they do."

"I expect both the Lormallians and the Humans to bring along a decent-size fleet to help protect their representatives, so our forces will not be alone, if it does come to a battle."

Admiral Larr walked over and gazed out the balcony at the capital city. It was busy as always, with just a hint of smog in the air. Efforts were already underway to completely clear the air. The smog was a direct result of how the Confederation had demanded they operate certain factories. "What do you think the Humans will offer us?"

"I don't know," replied Karn. He was a little apprehensive about that. "They have asked for as many representatives of the races aligned with us to be present for these meetings. Nearly every one of the worlds that are with us in this revolt are sending representatives. These meetings could be the most important we have ever held, particularly if we want to stay free of the Confederation."

"The Morag suffered massive losses in their attack on the Humans," pointed out Larr. "At the moment, I don't believe the Morag are in a position to attack. We have a few months to work on our fleet and to prepare ourselves for the next attack."

Representative Karn looked with alarm at Admiral Larr. "You believe the Confederation will attack us?"

Larr nodded. "As soon as they've rebuilt their fleets."

Karn took a deep breath. "I believe the Human Empire needs us as much as we need them. We must form an alliance of equality and respect, something we did not have with the Confederation. Many other worlds have approached us about joining our alliance. In one year's time, we could be as many as the Human Empire. If we can come to the proper agreements between the Humans and us, we would never have to fear the Confederation or anyone else again."

"We must learn from the failures of the Confederation," said Larr. "We must never treat another intelligent species as they have treated us."

Outside, the sun was setting, displaying a magnificent sunset. The lights of the city blinked on one by one, as darkness descended. Larr turned away from the window and spoke to Representative Karn. "The Humans have much to teach us. We must not be afraid to learn."

Karn nodded. "I am curious as to who they have sent to represent them. It will tell us much as to how serious they are in taking this meeting." Karn had no idea who the Human representatives were. It had been kept a secret to prevent the Morag from finding out. "Tomorrow we must finish our preparations to receive our guests. We have set up quarters for both the Humans and the Lormallians. Let's hope they approve of them."

The next day Councilor Reull's ship dropped from hyperspace, close to the planet. Ardon Reull was in the ship's Command Center and instantly saw numerous ships around the Visths' homeworld. "Whose ships are those?"

"I've identified 126 from other races, as well as some Human warships," answered the sensor officer.

"Can the Humans already be here?" Ardon wasn't expecting them until the next day.

"I don't think so," replied Captain Stord. "I believe this may be a squadron of Human ships assigned to keep these worlds safe from Morag attack. I have heard rumors of this from some of our contacts, who we still have on a few of the worlds in this section of space."

Ardon nodded approvingly. It showed him these worlds were serious about resisting the Confederation. He would have to ensure all these worlds understood that the Lormallians and the Zang and the Morphene were now neutral. "Contact Representative Karn and ask him where he wants our ship."

-

Twenty minutes later, the liner was docked to a large space station, and Admiral Keld had his ships in orbit at 15,000 kilometers. Keld had been surprised when Visth Admiral Larr had suggested that orbit. Larr, when questioned, had admitted that he was concerned the Morag might attempt to disrupt the meetings.

After getting his fleet into orbit, Admiral Keld decided to keep his fleet at a higher alert level, just in case. Just like Admiral Larr, Keld did not trust the Morag. They might make another attempt on Councilor Reull's life. If they did, Keld and his fleet would be ready.

-

Councilor Reull was in his suite of rooms that the Visth had furnished for him. They were very similar to what he would find on his homeworld. The Visth had done very well in making him feel comfortable. At the moment, he sat at the small conference table in the outer room, speaking with Representative Karn of the Visth and Representative Jagger of the Cajjun.

Representative Karn was speaking. "Is there any way you will allow us to produce our own telepathic nullifiers? We currently have over four hundred worlds that want freedom from the Confederation, with more contacting us every day. We need millions of the nullifiers to protect our governments and our militaries."

"Have you changed your shipyards to begin producing more warships?" asked Ardon. They would need warships to protect them from the Morag, the Zynth, and the Druins.

Karn looked at Jagger and then replied, "Yes, it won't be long, and we'll possess a very powerful fleet."

"Do you swear never to use that fleet against any Lormallian or Zang or Morphene world?"

Karn nodded. "Yes. Turn over to us the secret of the nullifiers, so we can make our own, and we will sign such an agreement. However, the Lormallians and the Zang and the Morphene must promise never to attack a world outside the Confederation, unless your worlds have been attacked first."

"I think that can be arranged," replied Ardon. What he didn't mention was that he had intended to give the Visth the secret of the nullifiers anyway. No way he could produce enough in the factories on Proxy Seven to meet the current demand.

Ardon leaned back in his chair. "No doubt the Humans will be attacking parts of the Confederation. The Morag made all the races of the Great Council do many horrible acts over the years. I don't know if the Humans, and even some of the other races who are here, will ever forgive us for what we were forced to do."

"It was the Morag," growled Jagger. "They are an evil race, and now they must pay for their crimes against all races. The Humans are coming, and I suspect, when it is over, not a single Morag world left will be inhabitable. They will burn them all!"

"Not just the Morag," said Ardon. "The Druins and the Zynth are extremely warlike. No doubt the Morag were behind this deadly turn in their evolution too, but now I'm afraid it's too late for either to go back. Something will have to be done about them as well. I know the Druins are personally responsible for billions of dead Humans. That's a big weight now sitting on their shoulders, and one I'm afraid they will never escape."

"It is a horrible thing the Morag have done," spoke Jagger.

Ardon nodded his head. "I'm afraid you're right. Even in the last meeting of the Great Council, the Druins still support the Morag, even though they are aware of the mind control. The Zynth are hesitating, but I expect them to side with the Morag as well."

-

They talked for a few more hours, with several other alien representatives stopping by. Finally they all agreed to call it a night, and they would all reconvene the following day, once the Humans arrived.

-

The ship carrying Prince Andrew and the escort fleet dropped out of hyperspace in the Visth System. Rear Admiral Carrie was not sure what to expect.

"Contacts!" called out the sensor officer. "We have a Lormallian fleet in orbit around the Visth homeworld. We detect 6 battleships and 13 battlecruisers. Scans indicate they are at a high alert level. Also detecting 27 unidentified battlecruisers and 212 support ships."

"Those will be the Visth and their allies," said Rear Admiral Carrie, as she eyed all the red threat icons on the tactical display.

"Admiral, also some Imperial warships are in orbit. We detect four Imperial dreadnoughts and twelve Imperial battlecruisers."

"I have Visth Admiral Larr on the comm," reported the communications officer. "He says all ships in orbit are peaceful, and we're to go into orbit ten thousand meters above their homeworld."

"Looks as if they're not taking any chances of this meeting being interrupted," commented Major Sullivan.

"A lot of civilian ships are in orbit as well," added the sensor officer.

Rear Admiral Carrie nodded her head. "Take us in, but I want the fleet to stay at Condition Two, until we're satisfied everything is as it seems. Also, see if we can contact one of those Imperial dreadnoughts. Perhaps they can tell us more about what's going on."

-

Prince Andrew and Kala were in the Command Center of the *Starburst*, as they neared the Visth planet. The *Starburst* was in the center of its protective fleet, surrounded by dreadnoughts.

"They only have a moderate defensive grid around the planet," commented Captain Orin Darlu. "We're detecting only a few hundred energy beam satellites and six missile platforms."

"What about their shipyards and space stations?" asked Andrew. Looking at the tactical display, he saw one large shipyard and two decent-size space stations.

"All are armed," reported the sensor officer. "The shipyard is heavily armed. Also quite a few civilian ships of multiple types are in a lower orbit. I'm surprised they were not ordered to land or to jump into hyperspace for their own protection."

"This should be interesting," said General Gantts, who had just entered the Command Center.

"We're being contacted," reported the communications officer. "Representative Stralon Karn is asking how many will be in our party, coming down to the surface for the negotiations."

General Lyra Gantts looked at Prince Andrew. "Want me to handle this?"

"Perhaps it's best. We don't want them to know I'm on board until the last minute."

Gantts nodded her approval. With that, she walked over to the communications console and spoke to Representative Karn.

After a few minutes, General Gantts returned. "All the arrangements have been made. We've been invited to come down this evening for a reception, and they have suites of rooms ready for us. The rooms have been modified to accommodate Humans."

"They should not have had to do too much," said Andrew. "The Visth are very similar to us." Andrew looked at the viewscreen, as they neared the Visths' homeworld. It was a beautiful world, comprised of about 40 percent water and the rest landmasses.

"Reminds me of Golan Four," said Kala, as she gazed at the viewscreen. "We may find we have a lot in common with the Visth."

"Let's hope so," replied Andrew. "However, we have a very big meeting with Lormallian Councilor Reull tomorrow. If we can keep the Lormallians and a few more of the Great Council races out of the rest of the war with the Morag, it could be a game changer."

"That may be easier than you think," said General Gantts. "From what I've heard, the Morag and the Lormallians are very close to a state of war as it is. The only thing stopping it is the number of Morag warships we destroyed when they attacked the Hagen Star Cluster and Golan Four. From the hyperlight messages we've been intercepting, we know the Morag have pretty well pulled back all their remaining forces into their section of the Confederation."

Representative Karn was waiting, as the vehicles carrying the Human representatives arrived. He knew General Gantts was one, and he had briefly met Gantts one time. He was curious as to who the others were.

The doors to the first vehicle opened, and four Imperial Guards with their purple robes stepped out and quickly moved to the second vehicle. Karn suddenly felt apprehensive. Surely they had not sent one of the three Royals. The door opened, and General Gantts stepped out. She was followed by a woman and a man, who Karn instantly recognized. It was Prince Andrew, third in line for the throne. Karn had watched their wedding, which had been broadcast by hyperlight transmission across an immense region of space, including the worlds of the Visth.

Upon seeing the prince, he instantly motioned for all those with him to bow. The Humans must be taking these negotiations very seriously to send someone as high up as the Prince of the Empire. After bowing, he quickly stepped forward to greet the prince and those with him. "I am honored that the Empire sent such a high-ranking individual as yourself to these negotiations."

Prince Andrew smiled. "We take these negotiations very seriously. I'm sure our goals are the same as yours, and that is to keep our people safe from the Confederation."

"You are correct," replied Representative Karn. "If you and your people will follow me, I'll show you to your rooms. We have a reception and a banquet set up for later tonight to allow you to meet some of the representatives from some of the other worlds aligning with us."

"I'm excited to meet them," answered Prince Andrew. "The Empire hopes this is the beginning of a fruitful and beneficial alliance for all our people."

"I should mention the Lormallian Councilor is already here. The Morag attacked his unarmed diplomatic ship. Fortunately his armed escort fleet managed to defeat them. There is some concern the Morag may attempt to disrupt these meetings as well. That's why we have such a large fleet in orbit."

"If they attempt to disrupt these meetings, our fleet will help in the defense of this planet," assured General Gantts. "We are prepared, in case the Morag dare to show up."

Representative Karn nodded. "Now, if you will follow me." Karn felt that, so far, everything was going well, particularly with a Royal here.

Councilor Reull realized these negotiations had suddenly swelled in their importance. Representative Karn had just contacted him and told him who the Humans had sent as their representatives. The Empire had sent one of its Royals, as well as its leading general from one of its core worlds to these negotiations. Reull knew now, with the attendance of Prince Andrew, that Reull's very civilization could be at stake. His plans for these negotiations had now changed considerably. One misstep and he could doom the Lormallian race. There was no doubt in his mind that someday the Humans would be the supreme power in this galaxy, and he did not want his worlds to become desolate wastelands, all due to the crimes the Morag had forced his people to commit in the past. He did have one important card he could play that might be the saving point for the Lormallian race.

-

Andrew and Kala were at the reception, where hundreds of dignitaries from different worlds were gathered. Kala wore a long and luxurious gown, while Andrew was dressed in a uniform with a purple cape designated for his position. Wherever they went, their four Imperial Guards were always close behind. At the moment, Andrew and Kala were walking around the large room, introducing themselves to various alien representatives. Some of the representatives were humanoid, and others were completely alien.

The representative from Drexid Seven resembled a large spider but possessed a pair of hands. The representative from Baxor Seventeen looked like a Human-size snail. Everyone in the room wore language translators to make speaking to one another easier.

Andrew currently spoke with Representative Daxol Aard, who resembled a large bat but walked upright on two legs.

"My species inhabits sixteen worlds," said Representative Aard. "For as long as we can remember, we have been slaves to the Confederation. Freedom is new to us, and it will take time for all my people to grasp what that means. We are currently expanding our shipyards, so we can build larger military ships to help keep my people and those in this alliance free."

"It is a worthy idea, freedom," replied Andrew, impressed. "What you and your fellow races are trying to do is quite noble, and the Human Empire will be more than willing to help you in any way it can."

-

Over the next two hours, Andrew, Kala, and General Gantts talked to numerous races. The diversity represented in this room was amazing. Some were humanoid species, very similar to Humans, to other species who were totally alien and almost frightening to even look at.

Finally Representative Karn announced the banquet would start and asked all representatives to take a seat. As soon as they were seated, the food began to be served. In some cases, it had been necessary for chefs from some of the representatives' worlds to help with the food preparation. Karn didn't want to accidentally poison anyone.

Andrew, Kala, and General Gantts were seated at the head table, along with Lormallian Councilor Reull. General Gantts had already spoken briefly with Reull and had promised a longer conversation with Prince Andrew later.

-

Councilor Ardon Reull sat next to Representative Karn, as they prepared to eat. Ardon had made his rounds in the banquet room and had received a rather cold response from the other representatives present. He could well understand the response, particularly since the Visth had furnished him with a small security escort.

Representative Karn stood, getting everyone's attention.

"I want to thank all the representatives from the different intelligent species who are here tonight. This is a special and hopefully a momentous occasion. We have Prince Andrew of the Royal Family from the Human Empire, his wife, Kala, and one of the leading military Imperial officers in the Empire, General Lyra Gantts." Karn paused, looking around the room.

"In the meetings we have scheduled for the next few days, we want to create an alliance that will protect all our worlds against Confederation aggression. As some of you already know, the Human Empire has just recently smashed the main Morag fleet, forcing it to flee from its worlds. Lormallian Councilor Reull is offering us the telepathic nullifiers, so the Morag can never control our minds or thoughts again." He gave a nod of appreciation to Reull.

"I should mention that, while many in this room have no love for the Lormallians, they were played by the Morag with their telepathic skills, just as everyone else. They were forced to do things that, in normal times, they would never have done. So I ask you, when you speak to Councilor Reull, do so with an open mind." Karn stopped and smiled. "Now, let's eat!"

Ardon leaned over to Karn, who now sat again. "Thank you."

Karn nodded. "If we are going to make this peace process work, we all must realize the Morag are the enemy, not the other races who they controlled."

"Very good speech," commented Andrew, who was on the other side of Karn. "I'm looking forward to these meetings."

Karn nodded. He looked at Councilor Reull and then back at Prince Andrew. "If the two of you don't mind, I would like to set up a short meeting between the three of us after this banquet is over."

Everyone agreed. Shortly it would be time to get down to business, and no one was quite sure where that would lead.

Chapter Four

Later that evening Prince Andrew, General Gantts, Representative Karn, and Councilor Reull met in a small conference room, specially set up for them.

Councilor Reull stood, a serious look on his face. "First, let me say that I must apologize for any harm my people have done to either of your races. We only became aware of the Morag's mental abilities after High Princess Layla and Rear Admiral Carrie broadcast the secret of the Morag telepathic skills in a hyperlight message."

"I'm curious," said Andrew. "What were the Morag's reaction to that broadcast?"

Ardon sat back down. "They were furious at first and very threatening. They pretty much told the other six races of the Great Council that, if they refused to do as the Morag demanded, those races risked being destroyed by the Morag fleets. After that, I went to Bator Prime to the archives and had my brother, who is the head curator, do some research. He found the secret of the nullifier buried in some secret files, along with what the Lormallian worlds were once like." Ardon grimaced, as he shook his head.

"I was both amazed and shocked to see what the Morag had done to our culture. They had erased it and had replaced it with something dark and evil. I swore then that I would do everything in my power to bring down the Morag. I found a Lormallian world where I could produce the nullifiers, and, since then, the Morag have wanted me dead."

"I suspect there is a lot more to your story than what you just told us," Andrew said.

Ardon smiled. "Yes, there is, but it would take a very long time to tell what all happened." Ardon reached into his pocket and took out a small computer disk, which he slid over to Andrew. "That was also in the archives. When the curators of that time so long ago realized what the Morag were doing, they hid much of the military research of that time." Ardon sighed.

"Once the curators were satisfied everything was hidden, they committed suicide, so the Morag could not read their minds and, therefore, could not discover the secret information cache on weapons research. The information on that disk is from a race that has long since gone extinct.

"It describes a beam weapon that destabilizes the bonds between atoms. For the lack of better terms, I call it an atomic disruptor. The beam will cut right through an energy screen and then destabilize the hull material of a warship. It will turn the hull into a dark dust, as the atoms lose their bonding ability. From what I've read, there is no defense against it."

General Gantts picked up the disk and turned it over in her hands. "This weapon could bring this war to an end."

Councilor Reull nodded his agreement. "The research is not quite complete, but enough is there that your Human scientists should have no problem finishing it and producing a workable weapon."

Andrew leaned back, staring at Councilor Reull. "Why not give this weapon to your own people? They could take over the Confederation with a weapon like this."

Ardon sighed and shook his head. "My people are not yet deserving. We're still far too close to the evil that has guided us for thousands of years. Even though I love my people, I could not risk giving them such a weapon."

Andrew folded his arms across his chest. "What do you want of us?" Andrew suspected there had to be a catch somewhere. Councilor Reull would not have turned over such valuable information without wanting something back in return.

Councilor Reull closed his eyes and then slowly opened them. He took several really deep breaths, and then he answered. From a folder in front of him, he took out a sheaf of papers and slid them over to Andrew.

He continued. "I want a promise from the Human Empire to spare the Lormallian race, as well as that of the Zang and the Morphene. I've researched the Zang ancient history, and they were once a very peaceful race, one dedicated to music and flying intricate dances in the air. The Morphene history was not readily available, but to this day they are very logical and trustworthy. My own race was once peaceful too and dedicated to the arts and the sciences. We were nearly to the point of making our worlds into literal paradises, when the Morag intervened. We wish for a chance for the races of the Lormallians and the Zang and Morphene to return to those days.

"Those documents contain a nonaggression agreement between the Human Empire, the Lormallian worlds, and the Zang and Morphene worlds. It also allows for future trade when this war is behind us. I realize it will take time to develop trust, but I firmly believe, if we work at it, that it can be done."

Andrew picked up the papers and was surprised to see they were written in their current Human language. He glanced through the pages, reading a few sections. "I need to have some experts, who are familiar with such documents, look over this."

Councilor Reull nodded. "I expected no less."

Andrew looked over at General Gantts and then spoke. "I believe we can work out some type of agreement. We would like nothing more than to see the Lormallian worlds and the Zang and Morphene worlds stay out of this conflict we have with the rest of the Confederation."

"There will be heavy fighting in the Confederation eventually," said General Gantts. "As long as the Morag have their military, they will be a danger to others. Whether that means destroying their worlds or just destroying their ability to conduct war remains to be seen."

"I understand," replied Councilor Reull. "I should also tell you that my government has authorized a massive increase of defensive grids to be emplaced around our worlds, plus the expansion of our fleets. All of this is being done not out of concern for you Humans but out of worry that the Morag will try to consolidate the Confederation by putting it completely under their control."

"We can understand that," answered General Gantts. "If the situation were reversed, we would do the same thing."

For the next several hours, they discussed the agreement that Councilor Reull wanted, as well as several other important matters. In the end, everyone was satisfied they were on the right track. Now it was only a matter of working out the finer details, some of which would be done back in the Empire on Golan Four.

Andrew finally returned to his suite, where Kala patiently waited. "Did you do anything while I was gone?"

Kala shook her head. "I wanted to go for a walk, but the Imperial Guard at the door suggested I stay inside, since so many strange and unknown races are in the building."

"You could have gone with me," said Andrew.

Kala shook her head. "No way. I had enough of that when we went on our little diplomatic cruise. I turned on the viewscreen, but there wasn't much that I understood."

Andrew laughed. "You saw some of the alien races who attended the banquet. Can you imagine being an ambassador to some of those worlds?"

"At least you would have a staff of Humans and a Human-built embassy."

"We better get to bed," suggested Andrew. "We'll have a long day tomorrow."

Kala nodded. "Councilor Karn has arranged for me to go on a tour of the capital tomorrow and maybe do a little shopping."

Andrew shook his head. "Make sure you take two of the Imperial Guards with you to help keep the crowds back. You're a Human, and you'll stick out in the crowd."

Kala smiled. "Councilor Karn has already arranged for my security. I will be just fine."

Later as they lay in bed, Kala turned toward Andrew. "I heard a few people mention the Morag might attack in an attempt to disrupt these meetings."

Andrew was worried about this as well, but he wouldn't tell Kala. "We have a big fleet in orbit, and we'll be just fine. Now get some sleep."

Kala snuggled up next to him and was soon sound asleep. Andrew put his arm around his wife and lay here, thinking. He wished Chancellor Stein had come along; there was so much to do. Fortunately Andrew had General Gantts to fall back on, and she was an experienced negotiator. Closing his eyes, he tried to fall asleep.

In orbit, Rear Admiral Carrie paced in the Command Center. She didn't like the current situation. In the morning, Carrie would contact the Lormallian admiral. She had spoken briefly with him earlier and had suggested, for precautionary reasons, they combine their fleets. She would also have the four Human dreadnoughts and twelve battlecruisers in orbit join her fleet. If the Morag did try to disrupt the scheduled meetings, she wanted to be ready.

Andrew and Kala were up early the next morning, both having a busy day planned.

"When do your meetings start?"

"After breakfast," answered Andrew, as he put on his shirt. We have several small meetings planned this morning, with various representatives. The main part of the meetings will be about all these alien worlds forming an alliance beneficial to all. That's why we're having the smaller meetings to iron out any differences first, before we have the larger meeting this afternoon, where all the various races will attend. This evening I have another meeting with Councilor Reull to discuss a number of items we're both concerned about."

"How do you think that meeting will go?"

"Probably not too bad. I believe that Councilor Reull wants what is best for his people, though he's afraid it'll lead to war against the Morag eventually."

"We want that, don't we?"

Andrew paused and looked at Kala. "I don't know. If the Lormallians were to lose, then the Morag would control an even larger region of the Confederation. The best option seems to be to keep the Lormallians and the Zang and the Morphene neutral, while using them as a threat against the Morag."

"Will you tell Councilor Reull about the upcoming attack from the Earth fleets?"

Andrew shook his head. "Not directly. I may just assure Councilor Reull that, if there are attacks in the Confederation by the Humans of the Empire or Earth, the worlds of the Lormallians and the Zang and the Morphene will not be involved."

Kala nodded, as she moved over to a large mirror to do her hair. She could call in a couple attendants, who had accompanied them down to the planet, but she preferred doing some things herself.

-

Morag Admiral Marcello neared the homeworld of the Visth with his fleet. Looking up at the tactical display, he studied the green icons surrounding his flagship. He wished his fleet were larger, but, due to the recent battle losses, the ships he had were all the High Council felt they could spare at this time. Marcello had twelve battleships, one Conqueror class battleship, and seventy-four battlecruisers. Normally that would be enough to handle any problems on the Visth-controlled worlds, but now he was not so certain.

What is this meeting we're supposed to break up? asked First Officer Kinslo.

Some of our informants have told us that many of the worlds in this sector are holding a meeting to form an alliance to resist the Confederation. Also supposedly the Humans and Lormallian Councilor Reull are meeting there as well.

The Humans? responded Kinslo, not looking pleased to hear that. *They will have some warships present.*

Possibly, replied Marcello. *However, Squadron Commander Zola was supposed to have intercepted Councilor Reull's ship and destroyed it.*

Kinslo nodded. *I hope he was successful. Councilor Reull has become a major problem for our race.*

That's why we decided to eliminate him.

What will the Lormallians do, if they find out?

Nothing. We've set it up so it will appear that Councilor Reull's ship met with misfortune and just vanished. They will never trace it back to us.

Two hours until we reach the target system, reported the navigation officer.

Admiral Marcello nodded. They would drop from hyperspace and attack all the civilian ships in orbit and take out any military vessels that might be present. Then they would bombard the capital and the surrounding region to ensure any of the representatives from the worlds attending this meeting were all killed. That would end this rebellion and set an example for all other worlds.

Andrew was in his fourth meeting of the morning when loud sirens sounded. Representative Karn looked surprised and then stood. "Those alarms indicate that Morag warships have been detected. If everyone will follow me, we have an underground shelter we can go to."

Andrew suddenly worried about his wife, as Kala was out somewhere in the capital city on a shopping trip. Even as Andrew thought about that, two Imperial Guards came into the room, taking up a protective stance on either side of him. "It's the

Morag," Andrew explained. "They will be attacking shortly. Do either of you know where Kala is?" The Imperial Guards carried small communication devices, so they could stay in contact with one another.

"She's already heading toward a shelter," reported one of the guards. "I've been in contact with Rear Admiral Carrie, and we have a sizable Morag fleet heading toward the planet. Admiral Carrie is already moving her fleet out to intercept."

-

Rear Admiral Carrie studied the tactical display. She faced twelve battleships, one Conqueror class battleship, and seventy-four battlecruisers. In her fleet, she had twelve dreadnoughts, six battleships, and fifty-eight battlecruisers, plus the four battlecarriers, which trailed the fleet.

"We should have a slight advantage," said Major Sullivan. "But not much."

"Have the battlecarriers prepare to launch," ordered Carrie, as she thought how best to use the attack interceptors. "Medium-range missile strikes only to begin with." Carrie would launch the interceptors, once the two fleets were engaged. The interceptors did a better job of destroying damaged vessels, rather than attempting to batter down the energy shields of undamaged ships. She wanted to hold down the losses of the interceptors, if she could.

"Engagement range in eight minutes," reported the sensor officer.

"Contact Lormallian Admiral Keld. I want to explain to him what I'm planning." Keld's ships were on the right side of the wedge formation. Since joining the two fleets, they had practiced a few fleet maneuvers, just in case the Morag showed up. Carrie was glad they did.

-

Morag Admiral Marcello was stunned when he saw the fleet coming toward him. *Are those Lormallian warships mixed in with that Human fleet?*

Yes, Admiral, replied the sensor officer. *Detecting nineteen Lormallian warships.*

Marcello knew now the mission to kill Lormallian Councilor Reull had failed. That failure would have some huge ramifications when he returned and made his report to the High Council. The High Council had never considered Reull might take a large escort of Lormallian warships with him.

Captain Setak, sent Marcello telepathically. Setak was the captain of the Conqueror class battleship. *We must destroy the Visths' capital city. That will be where Lormallian Councilor Reull and the Human representatives will be, as well as many others of various races who have come for this rebellious meeting. As soon as we engage, you will take ten battlecruisers as escorts and proceed to do so.*

Consider it done, replied Setak.

We will hold the Human and Lormallian fleets here, and that should allow you to reach the planet.

Five minutes to engagement range, sent the sensor officer.

Admiral Marcello buckled himself into his command chair. He knew there was very little chance he would survive this engagement. The odds just were not on his side. *All ships prepare to engage.*

-

Rear Admiral Carrie watched the viewscreens, now showing the Morag fleet. To her, it seemed as if it had only been a few days ago when she had been engaged against the Morag over Golan Four, and now here she was again. On the screens, Morag battlecruisers and battleships were clearly visible. A slight shimmer around them indicated active energy shields.

"Three minutes to engagement range," reported the sensor officer.

"Admiral, see how the big battleship has pulled back, with ten battlecruisers as well?" asked Major Sullivan. "They could attempt to go around our fleets to attack the planet itself."

Admiral Carrie looked closely at the tactical display. "Either that or they are holding those ships back for the end of the battle. Contact Admiral Larr and inform him the Morag may attempt to go around our fleets and attack the planet, particularly the capital, where all the representatives are." Larr was in charge of all Visth-allied fleet units.

Carrie wondered if she should risk sending the *Starburst* down to pick up Prince Andrew, Kala, and General Gantts. Unfortunately Carrie doubted if she had the time. She just hoped they were all in safe locations.

-

Lormallian Admiral Keld sat tensely in his command chair. He wondered if he should take his fleet, pick up Councilor Reull, and make a run for it. His primary responsibility was to protect the councilor. Of course that would be a betrayal to the Humans, trying to defend the entire planet from the Morag. With a deep sigh, he knew what the councilor would say. "Stand by for combat," ordered Keld. It was time to make a stand with the Humans.

-

"Optimum engagement range," called out the sensor officer.

"Fire!" ordered Rear Admiral Carrie, leaning forward in her command chair. She felt her pulse racing, and the adrenaline flowed through her body.

From the Human and Lormallian fleets, every vessel opened up with every weapon they had. The front of the Morag fleet formation exploded with light, as hundreds of antimatter warheads detonated, and fusion energy beams probed the wavering screens for a weakness.

All twelve dreadnoughts that Carrie had with her had particle beam cannons, and these were tearing through the energy shields in the front formation of the Morag warships. Hulls were ripped open, and internal explosions shook the Morag vessels. The Morag still had no defense against the Human particle beams.

Rear Admiral Carrie felt the *Exeter* shake severely, as several antimatter missiles detonated against the ship's energy shield. The damage control console stayed green, so she let out the breath she had been holding. "Continue firing," she ordered. This battle had a long way to go before it was decided one way or the other.

Lormallian Admiral Keld watched with interest, as the Humans' particle beams smashed through the energy shields of the Morag ships, causing massive damage. He saw hull material hurled into space, as the beams carved huge rents in the side of the stricken vessels. "Make sure we record everything we can on those weapons." Now he understood how the Humans had vanquished the Morag fleets. Supposedly the accelerator cannons the Earth Humans had were even more devastating.

Morag Admiral Marcello winced as five of his battlecruisers and one of his battleships were blown apart by the Human attack. His own ships fired back, and now the front of the Human and Lormallian fleets were covered in weapons fire. Already one of the Human battlecruisers had been destroyed.

Captain Setak, it's time for your task force to make its attack. Make the Morag proud.

We will destroy the enemy's capital city. Nothing will stop me.

Admiral Marcello nodded. If Setak could destroy the Visth capital, their little rebellion would fall apart.

Moments later, on the main viewscreen, the Conqueror class battleship and its ten-battlecruiser escort accelerated and steered around the growing battle.

Rear Admiral Carrie saw the large Morag battleship and its escorts begin to move and quickly contacted Captain Anderson on the battlecarrier *Orion*. "Launch all your attack interceptors and hit those eleven ships heading for the Visth homeworld. Launch your missiles from medium range. Your targets are the battlecruisers. Leave that big mother alone. I'll detach a couple dreadnoughts to take care of it." Carrie had planned on using the interceptors against the Morag fleet in front of her, but it was essential they destroy that huge Morag battleship. It could not be allowed to fire upon the planet. It also meant the odds had shifted slightly in favor of the Morag.

"Major Sullivan, dispatch the dreadnoughts *Darklight* and *Corona* to intercept and to destroy that battleship. Send four battlecruisers as escorts." Carrie was weakening her fleet, but she didn't believe that Admiral Larr could stop the battleship with just his ships. That Conqueror class ship was just too powerful.

-

Morag Captain Setak had broken free from the embattled fleets and neared the ships protecting the planet. The ships were forming up in front of his fleet, creating a barrier. The tactical display revealed the Visths' 27 battlecruisers and 212 smaller support ships. *We will attack their center and blast our way through*, sent Setak to the captains of his ten battlecruisers. *I just need to get this battleship in the clear long enough to fire our missiles at the capital*. There was no doubt in Setak's mind this plan would work. The battlecruisers would clear him a path, and then he would finish the mission with his battleship.

-

Coming in from behind the Morag were 640 attack interceptors, followed by 2 dreadnoughts and 4 battlecruisers. Their job was to eliminate the ten battlecruisers, so the dreadnoughts could use their particle beam cannons to destroy the battleship.

Captain Stephens had been promoted from lieutenant to captain and was leading the amassed squadrons. "We will fire half our missiles at medium range and the rest at point-blank range. If any battlecruisers still survive, we will go in and rake them with our energy beams. We must clear a path for our dreadnoughts."

"We'll get 'em," boasted Lieutenant Gains. "We just won't miss with our missiles."

Captain Stephens smiled. "We'll come in above them. That way, none of our missiles will come near the planet. We'll begin our attack runs in thirty seconds. Good luck and good hunting." Stephens knew, as close in as they would go, a lot of his crews would not return to the battlecarriers.

-

When the sensor console blared a warning, Captain Setak looked over at it. *What is it?*

Human small attack craft are coming toward us, replied the sensor officer. *Estimate over six hundred. Also two Human dreadnoughts trailing, escorted by four battlecruisers.*

Captain Setak knew the Human attack interceptors could be dangerous just because of the sheer amount of missiles they could launch. This changed his plans. He had intended to use his battlecruisers to blast a hole through the ships defending the planet, and now his battlecruisers would have to destroy the incoming squadrons of attack vessels. He knew the odds of him reaching the planet had just decreased substantially.

-

Visth Admiral Larr saw what the Humans were doing. They were trying to ensure none of the Morag ships could get close enough to launch their missiles at the planet. He admired their bravery, but their fleet was suffering for it, as the Morag now had a slight advantage in overall firepower. "I want twenty battlecruisers ready to attack the front of that incoming Morag formation. All other ships will stay in their current orbits to protect the planet from missiles." Admiral Larr did not want to see his planet ravaged, as the Morag and the Druins had done to so many others.

-

The Human attack interceptors reached medium range and launched half their missiles. Thirteen hundred fusion missiles headed toward the ten Morag battlecruisers. Small bright explosions in space marked where Morag fusion energy beams intercepted some of them. Moments later, the interceptor missiles struck the energy shields of the Morag ships. All ten of the Morag battlecruisers were lit up with light, as fusion energy gripped their energy screens in a death hold. Three of the battlecruisers saw their energy screens fail, and subsequent missile strikes sent all three to oblivion.

The interceptors dove on the remaining Morag ships and suddenly found themselves under intense weapons fire. Even a few antimatter missiles went off in their midst.

Captain Stephens took a deep breath, as he saw the small and brief fireballs lighting up space. Each fireball was an interceptor being destroyed. Men and women he had known for months were dying.

"Nearly there," reported the navigation officer.

Stephens nodded and then keyed his comm unit. "All interceptors go in close, and let's finish this."

The surviving interceptors split apart and dove on the remaining enemy battlecruisers. Space was once more lit up, as fusion explosions crawled over Morag energy shields. Energy shields began to fail, and, when they did, interceptors went in close and fired fusion missiles at the vulnerable hulls of the ships. Morag battlecruisers were torn apart, sending glowing debris flying through space. If the destruction wasn't complete, interceptors would go in close, strafing the ships, ensuring they were dead.

"All missiles have been expended," reported the weapons officer.

Captain Stephens took in a deep breath. "All interceptors, return to the battlecarriers. We've done all we can here." Looking out his cockpit window, Stephens saw only two surviving battlecruisers and the big Morag battleship. It would be up to the two trailing dreadnoughts and four escorting battlecruisers to finish off the Morag ships.

Looking at his tactical display, Stephens noted he had lost over two hundred of his interceptors. Going in close like they did always paid a heavy cost in lost interceptors and crews. Stephens just hoped many had managed to eject.

-

Morag Captain Setak was angry. The Human attack interceptors had taken out most of his battlecruisers. *Battlecruisers Arl and Mact, I want you to drop back and to protect this battleship from the Humans' new weapons. I'll attempt to take my battleship through the approaching Visth forces.* Setak had already noticed the twenty battlecruisers approaching from the planet.

Captain Setak looked over at the helm. *Increase speed by 40 percent. Tactical, launch missiles on my command and keep launching. Your target is the planet's capital city. I want it hit with as many missiles as possible.* Setak had already determined that he would not return from this mission, but he still planned on accomplishing it. He was a Morag, and a Morag did not fail.

-

The battleship suddenly leaped forward, as it accelerated toward the planet. Its weapons were focused on the incoming Visth ships, and soon their screens were lit up with heavy weapons fire. Two Visth battlecruisers near the center of the formation exploded, and the Morag battleship darted through the hole in the line. The battleship's energy screen was lit up, and a few fusion energy beams managed to penetrate, carving out deep gashes in the side of the ship. A few internal explosions blew out sections of the hull, sending debris flying across space.

Fire on the planet! ordered Captain Setak, seeing his opportunity. His battleship shook badly, and he knew it would not survive much longer.

From the ship, missiles began to launch, all targeting the planet. He never noticed the damaged Visth battlecruiser that suddenly slammed into his ship. In a massive explosion, both vessels vanished, as they were obliterated.

-

The defending ships began firing on the nearing missiles. Bright explosions in space indicated where some of the missiles were intercepted. However, a few made it past the ships. The defensive grid opened fire, but it was not strong enough to take out all the missiles. Two got through and headed toward the surface. In a massive explosion, the first detonated above the city. Fortunately, the city was protected by an energy shield, and the blast only caused the screen to flicker in a few places. But the second missile slammed into the weakened shield, causing it to fail. Deadly antimatter energy shot into the now-unprotected city.

The shield had held back most of the deadly power of the blast but not all of it. Even so, buildings caught fire, and some collapsed beneath the deadly but weakened blast wave. The entire city shook, causing a few more buildings to collapse. All the power in the city died, and most communication systems stopped functioning. Hundreds of thousands of civilians were trapped in underground shelters and in basements. Many of those caught out in the open were killed.

-

Kala was in a deep shelter, with her two Imperial Guards, when the antimatter missile hit, knocking down the energy shield. She felt the ground shake, and then the lights went out, only to come back on moments later.

"Do not be afraid," said her Visth escort. "The energy shield kept out most of the blast. While it appears there is substantial damage in the city, we avoided the worst of it. Word from above indicates the enemy ships that attacked the planet have all been destroyed."

"Is the larger space battle still continuing?"

"Yes, however, it should end shortly, as more ships are being committed to the battle."

Kala nodded. When the ground shook, she had never been so frightened in her life. She just hoped Andrew was okay. "How soon before we can leave this shelter?"

"Several hours at least," answered her Visth escort. "Many of the city streets are blocked, and emergencies services have just now been activated. They will notify us when it's safe to travel."

Kala knew she could do nothing else but wait. It would be a long afternoon.

-

Andrew was with Representative Karn and several other alien representatives in a deep shelter beneath the capital building. At least here, he had viewscreens, showing the chaos in the city and the ongoing space battle.

"Visth Admiral Larr is taking part of our fleet to reinforce Rear Admiral Carrie and Lormallian Admiral Keld," reported Visth Representative Karn. "This battle should be over shortly."

"Let's hope so," replied Andrew, as he watched the screens. "The Morag have demonstrated once again how deceitful they are and the danger they represent to this galaxy. They are a threat that must come to an end."

Representative Karn nodded. "After this attack, I fully expect all the worlds present and those who could not attend to sign the new alliance. We will have over four hundred worlds willing to join with you to end this nightmare."

"Have you decided on a name for your new alliance?"

"The United Worlds Alliance," answered Representative Karn. "Someday we hope to be as large as your own Empire."

"The trade agreement we discussed earlier will also be beneficial to your worlds as well as my own."

Karn smiled. "This will be the beginning of a new age for all of us, and soon we will no longer have to fear the Confederation."

Andrew hoped Representative Karn was right. However, Andrew greatly feared the war with the Morag had barely begun.

-

Lormallian Admiral Keld was immensely surprised by the particle beam cannon the Human dreadnoughts used. No wonder the Morag had been so soundly defeated when they had attacked the Hagen Star Cluster and Golan Four. Keld's flagship shook violently for a moment, and he saw several red damage icons appear on the damage control console. He had already lost two of his battleships and five of his battlecruisers. He suspected all the ships in his fleet had suffered some damage.

"Visth Admiral Larr is inbound," called out the sensor officer. "He has fifteen battlecruisers and sixty support ships with him. The two Human dreadnoughts and four battlecruisers are even now rejoining the fleet."

This would be the turning point. While the Human dreadnoughts had decimated the Morag's battleships, many of their battlecruisers still survived. With what remained of the Lormallian fleet and the Human fleet, victory was now assured.

"Continue the attack. I want every one of those Morag ships destroyed."

-

Rear Admiral Carrie was relieved to hear the capital had only sustained minor physical damage, as most citizens heard the alarms and evacuated buildings as soon as the Morag fleet had arrived. The *Exeter* shook constantly, as the enemy tried to bring down the ship's shield. On the viewscreen, another one of her battlecruisers was torn apart by Morag fusion energy beams. So far, the battle had been costly. Carrie had lost four of her dreadnoughts and thirty-one of her battlecruisers.

"Visth Admiral Larr will be here in two minutes," reported Major Sullivan. "Also the surviving interceptors have returned to the battlecarriers and are being rearmed."

Rear Admiral Carrie nodded. She had the Morag now. If they did not retreat, she would destroy their entire fleet.

-

Morag Admiral Marcello studied the tactical display. He was pleased when another Human battlecruiser icon suddenly swelled up and vanished.

We cannot defeat what's coming at us now, sent First Officer Kinslo. *While we can still cause considerable harm to the Human and the Lormallian fleets, the Visth fleet and the Human interceptors will finish us off.*

On another viewscreen, the capital city of the Visth was visible. Fires and considerable smoke covered the city, but it had survived Captain Setak's attack, although Setak and the Conqueror battleship had not.

Meanwhile Marcello's fleet had been hammered. He still had four battleships and thirty-two battlecruisers, though many of those were damaged.

Let us withdraw, he sent. *There is no longer any point to this battle. We must get word back to the High Council as to what has happened here.* Admiral Marcello knew the council would not be pleased to hear about the Humans and the Lormallians joining forces against his fleet, nor to hear attempts to kill Reull failed too. Marcello suspected this news would shatter the Great Council and possibly even lead to war against the Lormallians.

-

"Enemy fleet is entering hyperspace," reported the sensor officer, looking back at Rear Admiral Carrie.

Carrie felt the weight on her shoulders vanish. The battle was over, and they had won, though the victory had been costly.

"We'll hold here for an hour to ensure the Morag don't return. Have all ships begin what repairs they can. Contact Admiral Keld. I want to congratulate him on this victory." Rear Admiral Carrie wanted to ensure that the Lormallian admiral felt that his participation had been key to this victory and that his assistance was greatly appreciated. There was a chance that, someday in the future, they might need Admiral Keld again.

-

Andrew had been informed of the fleet victory and that the danger was past. "I've been thinking," he said. "The Morag have a tendency to attack cities and civilian populations. If you are interested, I can have the Empire furnish you with a fully functional defense grid to protect your home planet. I believe I can even talk the Imperial Council into including several ODPs as well. This would help to guarantee the security of your homeworld."

Visth Representative Karn was stunned by the offer. "We accept. It would be wonderful to live in the cities and to not be fearful of attack. Now, if you don't mind, we need to return to the surface and see if we can round up the rest of the representatives. We need to work out the trade agreements, as well as finish setting up our government structure for the United Worlds Alliance."

Andrew nodded. They would be here for several more days, before all the negotiations were complete. No doubt the Human Empire had gained a powerful ally in the war against the Confederation and the Morag. An ally they might sorely need as the war continued.

Chapter Five

The Morag High Council was in session and having an intense argument.

Admiral Marcello reports that, in the Visth home system, he came up against a combined Human and Lormallian fleet, sent Councilor Addonis. *It also appears that our attempt to eliminate Councilor Reull failed as well.*

We must attack the Lormallian worlds at once, replied Councilor Hiram. *They must not be allowed to side with the Humans.*

We don't believe they did, sent Councilor Delann. *It is evident they combined their forces to protect themselves from our fleet's attack of their planet.*

There is a greater problem, sent Councilor Addonis. *The Lormallians know we attempted to kill Councilor Reull. This will be brought up in the Great Council.*

Councilor Reull needs to be eliminated, sent Councilor Hiram. *His interference in our affairs must come to a stop.*

The other councilors looked at one another, until Councilor Brant responded, *The Great Council has served its purpose. Perhaps it is time to end it? If we do, the Lormallian councilor becomes less of a threat.*

Let us first seal our alliance with the Druins, the Lamothians, and the Zynth, replied Councilor Lomor. *We may need them in this war against the Humans. Then I agree. We end the Great Council.*

After listening to the others for a few more minutes, Addonis replied, *Agreed. I have been in contact with the Druins and the Zynth. They both will join in an alliance with us. The Lamothians are willing, if we allow them to take Humans for their feasts.*

That will only anger the Humans more, pointed out Councilor Delann.

Then they will be angry at the Lamothians, answered Councilor Addonis. *It will cause the Humans to attack the Lamothian worlds, weakening their fleets.*

How soon before our fleets are rebuilt? asked Councilor Lomor. *While we wait to attack, the Humans only grow stronger.*

True, answered Councilor Addonis. *However, we are strengthening the defense grids around all our planets and inhabited moons. New warships are coming out of our shipyards every day. It will be impossible for the Humans to conquer any of our worlds, without risking major losses to their fleets. When we are ready, we will strike and will end this Human menace once and for all. I will send Councilor Damora to pull us out of the Great Council—as well as the Lamothians, the Druins, and the Zynth. Damora will also demand explanations from the Lormallian ships firing on ours in the Visth home system.*

What about weapons research? asked Councilor Hiram. *Have we developed anything on that front? We must have a counter for the new weapons the Humans have developed.*

Our scientists estimate it will take two to three months to develop the particle beam cannon and the accelerator cannon that the Humans have used against us. It will then take four to six months to equip our fleet with the weapons.

Are we making any progress on developing any new weapons? asked Councilor Hiram.

Our scientists are working around-the-clock on new weapon technologies. We see some positive results, but we are still months or possibly years away from actually installing these new weapons on our warships. In the meantime, we must prepare for all-out war against the Human Empire. They are all that stands in our way of galactic domination.

We must destroy the Humans, sent Councilor Hiram.

-

Krista had returned to the Imperial Palace, after visiting nearly forty worlds between the Hagen Star Cluster and the periphery. She was currently in Layla's quarters, briefing her on what had been accomplished. "Out of the forty worlds I visited, thirty-six of them indicated they are willing to join the Empire."

"That's great," replied Layla. She was glad Krista was back in the Palace. It had been a little boring with her gone. "We've had several hundred other worlds agree to join. We're setting up some meetings in the House of Worlds to finish working out the details.

If all goes as I hope, within another four weeks, we will have nearly seven hundred worlds in the Empire."

"We're getting there," said Krista, smiling. She knew those numbers were a huge step forward in getting the Human Empire reestablished.

"We have another couple hundred that are still hesitant, but I firmly believe, when they see the benefits of joining the Empire, they will become members." Layla leaned back and looked curiously at Krista. "How did you like spending so much time with Mathew?"

Krista's face flushed, and her voice quivered slightly, as she answered. "Brenda kept a close watch on us. He wasn't allowed in my quarters, and, whenever we were together, Brenda was normally close by."

"Good for her." Layla laughed. "She'll be another Emira."

"I understand Andrew and Kala had a close call when they went to the Visth homeworld."

"Yes," answered Layla. She hadn't been pleased when she had heard about what had happened. "I suspect the Great Council is about to come to an end. Particularly with the Morag trying to kill the Lormallian councilor."

Krista let out a deep breath. "I'm ready for some peace and quiet. It's good to be home."

Layla nodded. She didn't tell Krista that Rear Admiral Collison and Rear Admiral Barnes would be setting out for the Confederation in a few more days. The war was not over; it was just changing to a different format. This time it would be the Confederation under attack.

-

In orbit on the shipyard, Derrick waited anxiously for the *Destiny* to be allowed to leave the repair bay. His ship was finally fully repaired and ready to resume its position as the flagship of Fifth Fleet. He watched from an observation lounge that overlooked the mammoth bay.

"She's as good as ever," commented Colonel Sheena Bryant. "Though the yardmaster did make a comment that you need to stop wrecking your flagship."

Derrick nodded. The last *Destiny* had nearly been destroyed, and Derrick had been lucky to survive. "We need to rebuild Fifth Fleet, as well as First Fleet. I'll recommend to Fleet Admiral Marloo that we bring both fleets up to full strength as soon as possible."

"What about the Earth fleets? Are we sending some ships with them when they attack the Morag?"

Derrick knew that both Earth fleets had taken substantial losses, while protecting the Hagen Star Cluster and Golan Four. "I'm thinking about sending Rear Admiral Carrie. I know she's been through a lot, but she's our best battlecarrier commander, and she knows everything there is to know about attack interceptor tactics. We'll add to her fleet and send them along with the Earth fleets."

"We need to have a name for her fleet. I know, at first, they were to be an auxiliary force, but they've played an important role in all the recent battles."

"Yes, we should," replied Derrick. "How about Eighth Fleet?"

Colonel Bryant nodded her head. "Fits in with the rest."

"I'll notify Rear Admiral Carrie, as well as Fleet Admiral Marloo."

Colonel Bryant's communicator buzzed. She answered it and spoke for a couple minutes, then turned toward Derrick. "The *Destiny* is ready to leave the bay. All they're waiting on is one of us."

Derrick smiled. "Take her out. I need to get down to Golan Four and to work out some details over these items we just talked about."

Colonel Bryant left, and there was a lightness to her step, due to going back on board the *Destiny*.

Stepping over to the large observation window, Derrick looked out over the *Destiny*. The mighty dreadnought was now more powerful than ever. Earth's accelerator cannons had been added to its multitude of weapons. It had taken an extra week to make the modifications necessary for those weapons, but now the *Destiny* was the most powerful ship in the known galaxy.

Derrick watched as a few shipyard personnel and several dozen work robots exited the bay. Suddenly all the running lights alongside the *Destiny* lit up. He knew that now they were just waiting for Colonel Bryant to come on board.

A few minutes later, red lights flashed in the bay, and the massive doors slid open, revealing the stars. The *Destiny* used her maneuvering thrusters to raise herself off the deck, and then the ship slid smoothly forward. In less than a minute, the two-thousand-meter-long vessel was free of the bay and was once more in her natural element, the cold harshness of space.

-

A full month had gone by since the attack on Golan Four. All the damaged Imperial warships had been repaired. A few had to be scrapped because the damage was too severe. New warships were rolling out of the shipyards all over the Empire, but it would be several months before all the losses in the battles were replaced.

Fortunately, during that time, new shipyards would come online, and many planets that had recently joined the Empire would also be building warships. In just a few months, the Empire would be ready to take the war to the Confederation. However, Earth was ready now.

Rear Admiral Marloo leaned back and lay down the reports, describing the expected production out of the Empire's shipyards. In front of him were Rear Admiral Barnes, Rear Admiral Collison, Rear Admiral Carrie, and Vice Fleet Admiral Masters.

"What are your current fleet situations?" asked Admiral Marloo. "Rear Admiral Barnes, if you would go first."

"My fleet was hit pretty heavily in the Hagen Star Cluster. Currently I have 833 battlecruisers, 178 dreadnoughts, 2 mobile repair yards, 32 supply ships, and 23 battlecarriers. There were some additional warships with the supply fleet."

"Rear Admiral Collison, I know you suffered even heavier losses, while defending this planet. What do you have in your fleet now?"

"With the supply fleet, I have 585 battlecruisers, 128 dreadnoughts, 2 mobile repair yards, 18 supply ships, and 15 battlecarriers."

Fleet Admiral Marloo nodded his head. "I want to thank both of you for the sacrifices you have made in defending the Empire. If you had not, I don't know if we would be here today. Rear Admiral Carrie, as I have told you earlier, we plan on sending your fleet along with the Earth fleets. We have also designated your fleet as Eighth Fleet."

Carrie nodded. "We have received some additional ships over the last few hours."

Derrick nodded. "I have sent you some of Fifth Fleet's ships. If we can destroy a large number of the Morag shipyards and hit a few other important targets in the Confederation, we might buy enough time for the Empire to build sufficient fleets so that a Confederation attack would be highly unlikely. Overall, you will have 30 dreadnoughts, 120 battlecruisers, 20 support ships— many of them carrying munitions and extra attack interceptors— as well as your 20 battlecarriers."

"One more thing," added Admiral Marloo. "I spoke to Fleet Admiral Reynolds, and, effective immediately, Rear Admiral Collison, you are promoted to the rank of admiral." With a smile, Admiral Marloo took out a small box and pinned the insignia on Collison's shoulders, then stepped back and saluted. "The three fleets are yours to command."

"Thank you, Fleet Admiral," replied Collison, returning the salute.

"I understand you plan on leaving in two more days?" asked Derrick.

"Yes, Admiral. We want to hit the Morag before they have a chance to start rebuilding their fleet. We're pretty certain they are still dealing with the damage we did to their ships."

"If you need anything else, let us know," said Fleet Admiral Marloo. "We're hoping your attacks will buy us four to six months. By then, we'll have the necessary ships to defend the entire Empire."

"We'll buy you that time," promised Collison.

Later Derrick was back in the Imperial Palace with Layla. They stood on one of the balconies on a sky tower, overlooking the city.

"What will the Morag do when we attack them?" asked Layla, as she leaned against Derrick's arm. It neared sunset, and a few of the city's lights were just now coming on. The capital never slowed down, not even in the middle of the night. As more worlds joined the Empire, it would only get busier.

Derrick smiled. "We're about to show them they're not as safe as they think they are. We're not going for their ships or their planets. We're going for their shipyards."

"I spoke to Andrew and General Gantts earlier. The Lormallian councilor gave them the possible design for a superweapon that an ancient race had designed thousands of years ago. It's called an atomic disrupter, and, if our scientists can finish the design work, it could easily end this war."

"I heard, but it could be months or even years before we have the weapon ready to test. Until then, we'll have to use the weapons we have now." He hugged Layla. "At least we have the hope of building a weapon that will end this war and that will keep the Empire safe."

Layla nodded. "Can you stay here at the Palace for a few days?"

"Yes, I have nothing planned for the next week. We can do whatever you want."

"Better be careful saying that. You never know what I might think of."

"Why don't we take the *High Kingdom* and go to Glimmer for a few days? I could use some time on the beach."

"I would love that," replied Layla. "They have the most beautiful beaches in the core worlds." It would be great to spend some quality time with Derrick, away from the hustle and bustle of the Palace.

Derrick smiled. "Then it's settled. I'll make the arrangements in the morning."

-

In the Confederation, the Great Council was once more in session. Everyone knew about the Morag's attempt to kill Councilor Reull.

"Why did your fleet join the Humans against ours, when we attempted to end the meeting of the rebellious worlds outside the Confederation? We could not get to the Visths' homeworld because of it." Councilor Damora stood, towering over the conference table. His eyes nearly glowed red with anger.

Councilor Reull stood, unafraid of the Morag. "Why did your fleet try to ambush my diplomatic ship and kill me? Never in the long history of our Confederation has one councilor tried to kill another."

"You were meeting with the Humans, which is a traitorous act against all the races here. The Humans are our enemies. You deserve to die!"

"I was meeting with them to ensure they understood that my people and the Zang and the Morphene were now neutral in this war. You and the Morag tread a dangerous path, one this council cannot tolerate."

Councilor Damora shook his head. "The Morag, the Druins, and the Zynth are no longer members of this council." Damora looked at the Lamothian Councilor. "What will your race do? Will you join us or stay with these other fools?"

70

"We will join you," spoke the Lamothian. "We want Humans for our feasts."

"And Humans you will have," promised Damora. With that, he stood and left the council chamber, followed by the others who had decided to remain with the Morag.

Lormallian Councilor Reull looked at Zang Councilor Crea and Morphene Councilor Klug. "Well, I guess that's it. The Great Council has finally been broken. I suggest our three races sign a nonaggression agreement against the Humans, as well as form an alliance to protect one another, if the Morag and their allies attack."

"We agree," said Councilor Crea in his birdlike voice.

"As do we," spoke Councilor Klug. "The Morag cannot be trusted. Someday I firmly believe they will come for all three of our races. With their telepathy, they are interested in one thing and one thing only. Power and control. It is a miracle you found the secret of the nullifiers, or we would still be under their power."

"We must move away from what the Morag have changed our races into," Reull stated. "Many of the planets in our individual sections of space view our races as being no better than the Morag."

"We agree," twittered the Zang councilor. "On our homeworld, we have found hidden archives that revealed what our worlds were once like. We plan on returning to those times, though it will take decades of reeducation of our people."

Morphene Councilor Klug, who was constantly shifting form but now resembled a humanoid, spoke. "I wish to send some scientists to the archives on Bator Prime to see what we can learn about our distant past. We have searched our worlds, and nothing describes how we lived before the advent of the Morag."

Councilor Reull nodded. "That can easily be arranged. I will even contact my brother and see what he can find. I do have a method to contact the Humans, and I will inform them that all three of our races plan to remain neutral in this war." His *method* was through the Visth.

"One more thing, from speaking to the Human Royal and General Gantts, I believe the Humans are already considering launching an offensive against the Morag. What that offensive will look like, I have no idea. However, I would suggest that all three of us keep our trading ships within our regions of space, so they don't get caught up in the fighting. All three of our controlled regions touch one another. Trade between the three of us and the worlds inside our regions can continue."

The other two agreed. "We must continue to build up our fleets and to fortify our worlds," added Zang Councilor Crea. "My own race is putting up defensive grids around all our primary worlds, as well as building new shipyards. If the rumored reports I have received are correct, the Morag race is far more numerous than we ever believed possible. Just something else they didn't tell us about. While we knew of their inhabited worlds, we did not know the extent of the number of moons they had terraformed and colonized. The Morag could easily have double the population we once thought."

This did not surprise Councilor Reull. "We also vastly underestimated the size of their warfleets. Even now, we believe they have over ten thousand still functional."

Morphene Councilor Klug shook his head. "They would not have needed such massive fleets, unless they planned someday to use them on us."

Lormallian Councilor Reull nodded. "I believe they want to control the entire galaxy. We were just a means to an end. I will set up a meeting place on Bator Prime for the three of us. Until this crisis is settled, one way or another, I suggest we meet once a week. We are entering very dangerous times, and it's possible none of us will survive." Councilor Reull also needed to send a message to the Visth about the Lamothians. The Morag would allow them to eat captured Humans in their planetary feasts. Reull imagined the Humans' reaction to this news would not be good.

One day later, Fleet Admiral Marloo was angry. He was in a small conference room beneath the House of Worlds. He was waiting on Admiral Collison to arrive. He had just received a message from the Visth that the Morag would allow the Lamothians to eat Humans in their ceremonial feasts.

The door opened, and Admiral Collison entered.

"Have a seat, Admiral," said Marloo. "I just received word that the Lamothians will start eating Humans in their feasts again."

"What!" said Collison, his eyes widening as he sat down. "I thought, after Admiral Masters destroyed one of their worlds, that was over with."

"So did I. Evidently the Morag agreed to allow them to have their Human feasts, as a bribe to keep them on the Morag side in this war."

Admiral Collison leaned forward. "What do you want me to do?"

Fleet Admiral Marloo took a deep breath. "As much as I hate to say it, I think we need to destroy another one of their worlds. We should make it plain that, if even one Human is used in their feasts, we will return and destroy all the rest of their planets."

Collison nodded. "I don't feel any leniency toward the Druins, not after what they've done to the Empire over the years, and they did attack Earth. Once we reach the Empire, I'll pick out one of their planets to destroy too, as well as broadcast a hyperlight warning. I'll see to it the Lamothians never eat another Human."

Admiral Marloo nodded approvingly. He shuddered, thinking about the billions of Humans the Lamothians had eaten in the last one thousand years. It was difficult to feel any leniency toward them at all. "Get the job done and return safely. This will be a new facet to the war, with us taking the war to the Confederation. This is not just an attack aimed at one planet but aimed at our enemies overall. Do as much damage as possible and know that, for every day you buy the Empire and Earth, the larger our fleets will be."

"Yes, Admiral. I realize what's at stake, and my fleets will buy the time you need."

They discussed a few more items and went over what they knew about the Druin and the Morag worlds. Due to accessing the computers on several destroyed Druin and Morag ships, they knew quite a lot, including the locations of all the Druin worlds and many of the inhabited planets and moons of the Morag.

With a deep sigh, Fleet Admiral Marloo looked Admiral Collison in the eyes. "It's time to take this war to the Confederation. Get it done, Admiral Collison."

Collison stood and saluted. "You can count on my ships and my crews. The Confederation has no idea what's getting ready to come their way."

On Glimmer, Derrick and Layla were lying on a beautiful secluded beach, with only a few people allowed admittance at a time. While other people were here, only a few dozen were around now.

"Promise me that you won't be leaving the Golan Four System to attack the Confederation," said Layla.

Derrick looked over at Layla, admiring the dark blue bikini she wore. It made her look even more alluring, and she filled it out very well. "Not for a while. But there may come a time in the war when I'm needed."

Layla let out a deep sigh and stretched. She had known what Derrick would say. "This war will still last for several more years, and there's no guarantee we can defeat the Morag."

"No, there isn't," replied Derrick, looking out over the azure-blue ocean waters. A few kids had some paddleboards and were constantly falling off. Derrick smiled and wondered if he and Layla would ever have children. They hadn't talked about it yet, but it would be nice, sitting here on the beach, watching their children play in the water.

Layla reached over and picked up the fruit drink on the small table between them. "I think we both needed this time away from the Palace. I'm afraid it will be a while before we can do this again, with all the worlds we're adding to the Empire. The next few months, we will all be very busy.

Derrick reached over and took Layla's hand. "It will be worth it. For every world that joins the Empire, the stronger the Empire becomes."

A few boats were out on the water. Several pulled skiers, and others just drifted. The weather was perfect, and Derrick could think of nowhere else he would rather be. "Let's take a dip in the ocean and then head for one of the restaurants. I could use a big juicy steak."

Layla hit Derrick playfully in the arm. "You're always hungry."

Derrick smiled. "It just gives me more energy for later."

Layla flushed and stood. "Maybe some ocean time will cool you off a little."

"Actually the water is quite warm."

Moments later, the two were in the water, splashing each other and laughing. For at least a little while, the worries of the Empire could wait.

Chapter Six

The next day the three fleets readied to attack the Confederation. All ships had been checked and loaded with sufficient munitions and supplies.

Onboard the *Mercury*, Admiral Collison's flagship, the Command Center was a beehive of activity.

"All ships report ready to enter hyperspace," reported Captain Billingsly. "The dreadnought *Johnston* just reached its assigned position in the fleet."

Admiral Collison took his seat and glanced at the viewscreens. Hundreds of ships were visible, all waiting for the command to make the transition into hyperspace. "Contact Fleet Admiral Marloo and tell him we'll leave in the next few minutes." Collison was anxious to get underway and to begin his real mission.

Collison then keyed his comm unit, connecting him to all his ships. "All vessels, we will leave shortly, so make final preparations to enter hyperspace. We have a short stopover near the Hagen Star Cluster, before continuing to the periphery, where we will begin our hyperspace journey to the Confederation."

Looking at the helm, Admiral Collison nodded. "Activate hyperspace drive."

Suddenly everything seemed skewed and out of focus and then instantly returned to normal. "Hyperspace insertion successful," reported the helm officer.

On the large tactical screen, more green icons appeared as all three fleets made the transition. Collison spent a few minutes cleaning up the formation and then relaxed. There was nothing to do for a little over a day and a half.

-

In the Confederation, Councilor Reull was meeting with the Lormallian Ruling Triad. "There is no doubt in my mind that the Morag would have eventually attacked us, if the Humans had not devastated their fleets first. There is no other reason for the Morag to have such large fleet formations. And they kept the existence of these ships a secret, even from us who shared the Great Council with them."

"I agree," said Mador Angst, the leader of the Triad. "And now the Morag, Zynth, Lamothians, and Druins have gone off and formed their own alliance. This is the end of the Great Council, and, after what we have learned about the Morag, perhaps it's for the best."

Councilor Reull nodded. "At first, their alliance will be for their own defense against the Humans, and, in time, I suspect we will be their next target. The Morag are extremely jealous that we control Bator Prime and all the information contained in the underground archives."

"We are increasing the defenses around Bator Prime," said Serrie Voll, the only female member of the Triad. "Should we assign a larger fleet there as well?"

Councilor Reull nodded. "I don't think we have any choice."

"Keep in mind we have lost a large number of ships, fighting alongside the Morag this past year," said the final Triad member, Birx Storl, bitterness in his voice. "We only have one complete fleet at the moment, and that is Admiral Garr's fleet. The fleets commanded by Admiral Keld and Admiral Zador are only at 60 percent strength."

"I suggest we get them up to full strength as rapidly as possible," said Angst. "We don't know what the future holds for us."

The other two members of the Triad nodded their agreement.

"We are already running our shipyards around-the-clock," pointed out Voll. "Even so, it will take us two to three months to rebuild those fleets."

"It must be done," said Reull. "Our very worlds may depend on it."

"I'll order the expansion of all our shipyards, beginning immediately," said Angst. "It looks as if, someday, we'll need as many warships as we can get our hands on."

Councilor Reull hesitated and then spoke. "I believe the Humans are about to launch a major offensive against the Morag, probably sometime in the next few weeks."

"Where would they get the ships from?" asked Storl. "While the Morag lost a large portion of their attack fleet, the Humans lost many vessels as well."

"The Earth Humans will attack," replied Reull. "Over half of their ships survived, and I firmly believe the two Earth fleets that helped the Empire were on their way to the Confederation but got rerouted at the last minute."

A look of concern crossed Leader Angst's face. "Are we in any danger?" He knew in the past the Lormallians had been responsible for many Human deaths.

"No," replied Reull. "I've seen to that in my recent trip to the Visth homeworld, where I met with Prince Andrew and General Gantts. They understand the Morag caused us to commit many of the atrocities that we did. It will be years, possibly decades, before they can fully forgive us, but, in time, I hope for us to become allies for the greater good."

The members of the Triad looked at one another and slowly nodded. "We must not do anything to further antagonize the Humans," said Leader Angst. "Councilor Reull, I've assigned you a permanent security detail. All members of the detail will wear telepathic nullifiers. It's very distressing that the Morag tried to kill a member of the Great Council. It further shows they cannot be trusted."

Angst continued. "We will also convert one of the light cruisers we've built for you to use as your personal ship. We're changing some of its interior to add an extra fusion power plant to greatly increase the power of its energy shield. From now on, wherever you go, you will have an escort of four battleships and ten battlecruisers. You are now our official liaison between us, the Zang, the Morphene, the Visth Alliance, and the Humans. At the moment, the Triad feels you are the only one they all trust."

"I'm not so sure how much the Humans trust us, but at least we have a start with them."

"We've been running videos of what our worlds were once like on some of the media stations," said Serrie Voll. "So far, we've received a very positive response."

"In the new school year, the curriculum will be changed to fit our new reality," said Storl. "Maybe in a few generations, we will see our worlds return to what they once were."

"Let's hope so," replied Councilor Reull. He knew his worlds had a lot of work ahead of them. He didn't say it, but he knew the Lormallian worlds and the Lormallian people would be dependent on the Humans winning this war.

Rear Admiral Carrie was in the Command Center of the *Exeter* when the fleet dropped from hyperspace. On the main viewscreen, the Hagen Star Cluster was plainly visible. It was a mass of stars that stretched from one side of the viewscreen to the other. Also Admiral Cleemorl was here with his fleet.

"Did you want to send a message to Admiral Cleemorl?" asked Major Sullivan.

"No, I'm sure Admiral Collison has already done that. Besides, the admiral will be busy getting First Fleet built back up. I know that Cheryl is on Tantula Five, and, from what I heard, she bought a very expensive house in the suburbs of the capital."

Major Sullivan started laughing.

"What's so funny?"

"I bet she's already setting up a chain of restaurants and entertainment clubs. She'll make another fortune off the clubs."

Rear Admiral Carrie frowned. "I've heard stories about those clubs."

"The fleet needs those clubs," replied Sullivan. "It's a great way to blow off a little steam and have a good time. The clubs have very good security, and they make sure nothing goes too far."

"Have you been to one?"

Sullivan nodded. "A couple times. They serve only the highest-quality drinks, and the prices overall aren't too bad. The entertainment is also pretty good."

"So I've heard," replied Carrie, blushing slightly. She knew most of the entertainers in the clubs were scantily dressed women. Each club also had a band that played music to dance to almost nonstop. However, if it kept her crews and pilots happy, she wouldn't object. She well understood the pressure many of them were under.

"I've got all the crews checking their hyperdrives and other key systems," added Sullivan. "We should have all systems checked in another two hours."

"Make sure of that. I believe Admiral Collison is giving us two and a half hours to finish our system checks. While we're waiting, go ahead and spend the next hour and a half sending out some of our squadrons. Some of those crews still need experience landing on a battlecarrier."

"I'll send the order to Captain Anderson, and I believe Major Conroy is aboard the *Orion* and will be coordinating the squadrons."

Carrie nodded. She knew Major Conroy very well. Conroy might be the best interceptor pilot in the fleet, next to Mathew.

-

"The *Orion* is sending out interceptors," reported Major Sullivan, sounding confused.

Rear Admiral Carrie looked at the tactical display, seeing the small green icons exiting the landing bays of several battlecarriers. They would form up into their squadrons and then make a complete orbit of Eighth Fleet, before landing back on the carriers. Then a second group of squadrons would take off and do the same thing.

"Takeoff and landing practice," commented Carrie approvingly. "We should probably be doing the same thing. Many of our crews are inexperienced, particularly in landing in a combat situation. When we drop out of hyperspace on the periphery of the Empire, we will stay for six hours, while we check out all of our ships' systems. During that time, I want as many interceptor drills run as possible."

Sullivan nodded. "I'll get them set up."

Admiral Collison looked at the viewscreens, showing various ships in his fleet. Battlecarriers, dreadnoughts, battlecruisers, and even one of the massive fleet repair ships were visible—a fleet set up for long-term action. He had no idea how long they would be in the Confederation. However, he had no intention of returning until he had accomplished his mission.

A little over two hours later, the fleets made the transition back into hyperspace on the way to the periphery of the Empire. After that, they would head for the Confederation and the fate that awaited them there.

Morag Admiral Voxx was now the senior admiral in the Morag fleet. All of his ships had been repaired, and his fleet had been augmented with new vessels. He now had 5,270 battlecruisers as well as 8 of the Conqueror class battleships in his fleet. He was confident the Humans would soon attack and had warned the High Council about that possibility. That's what he would do under the present circumstances. The Morag fleet was currently at its weakest and most vulnerable. The Humans would be foolish not to take advantage of this situation. Voxx did not think the Humans were foolish, so he was certain they would come.

Admiral Marcello was in command of 4,232 battlecruisers and 198 battleships, and 4 of the Conqueror class battleships. The remainder of the fleet was scattered across Morag space, protecting the more heavily populated worlds. Shipyards across Morag space had been kicked into high gear, as the Morag wanted to replace the ships they had lost in battle as quickly as possible. Even so, it still took a few months to build a fully functional warship. For those few months, the Morag worlds would be in danger.

-

Admiral Voxx was on board his flagship, pacing in the Command Center. *Where will the Humans strike?*

They could appear anywhere, answered First Officer Bale. *There is also a very good chance they could strike the Lamothians instead of us, if Councilor Reull has told them about the Lamothians' desire to once more eat Humans in their rituals. The Lamothians were fools to announce it like they did.*

Voxx nodded. The Humans had already destroyed one of the Lamothians' worlds. Why not another? *I think you're right. The question is, which world will they strike?*

You want to set a trap?

It should be easy. We send out a few unencrypted hyperlight messages, mentioning that feasts will occur shortly on a particular world, and, when the Humans come, we destroy their fleet. That will buy us the time we need to rebuild our fleets and to take the war back to the Human Empire.

First Officer Bale looked at Admiral Voxx. *The Lamothians might not like one of their worlds being used as bait for the Humans.*

It does not matter. If the Humans attack the Lamothian world, it will give us an idea of their fleet size and intentions. We can have a fleet sitting close by, and, once the Humans have engaged the Lamothian defenses, our fleet can jump in, pinning the Humans against the planet.

First Officer Bale looked confused. *But none of the Lamothian worlds have a decent defense grid around them.*

Not yet, but the world we'll use to lure in the Humans, we can help fortify. I'll speak to the High Council, but I'm sure they will agree to my plan.

Admiral Voxx sat back down, as he began to think about his idea. If he could trap the Human fleet and destroy it, the defeat would allow the Morag to completely rebuild their fleet before the Humans would dare to attack again.

Admiral Collison watched intently, as the last interceptor squadrons returned to their battlecarriers. They had been practicing takeoffs and landings and even a few spirited combat games against Rear Admiral Carrie's squadrons. Collison frowned, noting that Carrie's squadrons had won 72 percent of all the contests.

"Why are her pilots so much better than ours?"

"More combat experience," explained Captain Billingsly. "Rear Admiral Carrie handpicked many of the crews, with the aid of Major Lisa Conroy. Conroy is one of their top trainers, as well as an excellent pilot."

Collison nodded. "I'll contact Rear Admiral Carrie and ask if Major Conroy can be transferred to the *Athena* to work with Rear Admiral Barnes's crews. Once we arrive on the outskirts of the Confederation, we may spend a few days practicing battle maneuvers with the interceptors. They'll be key in our attacks against the Morag shipyards, and I would like to see as many of the crews as possible live through this."

Turning his attention to the main viewscreen, they were now leaving the Empire and entering the space that would take them to the Confederation.

Two days later, the *Mercury* received a directional hyperlight message from Golan Four.

"You're not going to like this," said Captain Billingsly.

Collison read the message and then wadded it up in his fist. "You've got to be kidding me. Don't the Lamothians understand what we will do to them? You would think they would understand that, after what Admiral Cleemorl did to Zaneth. Do they want to lose another world?"

"Fleet Admiral Marloo thinks the Lamothians are being set up. This message was transmitted with no encryption."

83

"Perhaps," replied Collison. "But we know the Lamothians do plan on using captive Humans in future feasts. We found that out from the Lormallian Councilor. That reason alone would justify attacking them."

"So," said Billingsly, looking at the admiral, "are we going to destroy a world?"

Collison frowned. "Maybe, or we could just turn this against the Morag. If they're attempting to set a trap, what if we just skip it and attack their shipyards? They must have at least one of their fleets committed to this."

"They would have to pull their fleet back to protect their worlds."

"Exactly, and, once that fleet pulls back, it will leave the Lamothian world open to attack."

"That would mean splitting our fleet."

"Yes, it would, but we have a good-size fleet."

Captain Billingsly looked thoughtful. "So what will we do?"

Admiral Collison leaned back in his command chair, crossing his arms across his chest. "We still have a few days before we have to decide. As soon as we drop from hyperspace, just outside the Confederation, we'll begin our interceptor drills, I'll give you my decision then. I also want to speak with Rear Admiral Carrie and Rear Admiral Barnes and get their opinions on what we should do."

On board the *Athena,* Major Lisa Conroy sat in a special command simulator, which allowed her to watch how her pilots were doing. At the moment, she had a full squadron on each battlecarrier in Rear Admiral Barnes's fleet sitting inside simulators. "Okay, people, as you know, the interceptors from Rear Admiral Carrie's fleet pretty well whipped your ass in all the battle scenarios we ran. I'm here to change that. Keep in mind that, even though these fights are in simulators, if anyone does something foolish, I'll see that you receive the appropriate punishment. Now all squadrons launch and form up into a loose formation above your battlecarrier."

Major Conroy launched as well, with the simulator making everything seem realistic. As soon as she was outside the *Athena,* she made a quick flyby of all the squadrons, checking on their formations. A few pilots were out of formation, and these she quickly reprimanded.

"Now watch me, and I want you to duplicate these moves in combat. Squadron Scorpion from the *Deneb,* I want you to try to shoot me down and don't collide with one another. Your goal is to eliminate me, before I shoot down your entire squadron."

-

"One interceptor against twenty," said Lieutenant Burr to his crew, as he and his wingman began a slow circle of Major Conroy's interceptor. "She must have some tricks up her sleeve. We'll hang back and see just what she does." Burr considered himself to be a pretty good pilot. However, he knew that Major Conroy was an instructor on Golan Four, and that alone made him respect her.

-

The pilots circled for a few minutes, keeping just out of range of Major Conroy's weapons. Finally two interceptors dove down from above her interceptor, firing nonstop. Conroy's interceptor suddenly darted forward, as it turned and twisted at the same time, using the small thrusters it was equipped with. Before the two incoming interceptors could make an adjustment, Conroy opened fire, stitching both interceptors with weapons fire. In two simulated fiery explosions, the interceptors disintegrated. Moments later, their dejected crews found themselves inside their simulators, their interceptors having been destroyed.

"Stay in your simulators and watch," ordered Major Conroy. "Perhaps you will learn something."

For the next thirty minutes, the interceptors were involved in a complex game of combat. Sometimes it was individual combat, and, at other times, Major Conroy took on up to four interceptors at a time. She quickly saw what the biggest problem was. They were flying their interceptors as if they were in two-dimensional space instead of three, as if they were in an atmospheric condition, instead of airless space. All they were thinking about was up and down. They didn't seem to realize their options in space were unlimited.

-

"I see," said Lieutenant Burr, as he watched Major Conroy make moves and turns that seemed impossible. "She's using space itself as a weapon. There's no air resistance, and she can turn on a dime. We've done too much practicing in a planet's atmosphere. I think I'm ready to take her down."

"If you say so," replied Lieutenant Carr from navigation. "She's just about eliminated everyone else. In another minute or two, she'll be coming for us anyway."

Lieutenant Burr quickly transmitted his attack plan to his wingman. "Okay, no point in delaying this. It's either her or us." Burr turned his interceptor downward, mimicking some of the attack runs he had witnessed his other squadron members make. He wanted to keep Major Conroy unsuspecting, until the last minute.

-

Major Conroy watched with a smile, as the final two interceptors made their attack run. She had been watching them on and off during the entire training exercise. If she were to be in for a battle, it would be from these two. Conroy had a strong suspicion the leader of the two interceptors had been watching her tactics and had carefully analyzed them. This was what she wanted, and now she would see what they had learned.

The two interceptors closed and began firing, just as those before them had. Conroy easily dodged the incoming rounds and put her fighter into a careful and calculated spin, as it climbed toward the two inbound interceptors. She was just about to fire, when both interceptors suddenly broke into a corkscrew move spinning wildly. She fired anyway and missed. The two interceptors now went into myriad sharp turns and dives, presenting only a small part of their interceptors to be attacked. Suddenly this had turned into a true three-dimensional battle, and Major Conroy grinned. Finally she had some competition.

-

Lieutenant Burr smiled, as he saw the major move away from the two incoming interceptors. By now she must have realized this would be no normal battle. He quickly contacted his wingman. "Come up underneath her, and I'll attack from above."

The two interceptors continued to fly in wild gyrations, until they were in position, and then they attacked.

-

Major Conroy saw she was in trouble. No doubt she could destroy one of the interceptors, but the second would probably take her out. Biting her lip, she prepared for combat.

-

The three interceptors closed and then began firing. Major Conroy managed to get some rounds into the lower interceptor, damaging it, and then she took it out in a final burst of fire. Its simulation exploded in a satisfying fireball. She quickly rotated her interceptor 180 degrees, but she had a sinking feeling it was too late.

Lieutenant Burr decelerated his interceptor for all it was worth and rotated his interceptor 90 degrees. He saw the major doing the same. The battle was now out of both of their control. The first one to get their interceptor lined up on the other ship would win.

Burr breathed hard, as he watched his targeting system. The major's interceptor was visible, and it was rapidly coming around. Just a few seconds more, and she would have him. "Target acquired," spoke the targeting computer. Without hesitation, he pressed the Fire button on his flight control stick, and weapon rounds from his interceptor leaped out to stitch the major's interceptor.

A moment later, he saw the major's interceptor finish its maneuver, and it began to fire on him. "Die, damn it," he said, as his rounds began to tear apart the major's simulated interceptor. In a satisfying fireball, the major's interceptor blew apart. Leaning back, he breathed out a long sigh of relief. Looking at his control panel, he saw his interceptor was pretty well shot up. Another few seconds, and the major would have won. "Damn, she's good," he said, shaking his head.

Major Conroy opened her eyes in her simulator. She smiled. She had found at least one interceptor crew who understood what she was trying to teach them. Now she needed to bring the others around. She would do three or four more sessions with this squadron and then have them begin training the others. With a little luck, she should improve their battle efficiency by 30 to 40 percent. If she could accomplish that, she would consider her training here complete.

Chapter Seven

Layla and Derrick had just returned from their trip to Glimmer and were meeting with Fleet Admiral Marloo and Chief Chancellor Stein in a large conference room in the Imperial Palace.

"How was your trip to Glimmer?" asked Chancellor Stein. "Was it as beautiful as you remembered it to be, Princess Layla?"

"It was even more beautiful than I remembered. Thank you for asking. It was nice to have some time to get away and to relax," Layla said, with a smile. "I am curious to know, how are Admiral Collison's fleets? Are they ready to begin their attack on the Morag?"

"There has been a new development," replied Admiral Marloo. "We've intercepted a hyperlight message, indicating the Lamothians are planning to use Humans in an upcoming feast to take place on their planet Xanther. Admiral Collison thinks this might be a trap from the Morag. Collison believes they plan to ambush Collison's fleet when they attack this Lamothian planet. His gut is telling him the Morag are luring them there to destroy his fleet and to keep him away from the Morag area of the Confederation."

Vice Fleet Admiral Derrick Masters thought for a moment, then replied, "That does sound like a good idea. The Morag seem to underestimate our ability to see through their carefully formulated plans. That could give us an advantage in this situation. What is Collison planning to do?"

"Currently he is examining his options. He is considering splitting his fleet into two groups. One group would head to the Morag-controlled part of the Confederation and attack the shipyards. This, he believes, will cause the Morag fleet lying in wait at Xanther to return to the Morag planets to defend their interests. When this happens, the second part of Collison's fleet will attack and destroy the Lamothian planet."

"He will destroy the planet?" asked Layla.

"Yes, that is his intention," replied Marloo. "As many Humans as they have consumed in their feasts, it's only fitting that we would destroy another of their planets. It will serve as yet another warning to the rest of the Lamothians. Not listening to our warnings comes with consequences. That is also when we could broadcast a message from you, warning them yet again of the consequences of using Humans in their feasts. If they offer even one Human in their feasts, we will return and destroy all their worlds."

"Do we expect their world to be heavily defended, after the Morag return to defend their planets?" asked Layla.

"No, we think they may have some moderate defensive grid. Also a few of their battleships may be in orbit. They could also have an armed space station as well. Nothing we can't handle," replied Marloo.

"How long until we expect Collison to enter Confederation space?" asked Derrick.

"He should be dropping from hyperspace later today in the periphery of the Confederation, and then they plan to do some more training with their interceptors. He also will discuss a battle plan strategy with Rear Admiral Barnes and Rear Admiral Carrie. They will let us know, once they have determined their plan of attack."

"Keep us in the loop," replied Derrick.

-

Admiral Collison's fleets dropped from hyperspace on the periphery of the Confederation. He immediately had Rear Admiral Barnes and Rear Admiral Carrie come over to his flagship, the *Mercury*.

"I've had a lot of time to think over the past couple days about our plan of attack, when we engage the Confederation. I want to split our fleets into two. Rear Admiral Carrie will go with me to attack the Morag's shipyards. We know where most of them are, thanks to our scientists boarding their wrecked ships above

Golan Four. I will need the battlecarriers and their experienced attack interceptor crews to have the most likelihood of destroying as many shipyards as possible."

"It will be my pleasure to follow you into battle and to destroy as many shipyards as we can. It is what our crews have been training to do. I would still like to do a few more training exercises with them before we depart," replied Carrie.

"We need to spend some time making sure all our ships are ready for the next part of our voyage, so you will have some time to train."

"Yes, sir."

"Rear Admiral Barnes will wait at the Lormallian star system, where we will stage the supply fleet, until we know the Morag have pulled out of the area around the Lamothian planet of Xanther. We have brought along some heavily stealthed scout ships that will find and monitor the Morag fleet. Once we locate them, we will execute our attack on their main shipyards. When the Morag fleet, lying in wait for our fleet to attack Xanther, hears of our attack on their shipyards, they will head back to defend their region of the Confederation.

"At that time, you, Admiral Barnes, will jump in and destroy their planet. Then you will transmit our message from High Princess Layla. Once you are successful in your destruction of the planet, you will move on to destroy one of the Druin planets. We have chosen the planet, Druin Seven, which neighbors the planet Vice Fleet Admiral Masters destroyed when he came to the Confederation last time."

"We will ready all our ships and get our battle plan together," replied Barnes.

"We jump into Confederation-controlled space in approximately three days," said Collison.

The meeting adjourned, and the rear admirals returned to their flagships to continue their attack interceptor training.

-

Back in the Hagen Star Cluster, Cheryl was as busy as ever, setting up a chain of restaurants and entertainment clubs. Currently the governor's wife, Lenora Dyson, and Cheryl were sitting down to lunch at one of her family-style restaurants.

"I love the food and the atmosphere of this restaurant of yours," commented Lenora.

"Thank you. It's one of Dylan's favorite ones. That is why I had one built here on Tantula Five. That way, we can enjoy it together," replied Cheryl, with a smile.

"How does he like the house you picked out in the suburbs?" asked Lenora.

"Oh, he's getting used to it. He spends most of his time on the *Themis*, tending to his fleet and keeping track of the Hagen Star Cluster. He wants to make sure his fleet gets back to its former size as soon as possible. Plus he intends to build up the fleets of the entire Cluster. He will never rest until the Confederation is no longer a threat," replied Cheryl.

"We are very appreciative of his determination," commented Lenora. "I think we all sleep more peacefully at night, knowing your husband is up there, protecting us."

Cheryl smiled and said, "Thank you. I'll be sure to pass that on to him as well."

-

On Morag Prime, the Morag High Council was once again in session. *Admiral Voxx, have you begun to execute your planned trap for the Humans at the Lamothian planet of Xanther?* asked Lead Councilor Addonis.

Yes, sir. The message has been sent out for the Humans to intercept. We expect them to arrive in about ten days. We will be lying in wait for them in the red dwarf system neighboring the Lamothian system. It is approximately a thirty-minute hyperspace jump from there to Xanther. We expect the Humans to come in and to scan the planet and to attempt to rescue Humans off the surface, before they attack the planet. This should give us plenty of time to get there and to catch the Humans off guard.

Sounds like a logical plan, replied Councilor Delann.

What about our defenses here? Should we heighten our defenses and pull more ships in to protect Morag Prime? asked Brant.

We are still in the process of constructing more and better orbital defenses, answered Addonis. *We have strengthened our defensive grids around most of our inhabited planets and moons. I will leave Admiral Marcello in orbit, around Morag Prime, which will give us a sizable fleet here, in case of an attack on our homeworld. I highly doubt the Humans will resist rescuing their own people though. They seem to be an emotional species. We will destroy them, before they have the opportunity to get to our part of the Confederation.*

Without a doubt, smiled Brant.

Derrick rushed to the underground Command Center, below the House of Worlds. "Has Collison made his final hyperspace jump into the Confederation yet?"

"He has not," replied Admiral Marloo.

"I have an idea. What if, instead of targeting the Lamothian planet of Xanther, like the Morag expect us to, we attack another of their worlds instead? I am confident the Lamothians will have most of their fleets in orbit around their world that is the bait for us. If we attack a different planet instead, it will catch them off guard. Potentially we won't face much opposition at all."

"That's an excellent plan, Derrick," said Marloo slowly, as he considered what Derrick had said. "I will transmit an encrypted message to Collison right away. Do you have a specific planet in mind?"

"Lamothia," smiled Derrick.

"The Lamothian homeworld?" Marloo said, a sly grin on his face. He turned and activated the holographic display of what was known of the Confederation space. Marloo and Derrick studied the map for a few moments, walking slowly around it.

Derrick added, "Another great thing about attacking their homeworld is that it's in a different star system than Xanther, so it will take them a little bit of time for the fleets to jump from there to Lamothia. I'll have to do some calculations, but I would guess about a forty-five-minute hyperspace jump."

Marloo smiled at Derrick again. "I like this idea of yours, even better with every passing minute. I will relay your idea immediately to Collison."

-

Admiral Collison had joined Barnes and Carrie on Barnes's flagship, *Phobos*, to observe the last battle simulation the attack interceptors were running. It still amazed him how well these pilots could maneuver their ships, the intricate way they wove and dove around each other at such high speeds.

He chuckled to himself. It's a good thing he wasn't expected to hop in and to fly one of those. He'd always been a little claustrophobic. The thought of climbing in one of those small interceptors wasn't his idea of fun. He was comfortable being in his command chair in the middle of the Command Center on his flagship. It was always a beehive of activity, everyone busy fulfilling their role. It took every single one of them to make everything run smoothly. He smiled to himself; everyone had their role, and his was to lead these fleets into battle.

These interceptors and their crews were vital to their mission. Fleet Admiral Derrick Masters had used them to his advantage when he had attacked and destroyed the Druin homeworld planet of Druin Six. Collison knew the Druins had their drones, which were a threat to the interceptors, but not as maneuverable. The Morag have their Interceptor Killers, intended to neutralize the interceptors. Thankfully it hadn't quite worked out that way.

The Lamothians, however, had nothing to defend their fleet and their planets against the interceptors. At least not that they had seen. Collison still had a lot to think about during the next leg of their journey. He knew that these attack interceptors would be vital to their success.

Many squadrons had been fighting mock duels out in the space between the fleets. It was very intense to watch, as they darted in and out and past each other at such speeds. The battle simulations they ran had dwindled down to two squadrons, the Black Dart Squadron from the *Orion* and the Scorpion Squadron from the *Daneb*. The admirals followed the action from the observation deck.

"Looks like these pilots and their crews are ready for this mission," remarked Collison, with a smile.

"They've made a lot of improvement over the last couple training sessions," replied Barnes. "We have Major Conroy to thank for that. She's made a big difference in their training. Our best squadron is the Scorpion Squadron. They are the ones who caught on first. They keep improving with each new battle they practice. Admiral Carrie's best squadron is the Black Dart Squadron. Those are the two left in their current battle simulation."

Turning from the view of the interceptors in their training, Collison said, "I have had a hyperlight message from Fleet Admiral Marloo. It seems Vice Fleet Admiral Derrick Masters has come up with another possible target for us to attack in the Lamothian star systems. He believes that we should attack Lamothia, their homeworld. It's in a neighboring star system to Xanther, about a forty-five-minute hyperspace jump.

"He thinks that most of the Lamothian battle fleets will be lying in wait for us at Xanther, which would leave their homeworld less defended than usual. This is our opportunity to take out their most populous planet. We would have a good forty-five minutes to scan the surface for Humans and to then bombard the planet, before the enemy fleets could reach us. We would still wait to enter the star system, until the Morag have left to head back to their area of the Confederation."

"That does seem like a good plan. Xanther could still be our backup plan, if we scan the star system where Lamothia is and detect too many enemy fleets," replied Rear Admiral Carrie.

"True, it's always good to have a plan B," mentioned Barnes.

"When do we make our hyperspace jump into the Confederation?" asked Carrie. She was excited and a little anxious about heading into the Confederation. She put on a brave front, but who knew what to expect when they arrived? Help would be a long way away, if they needed it. She swallowed the doubt that started creeping up.

She knew Collison was one of the best. Carrie knew they had a good plan and would fine-tune it over the next few days. She had faith in her fleet and the pilots who would help aid in their triumph over the Confederation and the Morag. She did look forward to destroying their shipyards. Hopefully they would do more damage than that. The more they could destroy, the longer it would take the Morag and their allies to rebuild.

That time would allow the Empire to rebuild and to strengthen its fleets. It would allow the Solar System more time to fortify all their colonies and cities. Plus build bigger and better fleets. Not to mention the training that went along with that. She knew that, when they returned to the Solar System, it would be ready to defend itself against any attack the Confederation might send their way.

Yes, victory seemed to be within their grasp. She smiled and turned her head toward Collison. "We are ready."

"We will start our hyperspace jump into the Confederation in twenty hours. I will give you the coordinates to the rendezvous point inside the very edge of the Lormallian-controlled area of the Confederation. We will not be near any of their core worlds. We will stay out on the periphery. I want to give us some time to make any needed repairs and any last-minute changes to our battle plan," said Collison.

"Will the Lormallians inform the other Confederation races that we have entered their system?" asked Barnes.

"We believe that the Lormallians will not interfere with our attacks on the Druins, the Lamothians, and the Morag," answered Collison.

"It's a relief to know that we have fewer enemies in the Confederation than we did before," said Carrie.

"I have sent our stealthed scout ships on ahead. Hopefully they will have some information for us by the time we reach our rendezvous point and make our repairs. I have sent some scout ships to the Lamothian-controlled star systems too, as well as the Druin and Morag systems," said Collison.

"We know from Fleet Admiral Masters's experience in the Zynth system that they can trace the radiation from a hyperspace jump. Do we know if the other races possess this same technology?" asked Carrie.

"That is unknown at this time," replied Collison. "The scout ships will stay in the asteroid belts, where available, and as far out as possible to avoid any chance of detection. We plan on sending them to the Lamothian area of space first to see if they can detect them. Then we will progress to the Druin-controlled and the Morag-controlled star systems. We should be arriving earlier than they expect us to, by at least a few days. This will give us a little more of an advantage."

"We will input your coordinates as soon as we have them," replied Barnes. "I will return Major Conroy to you, Rear Admiral Carrie, for you to have for the attack on the Morag. I believe we can handle the Lamothians and the Druins, now that we have had more training with our interceptor pilots."

"I'm glad she could improve your crews' skills." Carrie smiled.

–

The Lormallians, Zang, and Morphene councilors were meeting on Bator Prime. "Have there been any new developments since the last time we met?" asked the Morphene Councilor Klug.

"So far, we have not detected any Morag ships in our area of the Confederation," replied the Lormallian Councilor Reull.

"We have intercepted a hyperlight message discussing a Lamothian feast, where they will be consuming Humans," whistled the Zang Councilor Crea. "Are we to expect the Human Empire to react to that?"

Ardon Reull replied, "I would expect no less. It is probably what the rest of the Confederation expects as well. It might very well be a trap. A trap set by the Morag to destroy the Human fleets before they have the opportunity to attack the Morag. Why risk their worlds, when they can use others instead?"

"What shall we do if we detect Human ships in our systems?" asked Klug.

"We ignore them, give them a wide berth. Do not report them or send any hyperlight communications about them. We will not interfere. We are allies and have started to form a trust with the Humans and the Human Empire. We are not a part of this war. We want to be neutral. I do think that the Humans are our best hope at defeating the Morag and their reign on our Confederation."

"Will we aid them if the situation warrants?" asked Klug.

"Possibly. Have your fleets ready. We don't want to anger the Morag more than we already have, but I do fear that, when the Morag are finished with the Humans, they will come for us. If the Humans need our help, it may be in our best interests to help them. We will not engage unless needed. Leave some of your fleets in patrol of your systems and have one fleet ready to jump to aid the Humans, if need be," replied Reull. "Let's hope they don't need us though."

"All of our trading ships are staying in our star systems—to not be mixed up in anything," mentioned Crea.

"We will be ready," said Klug.

"How are your defensive grid installations coming along?" asked Reull.

"As expected. We should have them fully functioning in our main three-star systems in another six days," replied Klug.

"Ours are almost complete," twittered Crea.

"The ones here in our star systems will be finished in two more days," said Reull. "Our fleets are expanding every day."

"The Humans attacking the Morag will give us more time to build up our fleets and our defensive grids," replied Crea.

"Let's hope," answered Reull.

After a couple more hours of discussion and debate, they had decided to meet again the following week.

"I have brought some scientists with me to research the history of our race in the archives," said Klug.

"I have let my brother, Marlon, know they would be coming. He has already found some information to share with them," replied Reull. "I can take you and your scientists there now. Councilor Crea, you are welcome to have some refreshments and wait in the lounge, if you would like."

"I have much to do back at home, so I will return directly to my people. We have a war to prepare for. I want us to be as ready as we can be. Hopefully the Humans will not need us in this fight," replied Crea.

The three councilors left the chamber, with Reull and Klug headed to the archives, and Crea headed back to the Zang area of the Confederation.

Rear Admiral Cleemorl had just reviewed the most recent numbers he had received on his fleet. He had plans to not only get his fleet back up to the numbers he had before the last battle with the Confederation over Gideon but to increase those numbers. He also intended to increase the number of ships in the other fleets in the Hagen Star Cluster as well. He knew the Morag would return, and Cleemorl would once again be ready for them.

He was also considering the Earth Humans' fleets that would soon be attacking targets in the Confederation. They had showed up when he had needed them in the battle over Gideon, and Cleemorl wanted to return the favor. He knew they would most likely be tracked into hyperspace, when their mission was complete. Most likely a fleet of enemy ships would follow them back to the Empire.

If Cleemorl could be there when they dropped out of hyperspace, he could destroy the enemy fleet that followed them from the Confederation. Figuring out when and where they would need him would be his biggest challenge. They likely would have no more communication from Collison, until his three fleets were headed back to the Empire. Hopefully the Empire would have enough warning to strategically place a fleet where they could intercept the Morag fleet that would inevitably follow the Earth Humans out of the Confederation.

Cleemorl needed to think more about it and to formulate a possible plan of action. That way, he would be ready when they needed him.

Chapter Eight

Collison sat in his command chair, thrumming his fingers quietly. He turned to Captain Billingsly and said, "Take us into hyperspace." He felt the familiar lurch in the pit of his stomach, as the ship made its transition. He watched the screen in front of him, as all the other ships in the fleets made their transitions as well. It was a comforting feeling, knowing all those green icons were with him. They were leaving behind the Empire and headed into space—where few Humans had entered and had lived to return. This war would now shift to the Confederation for once. The start of a new era.

Collison knew this would be a long journey, having to drop out of hyperspace a few times before they reached their destination. He also had a lot of things to prepare for, although much of it was unknown. Thankfully they did have what they thought was an accurate map of the Confederation. It was a vast area of space, so many star systems and planets. Collison was not sure which planets and star systems were friendly and which were foes.

He stood and walked around the holographic display of the Confederation. With the information gathered from the damaged Morag ships and with what they had learned from Councilor Ardon Reull of the Lormallians, Admiral Collison, and Rear Admirals Barnes, and Carrie, along with their advisors, had decided upon a path they felt was the safest to get to their destination.

They knew the Lormallians, Zang, and Morphene were not a part of this war anymore. Collison knew that those three races were not happy with the Morag and that the Confederation had fractured. Collison would like to stay out of their space as well; no use chancing that new and untested alliance, especially if he didn't have to.

They knew from Fleet Admiral Masters's first trip to the Confederation that the Zynth have a way of sensing the radiation left behind from a hyperspace jump. Collison also knew the Lamothians had tracked Derrick through hyperspace and had followed him. Earth Humans and the Imperials had greatly improved their stealth capability on the scout ships since then, but none of these had been to Confederation space to see if the new technology would prevail. Could the scout ships be detected? That remained to be seen.

Their most significant advantage in the battle was the element of surprise. Collison knew the Morag were expecting them this time, but they had already been on their way to the Confederation when they had intercepted the hyperlight message about the Lamothian feast. Just thinking of the ramifications of that sent chills down his spine.

Hopefully it truly was a setup and not something that would happen. They should arrive a few days sooner than expected too, giving Collison's three fleets the opportunity to catch the Morag off guard. How many ships would the Lamothians have? How many did the Druins have left? They had left the Morag in the middle of the battle over Gideon.

At that time, the Humans had estimated one thousand ships still in those enemy fleets. Who knows how many the Lamothians and the Druins still had in reserve, patrolling their star systems? That left the Morag. The Humans counted only a little more than a couple thousand flight-worthy ships when the Morag left Golan Four. They've had time to repair and to strengthen that fleet since then. Plus there had been rumors that the Morag had a vast reserve fleet back in the Confederation. Some estimated close to ten thousand ships.

We have only a little more than 1,900—as well as more than 9,000 attack interceptors.

Collison's fleets could be significantly outnumbered in these attacks, but their success rested in having the best tactics. Collison liked to think of it as a game of chess. He had a lot of pieces to use in this game. He now needed to decide how and when to use them.

-

High Princess Layla Starguard stood, leaning against her husband, Derrick, on one of the sky towers at the Imperial Palace. Off in the distance, she saw dark clouds forming. The lightning was beautiful to watch, as the storm grew bigger and bigger. The capital city had been getting more and more rain since the Morag had hit Golan Four with their missiles. The ones that had hit the ocean were primarily responsible for their increase in storms. It would be years before their weather returned to normal. For now, she would revel in the beauty of the storm.

Her mind wandered to the Confederation and Admiral Collison. He would be making his final preparations soon and starting his attack shortly after that. She laughed to herself. The Morag have no idea a storm was headed for them. A big one. An angry one. Collison had traveled a long distance for this mission. *Thankfully he had detoured here to aid in our battle against the Confederation.* Their numbers and new weapons had really turned the tide of the battle—at Gideon as well as here above Golan Four. She shivered, thinking about the Morag's Conqueror class battleships. Who knew what destruction those could unleash?

"What's on your mind, Layla?" asked Derrick.

"I was just thinking about how thankful I am that Collison and Barnes arrived when they did. I hope they will have great success in their mission to the Confederation."

-

"I have every confidence in Collison, Barnes, and Carrie to do what they set out to do," replied Derrick. He didn't mention that a big part of him wished he were with them, in his new and improved flagship, *Destiny*. They could really inflict some damage to what was left of the Confederation. He sighed. He knew his place was here with Layla. There would be more battles to come.

Time was ticking closer to those battles every minute. With the success of the Earth Humans' fleets currently headed into battle in the Confederation, it would buy the Empire much-needed time to build up the Imperial fleets and to train more crews. They were also building more defensive grids, installing more ODPs and PDCs.

More and more planets and inhabited moons joined the Empire every day; at last count, the Empire was up to 637. The next meeting of the House of Worlds fast approached. He knew Layla had her hands full, preparing for the meeting.

-

Layla looked up at Derrick and smiled. She was thankful he was out of harm's way for now. She knew that wouldn't always be true, but she also knew she should enjoy these moments of peace as they came. No one knew what tomorrow would bring. She heard a loud rumble of thunder roll across the city. "Guess we better get inside. The storm is getting close."

-

Lormallian Councilor Ardon Reull was on a tour of the newly finished shipyard above Lormallia. The shipyard had recently been expanded, and missile defenses had been added. The space stations orbiting the planet had been heavily armed as well. Ardon hoped these defenses would never need to be used, but he also understood that, one day soon, the Morag would turn their anger to the Lormallians. Reull wanted to be prepared.

Every week more ships were added to their fleets. Time would be the main factor in whether they survived the upcoming battle with the Morag. If the Lormallians had enough time, their fleets would be big enough to defend their star systems. Their defenses would protect their planets. Their allies would have time to build their fleets and to enhance their planetary defenses as well.

Time, an enemy or a friend? Reull hoped time would be on their side. The one factor that could buy them more time was the Human Empire. He knew a Human attack on the Morag was imminent. Ardon knew his future and the future of his race was greatly dependent on the success of the Human Empire.

From the shipyard, he saw the planet down below. He sighed heavily. They had already finished the defensive grid around this planet, and he hoped it would be enough. The other planets in this system already had their defensive grids up as well. Every day they readied more and more for the attack that would come their way from the Morag.

Ardon still wrestled with the idea of if they should or shouldn't help the Empire in their attack. Revenge would come quickly from the Morag, and the Lormallians would be the closest to the enemy. Which meant they'd feel the brunt of the retaliation first. One thing the Empire had going for them was that they were far away from the Confederation. Earth was even farther than that.

Ardon took a deep breath and slowly let it out. He needed the Humans to win, but was it worth the risk to his people to help them, if the Humans needed it? Reull needed to address this with the Ruling Triad. Their next meeting was a few days away. At that next meeting of the Triad, they would discuss their options.

-

The smell of coffee eased the tension in Collison's head. An excellent hot cup of coffee would do him some good. He had a lot of plans and decisions to make by the end of the day. When was the last time he'd eaten? His stomach growled so loudly that he thought the entire cafeteria heard it. A nice hot breakfast would help settle his nerves.

A lot rode on his shoulders, as the admiral of this combined fleet. Who would attack where and when? Timing and position could mean the difference in life and death for hundreds, if not thousands, of people under his command, not to mention mission success or failure.

As he sat down at an empty table in the back of the room, the smell of his breakfast and coffee in front of him helped him to focus on what was ahead. He was so glad they had some fantastic cooks on his flagship. The wonderful smells of freshly made bacon and eggs reminded him of home. Earth was so far away, but having this food from home made this place seem a little more like home. Plus these biscuits and gravy were delicious—not as good as they were back home, made fresh in his kitchen, but it was a close second. Or maybe he'd been gone for too long.

-

Rear Admiral Barnes rested in her quarters. She knew the days ahead would be full of activity and preparations for the upcoming battles, so she had to sleep when she could. The thought of exploring parts of the Confederation that Humans had not been to before was pretty exhilarating. It's one of the reasons she became a pilot in the first place. She wanted to explore places near and far from Earth.

The opportunities she had capitalized on that got her here now were numerous. Things had worked out just right. Her mind was hard to quiet; sleep would evade her, until she could calm her thoughts. Barnes then let her mind wander back home, to her family and friends who remained on Earth. They were greatly missed, and she hoped that she would have the privilege of seeing them again one day.

As she faded off to sleep, her last thoughts were of her home on Earth.

-

Back in his office, Collison fine-tuned his battle plan. Lamothian fleets haven't fought their attack interceptors. He could use Derrick's strategy of engaging the fleet, while two battlecarriers jumped to the other side of the planet, launching all interceptors into the atmosphere. The Lamothians have no defense against interceptors—like the Druins have the drones, and Morag have the light cruisers.

What if the scout ships set off sensors all over the Confederation? The Confederation would have no idea where the Humans were coming from or going to. It would look like we were coming from all around them. Maybe all over the star systems of the Morag. Making it seem like the Morag were surrounded. Maybe Collison should spread out the Morag fleets all over the place, which would leave their shipyards less guarded. Collison could jump from one world to another, destroying as many shipyards as possible, ideally engaging the enemy fleets only if it couldn't be avoided.

There were lots of possibilities, and Collison still had time to make his final decisions. Collison wanted to make sure to look at all possible angles of how they could attack and when and where. The more options he had, the better, and then he could fine-tune them as time went on. He wanted to leave no idea left undeveloped.

The more possibilities they had, the better.

Chapter Nine

Collison and his Fourth Fleet, augmented by Third and Eighth Fleets, dropped from hyperspace just outside of the Lormallian-controlled star system. He looked up at the tactical display, as green icons appeared when Rear Admiral Barnes and her Third Fleet dropped from hyperspace. A few minutes later, even more green icons appeared as Rear Admiral Carrie and her Eighth Fleet reached the rendezvous point. "Captain Billingsly, scan the nearby systems for enemy fleets."

"Using our long-range scanner to scan the system."

Collison felt the tension in the air, as they awaited the results of the scan.

"Admiral, it looks like a Lormallian fleet is in the nearest system. Should I contact them to let them know we mean them no harm?" asked Captain Billingsly.

"No, not unless they make contact with us. I want to keep our hyperlight messages to a minimum to ensure they are not intercepted by the enemy. I am assuming that the Lormallians know we are not here for them. Keep an eye on their fleet formation. If anything changes, advise me."

Admiral Collison stood from his command chair and headed to meet with Barnes and Carrie. They had already planned to meet when they arrived at the rendezvous point to discuss their battle plan. Their meeting would take place here on the *Mercury* in the conference room. He assumed they were both en route to his ship.

Collison walked into the conference room and smiled as soon as he smelled the aroma of the appetizers prepared for them to snack on during their meeting. The smell of hot coffee lingered in the air. He surveyed the food, as he waited for the others to arrive. A meat and cheese platter sat next to the fruit tray. What he was most excited to eat though were the little smokies and chips and queso.

He closed his eyes and could almost hear the sounds of his family back home, as they enjoyed these snacks and had a family game night. He smiled and realized how much he missed home.

As he filled his plate, Barnes and Carrie walked in.

"Looks like you started without us," Barnes said, with a laugh.

"Didn't want you to have to wait in line," he said cheerfully.

They all laughed and chatted, as they filled their plates. Once the small talk and eating were finished, Collison got right down to business. He stood and turned on the holographic display. "I have had a lot of time to think about our different options for how to accomplish our mission. We have a few different plans to evaluate." They talked and strategized for a couple hours, making their battle plans and fallback options.

"Our final plan will mostly depend on what the scout ships have to tell us, correct?" asked Barnes.

Collison nodded.

"When should we hear from the scout ships?" asked Carrie, as they stood to head back to their flagships.

"I expect a report sometime this evening. Let's plan to meet here again tomorrow morning to go over the data we receive from them. Then we can fine-tune our plans and make our final preparations. Make all your repairs you need to. I want to start the next phase of our mission as soon as possible."

-

Ardon Reull finished his tour of a space station above another Lormallian planet. His assistant, Barlten Aveth, ran up to him. "Councilor Reull, we have detected a large Human fleet on the periphery of our system. What should we do?" He was breathless from running to find him.

Ardon turned to Major Cort and said, "Take me to the Command Center immediately."

Shortly they arrived at the Command Center. "Status report," commanded Reull, as they entered the room.

"We detect over two thousand ships in the Human fleet."

A smile slowly spread across Ardon's face. "This must be the Earth Humans' fleets coming for the Morag and their allies. They are a few days earlier than I expected. It's a good thing we have met with the Human Empire to make them aware of our intentions to stay out of this war."

"What should we do?" asked Major Cort.

"Have they sent us any hyperlight messages?" asked Ardon.

"No, there have been no messages."

"I assume they want to keep their presence a secret to surprise the Morag. Let's not send them any communications," replied Reull.

"How do we know they won't attack us for all the harm and destruction we've caused over the years to the Human Empire?" asked Major Cort.

"Let's show them that we are not a threat." Ardon paused, as he thought over the options for the best one. "Let's move our fleets away from that part of the system. Then they are reminded we are not a threat, while also acknowledging their presence in our star system."

"We will let the fleet know to move immediately to the other side of the star system," replied Major Cort.

Ardon smiled. This was a large fleet. From all reports, the Earth Humans had weapons the Morag could not defend against. Something called an accelerator cannon. This fleet was significant, but the Morag had a much more extensive fleet. Ardon took a deep breath. He hoped it was enough. He needed to meet with the Ruling Triad immediately and had many things to discuss with the Zang and Morphene councilors.

-

As Collison returned to the Command Center, he ran into Captain Billingsly.

"Admiral, I was just coming to inform you that the Lormallian fleet has changed positions."

"Are they headed this way, Captain?"

"No, sir. They are moving away from our location, to the other side of the star system."

"I take that as them saying, they are aware of our presence and an acknowledgment that they know we are not a threat to them."

"That is our consensus as well, sir," replied Billingsly.

"Have we had any reports from the scout ships yet?" he asked, as he entered the Command Center.

"None yet, sir. We expect some data soon."

Scout ship 125 had dropped from hyperspace just outside one of the star systems controlled by the Druins. Planet Druin Seven was located in this star system. It was the primary target the Earth fleet had selected to destroy. They had decided to leave hyperspace just outside the system in an abundance of caution, in case the Druins had a system in place that could detect them.

"Lieutenant Henley, anything on our long-range sensors?" asked Captain Laine.

"Nothing yet, sir," replied Lieutenant Henley.

"Take us in as fast as our sublight drive will take us. Keep us as near to that largest asteroid as possible. We need to get closer to take a more detailed scan."

All six crew members were on edge, as they moved into position.

"Lieutenant Henley, begin our long-range scans now," commanded Laine.

"Sir, I detect a Druin battle fleet on patrol in this system."

"How many ships?" asked Captain Laine.

"Just over eight hundred."

"Let's scan the planetary defenses," said Laine.

"Looks like they have a shipyard and two space stations orbiting the planet. All three of them are armed. It also looks like they have a defensive grid in place," replied Henley.

"Let's send this data to Admiral Collison and head back out slowly to where we jumped in. We will go to the next Druin-controlled star system and scan it. Maybe we can find a less-defended Druin planet to destroy." Captain Laine studied his map they had retrieved from the Confederation ships damaged above Golan Four.

-

Scout ship 368 dropped out of hyperspace outside of the Lamothian star system, where their home planet Lamothia was located.

"Lieutenant Maddox, what do we having on our long-range scanners?"

"Captain Hadley, I only sense a small Lamothian fleet of eighty-three ships."

Captain Hadley sat back down in her seat. "What about the planet? Is it protected by a defensive grid? Are there space stations or shipyards?"

"We need to move in closer to detect those defenses," replied Maddox.

"Take us in slowly. Watch that fleet for any changes in their positions."

"Engaging sublight drive."

After a few tense minutes Lieutenant Maddox replied, "It looks like no defensive grid is in place. Only two space stations and one small shipyard. The space stations are armed. It seems they are working to arm the shipyard."

"Let's send this data back to the admiral and move on to the next Lamothian system. We do expect the main Lamothian fleet to be nearby this next system. Let's be cautious. We don't want to lose our element of surprise," Captain Hadley remarked, as she took her seat in her command chair. *One down, three systems to go. Let's hope they all remain as uneventful as this one.*

-

Scout ship 255 dropped from hyperspace on the periphery of the Morag-controlled part of the Confederation. Sensor alarms immediately sounded.

"Lieutenant Pamela, report!" exclaimed Captain Malachi.

"Sir, we detect over five hundred Morag warships in this star system."

"Have they changed their positions any in response to our presence?" asked Malachi.

"They do appear to be changing positions, sir," replied Pamela in an unsteady voice.

"Let's use our sublight drive to get close to that uninhabited moon. Keep an eye on the fleet. If it looks like they've sensed us, we will get out of here."

-

Admiral Nortic, we sense some radiation from a hyperspace jump on the periphery of the system. It is very faint, and it barely shows up on our sensors.
Scan the system immediately!
I do not detect any ships on the long-range scanners.
Let's jump out there and check it out. We don't want any surprises.

-

"Lieutenant Pamela, let's scan this system and head to the next one," ordered Captain Malachi.

"Scanning now," reported Lieutenant Pamela.

Captain Malachi sat on the edge of his seat. Their stealth capabilities had not been tested in the Confederation. Suddenly alarms sounded, and red lights lit up on the console. "What is going on, Lieutenant Pamela?"

"Just finished the scan. Part of the Morag fleet has jumped to our previous location and is scanning the area."

"Let's get out of here then. We've got what we came for. Let's go to another star system without a Morag-inhabited planet."

"Transitioning to hyperspace now."

-

Admiral, we have found no ships on our scanners. Another very faint trace of radiation has been picked up nearest the moon by our sensors.
Take us there now.
They all had their focus on the tactical display.
Nothing shows up on the scans. It must have been nothing.
Should we report it? What if it were the Earth Humans?

*They don't have stealth capabilities advanced enough that we cannot detect
them. Let's return to our patrol. Keep watching for more spiked levels of
radiation, just to be sure though. We don't want any surprises.*

Yes, Admiral.

Scout ship 368 dropped out of hyperspace in the periphery of
the next system inhabited by the Lamothians. This system was
where the planet Xanther was located, where the Morag were
laying their trap for the Humans. The long-range sensors
immediately sounded. Red threat icons appeared on the screen.

Lieutenant Maddox turned to Captain Hadley and said, "It
looks like a Lamothian fleet patrols the system. They seem to be
more heavily orbiting the second and fifth planets in the system."

"Let's move in slowly for a closer look. I want to know how
many shipyards and space stations are in this system," replied
Captain Hadley.

As the ship used their sublight drive to slowly move closer to
the planets, the crew constantly watched the movements of the
enemy fleets for any changes in their behavior, indicating they'd
sensed their stealth ship. Thankfully nothing changed.

"Let's stop here, close to the sixth planet, and see what we can
discover of the second and fifth planet." The sixth planet was a
gas giant and uninhabited.

"Starting scans now of fifth planet," said Lieutenant Maddox.

All gazes were on the tactical display in front of them.

"Captain, it looks like forty-eight battleships are in orbit
around the fifth planet. Also two space stations and one shipyard.
I am sensing an energy shield around both space stations and the
shipyard. They are not currently activated."

"Can we detect if any Humans are on board any of these ships
or space stations? Also scan the planet," remarked Hadley.

"Scanning for Humans now."

Hadley had a sense of dread in the pit of her stomach. She
knew if they sensed any Humans, they likely would die a horrific

death before the fleet could rescue them. She realized she was holding her breath and slowly let it out.

"I detect no Humans in any of the ships, space stations, or the fifth planet."

Hadley let out a sigh of relief. "They must all be on the second planet, Xanther, for the feast that is to take place in five days. Let's move on to Xanther and see what information we can gather." She feared that they would probably discover a large number of Humans on Xanther. She prepared herself for what was to come.

Three hours later, they arrived close enough to the second planet to use their scanners.

Hadley took a deep breath and said, "Lieutenant, begin your scans." Hadley tried to calm her fears, as she swallowed the lump in her throat.

"Detecting fifty-seven battleships orbiting the planet, as well as one space station and two shipyards. All have energy shields that are not activated."

"Begin scan for Human life," Captain Hadley said slowly.

"I detect Humans on the space station as well as on the planet," replied Maddox.

"How many?" Hadley asked, with a sense of dread.

"Scanners detect one thousand Humans on the space station and a little over ten thousand on the planet surface."

"Where are they getting these Humans?" Hadley asked her crew. Everyone just shook their heads in puzzlement. It had been a while since any Humans had been taken from the Empire. The Confederation must have somewhere that they store a population of Humans to use at their disposal. Hadley felt the bile rise in her throat.

"Let's head to the next system. We must figure out where the Lamothians are getting the Humans from!"

Krista was getting ready to spend her evening with Mathew. She wouldn't be alone with him of course; Brenda would be their chaperone. Krista had tried on four different outfits, until she finally settled on one. They had made plans to dine at one of Cheryl's restaurants located close to the Imperial Palace that served Earth-style food. It was a popular place to eat, and usually getting a reservation there was not easy. She had connections though and could get right in. She thought to herself that being a princess sometimes had its perks.

Krista and Mathew settled into the booth in the back of the restaurant. Brenda was not far away, seated at the bar, probably thinking she could give them a little privacy in a public place like this. Of course Imperial Guards were posted outside as well.

"Have you eaten here before?" Krista asked Mathew.

"No, I have not had the pleasure of tasting Earth food yet. What would you recommend?" he asked.

Krista perused the menu for a few moments. "I plan on having the chicken parmesan. I have heard the spaghetti and meatballs are delicious as well."

"That sounds good to me," Mathew said, with a smile. He was glad he had this opportunity to spend some time with Krista. It would help distract him from the fact that many of his friends and crewmates were preparing to head into battle without him. He had been stationed on the *Orion*, a battlecarrier currently serving in Rear Admiral Lira Carrie's fleet. Mathew had helped train most of the attack interceptor crews on board. He wished he could be with them now but also understood why he couldn't be.

The waiter came and took their order. Krista was quite the talker this evening. She had so much she wanted to talk to Mathew about. He had been so busy lately, training new interceptor crews, that Krista had hardly had the chance to see him. He was a little distracted, but he was just glad to spend some time with her.

They weren't in any danger at the moment, which was a relief. The fighting had moved to the Confederation for a change, so they would just hear about it and not be facing imminent death if they were defeated. For now, he and Krista could relax.

She smiled at the waiter, as he brought their drinks and some bread to the table.

"What is this bread called?" Mathew asked Krista.

"It's garlic bread, and it's delicious."

Soft music played in the background, and the lights of the restaurant were muted. It was such a romantic place to eat. She hoped Mathew thought about their future as much as she did. Of course, with the Confederation rebuilding and undoubtedly planning another attack, their plans would have to wait. She would just relax and enjoy this day and hope they had many more of these to come.

They had a wonderful evening and talked for hours at the restaurant, until it was time for the restaurant to close. "This food was delicious, Krista. I hope we can come back here soon. That spaghetti and meatballs were amazing." He grabbed Krista's hand and looped his fingers through hers, as they left the restaurant.

Krista sighed, as she glanced at Mathew. Tonight was perfect. She couldn't wait to see him again. She hoped soon they could get away from their duties and spend more time together. She would be swamped over the next few days, preparing for the next meeting of the House of Worlds. Things were falling into place for her and the Empire. She just hoped it stayed that way.

Chapter Ten

Ardon Reull was back on Lormallia to meet with the Lormallian Ruling Triad.

"We have heard a sizable Human Empire fleet is on the periphery of our star system. Have we had any communication with the Humans?" asked the Leader of the Triad, Mador Angst.

"We have not, and I do not expect to hear anything from them," replied Ardon. "If I were them, I would keep hyperlight messages to a minimum, so as not to give away our position. Also they are here a few days earlier than I expected, so they benefit from an early attack. Maybe even before the Morag have positioned themselves where they intend to."

"Are we sure we are in no danger from these Humans?" asked Serrie Voll.

"Yes, I am confident that we have nothing to fear from them. What we need to consider is what our future holds. We know that, as long as the Human Empire is a threat to the Confederation, specifically the Morag, we will not become their primary target.

"I expect us to become the Morag target after they have conquered the Human Empire, as well as Earth. Then the Morag will come for us. So we benefit from these Human fleets having a successful mission. It would buy us valuable time to finish our defensive grids and to arm the rest of our shipyards and space stations."

The Triad was quiet for a moment, while they all considered this news. "What do you propose that we do?" asked Angst.

"I would like to consider if we should or should not help the Humans in their mission here. Their success benefits us. Their defeat hurts us. We have to weigh the costs against the rewards."

"If the Humans lose, and we helped them, the Morag will come for us swiftly and without mercy," Birx Storl remarked.

Ardon replied, "If we don't help the Humans, and they win, the Morag will still come for us. However, I don't think they would, not until they defeated the Human Empire and Earth, saving their fleets for the Humans initially."

"That would give us valuable time to build up our defenses and our fleets to a larger number to defend the star systems under our control," Angst replied.

Voll said, "If we help the Humans, and they win this battle, the Morag will still come for us. Maybe even before the Humans, since we are the closest to them."

"So that leaves the scenario of, what if the Humans lose, and we didn't help them? The Morag have then defeated one foe, and we move up the list. They still come for us," Angst said, with a sigh.

"The common end remains the same in all the scenarios. The Morag come for us," replied Ardon. "We just have to decide which scenario benefits us the most and which gives us the most time to prepare to fight the Morag."

"We also need to look to our future farther down the line. How do we strengthen our relationship with our allies? This includes the Humans and the Visth. We want to trade when this war is over. We want our future to be peaceful and to get our race back to what it once was, before the Morag came along."

"I believe our future is dependent on the Humans winning this war," Ardon said, with a grimace.

"This decision will determine our future," said Voll. "We should not make this decision lightly."

The Triad continued to debate among themselves and with Ardon for a few hours, finally deciding what they should do.

Admiral Cleemorl was in his quarters aboard his flagship, *Themis*. He had not slept well the night before, with the impending attack on the Confederation set to begin any day now. He wished the Empire could do more. Now that their fleet grew bigger each day, he was less worried about a Confederation counterattack. He walked slowly to the cafeteria to get his morning tea and breakfast. How could he help Collison? Cleemorl also didn't want to leave the Empire and the Hagen Star Cluster vulnerable.

"You look like you're deep in thought, Admiral," said Colonel Jase Bidwell, as he got behind the admiral in line for breakfast.

"Yes, sorry. I didn't see you there, Colonel. I've just been thinking about how we could help Admiral Collison and also keep this area of the Empire safe. They came through for us when we needed it. I'd like to return the favor."

As they filled their plates with a hot breakfast, they sat down together at an unoccupied table.

"Do you have any ideas how we can assist them?" asked Bidwell.

"I've been up thinking about it most of the night. I know his fleet is accompanied by his supply fleet, which includes mobile repair yards. I can only assume they will station the supply chain somewhere within the Confederation, where they can access it for resupply and to repair what ships they can. They are designed, as a fleet, for a long-term mission. My concern lies in when they return to the supply fleet. I think the Morag will follow them."

"The supply fleet would need to be in a safe part of the Confederation as well. Which limits their options," replied Bidwell.

"Battleships would be left with the supply chain but not enough to ward off a pursuing fleet of the Confederation." Cleemorl and Bidwell were quiet for a few minutes, while they thought over the scenarios.

"Maybe we could send part of the fleet to rendezvous where the supply fleet is, in case the Morag pursue Collison's fleet," said Bidwell.

Cleemorl finished his breakfast and headed with Bidwell to the Command Center. When they entered, they pulled up the holographic display. "Where would they leave the supply fleet?" asked Cleemorl aloud.

"Would Admiral Marloo know what Collison's plans were?" asked Bidwell.

"Wouldn't hurt to ask," said Cleemorl. "I will get ahold of him and find out what he knows. I will meet back here, once I have some answers—if there are any."

In the underground Command Center, beneath the House of Worlds, Admiral Marloo updated Vice Fleet Admiral Masters on the fleets' progress in the Confederation. "I have talked to Cleemorl. He is concerned that, when the three fleets jump back to the supply fleet, the Morag will pursue them. Cleemorl doesn't feel that they will have sufficient ships to defend this type of pursuit," said Marloo.

"He does have a good point," replied Masters. "What does Cleemorl want to do about it?"

Marloo chuckled. "He wants to take part of his fleet and be there to help, should the situation arise, like he thinks it will."

"Of course he does," said Masters, with a smile. "I would like to get in on that too, but Layla would not stand for that."

"Collison plans to leave his supply fleet here," Marloo said, as he pulled up the holographic display. He pointed to an area on the periphery of the Lormallian-controlled star systems.

"How long would it take Cleemorl to get there from the Hagen Star Cluster? Could he even get there in time?"

"It's two days to the periphery of the Confederation from the Hagen Star Cluster. Then another three days to the Lormallian star system, where Collison will leave his supply fleet."

"So, five days. When do we expect Collison to start his attack? He should be making his hyperspace jump to the Morag part of the Confederation within the next day. Their area of the Confederation is three days out from their current location. So, at a minimum, we have six days to get there." Derrick went silent for a few moments, while he considered the options. "Cleemorl would need to leave within the next twenty-four hours."

"That's correct."

"He'd be cutting it close, but it could work. How many ships does he intend to take?" asked Masters. "He can't leave the Hagen Star Cluster under-protected. The Confederation might be using this trap they set up at the Lamothian planet as a ploy to get our fleets out of the way for an attack on the Empire."

"Cleemorl has had the last few weeks to repair damaged ships. Utilizing the shipyards spread throughout the Hagen Star Cluster, he has recovered some of the ships he had lost in battle. His fleet is currently up to 908 battlecruisers and 102 dreadnoughts. It's growing every day. He is considering taking a task force about the same size as Rear Admiral Carrie's—120 battlecruisers and 30 dreadnoughts."

"Hopefully enough to aid the supply fleet but not too big that it weakens the Hagen Star Cluster," Masters said, as he thought over the numbers.

"He will split the remaining fleet in half. One half will be under the command of Rear Admiral Fulmar, and the other half will be commanded by Rear Admiral Manson," commented Marloo.

"How will we get word to Collison?" asked Masters.

"We won't. We don't want to risk the message being intercepted by the Confederation. We also don't want Collison depending on Cleemorl making it there in time, when he might not," replied Marloo.

"I hope this mission to the Confederation is a success," said Masters. "I will update Layla on the current status."

"Thank you. I will let you know when I hear anything else from the Earth fleets or Admiral Cleemorl."

Derrick decided to wait until later that evening to tell Layla about Cleemorl going to the Confederation. They had a lovely family meal with Andrew, Kala, Krista, and Mathew. It was nice to sit back and to relax a little. They had enjoyed a nice dinner, with some exceptional food that Andrew and Kala had requested the chef make. It was some of their favorite Earth meals. Sirloin steak with mashed potatoes and gravy. A green salad with a dressing he had not ever tasted before. Kala called it *Ranch*.

He thought the best part were the rolls, so delicious with that excellent topping Andrew insisted Derrick put on them, called butter. Earth Humans have some odd names for some of their food. Derrick figured Andrew and Kala thought that about their foods as well. Dessert was apple pie, apparently one of Andrew's favorites. It was good, definitely something Derrick would try again. Derrick knew Andrew and Kala really missed their home at times. Derrick knew how that felt. He had missed Golan Four, while he had been away at Pallas in the Solar System.

After the meal was over and the table had been cleared, he decided he'd better let everyone know the status of the Earth fleets and Dylan Cleemorl's intentions of heading to the Confederation himself.

"I met with Marloo today, and he updated me on the Earth fleets. They should have made it to the rendezvous point where they will leave their supply fleet, just on the edge of the Lormallian-controlled star system by now. They've sent ahead scout ships to collect information on where the Confederation fleets are."

"Sounds like things are going according to plan so far," replied Layla, with a smile.

"There has been one new development," Derrick said, with a pause. "Dylan has decided to head to the rendezvous point to help protect the supply fleet and to take care of any Confederation ships that might follow the Earth fleets back into hyperspace." He looked around the table to see everyone's response. They all knew Dylan very well and would be concerned for his safety.

"Does he have enough ships to take some and to leave enough behind to protect the Hagen Star Cluster?" asked Layla.

"Yes, he and Marloo have gone over all the details, and they are both confident in the plan," replied Derrick.

"It does sound like a solid plan. After all, if not for the Earth fleets arriving when they did, things may have gone differently in the Hagen Star Cluster and here above Golan Four. It's only fitting that we return the favor," replied Layla.

Andrew then said, "Our production of battlecruisers and dreadnoughts is at an all-time high across the Empire. We have more shipyards producing our ships than ever."

"Yes, as we add more and more worlds to the Empire, we are also adding more shipyards. We have a lot of worlds we need to defend, when the Confederation returns to attack us," replied Layla.

"I am sure Cheryl will not be happy with Dylan putting himself in harm's way again," remarked Krista.

"I don't envy him having that conversation with her," chuckled Derrick.

"I think Dylan has made the right decision. I know we will all remain concerned for his safety, as well as for the safety of all the fleets who have gone on to the Confederation to attack the Morag and their Confederation allies," said Layla. "They will be heavy on our thoughts over the next few days."

-

Cheryl knew something was going on when Dylan wanted to take her out to dinner at one of her nicest restaurants. She figured he either needed to apologize for something he had already done or something he was about to do. She had a feeling of dread deep down in the pit of her stomach.

The dinner went well, but she could tell he was abnormally quiet. She was the talker between the two of them, but he was quieter than usual. "So, what's going on? What's on your mind?" Cheryl asked.

"I have some news I need to tell you that you won't like," replied Dylan, a concerned look on his face. He gave her a small smile and then dove right in. "I am taking part of the fleet to the Confederation as a sort of safety net for Collison's fleets."

124

Cheryl went silent for a moment. She knew in her heart that it was the right thing for him to do; it didn't make it any easier for her though. "Okay. When do you have to leave?"

Dylan was surprised. He had assumed she would be much more upset and argue with him about it. She hadn't at all. He was speechless.

"Are you okay, Dylan?"

"Yes, I'm just surprised you are taking this so well."

"There's not much I can say that would change your mind. I also know it is the right thing to do. You know what you are doing, and, if you think you should do it, then I will assume it's the right thing for the Empire," Cheryl said, with a shrug. "I want you to be extremely careful and to not take any unnecessary risks."

"Of course. Thank you for being so understanding and supportive," replied Dylan.

"When will you have to leave?" asked Cheryl.

"Within the next twelve hours. The sooner, the better. It's a long trip there. We need to be there before they need us." Dylan stood. "I guess it's time I get you home. I need to be back up on the *Themis* within the next hour."

Cheryl and Dylan left the restaurant hand in hand.

-

Admiral Dylan Cleemorl headed straight for the Command Center when he returned to the *Themis*. "Colonel Bidwell, is our task force ready to transition into hyperspace?"

"We will be within the hour," replied Bidwell.

"Do we have the coordinates to where we are headed?" asked Cleemorl.

"Yes, sir. When will we head out?" asked Bidwell.

"We depart in one hour. We will stop at the edge of the Confederation to make any repairs to our ships, before we make the long jump to the edge of the Lormallian-controlled star system. Make sure all the other ships are prepared and have our jump coordinates," commanded Cleemorl.

"Yes, sir."

An hour later, the task force was ready to depart.

"Colonel Bidwell, let's make the transition to hyperspace." Almost immediately Cleemorl felt the pang in the pit of his stomach, as they made their transition.

-

Scout ship 368 slowly moved into their next Lamothian star system to investigate what defenses were in place.

"Lieutenant Maddox, let's scan the system."

Captain Hadley was still trying to figure out where the Humans on that last Lamothian planet had come from.

"Captain, the scans show activity around the fourth and fifth planets in the system. Only twenty-three battleships are on patrol in this system, with a lot more trading vessels and transport vessels. They are congregated more around the fourth planet."

"Let's move in for a closer look," said Hadley.

As they slowly moved toward the fifth planet, Hadley felt more and more tension growing in her head. She felt more unease. "What defenses does this planet have?"

Maddox replied, "Three space stations. No shipyards. According to our records, this is the planet Admiral Cleemorl destroyed after the Confederation attacked Highland Station and took all the Humans captive, one being his wife, Cheryl."

"Scan for life on the surface."

"No life has been found on the surface. It appears they are trying to clean the atmosphere," replied Maddox.

Hadley shook her head. Soon another Lamothian world would look like this. It saddened her to think of all the lives lost here. Humans as well as Lamothians. Plus the destruction of a planet. She sighed. She wished there was another way but also knew deep down there was no other way. "What progress have they made so far on restoring the atmosphere to what it once was?"

"It will be a long time before the planet can sustain life, according to our scans."

"Let's move on to the next planet," Hadley said, with a sigh.

As they moved closer to the fourth planet, Maddox started his scans. "It looks like they have two shipyards and one space station. No defensive grid is in place. I will scan for Human life now."

"One would think that after the Empire destroyed one of their worlds and a world of their allies, the Druins, that they would put up some defensive grids around their planets. We haven't seen one yet. Aren't the Lamothians supposedly one of the smartest races of the Confederation?"

"I believe that is true. Maybe they think it's not possible for us to destroy another world?"

"Maybe the Morag have been using their telepathy to make the Lamothians feel comfortable, and thus they feel no need for defensive grids. That way, in case the Morag ever turn on them, they're easier to defeat," Hadley thought aloud.

"I find no Humans on or around this planet, Captain."

Hadley shook her head. "Where are they getting them from then? We have one more star system to scan that has a planet inhabited by the Lamothians. Maybe we will find our answers there."

Chapter Eleven

Princess Layla was on her way to the House of Worlds to meet with the Imperial Council. The Council members had arrived a few days ahead of the House of Worlds meeting that would occur the following week. She was the last to enter the Imperial Council Chamber. As she did, the rest of the Imperial Council stood.

"Good afternoon, everyone. Please, be seated. We have a lot to cover today," said Layla. "Chief Chancellor Stein, what is our first order of business?"

"First, I want Vice Fleet Admiral Masters to update us on the status of our fleets and defenses," remarked Stein, as he turned to Derrick.

Derrick stood to address the council. "We have made significant progress, since the Confederation attacked us six weeks ago. The new shipyard above Golan Four is making great progress. When it is finished, which should be in another eight weeks, it will be the largest shipyard in the Empire. It will have particle beam cannons, as well as Earth's accelerator cannons. Our fleets grow in numbers daily. At last count, First Fleet was up to 908 battlecruisers and 102 dreadnoughts. Fifth Fleet has also gained more ships. It is currently up to 681 battlecruisers and 87 dreadnoughts.

"We have also started construction on some mobile shipyards, like the ones Earth developed to repair ships wherever we are. These will be invaluable, when we take the war to the Confederation."

Chief Chancellor Stein then turned to Prince Andrew. "How did your meeting go with Lormallian Council Reull, the Visth, and their alliance?"

Andrew stood, as he addressed the council. "It went well overall. The Morag did try to interfere of course. They tried to murder Reull before he arrived at the meeting. They also tried to attack the Visth homeworld, where the meeting was taking place.

They only caused minor damage, before our combined fleets overtook them. The Visth and their alliance—called the United Worlds Alliance—will set up a governing body, much like our House of Worlds. The Visth representative, Stralon Karn, and a few other representatives from the alliance will be observing our House of Worlds meeting this next week."

Governor Alex Therron of Bratol Three then asked Prince Andrew, "How did talks go with the Lormallian representative?"

Andrew replied, "They went well. He agreed on behalf of the Lormallians and the Zang and the Morphene that they would not attack a world outside of the Confederation, unless their worlds are attacked first."

"Do you believe him?" asked Governor Lindsay Littrel of Jalot Four.

"Yes, I do. Reull also wanted an agreement that would allow for future trade between our worlds, when this war is behind us."

"That is great progress," commented Governor Julian Bemire of Ambary Two.

"He also gave me some weapons research, found in the archives on Bator Prime. He did not want it to fall into the hands of the Morag or their allies. The research is not complete, but he had no doubt that our scientists could finish the research and produce a workable weapon."

"What type of weapon is this?" asked Littrel.

"It's called an atomic disrupter. There is no defense against this weapon," replied Andrew.

"A weapon that could end this war," stated Layla.

"That is our hope," replied Andrew. "I believe the Lormallians and their allies want to live in peace and to return their worlds to what they were before the Morag came along. Worlds of peace and prosperity, worlds where art and music and science are celebrated, not war and destruction. They know that we are their best hope in defeating the Morag and ending their reign of terror and destruction."

"It is a good feeling to know that the Confederation has fractured, and three out of the seven races want peace," commented Therron.

"How is the weapons research going on this new weapon?" asked Layla.

"It is going well. The scientists estimate another six months of research and development, before they would be ready to test the new weapon. Then, if tests go accordingly, it would take another three months to equip the battleships with them."

"So, what you're saying is that, in another nine months, we can end this war?" asked Bemire.

"That is what we hope for," replied Andrew.

"Our future is looking promising," remarked Layla. "We are adding more worlds to the Empire almost every day. We currently have 653 planets and inhabited moons as a part of the Empire." Layla couldn't help but smile. Her father had dreamed of a day when they could unite so many worlds under the guidance of the Empire. She saw his dream come true. She wished he were here to see his dream come to fruition. If only they could protect all of the Empire. As it grew in number, it also grew in vastness of space, all to defend against the Confederation.

"How will we protect so many worlds against the Confederation?" asked Dru Clarro of Vidon Seven.

Derrick looked at Layla, Andrew, and Chief Chancellor Stein. They all looked at him. So Derrick stood to answer. "We are providing as many defensive grid elements as we can to all worlds that join the Empire. In another four and a half months, we will have over six thousand battleships to protect the Empire. We are replacing all the defenses damaged in the last attack, as well as the military base on Gideon. We expect to have everything replaced within the next sixty days. At that time, we will start providing other worlds in the Empire with more defense satellites, missile platforms, ODPs, PDCs, and attack interceptors. Once we have replaced what was destroyed, we will start arming the rest of the Empire."

"Thank you, Derrick," replied Stein. "We hope that the Earth fleets currently in the Confederation to attack the Morag will buy us the time we need to prepare for the Confederation's next attack—or we might be prepared to go on the offensive ourselves."

Everyone liked the sound of that. A lot rode on the Earth fleets' success in the Confederation.

"When do we expect to hear word from Collison on how things are going?" asked Clarro.

"We will probably have some news before the meetings for the House of Worlds are finished," replied Stein.

The Imperial Council continued their discussions for another hour, before adjourning for the day.

As Layla and Derrick headed back to the Imperial Palace, she said, "So much is riding on Collison's shoulders. I wish we had more communication with him, so we knew what was going on. This not-knowing-anything is driving me crazy."

"I'm sure, once the battle starts, they will update us on how things are progressing," replied Derrick.

"Let's hope so."

-

Scout ship 125 slowly made its way farther into the next Druin system they were to scan. It was a yellow dwarf system that had three inhabited planets. Their long-range scans had shown moderate activity around the third, fourth, and sixth planets. The scans had shown a Druin fleet of around five hundred ships patrolling this star system. The scout ship was currently closing in on the sixth planet.

"Lieutenant Henley, what do we have on our scanners?" asked Captain Laine.

"We show a lot of trading vessels in the area around this planet. Also a shipyard with one space station. Both are heavily armed. Also a defensive grid is in place," replied Lieutenant Henley.

"Let's move on to the next planet," said Captain Laine.

A little while later, they approached the fourth planet.

"My scans detect two space stations and one shipyard, all armed. Defensive grid is in the process of being put up but is not complete," said Lieutenant Henley.

"We have a lot to report to Collison. We need to find a target that will be the easiest to destroy. We need to find a planet without a defensive grid and a small fleet patrolling the area. That would be ideal. Let's move on to the last planet inhabited in this system," said Captain Laine.

As they traveled to the next planet, the third one, using their sublight drive to make sure they weren't detected, Laine studied his map to try to find a star system with few Druin-inhabited planets.

After some thought, he had decided their next system would be the red giant system. It had only one inhabited world in it. It was closer to the Morag area of space but farther from the other races of the Confederation that weren't now a part of their alliance.

So maybe, just maybe, they hadn't had the opportunity to put up a defensive grid yet. With it closer to the Morag, maybe there wasn't a large fleet patrolling the system. They were running out of time to find the best target. Hopefully this next system would be the one they were looking for.

The scans of this third planet were similar to the previous one. One shipyard and one space station were heavily armed. The defensive grid was in the process of being put up. It was time to move on.

-

As scout ship 125 entered the red giant system, which Laine had picked out, a smile crossed his face. Their scans only detected twenty-five battleships in the system, along with some trading vessels and transport ships. As they made their approach to the third planet, which was the only inhabited one in the system, his face lit up even more.

"Lieutenant Henley, please scan the planet."

"Looks like no defensive grid is up yet. It also looks like the space station is armed, but the shipyard is not. They appear to be in the process of arming it now," replied Henley.

"It looks like we have finally found what we're looking for. A less-defended planet without a defensive grid," Laine said, with a smile. "What is the name of this planet, Lieutenant Henley?"

"Druin Nine," replied Henley.

"Let's get out of here and send all our data to Collison. We will continue scanning nearby systems to see if we can locate the rest of the Druin fleet. We've located about 1,300 battleships, so who knows how many more are out there."

Captain Laine finally found the rest of the Druin fleet patrolling a star system closest to the Lormallian area of space. This fleet was only one day's hyperspace jump from where Collison intended to leave the supply fleet. Laine needed to let Collison know this immediately. As soon as he got the word to him, he intended to stay and to monitor this fleet closest to the Human Empire fleet. They might not know it yet, but they would eventually figure it out.

The Empire fleet would have as much warning as possible, if Laine kept his scout ship here to monitor this enemy fleet. If they jumped out, Laine could give their fleet a pretty good heads-up before the enemy was upon them. Maybe enough time to move locations or to be prepared to fight. This was a sizable fleet; it just depended on how many Collison decided to leave behind to defend his supply fleet.

Laine had enjoyed exploring the Confederation over the last few days, but now the exploring was over. The battle grew near. This enemy fleet might respond to their planet being attacked, or it might attack the supply fleet. Only time would tell.

The Forgotten Empire: The Confederation and The Empire at War

Morag Admiral Voxx was having his last meeting with the Morag High Council, before their planned trap for the Confederation was set.

Admiral Voxx, is everything ready for your trap for the Human Empire? asked Councilor Addonis.

Yes, my fleet is ready to leave immediately following our meeting today, replied Voxx.

You will be taking a large-enough fleet to decimate these Earth Humans and their fleets. Even with the new weapons they possess, we should outnumber them enough for it to be a moot point. This time they will not have their planets and their planetary defenses to help them in their fight, said Addonis.

We are all but assured of a victory in the Lamothian star system. The Humans will never reach our part of the Confederation. We trust you to stamp out this nuisance that is the Human Empire. They will learn not to come into the Confederation. To do so means certain death, remarked Councilor Delann.

Are we planning on taking prisoners and giving them to the Lamothians? asked Voxx.

If it so happens that the situation warrants prisoners, then so be it. I, however, doubt that any ships will survive the battle to obtain hostages from, said Addonis.

It will be a swift and total destruction of their fleet. They will regret the day they decided to enter the Confederation. You know what to do and have the fleet to crush them. We expect total victory, with no Human ship escaping. If need be, chase them to the edge of the Confederation. Do not chase them outside of the Confederation, as I am certain an Empire fleet lies in wait, remarked Councilor Brant.

You have your orders, Admiral Voxx, and we will await your triumphant return to Morag Prime, where you will be celebrated as one of our most successful and best admirals of all time, said Addonis.

Admiral Voxx left the Morag High Council room. It was all on him to lead his race to victory. This was his moment, his destiny. He would bring pride to himself and his race by crushing these

Humans. After that, the Empire and Earth would be hesitant to enter the Confederation. The Morag would use these Earth Humans as an example for the entire Empire. No Human enters the Confederation and lives.

Visth Representative Stralon Karn was on his way, with a few other representatives of their United Worlds Alliance, heading to Golan Four to witness the meeting of the House of Worlds. Their new alliance planned to model their new government after the Empire's House of Worlds.

The House of Worlds had their upcoming meeting set for next week. Karn hoped they could learn a lot about how to structure their new alliance, which would give them the best chance at a successful future. He knew that the future that they hoped for was contingent on the success of the Human Empire, bringing the Confederation to its knees.

If Karn could do anything to aid in this process, he favored it. This was one thing he hoped to get a chance to talk about with the High Princess Layla or Prince Andrew. Prince Andrew seemed to be a very knowledgeable asset, when he had visited their homeworld to meet with the Lormallian Councilor Ardon Reull. Andrew was responsible for getting them a fully functioning defensive grid, which was now in place above their homeworld.

Karn hoped to talk to him about the ODPs that he had mentioned at their last meeting, as they were important to help guarantee the safety of his homeworld. He had already received a shipment of the nullifiers from Ardon Reull of the Lormallians. Karn expected another shipment soon. He had also received the nullifier plans from Reull, and production had started on a couple planets.

Karn glanced over at the tactical display; he had in his convoy some trading vessels and a few battleships. He had brought along one convoy of ships for their defense on the off chance they ran into a Confederation fleet. Karn knew at this time that was highly unlikely, but he didn't want to take the chance. The trading vessels were loaded with goods to trade with Golan Four. He wanted to prove to the Empire that they were a valuable ally and trading partner.

With a bit of luck, he would leave Golan Four with a few ODPs and a more solid alliance. The things they would learn from the Empire over the next week would be put to good use down the line in his own alliance. Hopefully the trading vessels would be loaded with valuable goods from this part of the Empire as they returned home. He was looking forward to a fruitful and productive week on Golan Four.

-

Scout ship 368 dropped from hyperspace, just inside the last star system controlled by the Lamothians, a red giant system. Only one planet in this system was inhabited, the fourth planet, being 80 percent water. The rest was one large landmass.

"Lieutenant Maddox, let's scan this system," commanded Captain Hadley.

"Only thirty-nine battleships in this system, Captain."

"Let's move in for a closer look. To my calculations, we've only come across 250 Lamothian battleships. Where are the rest of them? When they attacked Earth, they had a much bigger fleet," remarked Hadley. They had two unanswered questions still. Where were they getting the Humans, and where was their main fleet of battleships?

"Maybe they are waiting in a nearby system for the Empire to attack Xanther, and then they will help the Morag ambush them?" wondered Maddox.

"We need to find the fleet." As they moved in closer to the planet, Hadley examined her map of the Confederation. She knew she needed to explore the star systems closest to Xanther to see if she could figure out where the Lamothian fleet was. This would help Collison decide which planet to destroy.

"I detect one space station and one shipyard, Captain. Both are armed and have energy shields, but they are not activated. There is no defensive grid in place."

"Let's scan the planet and space station for Humans."

"Scanning now," replied Maddox. "My scans show no Humans on the planet or the space station."

Hadley was still puzzled over where the Humans were coming from. Maybe they could go back to Xanther and follow a transport ship, until they found where the Humans were being transported from. Yes, that's what she would do. First, however, she needed to find the main Lamothian fleet and report back to Collison. "Maddox, let's move on to this yellow dwarf system just outside of the Lamothian-controlled area of the Confederation. I think it would be a short hyperspace jump from there to Xanther. Let's see if we can find this fleet."

"Yes, Captain," replied Maddox.

Scout ship 255 dropped from hyperspace just outside of a Morag-controlled star system. According to the data retrieved from the damaged Morag ships left above Golan Four, this star system was home to four inhabited planets. These four planets each had two shipyards and two space stations. This was one of the star systems Collison's fleet would target.

With eight shipyards, it was too hard to resist.

What the damaged Morag ships didn't tell Malachi was where the Morag fleets were and in what numbers. This information was what Captain Malachi was here to find out. The scout ship slowly moved into the system, using its sublight drive. Progress was much slower this way, but they had already witnessed the Morag could sense radiation from a hyperspace jump. For this reason, Captain Malachi had transitioned out of hyperspace much farther away than last time from the system.

"What is on our long-range scanners?" asked Captain Malachi.

"We show a large Morag fleet patrolling this star system," replied Lieutenant Pamela.

"How large is large?" asked Malachi.

"Just over one thousand ships, sir," Pamela said, as she tried to swallow down her fear.

"Any movement in the fleet formation?" asked Captain Malachi, a hint of fear in his voice.

"No, sir, nothing yet."

"We need to see if we can get closer to use our short-range scanners on those shipyards. See if they are armed or have an energy shield protecting them. Lieutenant Pamela, let's slowly move closer," said Captain Malachi.

They all kept their gazes glued to the tactical display at all the red threat icons, as they slowly moved closer to the shipyards. After what seemed like an eternity, they were close enough to start their scans. "Let's run those scans, Pamela."

"Scanning now."

It was so quiet inside the ship that everyone heard Malachi's watch in his breast pocket, ticking the seconds by. It was a family heirloom that his grandfather had given his father, who had then passed it on to Malachi, just before he had taken command of this scout ship. A little piece of home, always close to his heart.

"According to the scans, both the shipyards and the space stations are armed. All of them also have energy shields."

"As I feared. Not as easy of a target as we had hoped." Captain Malachi chuckled. "Not that we thought it would be easy. We were all hoping they weren't armed or protected by energy shields. Let's go ahead and move slowly to the next planet. If this next one yields us the same results as this planet, then I think it will be safe to assume it's true of all the planets in this system. We can then move on to the next star system."

A couple hours later, they found the next planet also had their shipyards and space stations armed and protected by an energy shield. Captain Malachi decided to move on to the next star system.

After scanning multiple star systems ruled by the Morag and finding most of the shipyards and space stations armed and protected by an energy shield, and determining where most of the enemy fleets were, Captain Malachi decided it was time to report all their findings to Collison.

Malachi would then come and keep an eye on the largest congregation of the enemy fleet, which was in the star system containing the Morag homeworld of Morag Prime. Malachi knew twenty stealth scout ships had been assigned to scan and to explore the Morag-controlled area of the Confederation.

With 112 planets in 92 different star systems and 200 terraformed moons, Collison would have a lot of data to sift through.

-

Scout ship 368 exited hyperspace in the yellow dwarf system, not far from the Lamothian-controlled area of the Confederation. "What do our scans pick up?" asked Captain Hadley.

"Nothing, Captain. No ships in the star system. No battleships. Only transport and trading vessels," replied Lieutenant Maddox.

"Let's move in closer and scan for Humans on the inhabited planets."

"Yes, Captain."

Hadley knew her time was running out. She needed to report back to Collison. She had two more star systems to scan for the Lamothian fleet. It wouldn't take long to check these planets though.

As they moved toward the second planet, alarms sounded. "What's going on, Maddox?"

"Enemy fleet dropping out of hyperspace, Captain," replied Maddox.

"How many ships? Is it the Lamothians?" asked Hadley.

"No, Captain, it is a Morag battle fleet. Ships are still dropping out of hyperspace. The current count is over two thousand," Maddox said in amazement.

"Use our sublight drive to move away from the fleet. Let's move into orbit around this planet. If these other ships leave this system, we will too, at the same time. That way, nothing looks suspicious."

Shortly after they started orbiting the planet, the other transport and trading vessels began jumping out of the system. "How many Morag ships are in the fleet now, Maddox?" asked Hadley.

"Just over five thousand battlecruisers and battleships," Maddox said, with a hint of fear in his voice. "They have stopped exiting hyperspace."

"We need to report to Collison immediately. Let's jump out of here to the nearest inhabited star system," said Hadley.

-

Morag Admiral Voxx dropped from hyperspace in a yellow dwarf system, just outside the main star systems of the Lamothian-controlled area of the Confederation. This is where they would lay in wait for the Earth Humans to arrive at Xanther to stop the Lamothians from consuming Humans in their upcoming feast.

Voxx still had a few days to prepare the fleet, before the Humans were expected to arrive. He had intended to go over their tactics for the coming battle and work on some of their formations. Changing formations was so much easier than he'd imagined it was for the Humans.

With the Morag's telepathic abilities, they could move as one and change formations with no trouble at all. This was one advantage he had over the Humans. The Morag telepathic communication was instantaneous. The Humans would be without backup and without the extra help from their planetary defenses and orbital defenses. In a fleet-to-fleet battle, Voxx had no doubt the Morag were superior and would reign supreme.

-

Scout ship 368 exited hyperspace in a neighboring star system. Immediately alarms sounded. "Now what?" asked Captain Hadley.

"Another enemy fleet, Captain. It looks like we have found the missing Lamothian fleet," answered Maddox.

"How many warships are in this fleet? Let's hope it's fewer than in the Morag fleet," Captain Hadley said in a serious tone.

"Yes, there is less. According to my scan, 1,257 battlecruisers and battleships are in this Lamothian fleet," replied Maddox.

"All right, get us out of here to report our findings to Admiral Collison. I guess he will want us to observe the bigger Morag fleet for when they head back into hyperspace. Hopefully Collison's plan will work, and, when the Morag leave here, it will be to head home to defend their star systems," said Hadley. "Lieutenant Maddox, take us to hyperspace and drop us out in the next star system."

Lamothian Admiral Zahn prepared his fleet for the battle they would soon fight against the Earth Humans. He was looking forward to getting some revenge on these Earth Humans, after what transpired when the Lamothians had attacked the Solar System.

He did not like the Morag putting one of their worlds in danger. Zahn did not want his race being used as bait. Not that they had been asked. The Morag had already put their plan in action before the Lamothians had been notified of their role in this trap.

At least they had this perfect opportunity to destroy the Earth Humans' fleet before they could do much harm. The Humans had no idea what they would be facing. Between his Lamothian fleet and the Morag fleet, they had over 6,200 warships. He intended to let the Morag take the lead in this battle; he'd rather not lose any ships, if he could help it. The Morag had plenty to spare.

Of course the Morag would not be concerned with protecting the planet but with destroying the Human fleet. Zahn was glad he had a nullifier; no need to worry about Admiral Voxx trying to influence his fleet through him. None of the other ship captains had a nullifier; he was the only one.

He was confident they would defeat the Humans in this fleet, then would return to defeat the Empire, and thereafter on to the Solar System to conquer the rest of the Earth Humans' fleet.

-

Collison was summoned back to the Command Center, with reports coming in from all the scout ships. There was a lot of information to process, but thankfully he had the crew to do it. They now knew which Druin planets had more defenses than others and the location of their main fleet. That fleet was a little closer than he liked, but Collison didn't feel that they would come here, not once they started attacking their targets.

They also knew the defenses of all the Lamothian planets, as well as their primary fleet's location. Collison had the most scout ships out in the Morag area of the Confederation. He knew where the shipyards were and where the biggest Morag fleets were positioned. He had sent the scout ships back to monitor all the main fleets. They would notify him immediately of any movement in those fleets.

So now Collison had all the information he needed. All the chess pieces were now on the table. Time for him to make his final battle strategy and to launch his attack. He still had the element of surprise. They shouldn't be expecting the Humans to attack for another few days. The enemy fleets were in position but not ready for an attack.

Collison went back to his quarters to consider his moves. Things needed to coordinate just right for them to have the highest likelihood of a successful mission. He activated the holographic display, as he took a sip of his coffee. He knew it would be a long night. He slowly walked around the holographic display. It was a three-day journey to the Morag-controlled area of the Confederation. His part of the fleet would need to leave tomorrow. Barnes would need to wait another day to head to the Lamothian area of the Confederation. He paused; maybe he should have Barnes attack the Druins first, then go on to Lamothian star systems. Of course then she'd have a bigger fleet coming after her.

All the pieces needed to fit together just right. He walked around the display again and again, trying to fit everything together perfectly.

After hours of planning and deliberation, he had Carrie and Barnes join him on his flagship. They went over the proposed plan numerous times to make sure everyone was on the same page.

The only thing left to do now was get some sleep.

Chapter Twelve

As Rear Admiral Barnes returned to her flagship, *Phobos*, she kept running through her battle plan over and over in her head. Thanks to the scout ships, they knew where the main Lamothian fleet was. Collison had sent a scout ship back to that star system to monitor the fleet and to keep Barnes apprised of any enemy fleet movement.

According to the three admirals' calculations, the Humans would have less than an hour to attack the Lamothian homeworld of Lamothia, before the nearest enemy fleet could reach them. They thought that, with their accelerator cannons, they could destroy the shipyard and space stations quickly. A small fleet of eighty-three battlecruisers and battleships patrolled the system.

Barnes would have to keep them busy, while the battlecarriers launched the attack interceptors into the planet's atmosphere to destroy the planet. It had worked well for Fleet Admiral Derrick Masters, when he had destroyed the Druin planet; the Humans planned on it working well against the Lamothians.

Barnes just needed to attack the armed space stations and shipyard and keep the battlecruisers and battleships distracted long enough that the interceptors could launch their missiles and return to the battlecarriers. It seemed like a great plan; however, she had enough experience to know that sometimes plans went wrong.

Barnes returned to the Command Center on her flagship and briefed her crew on their mission. It would be a long night. She knew she probably wouldn't get much sleep. She decided to head to the cafeteria to put some food in her empty stomach. After she grabbed a chicken salad sandwich from the fridge and a sweet tea from the drink dispenser, she sat down to view the star system outside their ship.

She took a deep breath. The Confederation was so vast. It amazed her just thinking about it. To think that the Humans used to think Earth was the only planet with life on it. She laughed to herself.

She had another forty-eight hours before they needed to enter hyperspace. Collison would leave in a few hours. He needed to launch his attack first to pull back home the Morag fleet lying in wait for the Humans just outside the Lamothian star systems. Once the enemy was far enough away, Barnes would launch her first attack.

After her successful attack on the Lamothians, assuming her losses were minimal, she would then attack Druin Nine. Not their original target, Druin Seven, but, after the scans from the scout ships, Druin Nine was their easiest target. She chuckled. *Easy target.* She would be jumping closer to the Morag area of the Confederation.

She and Carrie and Collison did not believe the Morag would aid the Druins, not with the Morag shipyards being attacked. Not many battlecruisers and battleships were in that Druin star system, but Barnes knew it wouldn't take long for some Druins to arrive to aid their sister fleet.

Barnes would have about half an hour before the nearest fleet could reach her, bringing with them another five hundred battlecruisers and battleships. Even then, with a reinforcement Druin fleet, the numbers were on her side, assuming minimal losses in the Lamothian attack.

Collison advised her to send ships back to the mobile shipyards in the periphery of the Lormallian-controlled star system once they had reached 30 percent functioning of any energy shield or weapons store. It was easier to repair a ship than to replace it. They were here for a long-term mission, not just for a few battles.

Collison would leave behind some protection for the supply fleet. He wasn't sure if their damaged ships would be followed or not. If so, he wanted to be prepared. Barnes thought that was a good idea. She looked down at her sandwich; she hadn't eaten much. It would be a long night, a long night, indeed.

-

Rear Admiral Lira Carrie was trying to get some shut-eye before the big day tomorrow. The *big day* being the transition into hyperspace. When they exited, they would be in the Morag area of the Confederation. That's a place she had never been. A place, if she were honest, that she was afraid to go to. Thankfully they knew what to expect, since they had received the data from the scout ships about where the fleets were and where the shipyards were.

They needed to destroy as many of the shipyards as they could. Collison was a wise man; he had put together a solid plan. A plan Carrie would follow; it made the most sense. She kept telling herself that, but just something unsettled her.

They would start with the star system that had the most shipyards and then move to the next. It would be a hit-and-run sort of attack. Collison would destroy the energy shield, protecting the shipyard; then the attack interceptors would move in to destroy the shipyard. Collison would jump to the next target and destroy that energy shield; then Carrie would follow and destroy the shipyard, with the help of the interceptors.

Honestly she'd like to use some of the interceptors to hit the planets as they went along too. She would have to wait and see what they were up against. Carrie would like to give the Morag a taste of their own medicine.

-

Collison would leave behind twenty dreadnoughts and fifty battlecruisers to protect the supply fleet, which included four mobile repair yards and fifty supply ships. He hoped it would be enough. He had even considered the remote possibility that the Lormallians would come to their aid, if they were attacked here in their star system. The Lormallians wouldn't like the Morag or the Druins in their part of the Confederation. They just might chase them out.

Collison couldn't count on that, especially without communicating with them. He didn't want to chance that, in case his message was intercepted. It was a remote possibility though. He hoped any confrontation wouldn't happen here and put the Lormallians in a tough spot.

Collison had told Barnes and Carrie to send their ships back for repair once they reached 30 percent functioning levels on the energy shield or their weapons store. He hoped they could repair their fleet and stage another attack before returning to the Empire and then back to Earth.

Tomorrow. Tomorrow was the day they would start the next leg of this journey. They would drop out of hyperspace in a few days in a Morag-controlled star system. They had selected their first target, the one with the most shipyards.

From there, nothing would be easy. In all likelihood, the Morag would chase them into hyperspace, each time gathering a larger and larger fleet to tail them. Collison sighed as he finished off his last cup of coffee.

He knew he'd come up with the best strategy, based on their knowledge they had received from the scout ships. He couldn't help but feel the weight of his decisions on his shoulders. He was responsible for a large number of crew members on all their ships.

Collison knew not all of them would survive. He hoped that enough would survive to take this battle back to the Morag again and again, until the enemy had nothing left to fight with. The Humans would destroy as much of the Morag fleet and its shipbuilding capability to make sure the Humans never lost another minute of sleep in fear of when the Morag would return for their revenge. The reign of the Morag would come to an end. The sooner, the better.

The remaining councilors of the Morag side of the Confederation were meeting on the planet Druin Seven, which was the only inhabited planet left in that system. The other inhabited planet, Druin Six, had been destroyed by the Human Empire. A large fleet patrolled the system.

Councilor Damora of the Morag was not happy that the other councilors wore telepathic nullifiers. He wondered how many others had them as well. He would deal with the Lormallians before this got out of hand and everyone had one. He sat down at the head of the table.

Druin Councilor Clun sat across from the Lamothian councilor. He said, "I have heard that you are having another one of your feasts soon."

The Lamothian councilor smiled and said, "You have heard correctly."

Councilor Clun looked at Damora and said, "Won't this bring the Human Empire fleets here to the Confederation?"

"Yes, that is the plan. We have set a trap for them at Xanther. We will position our fleets outside of the Lamothian-controlled area of the Confederation. Once the Human Empire shows up, we will attack and ambush them. They think they will only face the Lamothians, but they are mistaken. We will destroy them," Damora said, while he pounded the table with his fist.

"How big of a Human fleet do we expect?" asked Clun.

"We believe some Earth fleets were on their way here when they sidetracked to help defend the Human Empire, as we attacked them there. Those are the fleets we believe will come here. They have lost some of their original numbers, and we will easily overwhelm them in a fleet battle," said Damora confidently.

"I am glad you are so confident in our victory. Our fleets will remain ready to defend our star systems," said Druin Councilor Clun.

Zynth Councilor Ralor Conn then said, "The Lormallians have been building up their fleets and putting up defensive grids above all their core planets. This goes against our agreement with them. What will we do about this traitorous activity?"

"Nothing yet. First, we will deal with this Human fleet, coming here to attack us. Once the Human Empire is no longer a threat, we will destroy the Lormallian fleets. They will be easy to defeat, when we combine our fleets. They won't stand a chance," replied Damora.

"What about the Earth Humans in the Solar System?" asked Clun.

"We will destroy their fleet coming to Xanther. That should stop them from returning to the Confederation ever again. We will hunt down all their ships and destroy them. There will be no survivors," replied Damora.

"There will be prisoners though, correct? Prisoners who will be transferred to us for our feasts?" questioned the Lamothian councilor.

"Of course," replied Damora. He knew there probably wouldn't be many prisoners; they would all die in the attack. He wouldn't mention that though. They would hunt them all down, allow no Human to leave the Confederation. He smiled to himself; the Earth Humans had no idea what was lying in wait for them. It would be their last battle; their days would shortly come to an end.

"When do we expect the Human fleet to get here?" asked Clun.

"Not for another few days, maybe four to five days," replied Damora.

"We will be ready for them," replied Clun.

After another hour of discussions, the Great Council of the Confederation, or what was left of it, adjourned to return to their homeworlds and to prepare for the coming battle.

Druin Admiral Falorr had received a message from Councilor Clun. The Earth Humans were suspected to be inbound for the Confederation. Most likely to the Lamothian area of the Confederation, but he thought it would be wise to raise the alert level of the fleet. No need to be caught off guard, if the Humans decided to target the Druins as well once more.

Admiral Falorr needed to reevaluate his fleet deployments. He assumed Druin Seven would be the prime target. Druin Six had been their homeworld, until the Human Empire had destroyed it. Now Druin Seven acted as their new homeworld. He was relieved that they had a defensive grid to protect Druin Seven.

Most of their other core worlds had them as well—only a couple didn't have a fully functioning defensive grid. They just hadn't had the time to get them all functioning yet. The shipyard and two space stations above Druin Seven were armed and had energy shields. They would be ready, if the Humans attacked Druin Seven. The Druins had learned from last time not to be too overconfident.

He would keep the central part of the fleet in the star system that contained Druin Seven. He would also keep a large number of battlecruisers and battleships in the most populous star systems that included Druin-inhabited planets.

He would need to assign a few more ships to the red giant system, where the planet had not finished their defensive grid yet. He would send another two hundred ships to aid them, if the Humans targeted their least-protected star system.

That would leave the fleet kept at the edge of the Druin system down to three hundred ships. They maintained that fleet there as their first line of defense against the former races of the Confederation—and the Humans.

They would be ready for this Earth Humans' fleet. There would be no surprises this time.

-

Morag Admiral Marcello patrolled the Morag home system, where Morag Prime was located. He was more than a little annoyed that the Morag High Council had sent Admiral Voxx to defeat the Earth Humans instead of him. Voxx had failed in the Human Empire. What would make them believe he wouldn't fail them again? Marcello was the superior admiral. He would not fail the Confederation.

He wanted to be the one responsible for crushing the Earth Humans' fleet. Rest assured that, when Voxx failed, Marcello would be here to prove that it should have been him to stand between the Humans and the Morag star systems, not Voxx. The more Marcello thought about it, the more he convinced himself the Humans would end up here.

Voxx would no doubt fail in the Lamothian star system. So Marcello needed to have his fleet on high alert. He would protect Morag Prime, and he would not fail.

-

Scout ship 368 was in the yellow dwarf star system just outside of the Lamothian-controlled area of the Confederation, where the Morag fleet was making repairs and preparing for battle. Everyone on board the scout ship was on edge. Most of the other vessels had left the system, when the Morag fleet had arrived.

Scout ship 368 had returned, after investigating the next star system, where they had found the Lamothian fleet and reported all their data to Collison. Now they had to observe the Morag fleet for any movement. If the Morag entered hyperspace, Captain Hadley had to inform Admiral Barnes immediately. Based on the direction of their hyperspace jump, she could tell if the Morag were headed back to the Morag area of the Confederation or the Lamothian area of the Confederation.

For Collison's plan to work the way he hoped, the enemy fleet must head back home to the Morag area of the Confederation.

The massive Morag fleet had scanned the star system a few times since they had arrived. Each time the crew on scout ship 368 collectively held their breaths. So far, they had not been detected. They were tucked in behind a moon, orbiting the second planet. Hadley knew it would be another few days before the Morag fleet would react to news of their area of the Confederation being attacked. So she and her crew had a lot of anxious waiting to do.

Captain Hadley found herself again wondering where the Humans had come from that the Lamothians had on Xanther for their upcoming feast. She had asked Collison for permission to investigate this question, once these initial battles were over. So far, the only races they knew of that could detect radiation from a hyperspace jump were the Zynth and the Morag. Thus more precaution was needed in and around their star systems and their fleets.

In the Lamothian and Druin star systems, however, the scout ships had gone entirely unnoticed. Hadley hoped to follow transport ships until she followed the right one to lead her to the answers she sought. Until then, it was a waiting game.

-

Captain Laine, aboard scout ship 125, observed the large Druin fleet patrolling their star system closest to the Human Empire fleet. There had not been much change in their movements over the last twenty-four hours. He was getting a little shut-eye when alarms sounded. "What's going on, Lieutenant Henley?"

"Some of the fleet is entering hyperspace, Captain," replied Henley.

"How many?" asked Laine.

"One hundred and counting, Captain."

"Which direction are they headed?" he asked, as he pulled up his map of the Confederation.

"Toward the Druin star systems. Not toward our fleet," replied Henley.

Captain Laine wondered if he should follow the fleet or not.

"They've stopped jumping. Two hundred battleships jumped out," commented Henley.

Now he wondered if he should stay or go. He decided he needed to know where this fleet was headed. Once he figured that out, he'd head back to watch the remaining fleet. "Follow them, Lieutenant Henley."

"Entering hyperspace now."

Derrick and Prince Andrew were meeting with the head scientist in charge of developing the new weapon technology which Councilor Reull had given them. They were in the research center in the underground military base on Golan Four.

"How is the new weapon development coming along?" asked Andrew.

"We have most of our weapons specialists working on this project," replied Canaan Roy. "We are making good progress. We still need to figure out a lot from what Reull gave us."

"Yes, he noted more research must happen before we had a workable weapon," replied Andrew.

"We have made some progress, and, based on what we have so far, we expect to have a weapon we can test in about five months. If you follow me, I will take you to the weapons development lab and show you around," said Canaan.

Canaan showed them around the lab, and they met a few of the scientists working on the project. Everything looked like it was progressing well, maybe even a little ahead of schedule.

"It looks like some good progress has been made on the project so far. This is the weapon we hope will win this war with the Confederation once and for all," said Derrick, as they left the lab.

"I am confident that will be the case. Once we have this weapon functional, there's nothing the Confederation has that can defend against it. It's a total game changer," replied Canaan.

"Yes, this is why we need it as soon as possible. Hopefully before the Confederation attacks the Empire again. We know it takes time to develop, but the sooner we have it, the better," replied Derrick.

"We are doing the best we can, Admiral," commented Canaan.

"Yes, I know. I also understand how important you all are to the continued freedom of the Empire, keeping us from the clutches of the Confederation," said Derrick. "We want you to have the time you need to make this weapon into all it can be. We don't want you to rush it. Your team of scientists are the best and the brightest we have. We are confident you will get the job done."

They thanked Canaan for his time and for his team's continued efforts in developing the new weapons.

-

Captain Laine dropped from hyperspace, not far from the Druin fleet. Everyone held their breath as they waited to make sure they didn't detect them. They hadn't been detected before, but one couldn't ever be too sure. They were in the star system that held Druin Nine, the planet Barnes planned to destroy. This morning only a few battlecruisers and battleships patrolled the system. Now it had over two hundred warships.

What had caused them to move part of their fleet here? Had they intercepted one of their hyperlight messages? He was confident they had taken all the proper precautions when communicating with the fleet. Now he had to decide what to do. He needed to let Barnes know what she'd be jumping into. What could he do to help?

After a lot of thought, he decided to monitor this fleet for a while. See if maybe this was just a routine stop, and the fleet would move on. He would wait twelve hours and then jump out to a different system to send his message to Barnes. If the fleet remained, he would return to monitor it, until it was time for Barnes to attack.

Twelve hours had passed, and the Druin fleet had not moved. It was time for Captain Laine to report the news to Admiral Barnes. He knew Barnes had a much larger fleet than the slightly more than two hundred Druin ships, but Laine didn't want Barnes jumping in blindly.

Chapter Thirteen

Admiral Collison was in the Command Center of his flagship. His crew anxiously awaited his command. They all knew that this hyperspace jump could be their last. They were headed for the Morag star systems. No known Human had ever entered that area of space. Let alone returned.

This was their mission. This is the reason they had left the Solar System. To take this war to the Confederation, to the Morag. No longer would this battle be close to home. This battle would now be close to their enemies' homes. Yes, the Morag would remember this day. Time for the next era of this battle against the Confederation to begin.

Collison took a deep breath and slowly let it out. He glanced at the tactical display, where all the green icons surrounded his ship. Friendly icons. He knew this display would be lit up with numerous red threat icons instead of just green ones in a few days.

From where they were, the Morag's star systems were a three-day hyperspace journey. Collison had decided on their targets and in what order and how the battle would progress. His moves were lined up. If only the Morag would react the way he thought they would, the Humans would win this battle. They would destroy enough shipyards, enough battleships, maybe even get a few missiles off to damage a planet or two. Not destroy, just damage.

Collison knew they wouldn't destroy a planet belonging to the Morag. Their fleet was too large. It would take too long to annihilate the shipyards, to destroy the space stations and the defensive grids in place. The Morag fleet would be on them before they could do all that.

If he could take out enough shipyards, it would make a massive difference for the future of the Human Empire and for Earth. Buy them more time to prepare and to build up their fleets. They were all depending on him to carry out his mission. He was determined to do his part, no matter what it cost him.

He looked around the room. This was his family away from home. He depended on these people, and they counted on him and his judgment to carry them through. He would not disappoint.

"Billingsly, transition us into hyperspace," commanded Collison.

"Yes, sir," responded Billingsly.

As the ship jumped into hyperspace, he felt the familiar pull in the pit of his stomach. He watched the tactical display as all the other ships going with him made their jumps into hyperspace too. Now all they had to do was wait. Three days of anxious suspense for what awaited them at the end of this hyperspace jump. Revenge, destruction, and, most important, hope.

The hope of a future free from fear. The hope to be free from fighting, from defending. The hope for the freedom of all Humans from the Confederation and their oppressive reign— and for other races as well.

The Humans would bring the Confederation to its knees. Give freedom to all the races oppressed by the Confederation. Collison smiled to himself. *Freedom*, such a powerful word. Earth had not been involved and oppressed by the Confederation for thousands and thousands of years. Yet Collison knew countless other races had. The Humans would fight this battle for every single one of them, Humans and non-Humans. To free every single life from the tyranny and deceit and evil Confederation, that's who Collison fought for.

Rear Admiral Lira Carrie watched as the ships all made their transitions into hyperspace. It was a good feeling to see so many ships in their combined fleet. She knew the fighting would be intense. She knew in all likelihood, when they returned to the supply chain, not as many ships would be with her. The battle plan was set, and she knew her role.

Carrie closed her eyes. The thought of going on the offensive for once felt good, and it made her smile. This was her destiny, to defeat the Morag. She was aware that it would take more than this one mission. It would take many, and she hoped she would be a part of them, a significant part of them.

Now what she needed was a nice cup of coffee and some food. She was starving. It would be a long three days between now and when they exited hyperspace. Hopefully the crew could all get some much-needed rest before the battle ahead of them.

As she walked to the cafeteria, she looked around at the crew she passed. She was thankful she had a good crew surrounding her. People who she could depend on. She was glad she could be here to support Collison and his fleet, as well as Barnes and her fleet—although her targets were different. Together, Collison and Carrie would target the Morag; they would cause the Morag to lose some resources. Resources the Morag needed to continue this battle against the Human Empire. The Humans would bring destruction and defeat to their enemy.

Three days. That's how long the Morag had left to feel safe.

Then the game would change.

Admiral Barnes watched as Collison's and Carrie's crews entered hyperspace. Barnes hoped she would see them again. As the green icons surrounding her fleet dwindled, she got a little more nervous. Barnes knew she had enough ships to complete her part of the mission. Having all three of these fleets here together though had been a comforting experience.

Now her fleet was on their own. They would wait a couple days, and then they would enter hyperspace themselves. Until then, her crew needed to rest and to get consistent nourishment. Thinking of food, she heard her stomach growl. Just as she left the Command Center, a hyperlight message came in.

"Admiral Barnes, we just received a message from Captain Laine onboard scout ship 125," Captain Borrel said, as she handed her the message.

As she read, her uneasiness grew. "Captain Borrel, Laine reports that a large part of the Druin fleet stationed near the edge of their star systems has moved to the star system containing our primary Druin target. The planet we are planning to destroy, Druin Nine."

"Will this change our target, Admiral?" asked Borrel.

"I don't think so. We will just have more of a battle on our hands than we expected," replied Barnes. "Please tell Captain Laine to continue monitoring the Druin fleet in the star system containing Druin Nine and to notify us of any significant change in their position."

"Yes, Admiral," replied Borrel.

"I will go over all the intelligence we have obtained on the Druin star systems, their defenses, and their fleet deployment. I will let you know if there will be a change to our battle plan, but, first, I need some food."

As she headed to the cafeteria, Barnes went over all the information she could remember. Sometimes she thought more clearly when she was on the move. She also knew a good meal would do wonders to clear her mind, so she could process this new information and make the best decision about which star system and which planet to target.

She slowly ate her lunch of fried chicken with green beans and her favorite part, mashed potatoes and gravy. It made a big difference, thinking on a full stomach, instead of thinking on an empty stomach.

Barnes headed back to her quarters to figure out what they should do. Once there, she activated the holographic display of the Druin star systems. Barnes slowly walked around the display, as she thought over what she knew. Fleets patrolled all three star systems that contained the Druins' core worlds. They had selected Druin Nine as the target, since it didn't have a defensive grid in place. It now had over two hundred battleships in the system, but the other Druin star systems still had larger fleets. Druin Nine remained the best target.

She could destroy the planet faster with no defensive grid in place. They would spend considerably more time, and most likely lose more ships, defending the battlecarriers from this larger Druin fleet, as Barnes launched their attack interceptors. It wouldn't take long for the other Druin fleets to arrive to aid in their defense of their planet. Barnes would have a small window of time to jump in and to get the job done, before they must jump out, to avoid facing the entire Druin fleet.

As Barnes continued to slowly walk around the holographic display, she thought about her fleet. She had just over 4,600 ships at her disposal. The vast majority of these were the attack interceptors on her 23 battlecarriers. Each battlecarrier had 160 attack interceptors onboard.

If they could maintain minimal losses in their attack on the Lamothians, she should have no problem destroying Druin Nine—assuming the Morag fleet headed home, and the Lamothian fleet did not pursue them. She frowned. A lot of *ifs* were in this scenario.

One thing remained certain. Their target planet would stay the same. Druin Nine would still face destruction in a few days. How many Druin battlecruisers and battleships were lost in the process? Well, that was up to the Druins. She reported back to Command Center to confirm their target and to make sure no new messages had come in.

Their course was set; the pieces were in place. Who would win this round? She was confident her crew and her fleet would come out of this triumphant.

The next day dawned quickly on Barnes and her fleet. All of her ships were prepared for their hyperspace jump. She had to time their jump to make sure to give Admiral Collison and Rear Admiral Carrie enough time to begin their attack. Once this had occurred, that would hopefully pull the Morag fleet away from the Lamothian area of the Confederation—if all went according to plan of course. Then Barnes's fleet would have fewer enemy ships to deal with in Lamothian space.

Barnes patiently waited for the designated time and then confidently told Captain Borrel, "Take us into hyperspace."

"Yes, Captain," said Captain Borrel.

Barnes watched as her fleet made the transition into hyperspace with her. It was reassuring to see so many green icons. Soon she knew a lot of red threat icons would show up on her display too. Hopefully no Morag ships though. Time would tell. She still had two days until she would know if Collison's plan had worked.

The Imperial Council once again met in the Imperial Council Chamber in the House of Worlds. As soon as everyone was present, Chief Chancellor Stein stood and turned to Fleet Admiral Derrick Masters. "Masters, could you please update us on the Earth fleets in the Confederation?"

Derrick stood and addressed the council. "Right now, all three fleets should have made their final hyperspace jumps. The battles should begin in about twenty-four hours. Then we expect to get updates from the fleets. Until then, we expect no communication from them. Admiral Cleemorl is still a few days away from the supply fleet. I will hopefully have more information for you at our next meeting."

Stein stood and said, "Thank you, Derrick." He then turned to Prince Andrew. "Any new updates on the weapon development since our last meeting?"

Prince Andrew stood and answered, "Yes, Derrick and I met with the scientists, and they are a little ahead of schedule. We are confident they will get the job done as soon as possible."

"That's great news," responded Governor Littrel of Jalot Four.

Princess Layla stood to address the council. "The representatives from the other worlds in the Empire have started arriving. We will host a special reception this evening to welcome those who have arrived. I hope that all the council will be available to attend. We need to make all the new members of the House of Worlds feel welcome."

Everyone nodded their heads and agreed to be there for the reception.

"In a few days, the representatives from the United Worlds Alliance will be arriving as well. We will host another special reception to welcome them," said Layla.

"So basically, what you are saying is, every night we will have a reception to welcome the new guests to Golan Four and to the House of Worlds?" asked Derrick, with a smile. "Great food and great company. I will be there!" he said, laughing.

Everyone laughed along with Derrick. As they continued their meeting, a few more essential items were discussed, and then they dismissed to prepare for the reception later that evening.

As High Princess Layla entered the grand reception hall in the Imperial Palace, she was greeted by hundreds of new faces. She smiled, as she walked to her seat next to Derrick. It was gratifying to see so many people representing so many worlds. The Empire was growing every day. She knew this would be a long night. She hoped, between all the council members, they could speak to each person here tonight. She wanted all of the new attendees to feel important and to not be overlooked. Each world represented here tonight was vital to the success of the Empire, now and into the future.

As the meal started, she looked around to take in everything. Krista had done a great job ensuring the room was ready for their guests. Everything was decorated just right, down to the flowers on each table. She leaned over to Krista and said, "You did a wonderful job getting the room ready. I am very proud of you."

Krista swelled with obvious pride.

161

Layla trusted her with more and more tasks as time went on. She had an eye for decorating, and Layla had put her to work doing something she was good at.

Krista felt more like an asset to her cousin tonight than she had before. She knew Layla would want her to meet and to talk to as many people tonight as she could. She was starting to get good at working a room.

She glanced at Mathew, sitting next to her. He was dressed in his uniform and looked as handsome as ever. He shifted a little uncomfortably, as he lifted his gaze and met hers. They shared a smile; she knew he didn't like getting put on display. That's how he felt when he had to sit at the head table. He felt like a lot of eyes were on him, he had told Krista. She gave him a quick wink and finished eating. It was a delicious meal, and everyone seemed to enjoy it.

Once everyone was done and the dishes taken away by the staff, Layla stood to make a toast. "I would like to thank each and every one of you for making the journey here tonight, however long or short that journey was. For some of you, this is your first time to visit our Imperial Palace and the House of Worlds. I want to extend a big welcome to you. We are so happy to have you here and to have you as a part of our great Empire. Please enjoy the evening and feel free to stay awhile and meet others from our great Empire. We have a bright future to plan and to look forward to, and we will do it together." She raised her glass and said, "To the Empire!" She slowly sat down, as the *clink* of glasses could be heard all around.

"That was a great toast, Layla," remarked Derrick.

"Thank you. I spent a lot of time writing and rewriting it," she said, with a laugh. She was so glad she had Derrick by her side. He was someone she could depend on and could lean on whenever she needed to. He always knew how to lighten her mood as well. As much as she tried to focus on this night and this reception, her mind kept wandering to the Confederation and the battle that would take place there soon. She pushed her worries from her mind, as she stood to greet as many people as she could.

A few hours later, Layla and Derrick finally left the reception. She was exhausted from being on her feet so long in these adorable shoes that weren't the least bit comfortable. After a good night's sleep, she would have Derrick check with Admiral Marloo to see if any updates came from any of the Human fleets in the Confederation.

Admiral Collison was making his final preparations. He had already had the fleet at Condition Three when they entered hyperspace. He would soon give the order to move to Condition Two. The last couple days had dragged slowly on. He was ready to start this battle. It had consumed his thoughts for so long that he grew tired of all the scenarios flying around in his mind. It was hard to shut that off so he could rest. He knew it was vital that he be fully rested. Once the battle started, sleep would be hard to come by—maybe for quite a long time—as he intended to attack the Morag many times over the next few weeks. This was just stage one.

They were safe as long as they were in hyperspace.

As he walked to his quarters to try to get some sleep, he thought about his family back home. He wondered what they were doing and hoped that someday he would see them again. He was doing this to protect them. To protect them from ever having to live in fear of the Confederation and the Morag, like countless other families had felt for most of their lives in the Empire. The Earth Humans were lucky, living on Earth, far removed from the Confederation.

Sleep would come eventually, and, when he woke up, it would be almost time for the battle to begin.

Midmorning the next day, Layla and Derrick headed to the Command Center, located under the House of Worlds. She had planned on sending Derrick by himself but then decided she wanted to hear directly from Marloo what was going on.

As they entered the Command Center, Marloo greeted them. "No news yet," he said. "We expect to hear something today."

Derrick sighed. "It's hard not knowing what's going on. It's a lot different being down here in the Command Center than up there in my flagship. I wish we could do more."

Layla shot him a stern look. "We are doing everything we can do, and, for now, your job is to stay safe here on Golan Four."

"I have no plans to go anywhere," Derrick replied, with a sly grin.

"You better not. Well, since no action is going on here at the moment, I have lots of other business to attend to. I will check back with you two after lunch," Layla said, as she headed out the door.

"Not much to do here but sit and wait," Marloo noted, as he pulled up the holographic display. He and Derrick studied it. Of course the map didn't tell them anything they didn't already know. They both sat down to wait.

Somewhere in the vast darkness that surrounded them was a world where Lamothians were going about their daily lives, not knowing it would be their last. Barnes knew that they deserved what was coming, for all the thousands, possibly millions, of Humans that they'd consumed over the last one hundred years alone. It made her sick to her stomach just thinking about it. What those people must have gone through. She shook her head in disgust.

Nope, she would not feel any sympathy for these Lamothians. "We will have our revenge," she muttered to herself. Then her mind turned to the Druins. How many Humans had they killed in the previous one hundred years? How many Human captives had they brought to the Lamothians, knowing what would become of them? How many other races had the Druins destroyed or exterminated because they didn't give the Confederation what they wanted or didn't meet their quota?

The Druins had kicked the hornet's nest when they had attacked the Solar System. *We will exact our revenge before their sun sets tomorrow. They will then know what it's like to live in fear. The fear of when we will return or what we might do next.* Yes, the tables were turning. They will regret the day they ever sent a ship to the Bacchus Region of space.

No, we will not sit idly by and wait for another attack. Today is the day we show them what the Earth Humans can do. We will bring the fight to them. No longer will it be our worlds at risk but theirs.

Chapter Fourteen

It was time, time to move the fleet to Condition Two. Collison stood in the Command Center, watching the various displays surrounding him. He nodded to Billingsly. "Take the fleet to Condition Two."

"Yes, sir," Billingsly replied.

Collison pulled up the holographic display and studied it for a few minutes. He mentally went through his moves. Where they would drop out, what their first target would be, what their second target would be, then the next and the next. How many targets they could damage or destroy all depended on the Morag and how many ships Collison lost along the way.

The following twenty-four hours would be long and hard. Collison looked around the room at his crew. He knew they wouldn't sleep or get much to eat until this battle was over.

He had another twenty minutes before they dropped from hyperspace into a Morag-controlled star system. He reviewed the data he had received from the scout ships. "Billingsly, I want us to drop out of hyperspace as close as we can to the fourth planet. Maybe we can get this first shipyard destroyed before they realize what's hit them."

His fleet had their assignments and knew what they were supposed to do. They wanted to destroy as many shipyards as possible. They wanted to avoid fleet-to-fleet battles, but Collison knew they were inevitable. This first star system was well protected. A total of eight shipyards orbited the four inhabited planets of this system. They would attack them all at the same time. Each task group had its specific targets. He hoped it would work like he thought it would. He hoped the Morag fleet would split up as well. Time would tell.

-

Admiral Carrie sat in her command chair on the edge of her seat. In less than five minutes, they would drop from hyperspace.

Her task group would attack the two shipyards on the first inhabited planet in the system, Morag Twelve. It wouldn't take long for the Morag fleet patrolling the star system to react to their presence.

Carrie's crew should get off a couple rounds of fire and deploy the attack interceptors before the enemy fleet was in range. With their accelerator cannons, it would only take a few hits to destroy the energy shields and to damage the shipyard. Then the interceptors would fly in to finish the job, while the rest of the task group defended the interceptors from the enemy fleet.

The plan was a solid one. Hopefully everything would go according to plan. Carrie would also send a hyperlight message to Golan Four, once the battle started, to let them know the attack had commenced.

This would be a long day but a rewarding one. She would make her family proud. She would do her duty and would complete her mission, no matter the cost.

-

Collison's task group dropped from hyperspace close to the fourth planet. Immediately alarms sounded. "Get us to that first shipyard quickly. Billingsly, how far is the nearest enemy ship?" asked Collison.

"They're jumping closer now. There are 1,028 Morag battlecruisers and battleships in this star system, Admiral."

"How close are we to weapons range of the shipyard?" asked Collison.

"Five minutes, sir. Three hundred Morag battlecruisers just dropped from hyperspace. They'll be in weapons range in ten minutes."

"Get the attack interceptors launched. Tell them to wait until we launch the accelerator cannons before they attack. We need to take down the shields first."

-

On board the battlecarrier *Freedom,* interceptors launched from the launch bay. At the same time, interceptors launched from three other battlecarriers too. Quickly over six hundred interceptors were ready and waiting to attack.

One of the group leaders of the squadron of attack interceptors, Lieutenant Garland, had her squadron ready to lead the attack on the first shipyard.

She knew she needed to wait until the accelerator cannons were launched to destroy the energy shields of the shipyard and hopefully damage it as well. That was their cue to launch their attack. Her squadron was ready.

Morag Admiral Ramgen was on his routine patrol when alarms sounded. He quickly raced to the Command Center and asked for a report.

A Human fleet has dropped from hyperspace. It appears they are headed toward our inhabited planets. They're split into eight groups.

How many ships? And why eight groups? There are only four planets. What's their target? Admiral Ramgen demanded.

Their target is unknown at this time. The Humans have over eight hundred ships, sir, replied his First Officer.

Split our fleet into four groups to intercept this pesky Human fleet. How stupid are they to dare enter our star system? Also notify Admiral Marcello and let him know we have a Human fleet in the Confederation. I thought Admiral Voxx planned an ambush for these annoying creatures in the Lamothian star systems, commanded Ramgen.

It looks like they are headed toward the shipyards, Admiral, said the First Officer.

We will make quick work of destroying this fleet. We more than outnumber them. Ramgen shook his head. It looks like he would be moving up in the ranks, after he destroys this Human fleet, instead of Voxx. Ramgen always thought he was far superior to Voxx. *How quickly will we be in weapons range?* His part of the fleet would attack the Humans now inbound to the third planet, Morag Fourteen. He had 250 ships with him.

Admiral, it looks like they've launched a lot of smaller craft from some of their ships.

I've heard about these smaller attack craft. How many? Ramgen asked.

Over six hundred, Admiral.

Ramgen paused. *With the weapons fire from the shipyards and our own, it won't matter. How long until we're in weapons range?*

Five more minutes, replied the Tactical Officer.

We must stop them before they destroy our shipyards. From there, they might think to attack our space stations and possibly our planets. Ramgen shook his head. Not on his watch would he allow any of that to happen.

As he watched the displays in front of him, the shipyards started to fire on the Human fleet. At about the same time, the Human fleet launched their attack as well. He watched in dismay as the Humans used a new weapon, one he had only heard about from Voxx. An accelerator cannon. Each ship seemed to have this weapon. It easily overloaded the energy shield protecting the shipyard.

The next ones heavily damaged the shipyard. Then the small Human crafts moved in and destroyed what was left of the shipyard. It all happened so fast. Such destruction so quickly from this weapon. There was no defense against it.

If it can do that to the shipyard, what would it do to his battlecruisers and his battleships? For a brief moment, he considered jumping out of the system to save his fleet, but he knew, without a doubt, the Morag High Council would execute him for that. If he were going down, he would do it with honor.

"We're in weapons range, sir," said Captain Billingsly.

"Have all the ships target the shipyard with their accelerator cannons," commanded Collison. The accelerator cannons could accelerate a projectile almost up to the speed of light. Each cannon was capable of firing once every thirty seconds. Every dreadnought and battlecruiser in the fleet was equipped with one pair of cannons.

"Target locked," said the tactical officer.

"All ships fire!" ordered Collison. He focused his gaze on the viewscreens. He realized he was gripping the arm of his command chair tightly and relaxed a little. He felt the ship shake slightly, as the cannons launched.

At the same time, the shipyard launched all of its missiles it could.

The entire command crew watched as the Human projectiles hit the energy shield of the shipyard. The energy screen lit up brightly as it was hit. It got brighter and brighter, until it finally overloaded and failed. As the next round of projectiles arrived, the shipyard took heavy damage.

Now the enemy's missiles from the shipyard struck the fleet, as bright flashes of light lit up their energy shields. Most held together, but a few holes emerged in a few battlecruisers. No significant damage resulted from the breach in the shields.

"All ships come about. Morag fleet will be in combat range in two minutes! Prepare to fire as soon as we have a target lock," commanded Collison. *We need to give the attack interceptors time to finish off the now-defenseless shipyard and destroy some Morag battleships in the process*, he thought, as a smile spread across his face.

-

Lieutenant Garland and her squadron of attack interceptors immediately launched their attack. She was not alone, as the other squadrons moved in to destroy what was left of the shipyard. She smiled at how effective those accelerator cannons were.

They had to dodge some weapons fire, getting through to the task force. Not too much for them to handle. The shipyard had no functioning defenses left and drifted in multiple pieces. The squadrons moved in and launched their missiles at the remaining wreckage. They didn't want to leave any pieces big enough that they could repair them. They wanted them to have to start from scratch on rebuilding these shipyards.

They quickly launched their missiles and returned to the battlecarriers. It was time to move on to the next target.

"Target locked on Morag battlecruisers!" cried out the tactical officer.

"Fire!" commanded Collison. Almost as soon as they fired, the Morag had as well.

"Missiles inbound!" yelled the tactical officer.

"Brace for impact!" said Collison.

His gaze was still glued to the viewscreens, as their projectiles from the accelerator cannons reached their targets. All across the Morag line of battlecruisers and battleships, their energy shields glowed brightly, before they overloaded and failed. Then the second round hit, and massive fireballs lit up space, as the ships began to blow apart.

Just then, the missiles launched from the Morag fleet arrived, and Collison's ship shook violently. The energy shield held.

"Launch another round of the accelerator cannons!" commanded Collison. One more round, and they would be about ready to head to the next system. He needed to check in with the other task groups. He hoped they were having as much success as he was.

As Rear Admiral Carrie moved into position over the planet Morag Twelve, the first planet in the system, she sent out a quick hyperlight message toward Golan Four.

"Admiral Marloo, the attack on the Morag has commenced. We will update you when we can."

She took a deep breath; she knew they were waiting for word back on Golan Four. It was hard not knowing what was going on; she had been in that position before. It felt good to be in this battle, instead of sitting on the sidelines.

"Major Sullivan, how close are we to engagement range?"

"Seven minutes," replied Sullivan.

"What about the Morag fleet patrolling the star system? Where are they?"

"It appears they have divided their fleet into four sections. One is headed to each planet. The fleet dropped out about thirty seconds ago. They're about ten minutes to engagement range."

"How many ships are we up against?" asked Carrie.

"Our scans show 228 Morag ships," replied Sullivan.

"We need to be ready to strike the shipyard as soon as we're in range. We will only have three minutes to destroy the energy shield and hopefully damage the shipyard before the enemy ships arrive. We should get two rounds of the accelerator cannon off before we need to turn to face the fleet. Make sure all the other ships are aware of what they need to do," commanded Carrie.

Carrie hoped the battlecarriers would have enough time to launch their interceptors before the Morag fleet started their attack. They would need time to launch, fly in, fire their missiles at the shipyard, and get back on board the battlecarriers.

As the Human fleet moved closer to engagement range of the shipyard, the shipyard opened fire on the fleet. Not much reached them yet, but it soon would. Carrie took a deep breath and steadied herself. "Prepare to fire." She watched the tactical display intensely, as she waited for the signal that they were in range. As soon as she heard the signal, she yelled, "Fire!"

All the battlecruisers and dreadnoughts in her task force launched their first round of accelerator cannon fire at the shipyard. Soon after the launch, the energy beam fire from the shipyard reached the Human fleet. Energy screens lit up the sky as the beams looked for a weak spot to penetrate the shield. Carrie watched as a few of them were successful. She pulled in a deep breath as ships disappeared from the display. Several ships had been blown apart in huge explosions of raw energy.

She closed her eyes and yelled, "Fire!" She was thankful the accelerator cannons could launch every thirty seconds. Each ship had two cannons on board. She was confident two rounds of the

Raymond L. Weil

accelerator cannon fire would do the trick and would destroy the energy shields and would do heavy damage to the shipyard. No energy shield could withstand the sheer power of the projectiles hitting their energy shield like that.

Carrie watched, as the first round of accelerator cannon fire hit the shipyard's energy shields. Space immediately lit up from the sheer intensity of the projectiles hitting the energy shield. The bright explosions lit up the sky, seemingly turning night into day. She had to shield her eyes from the intensity of the light. When she could look again, giant pieces of glowing wreckage littered the space around the planet.

As the second round of accelerator cannon fire arrived, the remaining pieces were disintegrated into oblivion. Carrie was surprised at how effective those two rounds had been. They didn't even need to use the attack interceptors this time. She let out a sigh of relief. She knew they would need them in the subsequent attacks.

Alarms sounded as the Morag fleet reached engagement range and fired their missiles and energy beams at the Human fleet. "Get us out of here!" commanded Carrie. She had achieved her goal of destroying the shipyard. No need to stick around to face the Morag in a fleet battle. She was well aware her task force would be outnumbered.

As her fleet transitioned into hyperspace, she felt that familiar pull in the pit of her stomach. She sat down in her command chair. Round one was over for her and her task force. She was unsure how many of her ships had been destroyed or damaged by the shipyard's ferocious bombardment of her fleet. "Damage report."

"I am working on that now."

She let out a deep breath and tried to relax for a moment. They had a couple hours of safety, before they exited hyperspace at their designated coordinates. She needed to take full advantage of the security that hyperspace gave her. No one could attack while in hyperspace. She needed to evaluate her task force. See how many ships they'd lost and how many needed to be sent back to the supply fleet and the awaiting mobile shipyards for repair. Then she would get a quick bite to eat.

-

Collison watched as his second round of accelerator cannon fire hit the Morag fleet. Energy shields lit up and failed quickly. At about that time, the second group of cannon fire hit the ships, causing catastrophic damage to the Morag front line. He smiled at how effective it was to have two cannons on each battleship. One to take out the energy shield and the other to destroy the ship.

His smile quickly faded as the Morag barrage of missiles and energy beam fire weakened the energy shields of several ships on his front line. Once the shields were weakened, they were vulnerable to failure. He watched in dismay as multiple ships were then hit by antimatter missiles and annihilated in giant explosions of light.

Collison quickly checked with the battlecarriers to confirm all attack interceptors had returned to the carriers. Once confirmed, he gave the order to all his task force to make the transition into hyperspace. He had lost more ships than he thought he would. It was time to regroup at the rendezvous coordinates and adjust their battle plan.

-

Morag Admiral Ramgen was almost to engagement range with the Human fleet that had attacked the shipyard above the third planet in this star system, Morag Fourteen. *Weapons ready. We must fire as many weapons as possible.*

The Human fleet had turned to face his fleet. It had been reinforced by the Humans who had attacked and destroyed the second shipyard above the planet. He now faced a little under two hundred ships. He swallowed, as he focused on the display in front of him. As soon as they were in range, he yelled, *Fire!*

For several moments, time seemed to slow, as Ramgen waited to see if the energy shields would sustain the inbound enemy projectiles. He focused his gaze on his displays in front of him. As the projectiles arrived at his fleet's location, the battlecruisers and battleships in his fleet glowed brighter and brighter, as their energy shields tried to ward off the attack.

One by one, they failed, and then the next projectile turned each ship into a massive explosion of molten wreckage. On his tactical display, his green icons disappeared one by one, faster than he could keep count.

He looked up to see how much damage they had caused the Human fleet. He smiled; well, at least they had weakened them some, as he noticed some wreckage among the enemy fleet. *How many did we destroy?* he asked his tactical officer.

We destroyed twenty-three battlecruisers and three dreadnoughts Admiral, replied the Tactical Officer.

He turned his hard gaze to the display and asked, *How many did we lose?*

Fifty-one battlecruisers and five battleships, he replied. *The Humans are preparing to launch the accelerator cannons again, Admiral.*

We lost two ships to every one of theirs we destroyed. At this rate, they will destroy all our shipyards in this system before we can destroy their fleet. We must ensure they do not leave this star system. It might take almost all our ships, and we will lose all eight shipyards in this system, but we will stop these pesky Humans here, Ramgen sent, as he pounded his fist on the arm of his command chair.

Admiral, they are firing again! said the Tactical Officer.

Fire! commanded Ramgen. He watched as the second wave of projectiles headed his way. They would not last long against these weapons. They needed to figure something else out. This would not work. He needed to rejoin his entire fleet. He sent the command to the other captains in his fleet, *Surround the Human fleet at the planet Morag Fourteen. It's time to destroy them. They won't even realize what hit them!*

Immediately the other captains in the fleet received his command and inputted the coordinates to Morag Fourteen. Shortly thereafter, they jumped to the planet.

-

Captain Drake saw the Morag fleet had been significantly damaged, as they engaged the Morag above the third planet, called Morag Fourteen. He, unfortunately, was losing ships as well. They had successfully destroyed both shipyards and had just launched their second wave of accelerator cannon fire at the attacking Morag fleet.

Time for them to jump out of this system. He had the coordinates to their first rendezvous location in a yellow dwarf system halfway to their next target. Here the fleet would meet up and access the damage done and evaluate their next move.

He watched as his accelerator cannon fire reached the Morag fleet and lit up their energy screens. They quickly overloaded and failed. Then the second projectiles hit the now-vulnerable ships and destroyed their targets. Massive fireballs could be seen, where once was an enemy ship.

The Morag fusion energy beams and fusion missiles reached his fleet, just as the last interceptors boarded the battlecarriers. He watched as numerous green icons disappeared from his viewscreen. He winced at the thought of how many lives had just been lost.

He pressed the comm button and said, "Time to move to our rendezvous location. All ships jump immediately."

-

Just as the other Morag ships jumped in to assist Ramgen above Morag Fourteen, all the Human ships above the planet transitioned into hyperspace. *Where are they going?* demanded Ramgen angrily. He had almost had his fleet in position to annihilate one of the groups. He had made a mistake in splitting his fleet. He should have gone after one target at a time. The

Humans would have suffered more losses that way. He would not make that same mistake again.

Should we follow them, Admiral Ramgen? asked his tactical officer.

No, it may be a trap. There might be more ships waiting on the other end of that hyperspace jump. We have no idea where they will end up. We will regroup and evaluate our losses. We must consult with Marcello and Voxx to decide where we think the Humans will attack next. Then we wait for them to attack and will extinguish them from the Confederation. They will live to regret this day. That day of reckoning will come swiftly and without mercy, Ramgen said in a cold voice.

I have received status reports from the rest of the fleet, said the tactical officer.

How many ships did we lose here above this planet? asked Ramgen.

We lost 108 battlecruisers and 11 battleships, replied the tactical officer.

What of the rest of the fleet? What are our total losses?

Total losses include 238 battlecruisers and 45 battleships destroyed, with 64 damaged.

Send the damaged ships to the nearest shipyard to be fixed, replied Ramgen. *I will have a conference with Voxx and Marcello as to what our next move is. Have the rest of the fleet prepare to jump to our next location, when I return.* He walked slowly from the room. His thoughts were already evaluating what he thought the Humans might do next. They obviously were trying to destroy the Morag's shipyards. So far, they had been successful, but whatever their next target was, they wouldn't be. Now to figure out which one that would be.

Fleet Admirals Marloo and Masters were in the underground Command Center, beneath the House of Worlds, when they received the message from Rear Admiral Carrie that the attack had commenced. They were both currently walking slowly around the holographic display of the Morag-controlled area of the Confederation. They had also received information from the scout ships and had updated their map.

Hopefully the next time they heard from the Earth fleet, it would be to tell them how many shipyards they had successfully destroyed. The fewer battleships they lost in each star system, the more shipyards they could destroy. Of course that assumed they could avoid the large Morag fleets. One was stationed around Morag Prime. The other was two days away, just outside of the Lamothian-controlled area of the Confederation.

Whatever the Humans planned to do, they had less than two days to do it.

Chapter Fifteen

As the Human fleets exited hyperspace in the yellow dwarf system, green icons lit up their tactical display. Unfortunately not as many as they had left with. On the positive side though, what was left of the Morag fleet they had battled against had not followed them into hyperspace.

Collison received the reports from all the task groups. All eight shipyards had been destroyed in that star system. He smiled. A successful mission, at least phase one had been a success. That star system had the most shipyards. The rest were more spread out. The rest would be more challenging. Now they'd be expected.

He was relieved they had not been followed by that Morag fleet. He needed to send a message to Golan and update Vice Fleet Admiral Marloo of phase one's success. He would wait until they were ready to make their next jump though, in case it was intercepted.

The task forces' reports revealed the loss of 142 battlecruisers and 18 dreadnoughts. They would send 30 battlecruisers and 3 dreadnoughts back to the mobile shipyards for repair. They would rejoin the fight eventually though. Collison was glad they had the mobile repair yards. The Empire was a long journey away. The Solar System even farther.

He would keep the fleet at Condition Two, just in case the Morag fleet did decide to attack them. In the meantime, he needed to grab a bite to eat. Rear Admiral Carrie would arrive shortly to go over strategy and to assess the damage done to the fleet. It could have been much worse. He was quiet for a moment, thinking of the lives lost.

As Carrie arrived on Collison's flagship *Mercury*, she went straight to the conference room. Collison was there, waiting on her. She smiled when she saw him. "Well, phase one was accomplished. What's our next target?"

Collison felt fortunate to get to work with Rear Admiral Lira Carrie. She was very good at what she did. She was also someone who was very focused on the goal. Their goal for this mission was to destroy as many Morag shipyards as possible. "Now that they know we're here and what we're doing, it won't be so easy," replied Collison.

"Why do you think they didn't follow us?" asked Carrie.

"My best guess is that they will go to other star systems to protect their shipyards. I'm sure they've notified their fleet that was setting a trap for us close to the Lamothian star systems. They are most likely headed back here now. That gives us less than twenty-four hours before another five thousand Morag warships arrive to defend their shipyards," said Collison.

"We better not waste any time then."

"Exactly. We need to let everyone finish what repairs they can. Then we must move on to our next target. We jump in two hours."

"Where are we going?" asked Carrie.

"To the red giant star system containing one Morag inhabited planet, Morag Forty-Two, with its two terraformed moons. According to one of the scout ships, two shipyards orbit the planet. It is armed and has an energy shield. The planet is installing some planetary defenses. We are unsure whether they are combat-capable or not. It is not the closest star system with a shipyard. Two are located closer, but I'm guessing that's where that Morag fleet we just battled will head, thinking it's our most logical next target."

"The Morag are supposedly a very logical thinking race. So it would make sense for us to be a little illogical to outwit them," replied Carrie.

"Precisely why we are targeting this red giant system first. We should have plenty of time to hit our target and to jump out before that Morag fleet could arrive."

"Did the scout ship report any warships in the star system?" asked Carrie.

"Forty-three were reported when the scout ship was here. That could have changed by now. When we exit hyperspace, I want all ships at Condition One," said Collison.

"Will we jump to another rendezvous point after that or to the next target?" asked Carrie.

"To the next target. My plan is to hit three different star systems in a row. Then rendezvous here to assess the damage. The second star system will be two star systems over from the first. We will bypass more shipyards to get there. It also has one inhabited planet, Morag Thirty-Seven, and three terraformed moons. Three shipyards are located in this system. It is protected by a Morag fleet of seventy-three battlecruisers that patrol two systems. If we get lucky, they won't be there when we arrive. If they are, we must defend the battlecarriers, while the interceptors go to work."

"The third target?"

"The third target is three systems farther, closer to Morag Prime. Hopefully they'll think we are moving closer to Morag Prime and will consolidate their fleets. Then we can more easily hit the star systems on the periphery of the Morag's part of the Confederation for our third attack within phase two. This star system has one inhabited planet, Morag Twenty-Six, and its two terraformed moons. There are two shipyards and a Morag fleet of eighty-six battlecruisers."

Carrie was quiet for a few moments, while she absorbed the plethora of information Collison just gave her. They spent a few more minutes going over strategy and battle plans, before she headed back to her flagship, *Exeter*. She needed to prepare for phase two of their attack.

-

Morag Admiral Voxx rested in his quarters, when he was paged to come immediately to the Command Center. This must be it. It must be time to kill the Humans, who have fallen for his trap. It was a few days earlier than expected, but they were prepared.

As he entered the Command Center, he saw the troubled look on the captain's face. *What is going on?*

The Earth Humans have started their attack, Admiral Voxx.

This is a few days early, but we are ready. Why do you look so worried? asked Voxx.

The Earth Humans did not attack the Lamothian world of Xanther. They are attacking the eight shipyards in Morag-controlled space containing Morag Twelve and Fourteen, replied the captain.

What? Voxx yelled angrily. How could this be? How could they not fall for his trap? It was a perfect trap. Humans were very emotional and made irrational decisions. How could they not try to rescue their fellow Humans, set to be a part of the Lamothian feasts in a few days? He took a deep breath to calm himself. This was a very unexpected development.

Shall we set a course toward our Morag star systems, Admiral?

How many Human battleships attacked our area of space? asked Voxx.

According to the reports we have received from Admiral Ramgen, a little over eight hundred.

Voxx went silent, as he considered his next move. It would take him two days to get back to the Morag-controlled area of the Confederation. It was doubtful by then that the Humans would still be attacking targets there. Well over five thousand Morag warships were in their area of the Confederation. Against eight hundred Human battleships? The Humans were more than outnumbered and seemed to be attacking Morag shipyards. Once Ramgen reported on the type of weapons used by the Humans, they would know what they were up against. Ramgen surely can handle more than eight hundred battleships.

Voxx remembered how the Earth Humans had two fleets that attacked them, while they were targeting the Human Empire. One came to the Hagen Star Cluster and the other to Golan Four. Each of those fleets easily had more than eight hundred battleships. Another Earth Humans' fleet must be out there somewhere. He just needed to figure out where.

We will not head back to our part of the Confederation. I suspect another Earth Humans' fleet is out there somewhere. This attack in our star systems might be a diversion to get us to leave this area of the Confederation. By the time we made it back, the Earth Humans would be gone. No, we will not take their bait. We will stay here and see what the other Human fleet does, said Voxx.

Yes, Admiral, replied the captain.

They probably have a ship watching us, remarked Voxx.

Admiral, we have scanned this system many times, and no ships have been detected, replied the captain.

It must be a stealth ship. The Earth Humans are far more advanced than the Humans in the Empire. It would be logical to think they have developed a stealth ship that we cannot detect, said Voxx.

What shall we do? asked the captain.

We should make them think we took their bait. Let's set a course toward our star systems. We will only jump to the other side of the Lamothian-controlled area of the Confederation. To the Human stealth ships, it will look like we're headed home. The Earth Humans will believe they have outsmarted us. They will soon find out how wrong they are, said Voxx coldly.

When shall we leave? asked the captain.

Prepare the fleet to enter hyperspace in one hour. I will try to contact Admiral Ramgen to confirm it is the Earth Humans who have attacked, answered Voxx.

Ramgen was in his quarters, having a conference with Admiral Voxx and Admiral Marcello.

What type of weapons were used by the Humans in their attack? sent Voxx.

Those cannons you had described from the attack on the Human Empire. The ones that the Earth Humans possessed. They were very effective. It didn't take long for them to destroy the shipyards. We have no defense against it, said Ramgen.

The Forgotten Empire: The Confederation and The Empire at War

It is as I expected. I believe another Earth Humans' fleet is out in the Confederation somewhere. They had two fleets that came to aid the Human Empire in our attack against them. If not for their interference, I believe we would have been victorious over the Human Empire, said Voxx.

What shall we do? asked Ramgen. *How do we destroy them?*

We have the numbers to destroy them. It may cost us, but we cannot let them survive this attack. If they are successful, it would only encourage the Humans to attack again. They need to learn that to come to the Confederation and to attack us means certain death, said Voxx.

They destroyed two of our warships to every one of theirs we destroyed. We estimate that they still have over six hundred ships left for their next target, said Ramgen.

With 1,500 warships, you could easily overwhelm them then. How many do you have left in your fleet? asked Voxx.

I have 681 ships left in my fleet, replied Ramgen.

Marcello, can you spare nine hundred of your fleet to reinforce Admiral Ramgen? asked Voxx.

Will you not be returning with your fleet? asked Marcello.

No, it would take us two days to get there, and I believe you and Admiral Ramgen will have them vanquished before I can arrive. I will wait for the other Earth Humans' fleet to attack their target and then exterminate them myself, said Voxx.

I can send Admiral Ramgen 900 warships. That will leave me with a little more than 4,300 warships to protect Morag Prime, said Marcello.

Now we must determine where the Earth Humans will strike next. Then we will destroy them, said Ramgen.

The Morag Admirals continued their strategizing for another few minutes, settling on one star system that they felt most likely would be the Humans' next target. If their goal were to destroy shipyards, the closest target to where they were, with the most shipyards, would be the system containing three shipyards with one inhabited planet, Morag Forty-Five, and its two terraformed moons.

Marcello would send his nine hundred ships to aid Ramgen there. It would take them a little longer to get there than Ramgen, but they felt they had some time before the next attack.

Let's go kill some Humans, Voxx said in a sinister voice.

-

Marcello was not pleased that he had to send nine hundred ships to aid Ramgen. Marcello wanted to be responsible for crushing these inferior beings. He knew the likelihood of them attacking Morag Prime was very remote. Ramgen would end up succeeding in his endeavor, most likely surpassing Marcello in the eyes of the Morag High Council. He wanted to defeat these Earth Humans himself, but it looked like he wouldn't get his chance this time.

Maybe Ramgen wouldn't survive this battle against the Earth Humans. The fleet Marcello would send to aid Ramgen was bigger than what Ramgen had left of his own fleet. Maybe there was still a way for Marcello to take credit for the success and move up in the ranks. Only time would tell.

-

The Morag High Council was once again in an emergency session on Morag Prime. *How dare the Earth Humans attack us in our star systems! They will surely pay a heavy price for what they have done,* said Councilor Delann.

What word have we received from Admiral Ramgen? asked Councilor Brant.

The Earth Humans successfully destroyed all eight shipyards in that star system. They did not even attempt to destroy the space stations or fire a single shot at the planets, replied Councilor Addonis.

What were our losses to our fleet that engaged them? asked Brant.

Admiral Ramgen lost 283 ships, and 64 were damaged and are currently undergoing repairs at various shipyards throughout our star systems, replied Addonis.

What damage did we cause the Earth Humans' fleet? Asked Brant.

Admiral Ramgen believes his fleet destroyed around 160 of their battlecruisers and dreadnoughts. An unknown number of battleships were damaged, replied Addonis.

Why did Admiral Voxx's trap not work? Asked Councilor Hiram.

Admiral Voxx believes that this Earth Humans' fleet is a decoy to try to get his fleet away from the Lamothian area of the Confederation. He believes, once they leave, the other Earth Humans' fleet will attack Xanther, replied Addonis.

Is he planning to head back here to help defend our shipyards? Asked Hiram.

No. He will jump out of the system the fleet is currently in, make it appear as if they are headed home. He believes the Earth Humans have some type of stealth ship monitoring their activities in the star system. Once he does this, he believes the Earth Humans will launch their attack on Xanther. He will only jump a few star systems over. Then he will wait for them to attack their target and then exterminate them, Addonis said, with satisfaction.

What about the fleet destroying our shipyards? asked Delann.

Admirals Voxx, Marcello, and Ramgen have determined the most likely target the Earth Humans will attack next. A system not far from the first attack, replied Addonis. As he spoke, he activated his holographic display to show which star system he referred to. *This system has three shipyards. Admiral Ramgen is currently en route to this location. Marcello has sent nine hundred ships to aid Ramgen in his defense of these shipyards.*

What if they are wrong, and the Earth Humans target a different system? asked Delann.

There was silence, while everyone considered the ramifications of the reality that this very well may end up being a complicated game, exterminating this Human infestation. If they were wrong, and the Humans attacked elsewhere, then they would successfully destroy more shipyards before the Morag fleet could reach them. Then it would once again be a guessing game as to where the Humans would attack next. Eventually the Morag would guess correctly, but how many shipyards would they lose first?

Should we divide Admiral Marcello's fleet into smaller fleets to spread out among our star systems? We'd have a better chance of catching the Humans quicker that way, commented Hiram.

That would leave Morag Prime vulnerable to the Earth Humans' attack. That is not an option on the table at this time, replied Addonis.

We should see a logical pattern as to where the Humans attack after a few more of those. Then we can more accurately predict their next target, said Hiram.

There is one fatal flaw in your reasoning, Hiram, said Addonis. *The Earth Humans and Humans of the Empire are not always guided by logic. It is possible that we will be unsuccessful in predicting their target before they strike.*

What shall we do? asked Hiram.

Let's follow the plan that Voxx, Marcello, and Ramgen have formulated. If it is not successful, we might have to consider creating another couple fleets out of Marcello's fleet to protect more of our shipyards, remarked Addonis.

Let's hope it does not come to that, said Brant, as he pounded his fist on the table.

-

Admiral Voxx was once again in his command chair in the Command Center of his ship. *Is the fleet ready to make our hyperspace jump?* he asked the captain.

Yes, Admiral. Everyone is ready, replied the captain.

Time for these Humans to realize that coming to the Confederation was a colossal mistake. One they will pay for with their lives. Transition to hyperspace, Captain, sent Voxx.

Voxx smiled, as he felt his ship make the jump. The Earth Humans had underestimated them. They thought his fleet would return home. They failed to realize that the Morag don't make decisions the same way the Humans do. Our choices are logical; theirs are not. This will be their downfall. He shook his head. He had them right where he wanted them. His trap would still work out as successfully as he had planned.

-

Ardon Reull was in a meeting on Lormallia with the Ruling Triad.

Admiral Garr was updating them on the hyperlight messages they had intercepted from the Earth Humans' ships, stationed on the fringe of the Lormallian-controlled area of the Confederation.

"From the messages we've intercepted, it appears that the Earth Humans have successfully destroyed eight Morag shipyards in one star system," said Admiral Garr.

"That's good news," remarked Mador Angst. "Hopefully they will have more success. The more they can destroy, the longer it will take the Morag to build up their fleets. That will allow us more time to build up our fleets and defenses."

"It also allows the Human Empire and the Solar System to continue to build up their defenses and fleets as well," remarked Reull.

"Any reports on how many ships they've lost or how many Morag ships they destroyed?" asked Angst.

"No. We only know that the Humans are sending damaged ships back here to their mobile repair yards for repair," replied Admiral Garr.

"Their fleet jumped out a day apart, so we are guessing they have two different targets. It is unclear what their second target is. However, I would assume it's Xanther in the Lamothian star systems, since that's where the feast is to occur, where they will be consuming Humans." Reull shook his head in disgust. "I am certain we will get more reports in soon."

"What if the Morag fleets follow the Earth Humans back here, when they leave the Morag area of the Confederation?" asked Serrie Voll.

"Then we will be ready for them. The Morag are not welcome here in our area of the Confederation. If they come here, we will assume it is to attack us. It is even likely that, if they did follow the Humans back here and attacked them, they might go ahead and come after us while they are here," replied Angst.

"Our fleets need to be ready for this possibility and to be prepared to defend our star systems," said Birx Storl.

"Based on when the first Human fleet left, we still have a few days to get our fleets into position, before they could return here," said Reull.

"Can we reach out to the Humans and ask them to warn us if their fleets are being pursued by enemy fleets? That way, we can get our fleets into position? We don't want them thinking we are getting our fleets into position to attack them," said Voll.

"As the time draws near, I will reach out to the Human fleet to offer our assistance, if the Morag fleets pursue them. Hopefully it won't come to that. If our fleets are there when the Morag arrive, we could always say we were preparing to defend our star systems from the Humans, not the Morag—depending on how large of a fleet is in pursuit," remarked Reull.

"Good. We have a plan. Let's get things in order, so we are not taken by surprise. Let's have the fleet ready to jump to the fringe of our system. That way, they are ready when we need them," said Angst.

The Ruling Triad, along with Reull and Admiral Garr, discussed a few more matters and specifics on their plan, before they dismissed their meeting and headed their separate ways.

High Princess Layla was in her office, when her husband, Derrick, entered. He was always amazed at how hard she worked. She was utterly consumed by what she was working on and didn't even notice Derrick had entered the room. He stood in the doorway, watching her for a moment, before interrupting her concentration. He then cleared his throat to subtly notify her of his presence.

Layla quickly looked up from her work and smiled at Derrick. "How long have you been standing there?" she asked curiously.

"Long enough to know the Empire is no doubt better in your capable hands than in any others," Derrick replied matter-of-

189

factly. "Are you ready for the meeting and the welcoming of the United Worlds Alliance?"

"Yes, I am. I will head over to the House of Worlds in a few minutes to greet them when they arrive," replied Layla. "Would you care to join me?" she asked, with a smile.

"It would be my honor," replied Derrick.

"Any news from the Earth fleets?" asked Layla, as she stood from her chair.

"Yes, that's one of the reasons I came by. We received a message from Rear Admiral Carrie that the attack on the Morag shipyards had commenced," replied Derrick.

"Were they successful?" asked Layla.

"We have not yet received another message from Carrie," Derrick answered. He watched Layla, as she walked toward him.

"Is that bad? Does that mean they were unsuccessful?" asked Layla, as a cold shiver ran down her spine.

"No, we don't expect to hear from them again, until the attacks are over. They wouldn't want their message to be intercepted, and their location jeopardized," replied Derrick.

Layla let out a big sigh of relief. "For a moment there, I was thinking the worse. How about next time you include that part of the message a little earlier in the conversation," she said, as she gave him a tiny pinch.

Derrick chuckled and promised to deliver the message in a more complete way next time. He took her arm, as they left her office, and headed to the House of Worlds to great the Visth and the rest of their new alliance.

At least this would keep him busy and his mind occupied for a little while. Not knowing what's going on with Admiral Collison and his fleet was very nerve-wracking.

-

Cleemorl was in his quarters, pacing back and forth in front of his holographic display. He wished he could send and receive messages without giving away his location. He knew Collison should have started his attack by now. He could already be on his way back from attacking the Morag shipyards.

Cleemorl was pushing his hyperspace drives to the limit. He was certain they'd need repairs when they arrived at their destination. Hopefully he wouldn't need them soon after their arrival.

He stopped and looked again at the display. The Morag area of the Confederation was so vast. They had 92 star systems with 112 inhabited planets and over 200 terraformed moons. The number of shipyards they had was not known. Plus they could have built more in the months since they last attacked the Human space. With the data the Humans had retrieved from the damaged Morag ships above Golan Four, they knew where some of the shipyards were located.

The rest would be filled in by the scout ships sent ahead of Collison's fleet. That information should be known and shared by now. His display wouldn't update though, not until he dropped out of hyperspace. It was probable that each planet had at least one shipyard. Possibly even the terraformed moons had them as well.

In order for the Morag to have so many battlecruisers and battleships, they had to have a sizable number of shipyards. More than the Empire had, more than the Solar System had. It was vital that Collison destroy as many of these shipyards as possible to give the Humans the time they needed to build up their fleets.

According to Cleemorl's navigator, they had a couple more days of hyperspace travel before they dropped out at the rendezvous coordinates, where the supply fleet awaited.

Cleemorl felt a sense of dread seep in slowly in the pit of his stomach. If Collison were pursued by a large Morag fleet, they'd be outnumbered, without any relief coming to aid them.

When the Morag left Golan Four, they still had over two thousand ships. It was safe to assume they would not have left their area of the Confederation unprotected, so they likely had a reserve fleet. Based on the size of the fleets they had used to attack the Human Empire, it was likely the Morag had another ten thousand or more warships still active in the Confederation.

Cleemorl swallowed his fear and took a deep breath. According to the data they'd gotten from the damaged Morag ships and from Ardon Reull, the Morag did have a large fleet. Cleemorl did not want to face the entire fleet. Cleemorl and his fleet would be annihilated, even with the accelerator cannons the Earth Humans' ships had.

If only they could make it appear to long-range scanners that they had a large fleet lying in wait to ambush the Morag upon their exit from hyperspace, then maybe they would not attack.

If Collison destroyed enough shipyards, the Morag might be more cautious with their fleet. They might not want to risk losing ships that they would have a more challenging time repairing or replacing. Cleemorl just had to figure out how to make it look like they had a considerable fleet, lying in wait.

A plan was taking shape in his mind. He just had to figure out how to implement it quickly, once Collison's combined fleet dropped from hyperspace where the supply fleet was positioned, trying to escape any Morag fleet following them.

Rear Admiral Barnes was enjoying her daily cup of coffee in the cafeteria, when she was paged over the comm system to come to the Command Center. She wondered what was going on. She wasn't expecting to hear from Collison at all, not until after her attack on Lamothia. Then she was supposed to send out Princess Layla's message to the Lamothians and afterward send a message to Collison, informing him of her victory. She hoped things were going well for Admiral Collison and Rear Admiral Carrie. They should have begun their attack on the Morag shipyards by now.

As she entered the Command Center, her communications officer said, "We have received a message from scout ship 368. Captain Hadley reported that the large Morag fleet positioned in the Lamothian star system entered hyperspace about an hour ago.

They appeared to be headed back toward the Morag area of the Confederation."

Barnes smiled. "Looks like Collison's plan worked after all." She felt a wave of relief wash over her. The Morag fleet was a large one; that was one less thing she had to worry about. Now she had to face only the Lamothian fleet patrolling the star system. Hopefully she could destroy the planet before the larger Lamothian fleet, lying in wait closer to Xanther, had time to reach the star system where Lamothia was located. It seemed the stars were in her favor after all. She would sleep easier tonight. Then tomorrow they would drop out of hyperspace near Lamothia and destroy it before anyone could stop them.

Scout ship 368 had watched as the Morag fleet had entered hyperspace. "Should we follow them?" asked Lieutenant Maddox.

"No, they may detect us when we drop out of hyperspace. Collison wanted us to head to Xanther and to observe the activities going on there. See if we can follow a transport ship back to wherever they are getting their supply of Humans from," replied Captain Hadley.

"Shall we plot our course back to Xanther then?" asked Lieutenant Maddox.

"Yes, let's get out of here and go solve this mystery," said Hadley.

She felt a sense of relief, as her scout ship transitioned into hyperspace. They had already established the Lamothians could not detect their stealth ship, so they would be safe and not have to worry about being detected.

As Morag Admiral Voxx and his fleet emerged from hyperspace, he immediately had the tactical officer run a scan to see if any ship had followed them.

We have not detected any ships, Admiral.

The Forgotten Empire: The Confederation and The Empire at War

Let's keep our scanners activated for a while to make sure we don't detect any radiation from a hyperspace jump other than our own. I wouldn't be surprised if whatever ship was spying on us follows us. If they do, we need to destroy them before they can get a message back to the Human fleet that we didn't, in fact, return to the Morag-controlled area of the Confederation, said Voxx.

We will keep the scanners activated, Admiral.

Yes, and we will reign supreme. These Earth Humans will soon be taught a very harsh lesson in reality about who really rules the Confederation.

Chapter Sixteen

Admiral Collison and his fleet were minutes away from dropping out of hyperspace in the red giant star system that held their next targets. His fleet had already moved to Condition Two and would shortly move to Condition One. He wanted to be on the highest alert, in case the Morag had managed to identify his next target. It was highly unlikely; for now, the odds would be in Collison's favor.

With every star system they targeted and with every shipyard they destroyed, the odds would eventually shift in favor of the Morag identifying a pattern. Collison was trying to be mindful in picking his targets at random, to not be logical about it at all, but that wasn't as easy as it seemed.

"Captain Billingsly, move the fleet to Condition One," Collison commanded. He would be ready for whatever awaited them in this star system. He hoped he had enough time to destroy the shipyards before the patrolling Morag fleet could engage them. Dealing with the patrolling fleet wasn't as bad as dealing with the larger fleet that he was sure waited for them somewhere. Hopefully not anywhere near this system. He knew, the next time the Morag found Collison's fleet, that the Morag fleet would likely follow them into hyperspace. The more shipyards he could destroy before then, the better.

As they dropped from hyperspace, alarms sounded.

"What do we have, Captain Billingsly?" asked Collison.

"Scans show thirty-seven battlecruisers and six battleships patrolling near the shipyards of Morag Forty-Two," reported Billingsly.

"Guess they know why we're here," replied Collison. "Take us in as close as we can get. We will engage the fleet, while Rear Admiral Carrie and the battlecarriers take out the shipyards."

Rear Admiral Carrie was not surprised the Morag fleet was already in position to protect the shipyards. The longer the enemy fleet could hold off the Humans, the more time it bought the larger Morag fleet to arrive. This meant destroying the shipyards would be up to her and her attack interceptors, while the larger part of the fleet held off the Morag ships. Carrie's crew was ready. They had planned for this.

As they moved closer to the planet and the first shipyard, Carrie and the battlecarriers held back a little. They would launch their attack from the safety of the rear of the fleet.

She watched as the fleet took the formation of ten ships high and sixty ships long. The dreadnoughts were in the center of the formation.

"Let's have the battlecarriers prepare to launch the attack interceptors. We will launch as soon as the fleet sends off their first rounds of accelerator cannon fire," commanded Carrie.

"The Morag fleet is two minutes from engagement range," said Major Sullivan.

Carrie took a deep breath to steady herself. The Morag fleet wouldn't last long up against the accelerator cannons. That weapon had really helped to even the playing field a little bit. Destroying their shipyards would help it even more.

Morag Captain Matiun was on patrol in a red giant star system and its one inhabited planet, Morag Forty-Two. He had received troubling reports from Admiral Ramgen that an Earth Humans' fleet had attacked and destroyed shipyards in one Morag star system already. Matiun was to be on the lookout for this fleet. Ramgen did not expect them to attack this system next, but the Humans did not always make decisions the way the Morag would.

Matiun only had forty-three ships in his fleet, but, if he had to, he could hold off the Humans for a little while. Hopefully long enough for help to arrive. He had positioned his fleet close to the one inhabited planet in this system. Two shipyards and its two terraformed moons all orbited the planet.

As Matiun was settling down for his evening meal, an alarm sounded. An uneasy feeling of dread crept up in the pit of his stomach. He rushed to the Command Center. There was only one reason those alarms would go off and only one enemy fleet in the Morag part of the Confederation.

He immediately sent a message to Admiral Ramgen. *The Earth Humans are attacking the red giant star system. They are currently dropping from hyperspace.*

How many ships? asked Ramgen.

Over six hundred, Matiun said coldly. He closed his eyes and then slowly opened them. No way he would hold them off long. He was too outnumbered. *How long until you can get here?*

Two hours, he said slowly.

Matiun let out the breath he had been holding. He already knew Ramgen was too far away to get here in time. Hearing it confirmed though made it more of a reality. He needed to take as many ships with him as he could.

We will head in your direction. They will likely hit a neighboring star system next. Hopefully we will catch up to them and annihilate them. Destroy as many of their fleet as possible. You have served the Morag well, Matiun, Ramgen said.

Matiun turned to his crew and said, *Let's get the fleet in a cone formation. We will hold on as long as possible and destroy as many enemy battleships as we can.*

As the command crew set about their tasks, Matiun sat down in his command chair. *We will launch our antimatter missiles and fusion energy beams as soon as they enter our extreme combat range. We need to batter down their energy shields and then obliterate these insufferable Humans.*

Five minutes until they reach our extreme combat range Admiral Matiun, said his tactical officer.

Stand by to fire, said Matiun.

Admiral Ramgen slammed his hand on his command chair. These Humans think they've outsmarted us, but we will get them.

When we do, nothing will be left of their fleet. We will hunt them down until they are all destroyed!

Plot a course for the neighboring star system of the red giant system. We cannot reach Matiun in time, but we can reach that area of space to be ready for their next attack, said Ramgen.

He would have this Human fleet destroyed in the next day, he was certain.

-

We are in extreme weapons range, Admiral Matiun, said the tactical officer.

Fire! commanded Matiun. He felt a slight shudder, as his battleship launched its missiles toward the approaching Human fleet. He watched intently as the fusion energy beams and antimatter missiles closed in on the enemy fleet. He took in a sharp breath as the Humans launched their first rounds of attack as well. Matiun had only heard of the accelerator cannons. Now he was seeing them in action.

Their fusion energy beams reached the enemy fleet first and battered down some of the energy shields of a few of their battleships. Soon afterward the antimatter missiles arrived and blasted the battleships into thousands of pieces. A satisfied smile crossed Matiun's face. Now they needed to shift their focus to the next ships and annihilate as many as they could in what time they had remaining. *Keep firing all weapons!*

-

Collison commanded the fleet to get into battle formation, ten ships high and sixty ships long. It shouldn't take them long to destroy this small Morag fleet. If only all the Morag fleets were this size instead of multiple thousands, it'd make defeating them that much easier.

As they neared extreme combat range, the Morag fleet opened fire. "Admiral, they've launched their missiles and fusion energy beams. Should we return fire?" asked his tactical officer.

"No, we will wait until we are close enough for our accelerator cannon fire to be effective," replied Collison. "How much longer until we reach our combat zone?"

"Two minutes, Admiral," replied the tactical officer.

"Have all of the ships lock on to their targets and launch their weapons as soon as we reach that combat zone," commanded Collison.

"Brace for impact!" shouted the tactical officer.

As everyone in the Command Center braced for impact, Collison felt his heart beat faster. The Morag had very effective weapons but nothing to match the accelerator cannons. Collison's fleet would decimate this Morag fleet, but not before they lost a few of their own. He closed his eyes and took a deep breath. When he opened them, he gazed intently at the displays in front of him.

As the fusion energy beams arrived at the inbound Human fleet, energy screens lit up, as they battered against the safety net that the energy screens provided. Most energy shields held up to the bombardment, but a few failed. As the antimatter missiles arrived, they quickly destroyed the ships that had saw their energy shields overloaded.

Collison grimaced as he saw a few green icons, representing his fleet, disappear. The bombardment continued as they moved ever closer to the defending Morag fleet. Once in range of the accelerator cannons, Collison ordered, "All ships fire!"

Captain Anderson was on board the battlecarrier *Orion*, awaiting the signal to launch the interceptors. The fleet was almost to engagement range. As soon as they launched their accelerator cannons, he would launch the attack interceptors. The plan was to have them go around the fleet and get in behind the Morag fleet. This fleet didn't have any of the smaller attack craft the Morag had developed to counter the attack interceptors.

The interceptors were to split in two groups, with half going to the closest shipyard and the other half going to the farther one.

They were to get in there, launch their payload of fusion-tipped missiles, and then return to the battlecarriers to reload. The hope was that, by this time, the Morag fleet would be destroyed, and both shipyards would be destroyed; then Collison's fleet could move on to the next target.

All 160 of Anderson's attack interceptor crews were ready and waiting for his command. No doubt some of them would not return. The shipyards were heavily armed.

As he watched the displays in front of him, the sky lit up as both fleets launched their attacks. If it weren't so deadly, some might call it beautiful. It didn't take long for the missiles to start their destructive explosions, as they hit the energy shields of both fleets. He closed his eyes for a moment to shield them from the intense light created by the attacking fleets. As he opened them, he commanded, "Launch the attack interceptors!"

All of the battlecarriers launched their attack interceptors. In a matter of minutes, over five thousand interceptors had been launched and were headed to the shipyards. It was an impressive sight to see. Each interceptor was armed with four fusion-tipped missiles. If each launched their full payload, over twenty thousand missiles would be inbound toward the shipyards in a matter of moments, which should definitely light up the sky.

-

Lieutenant Garland and her squadron had launched from their battlecarrier *Freedom*. Her squadron would attack the shipyard closest to the defending Morag fleet. As they headed toward the shipyard, she couldn't help but watch as the accelerator cannon fire reached the Morag fleet and started to decimate their energy shields. As the second round of accelerator cannon fire hit the now-unprotected ships, they were destroyed in massive explosions. All along the Morag fleet, massive fireballs lit up the space.

Garland shifted her focus back to her mission. No matter what was happening around her, her squadron had to get through and had to launch their missiles at the shipyard.

As they got closer, the shipyard started to launch their fusion energy beams at the approaching attack interceptors. All of the squadrons began their evasive maneuvers to avoid the onslaught of the energy beams.

Garland saw bright flashes of light around her. She knew interceptors were being hit and destroyed by the shipyard. They just had to get a little closer before they could launch their missiles.

The shipyard then started launching their antimatter missiles at the attacking interceptors. The interceptor pilots used all of their intense training to avoid being hit by the incoming fire. Only one more minute, and she could launch her missiles and get out of there.

More and more flashes of light occurred all around her. She kept her focus on the incoming fire. As she dodged another missile, the alarm sounded, notifying her that she was in range. She quickly launched her four fusion-tipped missiles and turned to head back to the battlecarrier. She didn't even wait to see if the missiles destroyed their target. All around her, she saw attack interceptors launching their missiles. She needed to get back to her battlecarrier *Freedom* and reload.

As Garland returned to *Freedom*, she couldn't help but notice that space was littered with the molten wreckage of destroyed ships. She hoped most of them were Morag ships, but she knew that, in all likelihood, some Earth ships were in the wreckage as well.

As she neared *Freedom*, she sent a message to her squadron. She needed a count of what was left. When they had started this attack, there had been twenty attack interceptors in her squadron. She now had only fourteen. There would be time to mourn the loss of her crew after this battle was over.

As she entered the landing bay, she noticed a lot of missing interceptors. She received the command from the captain that they did not need to relaunch but needed to reload for the next attack.

For now, her part in the battle in this star system was over. She needed some rest and to regroup with her squadron, before they reached the next star system. They needed to see what they did wrong and what they did right. They needed to learn from their mistakes. That way they could survive this attack on the Morag and live to see Earth and their families again.

-

Admiral Matiun's gaze focused on the displays in front of him, as the accelerator cannon fire reached his fleet. Within seconds ships had disappeared from the tactical display. The bright explosions lit up all across the front of his cone formation. He barely had time to process what had happened before the next round hit his fleet. They were being destroyed so quickly. Space was littered with debris from the destruction of his fleet.

Massive explosions riddled the formation, as more and more ships met their end in violent displays of sheer power. He was amazed at this new weapon the Earth Humans possessed. The Morag needed to get their hands on this weapons technology. If they were to defeat the Earth Humans, the Morag would need to defend against this new weapon and to develop one even better to annihilate all the Humans and their Solar System from which they came.

Within minutes most of his ships had disappeared. What ships remained were firing as many rounds as was possible. His heart pounded in his chest, as he saw the deadly Human projectiles headed straight at his ship. He watched as the first projectile hit his energy shield and overloaded it. He braced for impact. He heard a low rumble start from somewhere deep in the ship. It got louder and louder, until it consumed him.

-

Collison continued to intently gaze at the displays in front of him. A few more green icons disappeared. Then the first round of accelerator cannon fire hit the Morag fleet, immediately lighting up and overloading their energy shields. As the second round then hit those now-defenseless ships, huge explosions of raw energy erupted across the front line of the enemy fleet. Shortly after that, the next round hit and the next. Within minutes the enemy fleet defending the star system was no more. The space above the planet was littered with debris from the battle.

Collison turned his attention to Billingsly. "Have the attack interceptors destroyed the shipyards?"

"Yes, Admiral. They are returning to their battlecarriers now," replied Billingsly.

"As soon as they are all back on their carriers, let's move on to our next target," commanded Collison.

"We have about five more minutes, and we will be ready to enter hyperspace Admiral," replied Billingsly.

"In the meantime, let's get damage assessments from the fleet and send those ships too heavily damaged to get repaired by the mobile shipyards," replied Collison.

"Yes, Admiral," said Billingsly.

Captain Anderson had all of his remaining attack interceptors back on his ship, *Orion*. His attack interceptors had been involved in the destruction of the second shipyard. His best squadron, the Black Dart Squadron, had been instrumental in leading the attack.

Captain Stephens was the group leader of the Black Dart Squadron. Anderson had already spoken with Stephens. His entire squadron had made it back to the battlecarrier. Unfortunately the other squadrons hadn't fared as well. Out of 160 interceptors that had left his ship, only 123 had returned.

They had quickly reloaded and were prepared for their next mission. Thankfully they had managed to launch enough of their fusion-tipped missiles to destroy the energy shield of the shipyards and then destroy the shipyard in a series of massive explosions, as all the missiles hit the shipyard sequentially. The energy shield of the shipyard couldn't handle being hit by so many missiles at the same time. The shield had quickly been overloaded and had failed, as more missiles reached the shipyard.

Now the large pieces left of what had been the shipyard fell to the planet. With any luck, some of them would cause some damage on the surface.

His Command Center was a beehive of activity, as they accessed the damage done to the fleet and prepared for their hyperspace jump. They were waiting on the command to come from Collison. This red giant star system now had no shipyards; mission had been accomplished.

At present they prepared for the next attack, and thankfully they had some time, once they entered hyperspace, before they would arrive at the next targeted star system. Anderson knew his crew and his interceptor crews needed some rest and a good meal before this next attack.

Rear Admiral Carrie was proud of how well the attack interceptors had performed up against the shipyards. They had lost a few from each battlecarrier but still had most of their numbers intact. She was waiting for the final numbers to come in. She watched, as the last few returned to their battlecarriers.

Collison and the fleet made short work of the defending Morag fleet. Carrie had witnessed a few explosions across their fleet, signaling a destroyed ship. Not as many as it could have been if they'd faced a more extensive fleet. She knew that battle was coming too.

Hopefully they would have a big-enough fleet to continue to destroy more and more shipyards. The attack interceptors had been effective, while the fleet took care of the Morag battlecruisers and battleships. They would use that tactic again, until it wasn't feasible, as they would lose more and more attack interceptors. If the next system didn't have an enemy fleet patrolling it, the attack interceptors could rest, while the fleet destroyed the shipyards.

As long as they didn't run into a large Morag fleet, they would be fine. She knew Collison was trying to be random in his selection of targets, so the Morag couldn't predict where they'd go next. No doubt one of the large fleets was currently headed this way. Next time there would be a large fleet closer to their target. Hopefully not close enough to aid the targeted shipyards. So far, they had successfully destroyed ten Morag shipyards. A small dent in the total number, but it was something.

As the last interceptor landed in the launch bay, the fleet transitioned to hyperspace. It was time to head to their next target.

As the fleet made the transition into hyperspace, Admiral Collison asked, "Captain Billingsly, do we have all the reports in from the fleet?"

"Yes, Admiral. We received the last one just a moment ago. We lost 17 battlecruisers and 2 dreadnoughts. The reports from the battlecarriers indicate that we lost 495 attack interceptors," said Billingsly.

"Let's consolidate our squadrons and send the empty battlecarriers back to the supply fleet to resupply them with the extra attack interceptors we brought along. We might need them ready to help defend the fleet when we return," replied Collison. "What about damaged ships?"

"We had two damaged battlecruisers and one damaged dreadnought. They have already set off for the supply fleet," said Billingsly.

"We need to be on high alert in the next system. The larger Morag fleets will most likely be closer by this time. I am sure this fleet we just destroyed will have notified the other fleets of our location. They will be headed this way. Our plan of attacking a few systems over will hopefully keep us out of range of the larger fleet. We need to prepare for the worst-case scenario as well though—meeting a large fleet—as eventually we will do just that."

Admiral Ramgen had received a discouraging report from the space station in the red giant system. Admiral Matiun and his entire fleet had been destroyed by the Human fleet. The Humans had been successful in destroying both of the shipyards as well. The space station had reported the direction the Human fleet left as they entered hyperspace. Ramgen was trying to determine their next most likely target. It was logical that the Humans wouldn't attack the next system; they hadn't done that previously. He thought the Humans would be two systems over from the previous target. This was assuming the fleet hadn't changed directions once they entered hyperspace.

Ramgen's fleet would reach the red giant system of Morag Forty-Two in less than an hour, but now that the space stations had reported the direction the Humans were headed, there was no need to stop in that system. He would alter his coordinates and head toward the star system he expected the Humans to target. Ramgen was closing in on the Human fleet. He was sure of it.

Rear Admiral Carrie was trying to rest a little before their next attack. According to the numbers that Admiral Collison had sent her, their fleet was still strong. That last attack had not cost them too heavily. Well, not in ships. When she thought about all the lives lost on those ships, it was a much more sobering number.

This is what they had trained for, why a number of them had signed up. To travel to the Confederation and to be a thorn in their side. To teach the Confederation that attacking the Solar System and Earth had consequences. Consequences that the Confederation now faced. As she drifted off to sleep, her mind wandered to Rear Admiral Barnes. Carrie hoped Barnes would have great success in her missions and not meet much resistance.

Raymond L. Weil

Chapter Seventeen

Admiral Voxx studied his holographic display of the Morag's area of the Confederation. They had been wrong in where the Humans would attack. Admiral Matiun had paid the price for their mistake. Fortunately they now knew where the Humans had been recently and in which direction they were headed. Ramgen was closing in and would be nearer to where they suspected the next attack would be by the Humans. Ramgen would get them this next time. If not, they would need to split Marcello's fleet into smaller groups to have more fleets to find and to destroy the Humans.

Voxx then switched his display to the Lamothian area of the Confederation. He was only a short hyperspace jump from Xanther. It would take them about an hour to arrive there, once they received word that the Human fleet had entered their star system. He knew the Humans would feel the need to rescue the Humans held on Xanther, before they attempted to destroy the planet. The Lamothian fleet was positioned a little closer to the star system and could arrive first. Once the Lamothians engaged the Human fleet, that would keep the Humans occupied, until Voxx's fleet reached them. Then they would finish them off.

As he turned off his holographic display, First Officer Bale sent a message for him to come to the Command Center immediately. Guess it was time to kill some Humans.

As he entered the Command Center, he could tell something wasn't right. *Have the Humans entered the star system near Xanther?*

No, Admiral. We are getting reports that a Human fleet is exiting hyperspace near Lamothia, Bale said coldly.

Voxx slammed his hand on his command chair. *These nettlesome Humans will pay for this!* He paused as he thought for a moment. *How far are we from Lamothia?*

A two-hour hyperspace jump, Admiral, answered Bale.

So, not close enough, replied Voxx. *Set a course for Lamothia. Maybe we can determine their next move and follow them or, better yet, beat them to their next target,* commanded Voxx.

Admiral, said Bale, *could their second target still be Xanther?*

Voxx quieted, as he thought it over. *How many ships are they reporting that the Human fleet has?*

The report says that the Humans had 1,034 battleships, which exited hyperspace above Lamothia, answered Bale.

We have under 5,300 ships in our fleet. Let's split our fleet into two fleets. One will stay here, in case the Humans target Xanther next. The other one will head to Lamothia to find and to destroy the Human fleet. We would still have a considerable numerical advantage over the Human fleet. We can still crush them, even with half our fleet, said Voxx.

As Voxx settled into his command chair, he watched as half his fleet joined him in jumping into hyperspace. The other half stayed behind, with Commander Phobyis as their leader. Of course, Voxx could still control him with Voxx's strong telepathic abilities. He implanted a few commands in Phobyis's mind before they left. He wanted to ensure Phobyis did what he wanted him to do.

Now all Voxx could do was wait. Wait to see what the Human fleet headed toward Lamothia would do. So far, the Human fleet in the Morag area of the Confederation had not attacked a planet, only shipyards. Was that what this fleet would do as well? Or would they destroy Lamothia? The Humans had mentioned in the past that using Humans in the Lamothian feasts would result in the destruction of one of their planets. Time would tell. Right now Voxx had time, about two hours' worth of time.

Lamothian Admiral Zahn had just received word that the Human fleet they had expected to come to Xanther had exited hyperspace near their homeworld of Lamothia. "How can this be! Why did they not fall for our trap that we set for them at Xanther? Admiral Voxx is to blame for this. We left our homeworld exposed to danger, believing the Humans would fall for the trap."

His captain replied, "How many ships do we have orbiting Lamothia?"

"Eighty-three. And the Humans have a little more than one thousand," Admiral Zahn said slowly, as a chill came over him. "How long will it take us to reach Lamothia?"

"Just under two hours, Admiral," replied Captain Camdret.

"Let's head that way. We will likely not reach them in time, but we must pursue this Human fleet and make them pay for attacking our homeworld," said Admiral Zahn.

"Maybe they will not attack Lamothia. Maybe this is a trick to get us to leave Xanther exposed," commented the admiral's First Officer Vormalt.

Admiral Zahn paused, as he considered this possibility. "Even if that is true, we would still have time to get there. The Human fleet would no doubt try to rescue the Humans on Xanther. They most assuredly would not destroy the planet with Humans on it. That would buy us enough time to return to Xanther to engage the Human fleet."

"Then we should head to Lamothia then?" asked Camdret.

"Yes, let's set a course for Lamothia. Maybe the fleet protecting our homeworld can hold off long enough for us to get there," Admiral Zahn said in a doubtful tone.

As the fleet started their transition into hyperspace, First Officer Vormalt asked, "What about Morag Admiral Voxx? What are they doing?"

"I am not sure. Voxx is keeping communication down, since he doesn't want the Humans to intercept any messages he might send us," replied Admiral Zahn.

"Maybe they will stay here near Xanther, while we head back to Lamothia," First Officer Vormalt replied.

"We will have to operate under the assumption that we are on our own. If they show up and help us fight these Humans, then so be it. If they don't, then we will be prepared to annihilate the Humans ourselves," replied Admiral Zahn.

"By *annihilate*, you do mean capture them to add to our feasts, correct?" asked First Officer Vormalt.

"If that is possible, then yes. Our priority is to defend our planets from being destroyed by this inferior species," replied Admiral Zahn. "They've already destroyed one planet, and we only have five left. We cannot afford to lose another one."

Admiral Barnes had her fleet at Condition One. They would be dropping out of hyperspace in a few minutes. Their long-range scanners were already sounding alarms. According to the scans, the Lamothians had a fleet of eighty-three battleships still in the system that contained Lamothia. She breathed a sigh of relief that no other fleets were here. She knew she needed to destroy Lamothia as quickly as possible to avoid any other fleets having enough time to come to their aid. If no other ships were around, then no ships would follow them into hyperspace and could report their location to other enemy fleets.

She took a deep breath to steady herself, as her fleet dropped from hyperspace. She set her timer for sixty minutes. She should have at least that much time before any surrounding fleets had time to jump into this star system.

They had a lot of work to do in very little time. They did, however, have a solid plan. They would be using a strategy that Vice Fleet Admiral Derrick Masters had used, when he had destroyed a Druin planet not too long ago.

The Human fleet would engage the enemy fleet. Once that was overwhelming the enemy, the battlecarriers, with a few dreadnoughts and battlecruisers, would jump to the other side of the planet and begin the bombardment of the planet. It shouldn't be too hard, since they did not have a defensive grid surrounding the planet. The only defenses included the space stations and that shipyard that had energy shields, all armed.

Part of Barnes's fleet would be tasked with destroying the space stations and the shipyard, while part of Barnes's fleet engaged the enemy fleet. Luckily she had a sizable fleet that should eliminate this small Lamothian fleet of eighty-three ships pretty quickly.

"Any surprises that we didn't know about?" asked Barnes.

"Everything appears to be as reported by the scout ship. It looks like the shipyard is now fully armed. The space stations and shipyard have activated their energy shields," replied Captain Borrel.

"What is the Lamothian fleet doing?" asked Barnes.

"Moving into a wedge formation," replied Borrel. "They are positioned between one of the space stations and the shipyard. They will use their firepower to their advantage."

"Get the fleet into a formation that's ten ships high and one hundred ships long. Keep the battlecarriers and the ships that will protect them back behind the formation," commanded Barnes.

As the fleet got into formation, it closed in on Lamothia. "Five minutes to engagement range, Admiral," said Captain Borrel.

"Have all ships prepare to fire. Have part of the fleet target the Lamothian fleet and the other half target the shipyard and space station," commanded Barnes.

She sat on the edge of her command chair and gazed intently at the viewscreens in front of her. They more than outnumbered this fleet ten to one. She glanced at her countdown timer. She still had plenty of time.

—

Lamothian Admiral Declan was in charge of the partial fleet left to patrol their home star system, where Lamothia was located. He was more than a little annoyed that he wouldn't get in on any of the major battles expected to take place at Xanther. Admiral Zahn got to have all the fun. He would capture lots of Humans from the fleet expected to attack Xanther in a couple days. He'd probably even be allowed first pick at the feast.

Declan really wanted to see some action. All he ever did was patrol their home system. Not much ever happened here. He'd never even ventured out of the Confederation. At the time the

Humans had attacked Zaneth, Declan had been away on a training mission. He wasn't sure if he was lucky that he wasn't there or unfortunate for not being there to aid the fleet stationed there.

Morag Admiral Voxx had set a trap for the Humans over Xanther this time. It appeared to be a great plan, if only it weren't a Lamothian world at risk. They only had five inhabited planets left. They couldn't afford to lose another one. It would be better if the Morag had set the trap in the Morag area of the Confederation. They hadn't lost any planets.

Declan did recognize that the easiest way to lure the Humans in was with live bait. With their own species held here, the Humans couldn't help but try to be the heroes and come to their rescue. Yes, it was a great plan, as long as it worked like the Morag thought it would.

As Declan headed to his quarters to get some rest, the alarms sounded. He wondered what could possibly be making the alarms sound. As he reached the Command Center, he felt his blood coursing through his veins, and his heart beat faster. Something must actually be happening here. "Status!"

"Admiral Declan, a Human fleet is emerging from hyperspace," replied Captain Elsmed.

He couldn't believe his eyes. An actual Human fleet was here, in his star system. He tried to contain his excitement. In a more serious tone than he felt, he asked, "How many ships are in this Human fleet?"

"Over one thousand, Admiral," Elsmed replied in a cold voice.

Declan's pulse quickened even more, this time not out of excitement but out of fear. He only had eighty-three ships. What would he do? He had to think quickly; it wouldn't be long, and the Human fleet would be in weapons range. "Send a message to Admiral Zahn and apprise him of our situation. I guess Admiral Voxx's plan did not work. The Humans are here, where they weren't supposed to be, and they're two days early!"

"Yes, Admiral," replied Elsmed.

"Are any fleets close by?" asked Declan.

"No, none are close enough to get here in time," replied Elsmed.

"Send a request for aid. Maybe a Zynth fleet or a Druin fleet is near enough to come to our aid," said Declan. He swallowed and tried to regain control over his emotions. He needed to assume no help would arrive in time. What could he do to stall the enemy fleet from destroying his homeworld?

He looked at the display that showed the planet below. It was a blue-green planet with 60 percent water and 40 percent landmasses, four large landmasses in total. As he looked at the view of the planet, he saw the landmass he had grown up on. Would it still be there by the end of this day?

He quickly evaluated his options. He needed to rely on the shipyard and the space stations for their added firepower. They were all also protected by energy shields. That would allow them to fire off more rounds before they could be destroyed. "Let's move our fleet in between the space station and the shipyard. Inform the crews stationed on them to fire as quickly and as many rounds as they possibly can at this attacking fleet as soon as they are in range."

As he moved the fleet into formation, he received a message from Admiral Zahn. "Admiral Zahn said his fleet is preparing to head this way. They will be here in just under two hours," said Elsmed.

Declan thought over the possibilities for a moment. He knew he had only a very slim chance that they could hold off this fleet for very long. Let alone two hours.

"Admiral, two minutes until the fleet will be in engagement range," said Elsmed.

"Tell all ships to fire continuously once they reach engagement range," said Declan. "We want to destroy as many of their ships as we can. We must stop them from firing on Lamothia."

The Command Center went silent, as they all realized the ramifications of this battle. They were up against unprecedented odds; they had never faced an enemy fleet with such huge numbers against their smaller fleet. The Humans should not be here. They don't belong here; they should have never come to the Confederation. This is because of the feast.

The Humans had warned us that they'd destroy another planet if we used Humans in our feast. We didn't believe them. Maybe we should have. That was not something that was in Declan's power though. What he did have control over was his fleet. They would make this Human fleet pay for coming here. They would destroy as many as they could.

"The fleet is in range, Admiral," said Elsmed.

"Fire all weapons continuously on all ships! Make sure the shipyard and space station are firing as well," commanded Declan.

They fired their fusion energy beams and their antimatter missiles. Hopefully they could overload some of the Human energy shields and take out some of their ships quickly.

The Human fleet launched their attack at the same time they did. He had never seen weapons like this. What was it? As he watched the displays, the fusion energy beams hit the Human fleet. He watched as their energy screens lit up from all the power being released. A few failed, as the antimatter missiles arrived and blew a few of the ships into millions of pieces.

Then the Human fire reached his fleet. It immediately overloaded the energy screens, as the second round hit and destroyed the ships in massive explosions. He watched in horror as the ships around him were decimated. Shortly after that, he watched as his ship was targeted. The first strike took down his energy shield, like it was a primitive technology. As the second round hit, it destroyed his ship into more pieces than one could count.

-

Rear Admiral Barnes watched the countdown to engagement range. Her heart pounded in her chest, as it seemed to slowly reach zero. When it finally did, she commanded, "Fire!" She felt the ship shudder slightly, as the weapons launched. The Lamothian fleet fired at almost the same time. Space lit up with accelerator cannon fire from her fleet. The fusion energy beams and antimatter missiles lit up the other side of the battle, as they headed toward her fleet.

She slowly released the breath she had been holding. She knew she would lose some ships, as the enemy fire reached her fleet. Hopefully it wouldn't be very many.

The Lamothian fusion energy beams reached her fleet first, lighting up the energy shields of numerous ships. Only a few overloaded, and then were destroyed when the antimatter missiles arrived. The debris remaining of those ships blasted in multiple directions and hit the energy shields of nearby ships. Thankfully none of them failed.

Barnes turned her attention to the Lamothian fleet, as her accelerator cannon fire reached them. They instantly destroyed the energy shields of the targeted ships. As the second round hit those now-vulnerable ships, they disintegrated with brilliant explosions of energy.

At the same time, part of her fleet was focused on destroying the space station and shipyard. Intense firepower came from them. The second space station was located on the opposite side of the planet. It would be dealt with after these first two were demolished into nothing but space debris.

Barnes watched the displays, showing the space station and the shipyard. She was surprised by the firepower the Lamothians had coming from them. As she watched some of her dreadnoughts and battleships get erased from her tactical display, she took in a sharp breath. Even though they took on heavy fire, the part of the fleet targeting the space station and shipyard quickly overwhelmed the enemy's energy shields and blew their targets into oblivion.

The fleet systematically took out all the enemy targets located within their firing range. Rear Admiral Barnes then shifted her focus to the attack her battlecarriers had launched on the planet of Lamothia.

On board the battlecarrier *Daneb*, Captain Elliott quickly launched all his attack interceptors to destroy the Lamothian homeworld of Lamothia. The interceptors had not moved to the opposite side of the planet, since the only remaining shipyard was still in orbit there. They instead launched their attack from behind the fleet in the opposite direction. His best interceptor squadron was the Scorpion Squadron. He knew they would lead the other interceptor pilots in destroying the planet Lamothia.

As Elliott watched his tactical display, the green icons multiplied, as all the interceptors from all the battlecarriers were launched. Within minutes it displayed 3,680 attack interceptors. Each carried four fusion-tipped missiles that they would launch at the surface of the planet, once they cleared the atmosphere.

As the interceptors split into their various squadrons, they headed toward their designated targets. As they reached their targets, they launched their missiles and then headed back to their battlecarriers.

Within minutes the skies of Lamothia were lit up with over 14,000 missiles, all headed toward the surface of the planet. Once they reached the surface, massive explosions could be seen all the way up into space, where the Human fleet watched. The skies filled with debris and smoke from the explosions. Before long, the surface was no longer visible at all.

Captain Elliott watched as his last interceptor entered the launch bay. None had been lost. It was time to reload their weapons and to prepare for their next battle. That one would not be as easy. The Druins had defenses against the interceptors.

They would be more prepared for an attack than the Lamothians above Lamothia had been.

Barnes watched as Lamothia was destroyed. The attack interceptors were very effective. So many missiles hitting the surface of the planet was too much for any planet to survive.

Now time to relay the message High Princess Layla Starguard had given them. As the message played, Princess Layla could be seen in front of a purple cloth, with the large starburst on a background of stars—the symbol of the Human Empire. "Lamothians, billions of Humans have died because of you and your barbaric feasts. Your race does not deserve to live in freedom or in peace. We have destroyed another one of your worlds today in retaliation for holding another feast, where you planned to consume more Humans.

"It has become obvious to the Human Empire and to Earth Humans that you have no plans to end these feasts. You leave us with no choice. If even one Human is used in your feasts, we will return and destroy *all* your worlds. We have already destroyed two, and only four remain.

"Can you afford to lose more? I think not. Not even one more Human may be harmed, or the Human Empire and the Earth Humans will not rest until your species has been destroyed." As the image of High Princess Layla faded, only the insignia of the Human Empire remained—a large starburst on a background of stars as the Imperial March played. Then it faded too.

As the message came to an end, Rear Admiral Barnes had one thing left to do. One more space station to destroy, and she had just enough time to do it.

As the fleet jumped to the other side of Lamothia, they prepared to fire on the space station. Once they were in range, they launched a complete bombardment of the space station. The space station also launched all its weapons continuously. Barnes saw a few more of her green icons disappear from her tactical display.

As the space station exploded into a massive fireball, it was time for her fleet to move on to their next target. Now no witnesses could confirm which way the Humans were headed. Hopefully they wouldn't be tracked or discovered until they had arrived at their next target.

Barnes communicated with her fleet and instructed the ships too damaged to fight in the next battle to return to the supply fleet. "Captain Borrel, let's get out of here," Barnes said, as her fleet transitioned into hyperspace.

Soon nothing was left in the star system that held Lamothia, at least nothing living. Now it was a place of destruction, death, and millions of pieces of space debris.

As the fleet all made their jumps into hyperspace, Barnes turned to Captain Borrel and asked, "I hate to think of all the people who sacrificed their lives, who will be sorely missed." Barnes paused for a moment, her eyes closed. "How many ships did we lose back there?"

Captain Borrel said, "Between the Lamothian fleet's firepower, the space stations', and the shipyard's, we lost fifty-six battlecruisers and six dreadnoughts. We sent five battlecruisers and two dreadnoughts back to the supply fleet for repairs. No losses were incurred by the attack interceptors."

"That leaves us with 772 battlecruisers and 170 dreadnoughts, correct?" asked Barnes.

"That is correct, Admiral. We still have all 23 battlecarriers and 3,680 attack interceptors as well," replied Borrel.

"We will not be so lucky in this next attack, I fear. We will honor those who have fallen, when our mission is complete," said Barnes.

It was time to get some rest and to go over the plan for the next attack. In this next attack, they would meet with a much larger enemy fleet. Word of their attack would have reached the Druins by now. She was certain they would be on high alert. No

more surprise attacks. She would have a much more challenging
and costly battle on her hands next time.

-

Lamothian Admiral Zahn and his fleet exited hyperspace in the
star system that contained Lamothia. They were immediately
stricken with grief as they realized they were, indeed, too late. All
that was left was debris from what was once a small fleet of
battleships, two space stations, and the shipyard. Even worse was
their homeworld of Lamothia. The atmosphere was dark and
covered in a cloud of gray smoke, with no way to see the surface
of the planet.

Admiral Zahn had his communications officer try to contact
anyone still alive on the surface of the planet. After trying
unsuccessfully for over an hour, they decided there were no
survivors. It would be years before the atmosphere would be clear
enough to get down to the surface and to rebuild whatever was
left.

Admiral Zahn and his crew then received the message Rear
Admiral Barnes and her crew had left from High Princess Layla
Starguard. They all watched the message in the Command Center
in silence. Once the message was finished, everyone in the
Command Center turned to Admiral Zahn for his reaction and
direction. He looked around the room at his crew.

He then activated the communications system that allowed
him to talk to all the ships in his fleet. He addressed them all by
saying, "What we have witnessed today is a travesty. These
Humans blame us for their ravenous need for destroying anything
they don't understand or agree with. They are not worthy of the
air they breathe. We will hunt them down, and we will make them
pay for the tragedy they inflicted on our beautiful homeworld of
Lamothia.

"Many of us grew up here, and our families lived here in peace
and prosperity, until these simple-minded Humans decided to
extract their baseless cause for revenge. We will have the final say.

We will have the final victory. We will call on our allies of the Confederation to come together and to hunt down these feral beasts that call themselves Human. They will regret this day. I will not rest until they are extinguished from the Confederation!"

With that, the crew cheered in unison. Then they all set about their work; for now, their purpose had shifted. Now they needed to find this enemy and to crush them. Crush them before they had the chance to destroy anything else or any other planet in the Confederation.

Soon after they returned to their jobs, alarms sounded. "What do we have?" asked Admiral Zahn.

First Officer Vormalt answered, "A fleet is dropping from hyperspace, Admiral. It seems to be a Morag fleet."

"It must be Admiral Voxx," replied Admiral Zahn. "We have a lot we need to discuss."

Morag Admiral Voxx and his fleet dropped from hyperspace in the Lamothian star system that contained Lamothia. The Lamothian fleet, led by Admiral Zahn, had already arrived.

Soon after they emerged from hyperspace, they received the message left by the Human fleet from their Princess. As Voxx and his crew watched the message, he shook his head. *We've told the Lamothians to stop using the Humans in their feasts. They have brought this upon themselves.*

Bale replied, *Were the Lamothians going to use Humans in their feasts this time, or was that set up as part of the trap?*

Admiral Voxx looked at Bale, with an angry expression. *They were already going to do it. We just advertised it for them, to bring the Humans in for our trap.*

So now what? asked Bale. *Where will the Humans attack next?*

We have part of our fleet near Xanther, in case they show up there. So we need to consider other places they may attack.

Admiral, we are receiving a message from Lamothian Admiral Zahn, said Bale.

Let's see what he has to say, replied Voxx.

"How will we find this Human fleet that destroyed our homeworld?" asked Admiral Zahn.

"We left part of our fleet near Xanther, in case they attack there. Your fleet should head to your other inhabited system, the system that contains two of your inhabited planets. That will allow us to protect what planets you have left," said Voxx.

"Where will your fleet go?" asked Admiral Zahn.

Voxx grew concerned that this Human fleet would rendezvous with the one currently terrorizing the Morag shipyards. They could do a lot more damage with more ships joined into a combined fleet. Or, if this fleet attacked separately, the Confederation could lose even more shipyards.

"We will contact our allies and see if anyone has seen this fleet. I think we would have heard already if they had, but I will check to be sure. Then we will head toward the Druin area of the Confederation and then on to our Morag area. We are concerned the Humans will come for one of our planets next," replied Voxx.

"That sounds like a valid concern. All of our allies must be vigilant. Anyone of our worlds could be next," said Admiral Zahn.

"We will leave our other fleet close to Xanther for now. If we determine the location of the Humans, we may have to move our fleet. I will contact the Zynth, Druins, and Morphene to make them aware of this invasive species that is attacking the Confederation," said Voxx.

"We will head back to our system to protect the rest of our planets. Let me know if you hear of the whereabouts of this Human fleet," commented Admiral Zahn.

"Yes, I will," replied Voxx.

Shortly after that, Voxx watched as Lamothian Admiral Zahn and his fleet made their transition into hyperspace. Voxx took a few minutes to survey the damage the Earth Humans had caused here. They needed to be dealt with and quickly. He sent out messages to his allies to inform them of the attack on Lamothia and to be on high alert for the Human fleet.

As for him and his fleet, they would head back toward home. He would stop in the Druin area of the Confederation to check with Admiral Falorr. This would be much easier if they weren't wearing the nullifiers. He could get the information he needed much quicker. He held Lormallian Councilor Ardon Reull responsible for that. His days were numbered as well.

First things first: find the Humans.

Lormallian Councilor Ardon Reull was meeting with Admiral Garr. "What do we know of the Human fleet activities?" asked Reull.

"We have received a message from High Princess Layla Starguard of the Empire. Have you seen it?" asked Garr.

"I have not," responded Reull. As he watched the message from the Princess, a smile slowly spread across his face. "The Lamothians knew the consequences of using Humans in their feasts. It serves the Lamothians right for continuing to do so. I am impressed that the Humans went after their homeworld of Lamothia, instead of Xanther, where the feasts are being held," said Reull.

"What about the other Human fleet? Have we intercepted any more messages about how many more shipyards they have destroyed?" asked Garr.

"No. Unless the Humans send a message about it, we won't hear anything from the Morag. They would communicate with each other telepathically, and we would never know about it," replied Reull.

"Do you think the Humans will destroy a Morag world as well? Or do you believe they will only target the shipyards?" asked Garr.

"I do not think they will target a Morag planet. I am assuming they will stick to destroying the shipyards. They are making sure that it will take months for the Morag to rebuild their fleets. The longer it takes, the longer the Human Empire and the Solar

System have to build up their fleets and defenses. The same as us. We would highly benefit from that attack strategy as well."

"Let's hope they have great success then. The second fleet that attacked Lamothia, do we think they have another target?" asked Garr.

"Honestly it could be any of the races of the Confederation. I trust, per our agreement, that they will not attack those of us who have separated ourselves from this ongoing war. It would likely be another Lamothian target—or a Druin. The Druins have caused much harm to the Humans over the years. They also attacked the Solar System. Or the Humans could be meeting up with their other fleet to do more damage to the Morag," replied Reull.

As Admiral Garr received a message from his communications officer, he looked a little amused. "We have received a message, informing us of the destruction of Lamothia and asking us if we know the location of the Human fleet," Garr said in amusement. "Why would we tell them, if we did?"

Reull contemplated this new development for a moment. "If we don't respond, that may raise suspicions. We could respond with our condolences on the loss of lives and say we do not know the location of the Human fleet. This is all true. We do not know where they currently are."

"Yes, that sounds like the most diplomatic thing to do. Guess that's why you are a councilor, and I am an admiral," he said, with a smile.

They worked on the exact wording for a few moments and then sent the message back to the rest of the Confederation.

"What now?" asked Garr.

"We wait patiently and listen," replied Reull.

"We likely won't hear of anything going on from the Morag, only from wherever the second Human fleet attacks next," said Garr.

"Very true. Keep me posted of any further developments," responded Reull.

Captain Colin Avery was in charge of the supply fleet left behind by Collison and Barnes on the periphery of the Lormallian-controlled star system. Avery was on edge a little, due to some messages they had intercepted. Avery knew that Rear Admiral Barnes and her crew had been successful in destroying Lamothia. Avery had intercepted messages between the Morag and their allies in regard to that.

What had him on edge were the messages the Morag had sent to the other races of the Confederation, who were no longer in line with the Morag. Avery had intercepted a message informing the Lormallians of Lamothia's destruction and asked them if they were aware of the Human fleet's location. Avery wasn't 100 percent confident that the Lormallians wouldn't give up his location. What would Avery do if they did? Surely the Lormallians wouldn't want the Morag coming here to their star system? Avery hadn't yet received any more updates from Collison on his mission.

Avery estimated that the damaged ships from Collison's first attack would arrive in the next day. He would get more information about Collison's success from them. Avery knew there was a possibility that they would be pursued. The plan was that, if they were being followed, they would send a message ahead to let him know to be ready. He wanted to be prepared either way. He would move the fleet to Condition Two in about eighteen hours. Better to be safe than sorry. He expected the mobile shipyards to be very busy for the foreseeable future. This was a long-term mission.

As he looked at the holographic display to figure out where else the supply fleet could go, if the Lormallians had reported their current location, Avery's communications officer, Lieutenant Dan, intercepted a message.

"Captain Avery, I have intercepted a message from the Lormallians to the Morag," Dan said.

"Did they report our location?" Avery asked hesitantly. He felt the sweat beading on his brow.

"No, Captain, they did not. They said that they do not know the location of the Human fleet that attacked Lamothia," replied Dan.

Avery smiled. "It's all in the precise wording, isn't it? I hope the Morag do not read between the lines on their reply."

"At least now we can take one worry off our plate. The Lormallians do appear to be on our side," replied Dan.

"Speaking of plates, I'm hungry!" Avery said, with a laugh.

Chapter Eighteen

As High Princess Layla and her husband, Vice Fleet Admiral Derrick Masters, entered the Royal Court, a hush fell over the crowd gathered there. The Imperial March played as they slowly made their way to the front of the room. Princess Krista, Prince Andrew, and his wife, Kala, were already there, waiting. As they reached the front of the room, Layla turned to address those gathered here.

"Thank you all for coming on this beautiful day. Every day that goes by, we grow more and more powerful. We grow more and more ready to defend our Empire and those of our allies." At this point, she looked over at those assembled with the Visth, members of their new United Worlds Alliance. "We hope to make the Empire's and our allies' worlds into places where peace and prosperity are our way of life. Not war and tragedy. We aim to be meccas of trade and commerce, where all races can feel safe and protected."

Layla looked around the room and tried to look in the eyes of as many as she could while she talked. Her father had taught her how to carry herself and how to project herself when she spoke. He taught her how to make people feel like you're talking to them, even though hundreds of people were in the room. She smiled and continued.

"Tomorrow marks the beginning of a new era. This will be our first meeting of the House of Worlds since we defeated the Morag and the Confederation!" With that, cheers erupted all across the room. "The Morag now know what it is like to retreat in defeat. Rest assured though that they will return. They will rebuild their fleets and return to try to destroy the freedom we have found. To destroy the friends and allies we have made. We will be ready for them. We are united. We will succeed in defeating the Morag and their allies once and for all!"

She turned and smiled at Derrick. "We have a lot of business to attend to and an Empire to run. Make no mistake. That will not be an easy task. It will be hard and, at times, seem impossible. We will persevere. We will prevail. We will work together to make tomorrow a better day for our children and for their children. Thank you all for coming here tonight. Please stay as long as you like. We are all friends and allies here."

With that, Layla accepted a glass that Derrick handed her. As she raised it, she said, "To the Empire, our allies, and to our freedom from the Confederation!" All around the room, the *clink* of glasses were heard, as everyone toasted their future.

Layla smiled at Derrick.

Derrick said, "Wow. You are amazing. I was hanging on to your every word. How do you do that?"

"I come by it naturally," she said, with a laugh. She looked around the room and steadied herself. Layla knew it would be a long night. Most of the people here were hoping to get a chance to speak with her. She would do the best she could, but she knew there was no way for her to talk to everyone. Thankfully her family was here to help.

She sighed. She might as well get things started.

-

Admiral Cleemorl was hours away from dropping out of hyperspace in the star system where the supply fleet was supposed to be. He wanted to be prepared, in case already trouble was amiss. No telling what he might find there. Hopefully he would find ships being repaired in the mobile shipyards. Ideally they could tell him of Collison's great successes he had had, destroying Morag shipyards. And he hoped to hear of the successful destruction of a Lamothian planet and a Druin planet.

As long as everything went according to plan, there would be lots to celebrate. He was also well aware that things rarely went according to plan. No way the Druins or the Morag would allow the Human fleets to escape their star systems without following them.

Cleemorl just prayed he made it in time to be of some help. He also hoped it wouldn't be an enormous fleet that pursued Collison's fleets either. Cleemorl had brought a sizable fleet but not big enough to take on thousands of enemy ships. He took a deep breath as he looked at the tactical display in front of him, glad so many other green icons showed up on the display. He hoped it would be enough.

Admiral Collison was ten minutes from dropping out of hyperspace in the yellow dwarf system that contained their next target. He already had the fleet at Condition Two. They would momentarily be moving to Condition One.

Who knew what lay in wait for them in this star system? Would the Morag guess his plans? Collison did know his fleet needed to regroup and to make some repairs. He hoped that could wait until after they'd hit their three star systems as planned. They had finished one and had two to go.

He felt the tenseness in his shoulders and the mounting pressure of trying to do these hit-and-run attacks without accidentally coming face-to-face with the larger Morag fleets. How many shipyards could Collison destroy before his luck ran out? Was there a way to throw the Morag off course?

A thread of a plan started to weave itself in his mind. He would need to give more thought to this, and, right now, he didn't have the time. They'd hit these shipyards, and then he'd toy with his idea some more. Until then, it was time to move the fleet to Condition One.

A few short minutes later, Collison and his fleet emerged from hyperspace in the yellow dwarf star system. One inhabited planet, Morag Thirty-Seven, and its three terraformed moons were in this system, which contained three shipyards. He planned to split the fleet in three and simultaneously take out all targets. The alarm sounded, and Captain Billingsly said, "Admiral, the scans show seventy-three ships in orbit around the planet. All of them are battlecruisers."

"We will deal with them as we deal with the shipyards. The fleet will use the accelerator cannons to destroy our targets. We will save the interceptors for when we have more enemy ships to destroy than we do here," said Collison.

"I will inform the captains of the plan," replied Billingsly.

"How long until we are in range, Captain?" asked Collison.

"Eight minutes, Admiral," replied Billingsly.

As the fleet split into three groups, they closed in on their targets. The Morag fleet stuck together around the shipyard closest to Collison's group. Rear Admiral Carrie lead one of the other groups of ships to the shipyard on the far side of the planet. Captain Drake led the third group.

"One minute to engagement range, Admiral," said Billingsly.

"All ships lock on to their targets and fire on my command," said Collison.

Just before Collison gave his command to fire, the shipyard opened fire on his fleet. The inbound fusion energy beam fire lit up the space above the planet. Shortly thereafter, the antimatter missiles were launched toward his fleet as well. He'd be lying if he said all that enemy fire didn't intimidate him at all. He quickly gave his command. "Fire!"

As the fusion energy beams hit his fleet, they tore through some of the energy screens. They riddled a few ships with gaping holes in the hulls before the antimatter missiles hit and put an end to the hopes and dreams of those on board.

As more and more bright lights engulfed the fleet with their destructive power, Collison's accelerator cannon fire reached the enemy fleet, where explosions ravaged the enemy ships on the front line. More and more ships succumbed to the powerful punch of the accelerator cannons.

Between the enemy fleet and the firepower from the shipyard, Collison's fleet took on more losses than he anticipated. He knew they needed to get in and out of this system as quickly as possible, since the larger Morag fleet had to be closer by than last time.

They had only moved over two star systems from their previous attack.

He started to feel a little uneasy, as he watched more green icons disappear from the tactical display in front of him. He felt the ship shudder beneath him, as his flagship was hit with fusion energy beam fire. "How's our energy screen holding up?" he asked.

"It's at 90 percent, Admiral," replied Billingsly.

"Let's hope it stays that way," he answered. The enemy fire was dying down now that most of the Morag ships had been blown apart. Thus the shipyard sustained heavy firepower from the accelerator cannons. Their energy screen was quickly overloaded, and then the next rounds of accelerator cannon fire arrived and decimated the shipyard.

Now to finish the fleet. Only a few ships remained. As the rest of Collison's fleet turned their attention to those ships, they made short work of destroying them.

The Morag fleet stationed in the yellow dwarf system that contained Morag Thirty-Seven and three terraformed moons was on high alert. Captain Gambrel was in charge of the fleet already patrolling the star system. He had received the warning that a Human fleet had been in a star system nearby and had destroyed the shipyards there. Admiral Ramgen was currently on his way here to add his numbers to Gambrel's fleet, was forty-five minutes away. Gambrel was confident Ramgen would arrive in time.

As Gambrel surveyed his fleet and reviewed their positions, alarms sounded. A cold shiver ran up his spine. "Ramgen will not make it in time," he muttered crossly. Gambrel quickly sent a message to Ramgen, informing him that the Human fleet was currently dropping from hyperspace in his system.

Ramgen quickly responded, *I will be there as soon as possible. Hold them off as long as you can.*

Easy for him to say. He wasn't facing over six hundred enemy ships with only 73 battlecruisers. He strategized quickly. He knew he would need the firepower from the shipyards to supplement the fleet. He had his fleet move into formation near the closest shipyard to the enemy fleet. The Humans would have to destroy his fleet before they could reach the shipyard. He knew he needed to keep his fleet together. He needed the numbers. He quickly sent messages to the other ships to fire all weapons continuously, once the Human fleet was in range. That was only six minutes away.

He knew the battle would be over quickly. The Humans had a new weapon that they could not defend against. He had heard a lot about it and had hoped not to face it. It looked like this would be how he died. At least he could destroy more of this Human fleet. Eventually Ramgen would catch up to these parasites. Then the tide would turn, and they'd be outnumbered. Even with their new weapon, they wouldn't stand a chance. Gambrel relished the thought.

As the enemy fleet came in range, it split into three groups. He would not split his fleet. He would destroy this smaller group of ships. The numbers were now a little less threatening. Only 200 to 73, his fleet fired. They fired the first rounds before the Humans did.

As his fusion energy beams reached the enemy fleet, they searched out any weaknesses in the energy shields. A few were found, and, shortly afterward, the ships were disintegrated, as the antimatter missiles hit their mark. He smiled as destruction spread across the Human fleet.

His smile quickly faded as the Humans' weapons fire struck many of the ships surrounding his. It was like the energy shields weren't even there. They were useless against this weapon. The second round almost immediately hit those vulnerable ships and splintered the ships into millions of pieces, which in turn hit the energy shields of the ships closest to them. As their shields lit up like they were bombarded by tiny missiles, another round of the Humans' weapons hit more of his fleet.

He shifted his focus back to his display. Not many ships remained. For a brief moment, he considered getting out of here, to live to fight another day. As he started to give the command, his ship was hit by enemy fire. Before the navigation officer could enter the coordinates to jump, the second round blew apart Gambrel's ship.

Rear Admiral Carrie closed in on her target. The shipyard quickly opened fire on her fleet, as soon as they were in range. Space was alight with the energy the firepower produced. It definitely wasn't a good feeling seeing all that firepower headed toward her. She quickly had the fleet fire their accelerator cannons on the shipyard. It didn't take long before their energy shield was destroyed, and the accelerator cannon fire slammed into the shipyard, destroying it, as if it were made out of sticks. The debris littered the space above the planet and quickly fell toward the atmosphere of the planet.

Maybe it would cause the planet a little bit of damage, Carrie thought to herself. She was beginning to think they should take out a planet or two, while they were here. While they had a limited amount of time before the Morag fleets caught up with them, they needed to do as much damage as possible before then. She would mention her thoughts to Collison to see how he felt about it.

Captain Drake approached his designated shipyard that he would soon blast into oblivion. It felt good to have the superior firepower for once. Of course, being on top in weapons technology was likely a short-lived thing. The Morag did seem to be an intelligent race. Drake was sure, somewhere in their inhabited systems, some scientists were busy working on whatever weapons technology was bigger and better than what the Humans had now.

At that thought, Drake realized that this war with the Confederation would likely go on forever—with the side having the superior weapons technology being on top, until the other side developed a much superior weapon. The only other thing that would stop this war was a treaty.

From everything he had heard, the Morag thought of the Humans as an inferior species. So a treaty probably wasn't an option. Even if they could destroy all their shipyards, the Morag would rebuild them and then come after us again. It would lead to a vicious cycle of death and destruction for the Morag and the Humans.

Drake's part of the fleet soon reached the engagement range of the shipyard. The shipyard launched a full attack of all their weapons. He swiftly ordered the fleet to launch their accelerator cannons. As the fusion energy beam fire arrived at the front of his formation, it quickly searched for a weak spot in any ships' energy screens to exploit any weaknesses found. A few were found, and energy screens were destroyed, as the antimatter missiles arrived a short moment later, creating a massive explosion that could be felt by nearby ships.

The Humans' accelerator cannon fire reached the shipyard, quickly smashing through the energy shield and then slamming into the shipyard itself, causing catastrophic damage. Soon nothing was left that one could tell used to be a shipyard.

With his target destroyed, Drake headed back to rendezvous with Admiral Collison and Rear Admiral Carrie. Drake had sustained minimal damage to his task force and had accomplished his mission. Hopefully he could prove himself to Collison and Carrie. Drake hoped to one day be a rear admiral himself.

Morag Admiral Ramgen was right. He had predicted where the Humans would attack next. Yet he knew he couldn't get there in time. He now needed to figure out where the Humans would go next. And that was where he would head now. No need to go to the yellow dwarf system of Morag Thirty-Seven. He knew what would happen there. The Humans would destroy the fleet and the shipyards. That would be three more shipyards that the Morag had lost.

No, Ramgen would head to the next system he thought the Humans would target.

He examined his holographic display of the nearby systems. He knew the ones immediately adjacent to the one the Humans currently attacked would not be next. The Humans were predictable in that detail. They never hit two systems side by side. If they continued on their current trajectory, they would attack either the system where Morag 32 was or the system containing Morag 26.

They were two and three systems over from the Humans' current location. Both systems had similar targets. Each had two shipyards. He couldn't afford to be wrong this time. His only option was to divide his fleet. Each of the two systems had fleets patrolling them. Not large ones but larger than the ones the Humans were currently up against.

Ramgen sent the commands and the coordinates to his fleet. He would take 790 ships to Morag 26 that was three star systems away from the Human fleet's current location. He predicted the Humans would try to change their pattern of moving two systems over.

With the fleet currently patrolling that system, it would put his fleet up to 876 warships. He also had a few of the attack craft designed to combat the Humans' small attack craft. He would have the numbers. According to Gambrel's report, the Humans were down to just over 600 ships. Hopefully Gambrel succeeded in destroying some more, giving the Morag an even better numbers advantage.

Ramgen smiled to himself. The Human fleet's next jump would be their last.

–

Morag Admiral Voxx analyzed the newest information sent to him from Admiral Ramgen. The Humans were attacking yet another system with a small fleet patrolling it. This led Voxx to be even more confident that the Humans must have stealth ships patrolling the Morag area of the Confederation. How else could the Humans have known which systems to avoid and which ones to target?

This was unsettling. The Morag hadn't detected any enemy ships. Who knows how many there were or where they currently were? They could be watching the star system where Morag Prime was located. He immediately sent Admiral Marcello a message to scan the system for any anomalies. Voxx would need to investigate anything suspicious. Once these two Human fleets were annihilated, they would hunt down these stealth ships and destroy them. The first thing though was to find the Human fleet that destroyed Lamothia.

Ramgen seemed confident he would ambush the Humans in the Morag area of the Confederation, as they made their next attack. Ramgen's plan was solid. Voxx agreed with his strategy of dividing the fleet. They had considered getting more ships from Marcello, but they didn't want to weaken their defenses around Morag Prime. Plus the reinforcements wouldn't reach them in time.

Voxx was closing in on the Druin area of the Confederation. He was confident that the Human fleet he searched for would head there next. The only question was which system they would target. As he looked at his holographic display, he reviewed the information he knew. The Druins had been busy putting up defensive grids around their main inhabited planets. Only a few were not complete. He assumed the Humans would know this.

He looked over the Druin fleet deployments. One system stuck out to him. It was a red giant system nearest the Morag area of the Confederation. They did not have a defensive grid in place and had the smallest fleet patrolling it. That's where he would head. That's where he was confident the Human fleet was headed.

Voxx would destroy them; they had no idea his fleet was anywhere near there. That is where the Humans would meet their end.

–

Collison was satisfied with the efficient way they had quickly destroyed the three shipyards in the system. He had sustained the most losses when compared to Rear Admiral Carrie and Captain Drake. Collison had also been the one facing an enemy fleet. Carrie had mentioned to him her thoughts about destroying a Morag inhabited planet. He had told her that, for now, they would stick to their original battle plan: eliminate as many shipyards as possible.

He reviewed the ships they had lost in this star system. It was more than he had expected to. They had lost 46 battlecruisers and 3 dreadnoughts. Another 4 battlecruisers and 2 dreadnoughts had been damaged and had already started their trip back to the supply chain. Collison needed to utilize the attack interceptors more in their upcoming battles. He still had over 5,000 of them.

He knew he needed a diversion of some kind. He was confident the larger Morag fleet was closing in on him. He felt it. The plan that had started to weave itself in his mind before this latest battle had begun to take a better form.

He needed the stealth ships to distract the enemy fleets. To move the Morag away from his location. Collison needed a little bit of time and a safe haven for his fleet while he put his plan in motion.

He searched the tactical display for a star system with no inhabited planets, where his fleet could rest and repair. He settled on a yellow giant system farther away from his next target than where they currently were. He quickly sent the coordinates to his fleet. Soon after that, the fleet jumped into hyperspace.

–

Rear Admiral Carrie had discussed her thoughts about destroying a Morag inhabited planet, but Collison felt they should stick to the original battle plan for now. He had come up with an idea that he thought would detour the nearby Morag fleet, getting them to leave the area, thinking they were following the Human fleet, when in reality they weren't.

It sounded like a great plan, as long as the Morag fell for it. She knew Collison still had some details to stitch together, and it would take time to move all of the pieces into play. For now, they would jump to a yellow giant system that had no inhabited planets. They would make some repairs on their ships and get some much-needed rest.

Morag Admiral Marcello was less than pleased that the Humans had destroyed so many shipyards. This would slow down their shipbuilding; plus the Humans had destroyed numerous ships as well. The Morag still had his large fleet protecting Morag Prime, while Admiral Ramgen had over 1,500 ships, and Admiral Voxx had over 5,000 ships. The Morag still had over 10,000 ships left in their other various fleets. The remaining shipyards were still building new ships, so their warship numbers still grew.

Marcello knew that the Humans were most likely trying to delay their ship-making abilities to have time to increase their own numbers.

So far, the Humans had not targeted a Morag planet, which was surprising. They had destroyed Lamothia with another fleet. No one knew where that fleet currently was. Voxx thought he knew where they were headed and was headed there himself with his fleet. The Humans had a head start though, and, even if Voxx were correct, he would still be trailing them. They would have a larger Druin fleet to destroy before they could destroy the planet there, but the Humans might still succeed in doing that before Voxx could arrive.

From there, the planet-destroying Human fleet would be close to the Morag part of the Confederation. Would they head here next? Would they rendezvous with their other shipyard-destroying fleet and destroy more shipyards? The Morag needed to get rid of these pests and quickly. The only question was how and where. Where would they go next? How could the Morag beat them there?

Chapter Nineteen

Scout ship 368 was currently stationed in the Lamothian star system that contained Xanther. Captain Hadley hoped to follow a transport vehicle full of Humans to Xanther. She wanted to follow them back to where they came from to find the source, where the Lamothians were getting all these Humans.

Currently two transport vessels unloaded Humans onto the space station. Apparently the Lamothians had no intention of heeding High Princess Layla's warning about not using any Humans in their feasts. From what Hadley saw, the feast was still set to occur, and they still brought in more Humans.

She needed to get word to Rear Admiral Barnes. Maybe after she destroyed the Druin planet, she should head back here and destroy another Lamothian one. That's what the message from Princess Layla had said they would do, if this race used any more Humans in their feasts.

One of the transport vessels had finished unloading and slowly moved away from the space station. "Let's follow that one when it leaves. We need to find out where it came from," she said to Lieutenant Maddox.

"Yes, Captain," replied Maddox.

As the transport vessel entered hyperspace, scout ship 368 followed.

Shortly after they followed the transport vessel into hyperspace, Captain Hadley received an encrypted message from Admiral Collison. It was a new plan to fool the Morag. The problem was it involved the stealth scout ships, and she was already hot on the trail of her mystery that she was trying to solve. Hadley quickly sent an encrypted message back to Collison, informing him of her mission.

She decided to keep on her current course. The other scout ships could pull off Collison's plan without her. Hopefully she would receive a confirmation from Collison that she could continue on her mission. Until she was commanded otherwise, she would keep following this transport vessel.

Hadley also sent an encrypted message to Rear Admiral Barnes, informing her of what they had observed above Xanther.

-

Rear Admiral Barnes would shortly drop out of hyperspace near Druin Nine. She had just received a message from Captain Hadley about what was going on at Xanther. *How could they still be going through with the feasts?* she thought to herself. She would figure out what to do with the Lamothians after she destroyed Druin Nine.

The fleet was already at Condition Two. In the next five minutes, they'd move to Condition One. She evaluated her battle plan again and again. She wanted everything to go smoothly. Barnes knew they would face a larger enemy fleet this time. Plus the Druins had the AI-controlled attack drones to combat the Human's attack interceptors.

Barnes's fleet would have a battle on their hands this time. She hoped to distract the Druin fleet, while her battlecarriers jumped to the other side of the planet and launched their attack on the planet. This was the same strategy Vice Fleet Admiral Derrick Masters had used on the Druins. Therefore, good chance the Druins would expect this strategy. If that didn't work, she did have a plan B.

The time had come to move the fleet to Condition One. They would drop from hyperspace in five minutes. They had planned to drop out as close as they could to Druin Nine to hopefully catch the Druin fleet off guard. She ordered all her ships to immediately target the enemy fleet and to launch their accelerator cannons, once locked on a target.

Barnes then informed the battlecarriers to drop out of hyperspace on the far side of the planet and immediately launch the attack interceptors. Part of the fleet would be with the battlecarriers to protect them from any enemy fire. The plan was solid, and everyone knew exactly what to do. They also were aware of the contingency plans.

Barnes wanted to be in and out of this star system as quickly as possible; that way, there was no time for reinforcements to arrive. When they left this star system, they would jump out in the direction of the Morag area of the Confederation. Hopefully that would prevent whatever was left of the Druin fleet from following them. Rumor was that the Morag didn't like any other race in their area of the Confederation, even their allies.

From there, she had two options. They could head to the Morag area of the Confederation, attack shipyards, or head back to Xanther and destroy another Lamothian planet. First things first though. Time to destroy a Druin fleet and a Druin planet.

Part of Barnes's fleet dropped from hyperspace near Druin Nine. They immediately locked their weapons on targets and launched their accelerator cannons. Alarms sounded in response to the enemy fleet's presence. Over two hundred Druins battleships showed up on Barnes's tactical display. The enemy ships immediately raised their energy shields and launched their attack.

Rear Admiral Barnes watched as the first round of accelerator cannon fire reached the Druin battleships. Their energy shields had been activated before the projectiles hit the front line. As the accelerator cannon fire reached the Druins, it slammed into the energy shields with twenty-three megatons of raw energy.

As the second round hit the line of Druin battleships, large explosions detonated across the line. Ship after ship was blown apart, as round after round of accelerator cannon fire decimated the enemy fleet.

Barnes felt her flagship, *Phobos*, shudder, as a fusion energy beam cut through and destroyed a nearby battlecruiser. It exploded and sent debris crashing into nearby ships. Their energy shields lit up like fireflies at dusk. So far, her flagship had avoided any direct hits of the Druin's fusion energy beams or antimatter missiles fire. All around her, her fleet was bombarded by the enemy. They were inflicting devastating destruction on the Druin fleet as well.

She might be losing ships, but the Druins were losing far more. As she watched her fleet target and destroy one enemy ship after another, she hoped the rest of her fleet and the battlecarriers were faring as well as they were.

Captain Elliott on board the battlecarrier *Daneb* had his interceptor crews ready to launch, as soon as they reached their designated coordinates on the far side of Druin Nine. He had a group of battlecruisers and a few dreadnoughts that would defend his ship, as well as the other twenty-two battlecarriers. Thankfully these ships weren't defenseless. They were armed and had energy shields. Their primary objective was to house and to launch the attack interceptor squadrons. His battlecarrier was home to one of the best squadrons that reported to Rear Admiral Barnes, the Scorpion Squadron.

As the battlecarriers reached their designated coordinates, the attack interceptors commenced their launches. Captain Elliott watched as Lieutenant Burr, the pilot and leader of the Scorpion Squadron, launched from Bay One.

Alarms sounded as the Druin fleet responded to their presence. The Druins had 225 battlecruisers in the star system. Also a group of about 195 AI-controlled drones launched from some of their drone carriers.

Elliott had hoped they wouldn't have to go up against these drones, but it looked like they would. They more than outnumbered the enemy's drones, with 3,680 Human attack interceptors. The scans showed 65 Druin battlecruisers had jumped to the far side of Druin Nine to thwart the attack meant to destroy the planet. With them came the 195 drones.

Elliott watched as the drones rapidly maneuvered to a defensive position between them and the planet. Behind them in a wedge formation was the Druin fleet. The Human battlecruisers and dreadnoughts quickly moved to an attack position between the battlecarriers and the Druins.

As the attack interceptors darted on their erratic paths to avoid any enemy fire, weapons fire began to light up both sides of the fleets. As the weapons fire arrived at the Human fleet, energy shields lit up and slowly faded, as the Druins bombarded the front line. Elliott watched as many green icons disappeared from the tactical display in front of him.

The Humans' accelerator cannon fire hit the Druin fleet and decimated it. As the fleets were destroying each other, the attack interceptors went above the fight and headed to the planet. The enemy drones quickly went after them.

To Captain Elliott, it was like watching a great science-fiction movie on TV. The fleet was between him and the danger. So his battlecarrier was mostly safe. Their energy shields were up, and they watched the battle in front of them. He was on the edge of his seat, watching the fleets fire their weapons and then watching the ships get destroyed. He carefully eyed the tactical display, as red icons quickly disappeared.

As he shifted his focus to the attack interceptors, he saw the AI-controlled drones closing in on them. The drones were 40 percent larger than the interceptors. One benefit the drone had over the interceptors was that their energy shield protected the entire drone, while the interceptors only had a forward-facing energy shield. The drones were not as maneuverable as the interceptors were though. One single fusion explosion could take down the drone's shield.

The attack interceptors needed to get below the atmosphere and launch their four fusion-tipped missiles at the planet's surface. Then get back safely to the landing bays of the carriers.

As they raced toward the planet, the drones started firing at their targets. The interceptors flew erratic patterns trying to avoid being hit by the fire from the drones. As Elliott watched the action unfold, he couldn't help wishing he was in the thick of it with his interceptor pilots.

Lieutenant Burr of the Scorpion Squadron was headed toward Druin Nine, with an enemy AI-controlled attack drone closing in on him. He ordered his squadron to shift their focus to hunting down and destroying the enemy-controlled drones. If they could destroy them, more attack interceptors would survive to fire their missiles at the planet. Plus many of his friends were out here. If his squadron could destroy these drones, that would make their mission much easier.

He had twenty interceptors in his squadron. They all turned and started hunting the drones. Surprisingly the drones kept closing in on the interceptors headed to the planet. None of them turned to chase after his squadron. He guessed the AI had determined the threat to the planet was more imminent than his squadron's change of flight pattern.

One by one, they hunted down the drones. They each only had four fusion-tipped missiles. It took one to destroy the drone's energy shield and another to destroy the drone. Burr quickly figured out that his squadron of twenty could only destroy forty drones at most. He needed five more squadrons to help. Burr promptly sent a message to Captain Elliott, who quickly had five additional squadrons headed to eliminate the drones.

As Burr trailed behind a drone, he had to rely on all his hours of training to lock on to his target. Once the target-locked signal was heard, a fusion-tipped missile was immediately launched. The target drone was hit seconds later, and the energy shield flickered and was destroyed, as it was overloaded with energy. As the second missile hit momentarily after the first, a bright fireball fell toward the planet. "One down, one to go," said Burr.

As they followed the drone through its dips, curves, twists, and turns, he finally got another target locked on. He quickly sent the missiles toward the target and smiled as another bright flash lit up the space in front of his interceptor.

245

"Now let's return and reload, in case we need to head back out," Burr said to his navigation officer, Lieutenant Carr. As they returned to the battlecarrier *Daneb,* space was alight with bright flashes of light, like camera flashes going off all around him. He hoped most of those flashes marked the destruction of the drones but knew deep down that some of those were attack interceptors.

He swiftly checked in with his squadron, and then the reality of the situation hit him hard. They had lost four of his twenty attack interceptors in his squadron. It was a significant loss that would be felt for years to come. These were people who he had trained with and had spent a lot of time with. He knew their families. The silence filled the interceptor, as they made their way back to their battlecarrier.

Lieutenant Stone was trying her best to outmaneuver the drone that tailed her. She used every trick she knew and then tried them again. She sent out messages to interceptors nearby for help. Stone knew she had only minutes to outmaneuver this AI, or she'd get blasted into a million pieces. As she twisted and dove across the atmosphere of Druin Nine, an alarm sounded, notifying her that the drone had a target lock on her.

She felt a bead of sweat run down her forehead, as she pulled up quickly and dove down in a spiral motion to try to lose the target lock, before the missile impacted her interceptor. She saw bright flashes all around her as other drones and interceptors were destroyed. She didn't want to be one of them. She quickly changed direction again and again. She heard her heart beating loudly in her chest. She had succeeded in losing the target lock.

Now she had maneuvered herself in a position where she had a target lock on the drone. The missiles were quickly launched one after the other. Moments later, the enemy drone was blown into oblivion. Her crew cheered in excitement and relief. Then their celebration was shattered by the alarm of another target lock.

Another drone had them in its sights. The game started again, as the crew did what they could to outperform their enemy.

The game would not end in their favor this time, as the sound of an alarm indicating an incoming missile rang loudly. Shortly the hopes and dreams of the souls on board the attack interceptor were vaporized, along with their ship.

–

Captain Elliott kept his gaze on all the screens in front of him and all the data coming in. The attack interceptors had begun launching their payloads of fusion-tipped missiles toward the surface of Druin Nine. In total, over 13,000 missiles were now inbound for the surface of the planet.

The interceptors were returning to the battlecarriers, and then it would be time to get out of here, before any nearby enemy fleets had time to get to this star system to reinforce whatever was left of the Druin fleet that had been stationed here.

Elliott watched as the missiles hit the surface of the planet, causing huge plumes of smoke and debris that reached as high as the atmosphere. Soon he knew the entire planet's atmosphere would be full of smoke and debris from the explosions and the destruction caused by the fusion-tipped missiles. This planet would be uninhabitable for a long time.

As the last attack interceptor landed in Bay One, Elliott had the navigation officer put in the designated rendezvous coordinates. As they transitioned into hyperspace, he took one last look at the destruction they left in their wake.

Had they turned into heartless creatures like the Druins? *No*, he told himself. We haven't even scratched the surface of the harm, devastation, and destruction that the Druins had brought on the Humans. Maybe this would teach the Druins that the Humans were no longer a race that they could toy with or could use for their resources anymore.

We are strong, and we are united.

–

Rear Admiral Barnes had the rest of Third Fleet transition into hyperspace, as soon as she got confirmation that all attack interceptors were back on board their battlecarriers. She had picked out an uninhabited star system a safe distance away, in the direction of the Morag area of the Confederation, to have her fleet rendezvous. From there, they would decide what their next target would be—the Morag shipyards or the Lamothian planet of Xanther. She knew her fleet had some repairs to make. Barnes had already sent those too-damaged ships on their way for repairs in the mobile shipyards stationed on the outskirts of the Lormallian star system.

She currently reviewed the report on the number of battlecruisers and dreadnoughts they had lost. The battlecarriers had not sent her the numbers of how many attack interceptors had been lost. She feared that number would be high, with them having to fend off and to destroy the drones the Druins had deployed to counteract the interceptors.

They had lost 167 battlecruisers and 6 dreadnoughts. Barnes had sent 7 battlecruisers and 2 dreadnoughts to get repaired. They had been successful in destroying the Druin fleet as well as Druin Nine. She was confident no one was left to report the direction of their hyperspace jump to whatever fleet would soon arrive in response to the calls for help the Druins had sent out.

She needed to be cautious, just in case she was wrong. For now, she would review the battle while she got a bite to eat, then get a short rest, before they arrived at their rendezvous location.

-

Morag Admiral Voxx and his fleet dropped out of hyperspace in the star system that contained Druin Nine. What he saw was devastation. Debris surrounded what was left of Druin Nine. He could only assume that most of that debris was the Druin fleet. As his gaze shifted to the planet, he felt a growing sense of foreboding rise up inside him. He had the star system scanned for any trace of life. None was found.

As they quickly surveyed the damage, alarms sounded. *Who is dropping out of hyperspace?* asked Voxx.

The Druins, Admiral, replied Bale.

A little too late to help here, Voxx said in a cold tone.

Druin Admiral Falorr requests we help them hunt down this Human fleet, before they can destroy any more planets, said Bale.

Tell him we fear the Humans are now headed to the Morag area of the Confederation, and we plan to head that way after them. He should stay here in the Druin-controlled area of the Confederation, in case the Humans return. He needs to immediately notify us if the Humans are spotted, said Voxx.

He said he would make sure his fleet searches every area of the Druin-controlled star systems, Admiral. They will not rest until that fleet is destroyed, added Bale.

With the Lamothians and the Druins hunting this Human fleet, their days are numbered. Yet I do believe they will not find them. The Humans must have headed to our star systems to wreak havoc on one of our Morag planets as well. We will be the ones to find the Humans and to eradicate this invasion of this subordinate race. We will show them who the superior race is, and they will regret this day, the day they dared enter the Morag-controlled star systems of the Confederation, Voxx said, with a confident and determined expression on his face.

On scout ship 368, Captain Hadley had received Admiral Collison's permission to continue on her course of following the transport ship. The vessel had left Xanther over six hours ago and was still in hyperspace. She had no idea what to expect when they did finally drop from hyperspace. They needed to be ready for anything.

Hopefully, wherever it was, their stealth technology would keep them invisible to whoever was in the destination star system. Who knew what enemy lay ahead or what atrocities she might find? She was determined to figure out where these Humans were coming from though. If they could cut off the Lamothians' supply of Humans, that would be a step in the right direction.

Lamothian Admiral Zahn had returned to the star system where Xanther was located. He was surprised to see the preparations for the feast were still in full swing. Had they not received the Humans' message? Did they not take it seriously? Surely they couldn't afford to risk losing another planet. They were quickly running out of those. He would contact the leader of Xanther to find out what was going on.

Shortly after that, he had a commlink to the Lamothian councilor. "Did you receive the message from the Humans sent out shortly after they destroyed Lamothia?" Admiral Zahn asked.

"Yes, we did. We figured that we had already prepared to celebrate this feast, and we would not be deterred from it. The Humans think they can tell us what to do? Well, we will show them what we think about that. We will dine on their species starting tomorrow, with the opening day of our feast. Even now the Humans we have are being bid on and taken to the proper locations for the start of the feast," replied the Lamothian councilor.

"Are you not concerned that the Human fleet that destroyed our homeworld will come here and destroy Xanther for not heeding their warning?" asked Admiral Zahn.

"No, we expect you and our allies to hunt them down and to destroy them. They are not a threat to us if they are dead. Or better yet, captured for the next feast," responded the Lamothian councilor.

"We do not know the current location of the Human fleet. Admiral Voxx sent us a message not long ago, informing us the Human fleet destroyed a Druin planet, Druin Nine. Not a single Druin was left alive in the star system. So now Admiral Voxx believes they are headed to the Morag area of the Confederation to exact their revenge on them as well. We came back here in case the Humans return here. All of our allies are on high alert for any sign of this Human fleet," said Admiral Zahn.

"Sounds like we are safe then to continue with our feast," answered the Lamothian councilor.

Admiral Zahn took a deep breath and said, "We will remain on high alert, for I am certain the Humans will come here to punish us for this feast."

Chapter Twenty

Morag Admiral Ramgen grew concerned that he had picked the wrong targets again that the Human fleet would attack. *They should have been here by now,* he thought to himself. *Where could they be?* He had no reports of them being spotted in any other star system. He could think of only two explanations for their absence. Either they had headed back home, which didn't make much sense, since they still had a sizable fleet left to attack more shipyards. Or they had stopped somewhere to make repairs before their next attack.

If that were the case, Ramgen could still have the right systems protected after all. Logic told him that the best course of action in the meantime was to stay put. The two star systems his fleet were currently staged to defend were still the most likely next targets of the Humans. Until they had been spotted elsewhere, Ramgen would continue his course, staying where he was. This was the best place to most likely come into contact with the Human fleet. He had the numbers to defeat them. He just had to find them, or they had to find him.

Admiral Collison's plan slowly came together. The fleet finished up some last-minute repairs before their next hyperspace jump. The scout ships were assembling around the fleet. The first phase of his new plan involved the scout ships finding the location of the large Morag fleets patrolling the area. Once they were found, the scout ships would reassemble and hopefully make it appear that they are scanning some star systems in a divergent direction to the actual one the fleet would take. The scout ships will then hopefully take the enemy fleet on a wild goose chase, before disappearing safely.

Collison was aware that, as soon as his fleet started attacking his target, the Morag would realize they had been fooled into taking the bait away from the target. Hopefully Collison's fleet would have enough time to attack one or possibly even two more star systems, before the Morag fleet could reach them.

Collison stood with his arms crossed and a furrow across his brows, as he studied the holographic display in front of him. The selection of his following targets was crucial to their success. He needed at least a couple options, dependent on the current location of the Morag fleet. He still had the third target he planned to attack, so he would keep that as an option and then add another star system to that plan.

He slowly walked back and forth, studying the image of the Morag area of the Confederation, Collison could go multiple places from there. He knew he needed to stay away from Morag Prime. It was very heavily defended and had the numbers there to split the Morag fleet and to send some to hunt down his fleet, if they felt Collison were close enough. He already had one large fleet chasing him. He didn't want to add to that.

Also the Morag fleet lying in wait for them near the Lamothian planet of Xanther hadn't been seen by the scout ships in a while. That Morag fleet most likely headed back to Morag-controlled space and would be in the hunt for Collison's fleet at any moment as well. So it would be safe to assume he now had two large enemy fleets looking for his.

He walked around the holographic display a few times, before coming to a stop. He had hoped his target would jump out at him, but it had not. He also needed *not* to be very logical about his target either, so the Morag couldn't figure it out and be waiting for Collison.

As he walked around the image again, his plan began to take form. His first option would be to attack the third star system from his last plan that he hadn't gotten to yet. From there, he would head back in the direction they had come and hit a star system they had previously passed over. Depending on the location of the enemy fleets, assuming the scout ships could find them, Collison would have a third star system on his plan as well.

They would head back the other way again and target a star system one over from their first target. It would be a lot of back-and-forth, but hopefully the Morag wouldn't catch on in time to catch them. Plus it didn't make a lot of logical sense to jump back and forth that way either. The Morag would hopefully assume the Humans would be picking up some more star systems in a linear fashion that they had skipped as they headed back out of the Morag-controlled star systems.

Collison smiled as he finalized his plans and then relayed them to his fleet. Now he needed to put his plan into action. That started with the scout ships. He would have them methodically check each star system, moving out from the one they were currently in. Once the Morag fleets were discovered, the next phase of Collison's plan would begin.

High Princess Layla Starguard made her way toward the House of Worlds. The meetings had been in full swing for a couple days now. She had been immersed in meetings nearly all day since the House of Worlds session had begun. She was very thankful that all the decisions did not fall on her shoulders but were shared with the Imperial Council.

They still had a lot of work to do and lots of important items on the agenda. She was anxious to hear from the Earth fleets in the Confederation, but, so far, they hadn't received any word on their progress. She couldn't decide if that was a good sign or a bad one. The best thing she could do was keep herself busy, and that would be easy to do today with her full schedule.

Hopefully Derrick would have an update for her soon. He was headed to the underground Command Center located beneath the House of Worlds to meet with Admiral Marloo.

As Layla entered the main chamber of the meeting room in the House of Worlds, she couldn't help but be amazed. So many worlds were represented here, and she was so thankful. She spent her days meeting with the leaders from different planets and hearing their concerns and suggestions. Many committees had been formed to start working through some specific issues and to make recommendations for how to proceed in improving those issues. Today she would meet with a few of these committees to see how she could be of assistance.

Derrick walked swiftly to the underground Command Center, where Admiral Marloo awaited his arrival. When he entered the room, a beehive of activity greeted him. "Any news?" asked Derrick.

"Yes, we have intercepted some hyperlight messages about the destruction of Lamothian home planet Lamothia, as well as Druin Nine," replied Marloo, as he examined his holographic display. Two more Confederation planets had been destroyed. That left the Lamothians with only four.

Derrick thought they'd be better off if no Lamothian planets were left, but, for now, he would settle with one less. "Anything from Admiral Collison?" asked Derrick.

"No, no news from Collison," replied Marloo.

"What about Admiral Cleemorl? Has he arrived at the supply fleet yet?"

"We haven't heard from either," Marloo said, "but I am sure they are being cautious and won't send any hyperlight messages to protect their locations."

They both studied the map of the Confederation. It was so vast. If only they could make peace with all the Confederation, they'd all benefit from it. Unfortunately the Druins, Morag, Zynth, and Lamothians would never settle for peace. They thrived on war and destruction.

Only now those Confederation races were experiencing the other side of that for once. They were being attacked in their star systems, as opposed to attacking Humans in ours. Derrick hoped the Earth fleets would be successful in destroying a large number of Morag shipyards. The Humans future depended on slowing down the Morag's ability to make such large fleets so quickly. The

Humans just needed time, and hopefully the Earth fleets were getting them some.

Captain Avery of the Humans' supply fleet sifted through the messages they had intercepted from the Confederation. It sounded like Rear Admiral Barnes had successfully destroyed Lamothia and Druin Nine. Avery wondered where she would go from there.

His thoughts were interrupted by an alarm sounding. His heartbeat quickened, and his throat went dry. He swallowed and closed his eyes for a moment, as he calmed himself. "What do we have?"

"Ships dropping from hyperspace, Captain," replied Lieutenant Dan. Silence filled the room, as the icons began to appear on the display. When they turned green, a sigh of relief could be heard from everyone in the Command Center.

Avery sat down in his command chair. "Let's move to Condition Two, in case they are being chased by an enemy fleet," commanded Avery.

Tensions rose again, as they all directed their attention back to the tactical display. As more ships emerged from hyperspace, they received a message from Captain Strong, leading part of Collison's damaged ships back here for repair.

"Captain Avery, we are the first ships coming in from Admiral Collison's first attack on the shipyards in the Morag area of the Confederation. We need repairs to be ready for whatever comes next," said Captain Strong.

"Can we assume that Admiral Collison had success in destroying the shipyards?" asked Avery.

"Yes, we destroyed all eight shipyards in that star system. The rest of Fourth Fleet stayed to destroy more in other star systems. We haven't heard anything from them since we left. I assume they're still having success. We likely will see more and more ships returning for repairs," commented Strong.

"Let's get the first ships in then. We'll start with the least-damaged ships and then go on from there," said Avery. In all, Strong had arrived with thirty battlecruisers and three dreadnoughts to be repaired. Avery had four mobile repair yards at his disposal. With thirty-three ships to repair, it would take some time.

As the mobile shipyards began their repairs on the ships, alarms sounded again. Avery knew it was too soon for more ships to be coming in from Collison's fleet or Barnes's fleet.

"Captain, ships are dropping from hyperspace behind us," said Lieutenant Dan. As Captain Avery was about to move the fleet to Condition One, the icons turned green. "Who is that?" asked Avery.

"Receiving an incoming message from Admiral Cleemorl, Captain," Dan said, with more than a hint of relief in his voice.

"What is he doing here?" asked Avery.

"Seems he came to help defend the supply fleet, in case the Human fleets are followed back here by the enemy," said Dan.

"That's a relief. I think I will sleep more soundly with Admiral Cleemorl and his fleet here," said Avery. "How many ships did he bring with him?"

"On the tactical display are 30 dreadnoughts and 120 battlecruisers," replied Dan.

"When you add in our twenty dreadnoughts and fifty battlecruisers, we have a good-size fleet here to protect us. Hopefully they won't be needed," Avery said in a grateful tone.

"Should we contact the Lormallians to assure them we are not a threat?" asked Dan. "Now that more battleships have shown up?"

"No, let's keep our eye on their fleets. If they weren't threatened by us before, I don't think Cleemorl's fleet will threaten them now. If you see any movement in their fleet positions, let me know," said Avery.

-

Admiral Cleemorl was relieved to have made it to the rendezvous location before Collison's fleet. It did appear Collison already had some ships that needed repairs and were sent here to the mobile shipyards. From what Cleemorl had learned from these returning ships, Collison had successfully destroyed eight shipyards in his first star system that he had targeted. Hopefully he had met with more success after that. Most likely, more and more ships would come in for repairs over the next few days, as the fighting escalated.

Cleemorl had also been updated that Rear Admiral Barnes had successfully destroyed both Lamothia and Druin Nine. Also discussions were had as to what Barnes might do next. Would she go on to the Morag area of the Confederation or head back to destroy Xanther? A scout ship had reported that the feasts were still being prepared for. Cleemorl didn't understand how the Lamothians wouldn't heed the warning High Princess Layla had sent them. They deserved what was coming for them, no doubt about it.

He was also interested to hear a scout ship was following a transport vessel that had delivered Humans to Xanther for the feast. Who knew where that would lead them? And what new problems would arise from that?

For now, his fleet needed to make a few repairs and to get some rest. They must be ready for what might be headed their way.

His thoughts drifted to Cheryl and what she was doing now. He wished he could speak to her and could let her know that he had arrived safely. The need to remain undetected prevented him from sending a message to her. No need to take the chance his message might get intercepted by the enemy.

He smiled, as he thought about how she was probably keeping herself busy with her businesses. She had a passion for what she did, and she was very good at it. He hoped that everything was aboveboard this time and that she was not dabbling in anything illegal.

Cleemorl looked forward to his future with Cheryl. As soon as this war was over, if it ever was, he'd spend more time with her. If only they could destroy what was left of the Confederation, they could all move on with their lives. Move on to having families and living a life of peace.

Well, no use daydreaming about it now. He had work to do.

Lormallian Councilor Ardon Reull had just been briefed about the activities of the Human fleet stationed at the edge of their area of space. It looked as if some ships had returned for repairs. He wondered if these ships were from the fleet attacking the Lamothians and Druins or the one that left first and was hopefully doing some damage in the Morag area of the Confederation.

As he contemplated those possibilities, he was informed another fleet was dropping from hyperspace. This fleet appeared to have come from the direction of the Empire. More ships? Ardon wondered what they were planning to do now. Maybe this fleet was to help supplement those that had been destroyed, or maybe they were there as a backup to defend the fleet stationed nearby. Time would tell. For now, they would watch and wait.

Professor Charles Wright was with a small fleet of ships headed from Earth to the Empire. He needed to speak directly with his daughter, Kala. Charles was an archeologist and had been working on an important dig on Earth. He had been searching for a clue connecting the Empire to Earth. He had discovered some incredible things over the last few weeks. Some things he couldn't wait to tell Kala and her husband, Andrew, about. Charles had a lot of questions and hoped that High Princess Layla might point him in the right direction to get the answers he sought.

Charles missed his daughter. He hadn't seen her in person since her wedding to Andrew. It was odd to think of Andrew as a prince. Hopefully his position in the Empire would help the professor solve his mystery.

He had unearthed some amazing discoveries, which, of course, lead to more questions than answers. The answers had to be in the Empire. He was determined to find them. On the plus side, he would get to see and to spend some quality time with his daughter.

The trip from Earth to Golan Four was a long one. Weeks of hyperspace travel. As he thought back, he was amazed at how far Earth had come in such a short time. Thanks to the life-extending drugs the Imperials had, Charles had been able to live a much longer life than he had ever expected to.

With that extra time, he had been able to dig and to excavate in more areas, which lead him to his most recent discoveries—and the answers to which he knew lay somewhere in the Empire. They just had to be there. He was on the brink of a find that could change the history books.

For now, all he could do was sit back and relax, until his long journey brought him to Golan Four and to his beautiful daughter. Then he would start putting more pieces of the puzzle together, until he figured out where the clues would lead him next.

-

Scout ship 255 dropped out of hyperspace in the star system Collison planned to attack next. Immediately alarms sounded.

"Lieutenant Pamela, report!" commanded Captain Malachi.

"Captain, I have over eight hundred Morag warships showing up on our scans of the system," replied Pamela.

"Any reaction to our presence?" Malachi asked, as he gripped the sides of his chair so tightly that his knuckles turned white.

"Not yet, Captain," Pamela answered.

"Let's move on to our next star system then. Send our encrypted message back to Collison. It's a good thing he decided to make some repairs and regroup before coming here. They're set to ambush us here," said Malachi.

As they entered hyperspace to head to their next star system, Malachi wondered if they'd run into any other Morag fleets. Maybe they'd found the only one hunting them. If they could stay clear of this one, they'd be good.

Admiral Ramgen, we are sensing some radiation leftover from a hyperspace jump on the periphery of the star system, said his tactical officer.

Take some ships and check it out, Ramgen replied. This could be the Humans stealth ships that didn't show up on their scans. If one was here, it would report back to the Human fleet, and it would steer clear of this star system. He slammed his hand down on his command chair, nearly breaking it. A few crew members jumped a little at the loud sound it made. Gazes were quickly averted, and everyone set about their work.

As the crew waited for word from their recon ships sent to check the area where the radiation had been detected, Admiral Ramgen studied his holographic display. What were the Humans doing? They must be repairing ships somewhere relatively close by. Based on the location of their last attack, and given the time between then and now, Ramgen narrowed down the Humans' possible locations.

No reason for them to stop their attacks yet. They had lost ships but not such a significant number that they would retreat. No inhabited star systems had reported the presence of the Human fleets, so they must be hiding in an uninhabited star system or one without a constant Morag presence in it. One of the inferior races that they ruled over?

Ramgen walked around his holographic display. He needed to narrow down the possibilities more. Maybe send out some scout ships of his own. He knew only a few uninhabited star systems were near enough to be a safe haven for the Humans.

As far as star systems that might not report the presence of the Humans, that would most likely be the Barsoons or the Creetins. The Creetins spread out over twenty-two star systems. The Barsoons did not have that vast of an area.

Admiral, the ships have not found any more evidence of a presence in the star system, said his tactical officer.

Just as I suspected. They probably made a note of our fleet location and then moved on to the next star system, replied Ramgen. *I want to send some of our own scout ships to the six uninhabited star systems nearest to our location to see if we can find this Human fleet before they move on to their next target.*

Yes, Admiral, we will start the search immediately, replied his tactical officer.

Ramgen smirked. He would find the Humans first and then ambush them, before they had a chance to destroy any more shipyards.

Collison had received some reports from the scout ships. So far, the only sizable fleet was the one in the star system he had intended to target first. He let out a sigh of relief. If they had gone on to that star system, instead of stopping for repairs, they would have come face-to-face with that Morag fleet. The scout ships had also found another Morag fleet close to the same size as the other in a neighboring star system. Now Collison just needed to avoid those two fleets at all costs.

So he must reevaluate his plans. He could still target that star system, just not first as he had originally intended. He would head back toward his first target and pick a star system to target that they had skipped over.

He also needed scout ships to monitor those two large Morag fleets. He must know when they left and which direction they headed. Then he would head the other way and would target another star system than the two the Morag fleets were currently in. Hopefully the Morag fleet would chase them but not have the opportunity to catch them. Collison could play cat and mouse all day, as long as the cat never catches the mouse, that is.

"Let's have the scout ships head in the direction of Morag Prime. I want them to all drop out of hyperspace in the same star system. Hopefully that will cause the Morag fleet to move toward them and farther away from our next target," Collison said. "Also have the scout ship that found that fleet in one of our target areas head back there to monitor it."

Captain Malachi on board scout ship 255 had not found any sizable fleets in any of the other three star systems they had painstakingly investigated. He had just received his message from Collison to head back and monitor the large Morag fleet. He shuddered at the thought of going back there. They knew the Morag could detect radiation from a hyperspace jump. Which meant they would know the scout ship were there. The question remained if the Morag could zero in on where the Human ship was. Malachi could drop out of hyperspace at the edge of the adjacent star system and move into the star system without using a hyperspace drive. That would take a lot more time though, and time wasn't exactly on their side. He shook his head; the option was clear. They'd have to hope the Morag couldn't zero in on their location.

His crew was somber, as they headed back to monitor the Morag fleet. They all knew what was at stake here. They were also all very aware of the risks. This is what they had signed up for. They had volunteered to come with Admiral Collison on this mission. To explore new star systems, at least not explored by any Humans. They had done that—exploring star systems no Human had ever been to before.

Each and every star system they explored was unique and awe-inspiring in their own way. It was eye-opening to see how vast the Confederation actually was and to accept the fact that the Morag had so much power and influence over so large of an area. It was more than a little intimidating.

The scout ships were headed to a white dwarf system, containing Morag Three, opposite where Collison intended to go. Once they were all in position, they would take down their stealth shields and jump into the star system that contained Morag Three. If Collison's planned work, the scout ships would have a very large Morag fleet in pursuit of them. They would head in a divergent direction than Collison's fleet intended to take. Eventually they would reengage their stealth shields and effectively disappear—if everything went according to plan.

A group of Morag scout ships dropped out of hyperspace in an uninhabited star system. They quickly ran their scans and headed to the next system. Captain Lenot was in charge of this little hunting expedition. He was determined to locate their target. They had already checked two other star systems and found no Human fleet. They had three to go. He knew he would find them and then would quickly report to Admiral Ramgen their location. Afterward Ramgen and his fleet would release havoc on these imbecile Humans.

Ramgen paced back and forth in his Command Center. How could these Humans be so hard to find? Why was it taking so long to destroy this fleet? How many more shipyards would they destroy before he caught up to them?

Admiral, I detect more radiation from a hyperspace jump. Nothing is on my scans though, said the tactical officer.

He rolled his eyes. They must want to keep tabs on where his fleet was. He carefully thought over his options. It was doubtful he could hunt down this stealth ship. However, he could fool this ship into reporting his direction when he transitioned into hyperspace, changing directions shortly after that. He doubted the Human ship would follow them into hyperspace. He slowly thrummed his fingers across the arm of his command chair. *How can he use this to his advantage?*

Should we send ships out there to investigate? asked the tactical officer.

No. We will let them believe they have not been detected. Then we will fool them when we leave this star system, replied Ramgen.

Have the ships we sent to scout the uninhabited star systems found anything yet? asked the tactical officer.

No, not yet. They are dwindling down their targets. I am confident they will find this fleet shortly, said Ramgen. *And, when they do, the Humans will never even see us coming.*

Captain Malachi and scout ship 255 had just exited hyperspace in the star system where one of the large Morag fleets was stationed. "Lieutenant Pamela, what do our scans show? Any changes?"

"Yes, Captain, fewer ships are here than last time," replied Pamela.

"By how many?" Malachi asked, a hint of concern in his voice.

"Fifty-seven, Captain," Pamela responded.

"That's odd. Where would they have gone?" Malachi thought out loud. "And why?"

"Do you think they went in search of us?" asked Pamela.

"I doubt it. But they may have gone in search of our fleet. We need to send an encrypted message immediately to Collison and notify him of the situation. Has the fleet moved any in response to our presence?" asked Malachi.

"No, Captain, no response," Pamela replied.

Malachi thought that was a little odd, but he was thankful nevertheless.

"Admiral, we've received an encrypted message from scout ship 255. Some of the Morag fleet has disappeared," said Billingsly.

"That's odd," Collison said, with a flash of concern on his face. "Where would they have gone?"

"Captain Malachi believes they have gone in search of us," said Billingsly.

"How many ships?" asked Collison.

"Fifty-seven, Admiral," replied Billingsly.

"This could complicate our plan, but the chances of them finding us remain slim," remarked Collison. "Let's continue with our plan and increase the alert of the fleet. Hopefully we won't be receiving any uninvited guests anytime soon."

Chapter Twenty-One

The scout ships, led by Captain Laine, were almost ready to exit hyperspace in the white dwarf system that contained Morag Three.

"All ships, lower your stealth shields. We will exit hyperspace in five minutes. Remain on high alert," said Captain Laine. He was very uneasy about this mission. However, he was confident that, once they jumped out of the star system and raised their stealth shields, they couldn't be followed. Laine just did not like the feeling of being exposed, when he was used to being hidden.

As they emerged from hyperspace, their alarms sounded. "Captain, sixty-four Morag battleships are in this star system," reported Lieutenant Henley.

"Have all ships prepare to jump into hyperspace and raise their stealth shields at the first sign of that fleet entering hyperspace. They'll be on us very quickly," said Captain Laine.

"Captain, half of the Morag ships just transitioned to hyperspace," said Henley in alarm.

"Get us out of here!" commanded Laine.

"Yes, Captain," replied Henley.

Everyone held their breath, as they transitioned to hyperspace and then raised their shields. They were pretty confident that the Morag couldn't trace them once they reengaged their stealth shields, but there was always a chance.

All gazes were on the tactical display. The Morag had indeed followed them into hyperspace. Now that they had raised their stealth shields, they needed to change directions to see if the Morag followed them.

As the navigation officer input the new coordinates, Captain Laine felt his heart beat faster. This was the moment of truth. Would it work? Or would this be the beginning of the end for them?

As the scout ships changed direction, they all watched if the Morag would continue to follow or if they would stay on their current course. All their gazes were glued to the screens. Then cheers erupted as the Morag fleet did not change directions and follow them. Captain Laine let out a huge sigh of relief.

Hopefully Admiral Collison's plan would work like he hoped it would. Captain Laine needed to inform Collison of their success. Now, if only the rest of the Morag fleets would react like Collison thought they would.

Morag Captain Helbum was tasked with protecting the star system where Morag Three was located. He had a small fleet of sixty-four battleships. He was not too concerned with running into the Human fleet, and they were not anywhere near their location. He couldn't believe Admiral Ramgen hadn't located and destroyed the Humans yet. Ramgen should have never let them escape the first time they attacked. He should have followed them into hyperspace, and then the larger fleets could have crushed them. That was his fatal flaw, and now he could only react to the Humans' next move. They had lost valuable shipyards as a result of Ramgen's incompetence.

Suddenly alarms sounded, capturing his attention from his thoughts. *Demar, report!* ordered Helbum.

Captain, we have ships exiting hyperspace. They appear to be Human ships, although not ones we've observed before, replied Demar.

How many? asked Helbum.

Forty-seven, Captain, replied Demar.

Are any more ships still exiting hyperspace? asked Helbum.

No, sir, that's it, said Demar.

Let's go investigate these Human vessels. Have thirty of our battleships escort us. Let's see if they came to fight or just to scan our system, said Helbum.

Helbum waited, as they jumped to the edge of the star system, sending a message to Admiral Ramgen. *Admiral, we have a group of forty-seven Human ships that just exited hyperspace near Morag Three. We are headed to investigate.*

Let me know what you find, replied Ramgen.

As the Morag ship exited hyperspace near the Human ships, the Human ships jumped into hyperspace. *Follow those ships!* commanded Helbum. He would not make the same mistake as Ramgen. He had come across Human vessels, and he would not let them escape.

As they followed them into hyperspace, Helbum contemplated where the Humans must be headed, based on their current trajectory. It appeared the Human ships were headed in the direction of Morag Prime. This really was an inferior race. They could not possibly believe they even stood a chance in attacking Morag Prime. Admiral Marcello had a considerable fleet there.

Helbum sent another message to Admiral Ramgen, updating him on Helbum's current coordinates and the Humans' possible destination.

Shortly after all the ships transitioned back into hyperspace, the Human ships disappeared. They were on the scanners one moment, and, the next moment, they were gone. "How could this be?" Helbum muttered to himself.

What should we do? asked Demar.

Helbum thought over his options. They could stay on their current path and hope to find the Human ships again, or they could head back to Morag Three. Since they left, it was more vulnerable to attack.

Yet he needed to find the Humans. He slammed his fist down. They would not outsmart him. He would search for them in every star system from here to Morag Prime if he had to. *Drop out of hyperspace in the nearest star system. We will quickly scan it and then head to the next one. We will continue this course until we find these Humans.*

He sent a message to Ramgen. *The Human ships have disappeared off our tactical display. We have no way to track them. I will check every star system between here and Morag Prime, until I find them.*

It must be their stealth ships. Unfortunately they will be almost impossible to find. They will not show up on your scans, even if they are there. This must

*be an attempt at a diversion of some sort, to get us to believe they are headed
to Morag Prime for an attack. They would be senseless to attack us there.*

*We must not fall for their trap. I do want you to search for the Human
fleet but not in the direction of Morag Prime. Head toward my location. You
will not find the ships you seek, but you just might find the Human fleet that
is attacking our shipyards. Only search uninhabited star systems and ones
inhabited by other races. If the Human fleet was in a star system inhabited
by the Morag, we would know about it,* replied Ramgen.

Yes, Admiral. We will start immediately, replied Helbum. He
wanted to be the one to find the Humans. As he examined his
holographic display of the Morag-controlled area of the
Confederation, he plotted a list of alternate star systems to search.

-

Morag Admiral Ramgen knew he needed more ships out there
to search for the Human fleet. He would ask Admiral Marcello
for more ships. He also needed to check in with Admiral Voxx to
determine his location.

He started with Voxx and quickly sent a message. *Where are you
and your fleet currently located?*

*We are nearing Morag-controlled star systems. Then we will begin our
search for the Human fleet,* replied Voxx.

*I have sent some ships out to search for the fleet. They are searching
uninhabited star systems and star systems that do not have a Morag-inhabited
planet in them. We must not assume that other races subjugated to us will
automatically report the presence of the Human fleet,* sent Ramgen.

*Yes, that is a good plan of action. We will do the same. I will divide my
fleet that I have with me into three groups of roughly eight hundred ships. We
will search everywhere, until we find them or until they attack another
shipyard. Then we will converge on them and destroy them,* said Voxx.

*I will send a message to Marcello and have him send some search groups
out from Morag Prime. With all of us searching, it won't take long for us to
find them. If the Humans attack before we find them, with us spread out
searching for them, we should have a fleet near enough to respond and to
engage them reasonably quickly,* said Ramgen.

Yes, their attacks will end today. We will destroy them, said Voxx.

-

Morag Admiral Voxx closed in on the Morag-controlled star systems. In a couple hours, he would be there. Now he needed to determine where he would begin his search for the Human fleet. He hadn't informed Admiral Ramgen that likely two Human fleets were in their star systems now. He would find this fleet he was searching for before they could destroy any shipyards. As long as Ramgen did his part and found and destroyed the other fleet, their problems with the Humans in the Confederation would quickly come to an end.

Voxx evaluated his options carefully. The Morag inhabited 112 planets in 92 different star systems. The other Human fleet had already attacked three of the star systems. He doubted they would venture very close to Morag Prime, so that lowered the possibilities there as well. Based on where Ramgen was located, that reduced the number of star systems Voxx would need to search. He doubted the Humans would be far from one of the Morag-inhabited star systems.

Most likely, the Human fleet Voxx was hunting would drop from hyperspace in an uninhabited star system to make repairs and to select their next target. Now to figure out which one that would be. If Voxx divided his fleet into three, he could check three star systems at a time.

Which ones would he target first? He considered his options and weighed the possibilities. The most obvious ones the Humans would probably avoid. So Voxx would too. Maybe he would get lucky, and they could find and destroy the Humans before they had a chance to attack any shipyards or, worse, destroy another planet. Voxx carefully selected his first three uninhabited star systems and relayed the information to his fleet.

-

Rear Admiral Barnes had selected an uninhabited star system in the Morag area of the Confederation to drop out of hyperspace and to make any repairs to the fleet that needed to be done. She did not know where Admiral Collison and Rear Admiral Carrie were or where they had been. They were not communicating to help keep the Morag from discovering their locations. She was essentially flying blind. She would need to make repairs as quickly as possible and then select which star systems and shipyards to target.

She slowly paced around the holographic display of the Morag area of the Confederation to figure out what their targets would be. There was a chance she would pick one that Collison had already destroyed. That would be something they'd quickly discern with their scans.

Barnes always thought more clearly when she was moving. As she weighed her options, she stopped and scrutinized the star systems closest to where they would be. That would be where she would start. One star system held the inhabited planet of Morag Seven. It had two shipyards in orbit around it. It also contained two terraformed moons that each had one shipyard in orbit. They could destroy four shipyards in one star system. Considering that the Morag already knew the Human fleet was targeting shipyards, she needed to assume this star system would be at least mildly defended with a Morag fleet.

Hopefully Collison was far from her target, and most of the Morag fleets would be chasing him. The appearance of her fleet would pull some heat off Collison. From there, they would need to make more repairs, so she selected their next rendezvous location.

Her plan was made, and now the fleet must move to Condition One. In less than ten minutes, they would emerge from hyperspace.

-

Morag Admiral Ramgen was discussing strategy with Admiral Marcello. *We must send out task groups to locate and to destroy this Human fleet,* said Ramgen.

I will send out two groups of 800 ships. That will still leave me with over 1,900 ships to defend Morag Prime, which should be more than enough. I will send them out in search of this fleet. They will fan out from here, thus covering more areas of our star systems. When the Humans attack, we will have more fleets out there patrolling, and one will most certainly be within range to react quickly enough to engage the enemy, replied Marcello. *We will start immediately.*

When Ramgen finished communicating with Marcello, Ramgen thought more about the stealth ships leading Captain Helbum in the direction of Morag Prime. Maybe Ramgen should jump over one star system in that direction. That would make the Human stealth ship watching him think that they had taken the bait and were headed toward Morag Prime as well.

Maybe by moving over one star system, the Human fleet would feel that the coast was clear and would then attack here. Ramgen would be close enough to ambush them before they had time to finish destroying the shipyards. He would leave the ships here that had been patrolling when they arrived. The rest would jump to the star system that contained Morag Thirty-Two.

Collison was ready to make his hyperspace jump to his first target. He had heard from Captain Laine and hoped the Morag fleets would head in the direction the stealth ships were headed, which was away from where he was headed. It would also clear up another one of his targets. He had just heard from Captain Malachi on scout ship 255, who had reported that the large fleet patrolling that star system had entered hyperspace in the direction of Morag Prime.

So far, things were going according to plan. Collison prepared his fleet for their next target. They would be targeting a yellow dwarf star system that held one Morag inhabited planet. This planet was Morag Five. Two shipyards were in orbit around the planet. The system also contained one terraformed moon, which had one shipyard.

At last report, this star system had a small Morag fleet patrolling of fifty-eight battleships. If Collison's fleet were successful, they would destroy the enemy ships and all three shipyards. He knew he needed to depend on the attack interceptors to destroy the shipyards as much as possible. All the shipyards were armed and had energy shields in place.

Each ship had its assigned targets and knew what was expected of them. Collison was confident in his plan and his fleet. They would begin their hyperspace jump to their next target in the next five minutes. He sat in his command chair and quietly watched his crew, hard at work.

Collison had a fantastic crew, who were like a family to him. He had worked with them for a long time. They worked like a well-oiled machine. Everyone knew their roles and what their strengths and weaknesses were. They filled the gaps when needed and worked great under pressure. He smiled and said, "Captain Billingsly, take us into hyperspace."

"Yes, sir," Billingsly replied.

The ships began entering hyperspace, their destination determined and their future riding on avoiding the large Morag fleets.

Unbeknownst to Collison and his fleet, just as the last few ships entered hyperspace, other ships exited hyperspace in this uninhabited star system.

Morag Captain Lenot and his group of battleships had just hit the jackpot. As they were exiting hyperspace, they witnessed the last few Human ships entering hyperspace. He noted their direction and immediately followed them. He was confident they were far enough behind that they wouldn't be noticed. He only had a small contingent of ships. Not enough to challenge this Human fleet. However, it was enough to track them and to hopefully rendezvous with Admiral Ramgen, where they would obliterate these witless Humans.

Lenot immediately sent Admiral Ramgen a message. *We have located the Human fleet. They have just entered hyperspace headed in the direction opposite to where your fleet is located. It would lead them to a few possible targets. We are following them.*

Excellent work, Captain Lenot. Our fleet will head in that direction immediately. Notify me immediately if the Human fleet changes course or drops out of hyperspace, responded Ramgen. *I will notify Admiral Voxx and have all fleets in the area on high alert.*

Admiral Voxx was minutes away from exiting hyperspace in one of the three systems he had concluded the Human fleet might take refuge in.

He had just received a message from Admiral Ramgen. The good news was that the Human fleet Ramgen was after was headed straight toward Voxx. If everything worked out, he would have enough time to destroy the first Human fleet and then prepare to destroy the second Human fleet.

He smiled coldly. It was finally time to kill some Humans. He had waited long enough. The time had come. He would show no mercy.

Rear Admiral Barnes and her fleet finished up some repairs before their next hyperspace jump. They would jump in the next five minutes. She was ready to destroy some Morag shipyards. The more they could destroy, the better. With her fleet and Collison's and Carrie's all destroying shipyards, they'd cause more damage to the battleship-making ability of the Morag.

Her target had four shipyards. She had already informed her fleet of their tasks and specific targets. The attack interceptors would be pivotal in this upcoming battle. According to the data the scout ships had relayed to them before they had jumped from the Lamothian area of the Confederation, this star system had a Morag fleet of forty-six battleships patrolling it. Nothing they couldn't handle.

The Forgotten Empire: The Confederation and The Empire
at War

As the time neared to make their transition into hyperspace, she sat down in her command chair. She was fortunate to have this opportunity to come to the Confederation and honored to be entrusted with the responsibilities given to her. She would make them all proud, the ones who trained her, the ones who served alongside her, as well as her superiors.

Rear Admiral Barnes was ready to head toward their first Morag target. Her heart beat faster in her chest. The Morag were a fierce opponent, and she knew she would be fine, as long as they weren't sufficiently outnumbered. She turned to Captain Borrel. "Captain, take us into hyperspace. Let's go destroy some shipyards," she said, with determination and confidence.

She felt the familiar twinge in her stomach, as her ship entered hyperspace. She laughed to herself, as she remembered the first time she had felt that feeling. It had taken some getting used to. Now she barely even noticed it. She smiled to herself. What she was doing was important and would make a difference in the fight against the Confederation. Hopefully teach the Confederation to stay away from Earth and the Solar System. It would also buy more time for the Empire to bolster its defenses and its fleets.

She had a couple hours of downtime, before she needed to prepare the fleet for the exit from hyperspace and the imminent attack on the shipyards. Everyone already knew what their positions and targets would be. She would take the opportunity to get a little rest.

Shortly after the last Human ship left the star system, Voxx and part of his fleet began exiting hyperspace. They immediately scanned the system. *Admiral, I detect radiation from a hyperspace jump on the periphery of the star system,* said Bale.

Voxx slammed his hand down on his chair. *We must have just missed them. Is there any way to tell which way they headed?* Voxx asked.

No, Admiral. Based on where they were located, we could make a logical determination of the most likely direction they headed. He pointed to the display in front of him and said, *the radiation is located in this area of the star system. It would make sense that they would be on the side closest to where they will head. Based on that reasoning, I would assume they are headed in this direction, toward one of these star systems here.* He pointed to the most likely star systems he felt the Humans would attack.

Bring up the holographic display. Let's analyze the possible targets that the Humans would most likely select. Which star systems have the most shipyards? That's where I will assume they will head, said Voxx.

After a few moments, he had narrowed down his possible choices to three star systems. He already had his fleet divided into three groups, so each one would head to a different star system. Hopefully they would find the Human fleet and then destroy them.

Let's prepare to jump to our designated star system as soon as possible. We have a few ships finishing up their repairs, and then we will make our way out of here, commanded Voxx.

After the ships completed their repairs, the fleet made their jump into hyperspace.

Voxx sat back in his chair. The Humans had no idea the Morag were coming for them. He estimated that the Humans would not have enough time to destroy all of the shipyards before Voxx arrived to wipe them out of the Confederation.

Admiral Collison was getting a hot cup of coffee when he was paged to the Command Center. As he quickly made his way back, his mind ran wild with different possibilities of why he was being paged. It wasn't time to drop out of hyperspace yet. So what could it be?

As he walked into the Command Center, he could tell by the look on Billingsly's face that something was wrong. "What's going on?" he asked.

"Admiral, we are being followed," Billingsly said gravely.

"How? How could they find us when we're in hyperspace?" Collison asked.

"It appears they followed us as we made our last jump into hyperspace. A couple of our battlecruisers reported alarms sounding as they made their jump. This fleet must have followed us from there," Billingsly replied.

"How many ships?" asked Collison.

"Fifty-seven, Admiral. Not too many that we couldn't handle," replied Billingsly.

"The problem is that they have likely informed the larger Morag fleets of our location and direction. All of the fleets will now be inbound to this area of the Confederation," Collison said gravely. "We have not destroyed enough shipyards yet. We need to do more."

Collison walked over to his holographic display and studied it for a moment. Then he said, "We will have to do it quickly, before they have the chance to make it to our location. We must be very efficient in our attack. Assuming that Morag fleet stationed where Captain Malachi last saw it was headed in the direction of Morag Prime, we should have plenty of time to destroy our targets."

He had his brows furrowed and his hand on his chin, as he continued his thought process aloud to his crew. "We still should assume there might be another fleet nearby. We need to attack aggressively and get in and out of there quickly. If we can destroy all the enemy ships before the other fleets arrive, they will have no idea where we went after that. Then we remain safe to attack another target elsewhere."

As he took a few steps around the holographic display, he knew he needed to reevaluate his plan of attack. The quicker they could get in and out of the star system, the better. He still had a couple hours to refine his game plan.

"I will be in my quarters, if I am needed. I need time to rethink our plan of attack, to see if there are ways to make it more efficient," Collison said to his command crew.

-

Admiral Cleemorl watched and waited, as more and more ships returned from other parts of the Confederation. Battlecruisers and dreadnoughts arrived from Lamothia, as well as parts of the Morag area of the Confederation. The most recent ships had arrived from Druin Nine. The information they had so far was all reasonably positive. Rear Admiral Barnes had successfully destroyed Lamothia and Druin Nine. She had then left in the direction of the Morag-controlled star systems. She had decided to help Collison and Carrie destroy more shipyards.

As for Collison and Carrie, so far, with what they could gather from each ship coming for repairs, the two admirals had successfully destroyed thirteen shipyards. Every single one they could destroy would make a difference in the abilities of the Morag to produce more battleships.

Cleemorl wished they could somehow destroy them all, but that was nearly impossible. Almost every one of the Morag's ninety-two star systems surely held at least one shipyard. With the three Human fleets acting now as two separate fleets, all destroying shipyards, they could do more damage twice as fast.

With the last few ships that had arrived from the Morag-controlled star systems, they now had forty-eight battlecruisers and ten dreadnoughts in line for repairs or getting repairs. The least-damaged ships were repaired first. That way, they had more available to fight, if they needed it. So far, nineteen battlecruisers and six dreadnoughts had been repaired and were battle-ready.

Admiral Collison had also sent three battlecarriers back for resupply. The fifty supply ships had attack interceptors on board that would resupply the three battlecarriers. They would then wait for further orders. It would take them too long to get back to the Morag area of the Confederation.

Cleemorl also knew they needed to deal with the Lamothians and Xanther. They had not heeded High Princess Layla's advice about stopping their use of Humans in their feasts. If only Cleemorl had brought a bigger fleet, he would take care of it himself. In all likelihood though, the Lamothian fleet was

patrolling that star system. The Humans would have to combine
all their fleets to take on the full force of the Lamothian fleet.

Hopefully Collison, Carrie, and Barnes would have large-
enough fleets left to challenge the Lamothians, before they left
the Confederation.

Morag Captain Helbum was headed to where the Human fleet
was likely headed. No need for him to search for them anymore
since they had been found. He wanted a piece of the action. As
soon as Admiral Ramgen had informed him that Captain Lenot
had located the Humans, he had changed his course.

Based on his calculations, Helbum would get there shortly
before Ramgen did. Helbum only had 31 ships with him, but that
would add to the 58 ships already patrolling that star system. Plus
Captain Lenot had a reported 57 ships with him. That would give
them 146 ships to hold off the Human fleet, until Ramgen or
Voxx could get there.

Captain Helbum smiled a chilling smile. *It looks like we will get to
kill some Humans after all.*

Chapter Twenty-Two

High Princess Layla and her husband, Fleet Admiral Derrick Masters, were headed to a meeting with the Imperial Council. Admiral Marloo had informed them that he had some news of the fleets in the Confederation.

They both walked quickly, with excited anticipation. "What do you think the news will be?" Layla asked.

"I'm not sure. His voice sounded upbeat, so I am taking that as a good sign," replied Derrick.

They slowed down, as they reached the door to the Imperial Council Chamber. They glanced at one another, and then one of the guards opened the door. The room was already packed with the rest of the council.

Layla and Derrick quickly greeted everyone and took their places at the table. They then looked to Chief Chancellor Stein.

"Good morning, everyone, and thank you all for coming so quickly to this emergency meeting. Admiral Marloo has an update for us on what is going on in the Confederation," said Stein, as he looked around the table.

Admiral Marloo stood and said, "Thank you, Chief Chancellor Stein. I have received an encrypted communication from one of the scout ships. The news is good. Planets Lamothia and Druin Nine have both been destroyed. There were minimal losses to Barnes's fleet. Collison and Carrie have been busy destroying thirteen shipyards so far in the Morag-controlled area of the Confederation, also decimating any warships in the star systems that they targeted.

"To date, none of our three fleets have had a run-in with the larger Lamothian, Druin, or Morag fleets. Although we can be sure, all of these enemy fleets are doing all they can to hunt down ours. We have also learned that the Lamothians on Xanther have still carried out their feasts, which unfortunately included Humans."

A collective gasp came from everyone as they deciphered the true meaning of his words. "What will we do to the Lamothians now?" asked Governor Littrel of Jalot Four.

All gazes turned to High Princess Layla. She stood and said, "We warned them what would happen if they continued using even one Human in their feasts. They defied us and did it anyway. We must follow through with our threat to annihilate them from every planet and every star system."

Heads nodded all around the table. Admiral Marloo stood and said, "I am not sure Collison, Carrie, and Barnes will have big-enough fleets left to take on the full Lamothian fleet. In order to do what you want, we would need to send more ships to the Confederation."

"How large do we believe the Lamothian fleet is?" asked Governor Therron of Bratol Three.

"We had a scout ship monitoring them for a time. At last count, the Lamothians had 1,257 ships. There's also the possibility that the Druins, Zynth, or Morag fleets might come to their aid as well," replied Marloo.

"In which case, we could quickly be outnumbered," replied Derrick. "It is also a possibility that their allies would stay out of the fight. They might see it as a losing battle. They might not want to risk their fleets being destroyed or losing what numbers they have left."

"That's some big *ifs*," said Littrel.

"Do we know how much of Third Fleet, Fourth Fleet, and Eighth Fleet are still battle-ready?" asked Therron.

"According to the scout ship, Third Fleet has a little more than 750 battlecruisers and dreadnoughts. Plus the 23 battlecarriers. It is unknown how many attack interceptors are left with that fleet," responded Marloo.

"Still a sizable fleet then," remarked Therron.

"As for Fourth and Eighth Fleets, they have approximately 550 battlecruisers and dreadnoughts left, with 32 battlecarriers.

The scout ship's message indicates 3 battlecarriers were sent back to the supply fleet to reload with attack interceptors. The specific number of attack interceptors remaining with those fleets are also unknown," said Marloo.

"If we sent a large fleet from here, that would leave the Empire more vulnerable. The other Confederation races might take that opportunity to attack us," said Littrel.

Silence filled the room, as they all quietly considered their options. "How long would it take a fleet to reach Xanther from here?" asked Therron.

"It would take us a good week," replied Marloo. "By that time, the fleets in the Confederation might be finished with their attacks."

"How is our shipbuilding coming along? How many ships do we have now? We don't want to jeopardize our fleet numbers on something that could wait a little while. We know the Morag will build up their fleets to come back to the Empire to destroy us. I agree that we do need to follow through on our promise to annihilate the Lamothians from the Confederation, but maybe it's something that has to wait—at least until we have our fleets large enough to defend the Empire as well as our allies. Then we will punish the Lamothians," Chief Chancellor Stein said. "All in due time."

"Derrick, what's the status on our fleet numbers?" asked Layla.

Derrick stood and said, "First Fleet is now up to 1,036 battlecruisers and 123 dreadnoughts. We have added more battlecarriers to their fleet with a full contingent of attack interceptors. Each battlecarrier can hold 60 attack interceptors. So First Fleet has a total of 10 battlecarriers and 1,600 attack interceptors. As we finish more and more battlecarriers, they will be distributed throughout the fleets."

As Derrick continued his update on the fleets, an idea struck him. He would have to discuss it with Marloo later. "We are currently training attack interceptor crews for the new ones we are building. Major Mathew Barkley is in charge of training the new crews. He reports that the training is going very well."

Derrick stopped and took a quick sip of his water. All of this talking was making him thirsty. "Fifth Fleet has 742 battlecruisers and 98 dreadnoughts, plus 4 battlecarriers have joined that fleet, with its 240 attack interceptors onboard. So Fifth Fleet has a total of 11 battlecarriers and 1,760 attack interceptors."

Derrick continued. "We are also increasing the size of Eighth Fleet, even though the main part of this fleet is with Rear Admiral Carrie in the Confederation. We want her to have a large fleet waiting on her, when she returns from her successful mission to the Confederation. The numbers I will give you here for this fleet do not include what Carrie has with her in the Confederation. We have 40 battlecruisers and 15 dreadnoughts and currently 2 battlecarriers with a total of 320 attack interceptors.

"Ideally we would like to resupply Collison and Barnes as well, but first we have to build up our own fleets. What they are doing in the Confederation will buy us some extra time. Hopefully it will be enough."

As Derrick started back to his seat, he decided to voice his idea. "I do believe the Lamothians' actions require an immediate response, so that the Empire's word remains strong and true. And, if there were a way to keep the fighting in the Confederation, it would keep the Empire safer—if we could do it without putting our planets at risk." He felt better now that he had voiced his idea, although he knew Layla wouldn't like the idea of him going to fight in Confederation space.

"We know the Druins have fleets of at least 2,000 ships," Marloo added. "The Morag have over 10,000 at last count. The Lamothians have a little more than 1,200, as mentioned earlier, and we are not sure about the Zynth. At last count, they were down to just under 2,000. I don't think we are ready to take the battle to the Confederation. If we met up with one of the large Morag fleets, it would be devastating, even with our current superior firepower. Now maybe, once we have our new weapon ready, the atomic disrupter, we would have the firepower to annihilate a huge fleet, such as the Morag have. I do think we could go toe-to-toe with the other Confederation races though," said Marloo.

"I guess the question remains," commented Therron, "do we have enough ships to send to the Confederation? If we do this, it must be soon. If the fleets could regroup at the supply fleet and then attack the Lamothians, we might have the numbers to destroy them and to take them out of the numbers the Confederation has."

Everyone on the Imperial Council turned to Layla, Derrick, and Marloo. Derrick said, "I don't think the Morag will attack us here while we have ships in their star systems attacking them. They won't risk leaving Morag Prime vulnerable. The Lamothians and Druins are on guard for our fleets as well. So, the only wild card we have to worry about right now is the Zynth. Do we have enough ships left here to defend against them? I think all the other races of the Confederation have their hands full right now."

Layla was quiet, as she thought over all of what had been said. She didn't want Derrick going to the Confederation. She did want the Lamothians to pay for what they had done. She also didn't want to risk leaving the Empire under-protected. "If we send a fleet from here now, don't we risk missing the three Human fleets there, if they decide to return? Then the fleet we are sending wouldn't be large enough to overtake the Lamothians."

"What if we send more of First Fleet, since they are closer?" asked Derrick. "We can send an encrypted message to the scout ship on the Confederation's periphery, and they can get word to the supply fleet. Then we can send part of Fifth Fleet and the small part of Eighth Fleet to beef up the First Fleet that remains in the Hagen Star Cluster.

"Meanwhile we will continue making more and more ships that can add to the protection of Golan Four and our core worlds. We also need some of those scout ships to be watching and following these Confederation fleets. Then we will have a heads-up if the enemy fleets head this direction and can then recall our fleets in the Confederation," said Derrick.

He turned to look at Marloo. "Plus, as long as we are holding meetings for the House of Worlds, the Visth and their allies will remain here as well. Their fleets aren't far from here."

Marloo raised an eyebrow, as he thought over what Derrick had said. "I hadn't thought about the Visth and the United Worlds Alliance having their fleets nearby. That does offer us more protection. What if the meetings end before our fleets return? Or what if our fleets do not return? Does that leave us vulnerable?"

"Yes, it would. However, I think this is a gamble we must take. The opportunity is there. We have the fleets available. Cleemorl is already in the Confederation to lead this fleet," said Layla.

Andrew added, "Also note that Kala's father is on his way here from Earth, with a contingent of battleships escorting him. They are meant to help replace losses from the fleets attacking the Confederation. I believe there are 200 battlecruisers, 65 dreadnoughts, and 5 battlecarriers," said Andrew.

"This is not a decision made lightly. It is also not my decision to make. We are a council, and we will vote on it. All in favor, raise your hand," Layla said, as she looked around the room.

Derrick raised his hand alongside Layla's; then everyone's hand joined in the vote. At last, Marloo said, "With the Visth here, we have a hedge of added protection. We should use that to our advantage while we can."

"Should we discuss the situation with them? Or leave it a secret until it matters?" asked Littrel.

"We wait and see. The meetings of the House of Worlds will last another few days. Then we will have a big reception to celebrate the closing of this session. We can then ask the Visth and their alliance to stay and to discuss what they've learned and what they need from us," Layla said, as she turned to Prince

Andrew. "Andrew, didn't the Visth still want something from us?"

"Yes, they were hoping to get some ODPs. Stralon Karn has already asked me about them," replied Andrew.

"Then let's get them for him. Even though they might have to stay another week or so after the House of Worlds session is over, for us to finish building them," Layla said, with a sly smile on her face.

"Looks like we have a plan," said Marloo. "How many ships do we send to the Confederation?"

"First Fleet had more than 1,000 battlecruisers now and over 120 dreadnoughts. Let's send 600 battlecruisers and 75 dreadnoughts. Also send 2 battlecarriers currently with First Fleet and the attack interceptors that they house. We will immediately reposition some of our fleets here to supplement the Hagen Star Cluster. We can say First Fleet is headed to do some training drills, if anyone asks," said Derrick.

"We will send Rear Admiral Fulmar with this fleet to meet up with Cleemorl at the supply fleet. We need to get the ball rolling quickly on this. Time is of the essence," said Marloo.

"In that case, meeting adjourned," said Chief Chancellor Stein.

"Derrick, come with me to the Command Center to set this plan in motion," Marloo said.

Derrick leaned over to Layla and said, "Sounds like it might be a long night." Then to Marloo, he said, "I'm right behind you."

Marloo and Derrick had everything organized and implemented pretty quickly. When Layla came to check on them after dinner, they were just finishing up. "How is everything going?" Layla asked.

"First Fleet will head to the Confederation in the next two hours. We've already informed the part of Fifth Fleet and the part of Eighth Fleet that are here to head to the Hagen Star Cluster to supplement what will remain of First Fleet. They will leave here in about two hours as well," said Derrick.

Marloo added, "We've also sent an encrypted message to the scout ship stationed at the edge of the Confederation. They will send the encrypted message on to another scout ship and then to Admiral Cleemorl. Hopefully everything will work out according to plan."

"I feel like we've done the right thing," Layla said reassuringly. She was so relieved that it wouldn't be Derrick leading this fleet of ships to the Confederation.

"Yes, I agree," said Derrick. He smiled at Layla. He knew she was glad he wouldn't be the one going to the Confederation. "Let's call it a night. Not much left we can do from here."

-

"Good night," Marloo said to Layla and Derrick, as they headed out of the Command Center. Marloo hoped things would work out as planned. Otherwise they may be in a world of hurt.

-

Admiral Cleemorl was examining the work done on a dreadnought in one of the mobile repair yards. The ships were being repaired reasonably quickly. He must let Fleet Admiral Marloo know that they needed to build a few of these mobile repair yards for their fleets for when they came to the Confederation. Otherwise repairs would be pretty far away.

With the mobile repair yards here, they could repair the ships and then have them battle-ready again, without returning to the Empire for supplies or repairs. They could sustain an extended mission, assuming the enemy didn't locate them. With that thought, Cleemorl decided he better start looking at alternative locations for the fleets to rendezvous, in case this location was compromised.

They should offer something to the Lormallians in return for their silence. They had thus far not reported that the Human fleet was on the periphery of one of their star systems. He should send some representatives over to speak to the Lormallians and to possibly negotiate some trade with them. That would further incentivize them to stay quiet about their presence.

He wished he had brought someone who was gifted at diplomatic relations, but, in all reality, it probably fell to him. He would need to organize this rather quickly, before the fleets terrorizing the Morag returned.

As he walked around the mobile repair yard, he felt encouraged. The Earth Humans had come a long way in terms of technology. He was thankful the Human Empire had the Earth Humans as allies. They were all in this together. More than ever, Cleemorl was glad he came to aid the fleets here in the Confederation.

As he finished up his tour, one of the officers approached him. "Admiral Cleemorl, you have received a message from Colonel Bidwell. He received an encrypted message from the Empire. He requests your presence back on your flagship immediately," said Lieutenant Brown.

"Please send Colonel Bidwell a message that I will be back on the *Themis* shortly." He wondered what was going on. He shuddered, as all the possibilities ran through his head. Was it Cheryl? Was something wrong with her? Was the Empire being attacked? He quickly made his way back to his flagship.

Once on board, he kept his face hard as iron. He wanted to be prepared for the bad news. It had to be bad, and he had that terrible feeling in the pit of his stomach. He didn't want his crew to see him falter. "What does the message say?"

"The Empire is sending part of First Fleet here to the Confederation to beef up the fleets here. They want us to destroy the Lamothians for not heeding High Princess Layla's words," replied Bidwell.

Cleemorl felt a rush of relief run over him. This was great news. "How many ships are they sending?" he asked.

"They are sending Rear Admiral Fulmar with six hundred battlecruisers and seventy-five dreadnoughts. Plus two battlecarriers loaded with attack interceptors," responded Bidwell.

"Won't that leave the Hagen Star Cluster vulnerable to attack?" Cleemorl asked hesitantly.

"He said they are redistributing the other fleets to pick up the slack. They said no need to worry," replied Bidwell.

"Well, when shall we expect them?" Cleemorl asked.

"The ships will be here in about five days," said Bidwell. "Our orders are to wipe out all Lamothian planets and their fleets."

"Sounds like we have some planning to do, Captain." Cleemorl pulled up the holographic display and began to analyze the Lamothian area of the Confederation. He had a lot of things to decide in the next five days. "We need scout ships in that area of the Confederation. We need to know what we are up against."

"I will get them headed there now," replied Bidwell.

As Cleemorl looked at the number of ships he had available, he smiled to himself. Even if Collison, Barnes, and Carrie weren't back yet, Cleemorl and Fulmar would still have a good number of ships to take to destroy the Lamothians. If they also took the three battlecarriers here and the ships that had already been repaired in addition to what was coming, it would be a good-size fleet.

Plus they had another five days to make more repairs and to get more ships battle-ready. He didn't want to take all the available ships though. They may be needed here, if the other fleets are pursued. Maybe they would hear something from Collison, Barnes, and Carrie soon.

He also needed to arrange for a diplomatic mission to visit with Lormallian Councilor Ardon Reull. Cleemorl's to-do list just grew. He smiled to himself. This was an excellent day for the Empire. He would send a message to the Lormallians to arrange a time to meet with Reull. It would probably be a good idea to inform him that more ships were coming. Cleemorl didn't want them to be alarmed or to feel threatened by the Humans in any way. That would not be beneficial to their alliance at all.

Lormallian Councilor Ardon Reull was meeting with his admirals when his assistant, Barlten Aveth, interrupted to deliver a message to him. He leaned over to him and said, "We have received a message from Admiral Cleemorl of the Human Empire, requesting a meeting with you. He is with the latest fleet that arrived a few days ago from the Empire."

"This is good news. When would he like to meet? Does this message say anything about what he would like to discuss at this meeting?" asked Ardon.

"It said he would like to meet at the most convenient time for you but also said he would like it to be as soon as possible," replied Barlten.

"Great. Let's set up the meeting for this afternoon then. I would invite him for dinner. However, I am not sure what to serve a Human to eat. So, let's avoid anytime where it would be expected of us to serve him refreshments or snacks. No need to risk offending him and jeopardize our alliance," responded Ardon.

"I will respond to the message immediately and then get everything set up for your meeting with the Human Admiral," said Barlten.

As Barlten left the room, the discussion shifted to why the Human Admiral might want to have this meeting. Lormallian Admiral Garr spoke his thoughts first, "Maybe they are in need of assistance in some manner. They may need some supplies for their fleet stationed at the edge of our star system."

"They could need our help defending them against the other races of the Confederation. Wasn't that one of the scenarios we were concerned would occur?" asked Admiral Keld.

"Yes, it could be any of those things. I would think that if their fleets were being pursued by any race of the Confederation, we

would have heard about it already. The Confederation race would
be asking for our assistance," replied Ardon.

"You believe the Morag would ask for our assistance in
pursuing the Humans?" asked Admiral Zador.

"When you say it that way, it does sound a little illogical. That
could be why the Human admiral wants to meet quickly. To ask
our assistance in fighting off the Morag or the Druins," said
Ardon.

"What will you say? If that is what he is asking of us," asked
Admiral Garr.

"That is a good question. I would need to discuss it with the
Ruling Triad before I gave an answer. That would buy us a little
time to determine our course of action," replied Ardon.
"Speaking of the Triad, I need to inform them of this meeting
with the Human admiral. They may want to meet with him
themselves. Or they may prefer to wait until after I have
determined the reason for this meeting."

"Good luck. Please keep us informed as to how the meeting
plays out," requested Admiral Keld.

"I will. Why don't we plan to meet this evening to discuss the
meeting and to delve into our strategy?" asked Ardon. The
admirals agreed to meet with Ardon later in the day.

Now to inform the Ruling Triad, Ardon thought to himself.

-

After informing the Triad of the impending meeting with the
Human admiral, Ardon busied himself with the preparations for
that meeting. He wanted to make sure everything was set, just as
it should be.

Time went by quickly, and, before he realized it, the time had
come for the meeting. He waited for the Human admiral to arrive.

-

Admiral Cleemorl was just landing on the Lormallian
homeworld of Lormallia. It was a rather beautiful planet.
Cleemorl wore a translator device that would allow him to more

easily communicate with Councilor Reull. Cleemorl didn't want to take the chance that something would get misunderstood. Things could get bad pretty quickly for them if things were miscommunicated.

He was escorted into a beautiful building that had lots of detailed architecture. The building looked very old but very well kept. He had brought with him a few Marines who were on board his flagship. He didn't want to seem paranoid but didn't want to take any chances either.

After walking down a large hallway and through a courtyard area, he was escorted into a conference room. Inside was Councilor Ardon Reull. Cleemorl had heard a little about him from Prince Andrew. He had met with Ardon not too long ago to discuss their alliance, where Ardon had passed on weapons technology that the Empire was currently developing into a workable weapon. This weapon would be the one that would end the war.

"Good afternoon, Councilor Reull. It is an honor to meet you. I have heard great things about you from Prince Andrew, as well as Visth Representative Karn," Cleemorl said, as he entered the room.

Ardon motioned for him to have a seat at the table. "We would like to officially welcome you to Lormallia, Admiral Cleemorl. We hope that you will enjoy your time here," Ardon said, as he sat down himself.

"I am sure you are wondering why I requested this meeting. I would like to discuss a few matters with you. First, we truly appreciate you allowing our fleets to station on the edge of your star system. It has been a safe haven for us, and we will not forget it. Second, we would like to update you on what we are doing here. I am sure you are already aware that our fleets have destroyed Lamothia as well as Druin Nine. We also have a fleet destroying shipyards in the Morag-controlled star systems." When Cleemorl said they were destroying Morag shipyards, he noticed Ardon smile.

"That is great news, Admiral Cleemorl. The Morag have such a large fleet. Larger than any of the other races of the Confederation were aware of. They have kept lots of secrets from us over the years. Not to mention their telepathic abilities that they used to control us for so long. It is good to know that the Morag are being attacked," Ardon replied. "This will slow their battlecruiser- and battleship-making abilities, which is good for us all."

"Yes, that is the intention. We know we cannot win in a fleet-to-fleet battle at this time. The Morag fleet is too large. If we can slow down their ability to make more ships as quickly, that gives us time to build up our own defenses and fleets as well. This also allows others, not only ourselves, to do the same," replied Cleemorl.

"That is something we are grateful for. We are on the same side of this war. We know that eventually the Morag will come for us. We are currently doing the same thing as the Human Empire, building up our defenses and our fleets. We still won't be large enough to take on the Morag alone," said Reull.

"Our scientists are still working on that information you gave to Prince Andrew at your last meeting. We truly appreciate that data. We hope it will be the push that will tip us over the mountain, the turning point that will finally allow us to defeat the Morag," commented Cleemorl.

"How many shipyards have your fleets been able to destroy?" asked Reull.

"Our information is dated, coming from ships to be repaired from these battles. You are aware of how long it takes to get from the Morag area of the Confederation back to here. So, per the last ships to arrive here for repairs, we had destroyed thirteen Morag shipyards. We would like to get a lot more than that, but that all depends on how long our fleets can keep dodging the large Morag fleets."

"So your fleets have not run into the Morag fleets yet?" Reull asked, with a bit of relief in his voice.

"No, they have not. Only small patrolling fleets that weren't very large. We are not communicating directly with our fleets in an overabundance of caution. We do not want the Morag intercepting our messages and figuring out where our fleets are or where we are," Cleemorl remarked.

"That is a smart plan. It is better the Morag never know where you were staging from. I fear that would bring their wrath upon my race even faster," replied Ardon.

"We are aware of that possibility. Unfortunately we are located too far away to be of much assistance if and when the Morag did attack. The hope is that we will destroy them before they turn their wrath upon anyone else."

"So, what is it that we can do for you now?" asked Reull.

"I was hoping to begin trading with you. We do not currently need anything for our fleets or our supply fleet. I thought it might be beneficial to start a trade agreement, while our fleets were here in the Confederation. With us nearby, our trading vessels would feel much more comfortable. Would it be possible for you to get a list of goods you would like to trade with the Empire?"

"That would be wonderful. Such a great idea to start, while your fleets are here. I will get a committee formed immediately to begin working on your request. Is there anything else we can do for you?" asked Reull.

"One last thing," Cleemorl said, with a pause. "We have more ships coming from the Empire. High Princess Layla and our Imperial Council will immediately follow through on their threat to the Lamothians, since they went ahead with their feast and used Humans as a part of those celebrations. Thus, we have no other choice but to act swiftly. The Empire is sending more of my fleet here to get that job done. We did not want you to feel threatened in any way, when more battleships appear. We are in no way here to harm or to threaten you or your people. Our problems lie with the Morag, Druins, Lamothians, and the Zynth. Not with the Lormallians," said Cleemorl.

Reull was quiet for a moment before he said, "Thank you for letting us know the situation, Admiral Cleemorl. We appreciate your honesty. We will continue to keep our fleets on the other side of the star system. Please let me know if we can do anything else for you."

"Yes, I will. Thank you for meeting with me today and taking time out of your day. I am sure you are very busy," Cleemorl said, as he stood to go.

Reull walked with Cleemorl out to his transport ship. Cleemorl was very satisfied with how the meeting had gone. Now he had to plan for the destruction of the Lamothians.

Chapter Twenty-Three

Morag Captain Lenot smiled, as the Human battleships exited hyperspace in the star system which held Morag Five. He quickly informed all other Morag fleets in the area of the location of the Humans. This would be so easy now that they knew where the Humans currently were. He and his small fleet of fifty-seven battlecruisers would exit hyperspace in roughly twenty minutes. Hopefully the fifty-eight ships already patrolling that star system could keep the Human fleet occupied long enough for them to get there.

He checked in with Admiral Voxx first. *How quickly can you get here?* asked Lenot.

I have my fleet split into three task groups of about eight hundred ships. The one closest to you will arrive in the yellow dwarf system in approximately forty minutes, replied Voxx.

We will do our best to keep the enemy fleet engaged until your fleet arrives, said Lenot. He then reached out to Admiral Ramgen. *How far away is your fleet from the star system the Humans have selected as their next target?* asked Lenot.

We are still ninety minutes out. We are pushing our hyperdrives to the limits. Voxx and his fleet will assist you in destroying these Humans in our Confederation. Whatever you do, you must keep one ship safe to follow them, if Voxx doesn't appear in time, commanded Ramgen.

I will hold back a couple ships at the periphery of the system. They will follow the Human fleet, if the rest of us are destroyed, said Lenot.

Captain Helbum is also en route to your destination. He should arrive shortly after you do. He has with him thirty-one battlecruisers, said Ramgen.

That is good news. We will certainly hold the Human fleet there until Voxx's fleet arrives, Lenot said firmly.

-

Admiral Collison was moments away from exiting hyperspace in the yellow dwarf star system that held Morag Five. With the group of Morag ships tailing his fleet, he knew he wouldn't have

long to destroy the three shipyards in this star system. He had
discussed his strategy already with Rear Admiral Carrie as well as
Captain Drake. They would again stay out of range of the
defensive grids of Morag Five.

With three primary targets to destroy, they would each have
their hands full. The scout ships had previously reported 58
Morag battlecruisers patrolling this system. When adding in the
57 Morag ships tracking them, Collison's combined fleet would
have 115 enemy battlecruisers to destroy and the three shipyards.

The fleet was already at Condition One and had begun to drop
from hyperspace. They had planned to drop out as close as
possible to their targets. After a quick scan of the star system, they
found that the fleet was stationed above Morag Five with the two
shipyards orbiting it. Admiral Collison would take a task group of
ships to destroy the fleet, while Captain Drake went around to
the other side with a group of battlecarriers and launch the attack
interceptors to destroy the two orbiting shipyards around the
planet.

Rear Admiral Carrie would take a task group of ships to
destroy the shipyard that orbited the terraformed moon. Her
battlecarriers would launch the attack interceptors to demolish
the shipyard, while she defended the carriers.

It was a great plan, as long as it was executed quickly. They all
knew that multiple enemy fleets were inbound to their location.
The quicker they could get in and out of this star system, the
better. Leave no enemy ship intact that could track them into
hyperspace—that was the secondary goal, after the primary goal
of the destruction of the shipyards had been completed.

Admiral Collison and his group of two hundred battlecruisers
and fifty dreadnoughts dropped out close to Morag Five. The
fifty-eight battlecruisers patrolling the area immediately fired on
his fleet.

"Captain Billingsly, lock on to a target and launch our
accelerator cannon fire!" Collison commanded. He was on the

edge of his command chair, gazing intently at the tactical display in front of him. If he could get off a few rounds of accelerator cannon fire before the enemy fleet tracking him came in, then Collison had a higher chance of destroying all enemy ships quickly, with minimal loss to his fleet.

As the space between the fleets lit up with streaks of light from the launched attacks, the Morag's fusion energy beam fire reached Collison's front line. The beams looked like branches of lightning, as they hit the energy shields and quickly searched for any weaknesses. Only a few were found, and then as the energy shield was overloaded, the antimatter missiles arrived to finish the job. The space around the fleet was lit up with big fireballs, as the ships were blown apart.

The accelerator cannon fire reached the Morag fleet and swiftly annihilated the energy shields; then the second round arrived and blew the ships into oblivion. Soon space was littered with millions of pieces of debris from what once was the Morag fleet.

A few more Human ships were blown apart before the rest of the Morag fleet was decimated. As Collison and his part of the fleet turned to face the impending arrival of the trailing fleet, the Morag began to emerge from hyperspace and immediately fired all their weapons.

Collison's flagship, *Mercury*, shook, as the ships around them were demolished. Space was ignited with the light from the firepower released by both of the fleets.

"Captain Billingsly, how are our shields holding up?" asked Collison.

"So far, holding at 90 percent, Admiral," replied Billingsly.

"Not too bad. Let's finish them off, before we lose any more ships." He knew that all the debris floating about was not only that of the enemy but of his fleet as well. Always sacrifice was a part of war, but Collison had no plans to sacrifice any more than he had to.

The accelerator cannons were absolutely remarkable in their effectiveness. With the ability to launch two projectiles from the two cannons affixed to each ship and to launch the projectiles every thirty seconds, the enemy didn't stand a chance. The Morag shields were destroyed as easily as slicing through butter with a knife. Now, if only they could destroy the shipyards before any other fleets arrived.

Simultaneously, as Collison and Captain Drake were in the midst of their own battles, Rear Admiral Carrie arrived within firing range of the shipyard in orbit around the moon. The battlecruisers and dreadnoughts entrusted to her were in a defensive formation in between the shipyard and her battlecarriers, as they launched their attack interceptors.

The battlecarriers immediately launched the attack interceptors. Carrie and her task group launched a round of accelerator cannon fire at the shipyard, which had begun launching its fusion energy beam fire and antimatter missiles at her fleet. If she could destroy the firepower the shipyard possessed, it would make the jobs of the attack interceptors that much easier and quicker. Plus they would lose a lot less of them. They could do some repairs of the interceptors in their battlecarriers, but way out here in the Morag area of the Confederation, they were not easy to replace.

With Admiral Collison engaged in a fleet battle with the Morag fleet patrolling the system, it left her with only the shipyard to contend with. The space station that orbited the moon was armed and had an energy shield, but it was not within range. One less thing for her to worry about.

Carrie focused her attention on the weapons the shipyard launched at her fleet. The space around the moon lit up brightly, with all the intense weapons fire launched. As the accelerator cannon fire reached the weapons turrets of the shipyard, it quickly battered down the shield and pummeled the weapons turrets. As the next round hit their marks, the turrets were turned into unrecognizable twisted melted wreckage.

Now that the fusion energy beams were out of commission, she turned her focus to the antimatter missile tubes toward the center of the shipyard. Carrie had her fleet target that portion of the shipyard. The Morag were launching their antimatter missiles as quickly as they could. A full barrage of antimatter missiles bombarded her fleet. As missile after missile battered down the energy shields of multiple battlecruisers, their shields glowed brighter and brighter before overloading completely. They were then slammed with antimatter missiles, resulting in brilliant flashes of heat and light, which completely consumed the vessels. Battlecruisers simply vanished from her tactical display right before her eyes.

As the attack interceptors swarmed toward the shipyard, the accelerator cannon fire obliterated the antimatter missile tubes, rendering the shipyard utterly defenseless.

The attack interceptors flew in and locked their targets on what was left of the shipyard. They launched their four fusion-tipped missiles and then immediately returned to their battlecarriers. As they did, space was alight with brilliant explosions, as the shipyard was blown into one million pieces of flaming debris. The debris was pulled toward the terraformed moon and soon lit up the moon's artificial atmosphere, like fireflies at dusk. Most of the pieces were destroyed before they could hit the surface.

As the attack interceptors landed in their designated bays, alarms sounded on Carrie's tactical display. "What do we have now, Major Sullivan?" Carrie asked, a sense of foreboding creeping up her spine.

"The Morag battlecruisers that were tailing us have arrived. Admiral Collison is firing on them now," replied Sullivan.

"What about Captain Drake? Has he destroyed the other two shipyards? Or shall we go aid his efforts?" Carrie asked. She was a little surprised Collison had sent her to destroy the one shipyard that orbited the moon while he had decided to send Captain

Drake to destroy the two that orbited the planet. However, there was no better proving ground for an up-and-coming captain on his way to rear admiral than in the thick of battle in the middle of a hostile star system. Not to mention he had plenty of help at the push of a button, if he needed it.

"It looks like he has it under control," replied Sullivan.

"Good, let's jump over and relieve Collison then," Carrie said, as she sat down in her command chair. "Also get me a report of what we lost back there at the moon. I need to know what is still combat-capable for whatever comes next."

"Yes, right away," said Sullivan.

As the task group entered their short jump to aid Collison, Carrie breathed a sigh of relief. Things seemed to be in hand here. Now they could shortly move on to another Morag star system and annihilate more shipyards.

Carrie had her fleet drop out just on the left flank of the Morag fleet. She immediately launched a full broadside of accelerator cannon fire at the enemy ships. The ships were quickly wiped out of the system, as piles of molten wreckage and carnage floated toward the planet down below. Most would be destroyed by the defensive grid that protected the planet. The rest would likely burn up in the atmosphere. *That's too bad*, Carrie thought to herself.

Morag Admiral Lenot had commanded all his ships to fire as soon as they were in range. He needed to destroy as many enemy ships as possible.

He noticed that the Humans had split their fleet into three sections. He would focus on the largest of the fleet groups. It was the one closest to him. Sweat ran off his brow, as they fired their first round of fusion energy beams and antimatter missiles. The weapons fire slammed into the front line of the advancing Human fleet.

As the pressure on the energy shields increased, they failed and allowed in the antimatter missiles to demolish the ship. Battlecruisers were battered by numerous antimatter missiles. His large red eyes focused on the display in front of him, as one red threat icon after another disappeared from the display.

The Humans' accelerator cannon fire reached his fleet and quickly penetrated their energy shields. Lenot's eyes grew wide with the pure power the projectiles had. His flagship shook violently, knocking Admiral Lenot to the deck. He stood back up and gazed at the damage control console and all the glaring red lights now flashing.

He quickly gave orders again. One moment he was speaking, and, the next, a brilliant flash of light swept through the Command Center and blew it into oblivion. His fleet ceased to be.

As Admiral Collison handled the Morag fleet, Captain Drake and his task group descended upon the shipyards. The 108 battlecruisers and 30 dreadnoughts lined up in a globe formation to protect the 20 battlecarriers. The ships immediately fired at the closest shipyard, as the attack interceptors launched from their battlecarriers. The shipyards had their energy shields up and began firing their fusion energy beams and antimatter missiles at the fleet as soon as they arrived in the immediate vicinity of the shipyard. The antimatter missiles and fusion energy beams rapidly tore a half-dozen battlecruisers into flaming debris.

The accelerator cannon fire pulverized the shipyard's energy shield, and then the fleet focused its fire on the weapons turrets. Once one was destroyed, they all focused their fire on the next and the next, until the shipyard was defenseless to the oncoming attack from the interceptors.

As the interceptors moved in to launch their fusion-tipped missiles at the defenseless shipyard, alarms sounded on the tactical display. "Report!" said Captain Drake.

"Morag ships emerging from hyperspace, Captain, the fleet that was tailing us through hyperspace. Admiral Collison has turned to fight them," replied Lieutenant Starr.

"Let's get this shipyard destroyed and move on to the next one. We need to be out of here before the larger fleets have a chance to get here," said Drake.

As his gaze shifted back to the attack interceptors, he saw hundreds of streaks moving through space toward the shipyard. The interceptors had already launched their missiles and were headed back to rearm, before they attacked the next shipyard.

Once all the interceptors were back on board their battlecarriers, they jumped to the location of the other shipyard that orbited the planet. It would take them ten minutes to rearm the attack interceptors. Drake was glad that the defensive grid was not in range of the shipyards. One less thing he had to worry about.

Intense weapons fire broke out, as they came in range of the shipyard. His fleet immediately opened fire and focused their accelerator cannon fire on the shipyard's energy shield. It was quickly battered down from the massive hail of projectiles launched at it.

Once the shield was down, they shifted their concentration to the weapons constantly launched from the shipyard. As the fusion energy beams struck Drake's fleet, the battlecruiser positioned close to him was torn apart and blown into a glowing pile of wreckage. Drake winced at the sheer amount of firepower coming from the shipyard. The shipyard was well-armed.

They again focused their fire on one weapon at a time. Once it was destroyed, the fleet shifted their attention to the next one. After they were all out of commission, the attack interceptors again swooped in to finish the job of turning the shipyard into a mass of glowing debris.

They then quickly flew back to their battlecarriers to rearm for the next attack.

"How are Collison and Carrie doing?" asked Drake.

"Carrie has destroyed her shipyard and has jumped over to help Collison finish off the Morag fleet that had tailed us," replied Starr.

"Looks like we will be headed out of here soon. What did we lose?" asked Drake.

"We lost sixteen battlecruisers and four dreadnoughts, Captain," replied Starr.

"Have any damaged ships begin repairs, as we wait for Collison to send us the command to enter hyperspace. It looks like he and Carrie have that Morag fleet well under hand," remarked Drake.

"We have two battlecruisers working on quick repairs," replied Starr.

"Scan the system to see if we are missing anything, while we wait," said Drake. They didn't need any surprises.

"Appears two Morag battlecruisers are hiding out in the periphery of the star system, Captain."

"Bring them up on the screen. They must be hiding so they can follow us to our next destination. Inform Collison we will go annihilate the threat," said Drake. "Have the ships working on repairs stay here until given the command to enter hyperspace from Collison."

The task group under his command then jumped to the periphery of the star system. Once in range, they quickly blew the two ships into oblivion. As Captain Drake sat back down in his command chair, alarms sounded.

-

Carrie was going over the reports of the ships they had lost when alarms sounded. Her heart skipped a beat, and sweat began to bead on her forehead. Her gaze shifted to the tactical display in front of her. Had the larger Morag fleets had enough time to get here?

"Major Sullivan, what do we have?" asked Carrie.

"Looks like a fleet of Morag ships is dropping from hyperspace," responded Sullivan.

"How many?" Carrie asked, as she tried to suppress the fear from her voice. She closed her eyes briefly and then reopened them to focus her gaze on the tactical display in front of her. She stood and braced herself for what was to come.

"Thirty-one battlecruisers," replied Sullivan. "No more have dropped out of hyperspace with them."

"Captain Drake has sent us a message that he has destroyed the two Morag ships hiding in the periphery of the star system and that he will deal with this small contingent of Morag battlecruisers," said the communications officer.

"Glad he scanned the system to search for any ships. They were probably lying in wait to follow us, when we jump to the next system." She realized that maybe Drake would make a good rear admiral someday.

While Drake took care of the newest enemy fleet, Carrie finished her review of the losses from the day's battles. They had lost a total of twenty-nine battlecruisers and five dreadnoughts. She sent her reports over to Collison. They were quickly running out of time; she felt the growing anticipation of meeting the larger Morag fleets. It was bound to happen eventually.

-

"Report!" Drake ordered. He felt the goose bumps rise on his arms. They weren't expecting any other fleets from neighboring star systems, which meant this had to be one of the larger Morag fleets. Just how many there would be, none of them knew.

"There are thirty-one battlecruisers, Captain. No more ships are dropping from hyperspace. That appears to be all of them."

"Let's jump in behind them and eliminate this threat. It should be reasonably easy. Their attention will be on Collison's and Carrie's fleets," remarked Drake.

The enemy ships did not seem to be in a hurry to engage the fleets. This made Drake uncomfortable. Why would they wait? The answer he came up with sent chills down his spine. "There must be more shortly behind them. They seem to be waiting for something."

"What should we do?" asked Lieutenant Starr.

"Let's engage them. We will destroy them before their help arrives, so then we can get out of here," replied Drake.

Drake and his task force quickly descended upon the fleet. Once they were in engagement range, they launched a full bombardment of their accelerator cannon fire. The battle grew in intensity, as the Morag ships turned and fired upon the fleet. Massive explosions of pure energy rocked the energy shields of Drake's task force. Several energy shields collapsed, allowing antimatter missiles to turn the ships into shattered pieces of molten metal.

The enemy fleet was quickly annihilated.

"How are Collison and Carrie doing?" asked Drake.

"They've just finished off the last ship," replied Starr.

As if right on cue, Collison ordered the fleet to enter hyperspace. "All ships immediately head to our next coordinates," he commanded on the comm.

"Let's get out of here!" said Drake.

As the fleet jumped out of the system, Captain Drake once again evaluated what he had lost. An additional eight battlecruisers and two dreadnoughts had been destroyed.

Part of Morag Admiral Voxx's fleet headed to the yellow dwarf system began emerging from hyperspace. The commander had the tactical officer quickly run scans of the system. It was apparent from what they saw that the Humans had already been here and had already left. Debris surrounded the planet, tangled messes of molten steel and glowing debris from what once had been shipyards and battlecruisers.

The space station had been left intact. From them, the commander could determine in which direction the enemy had headed when they left the system. They hadn't missed them by much. So close! The commander entered hyperspace in the same direction the Human fleet had headed. Hopefully he could determine where they were headed next.

Admiral Collison was going over his fleet losses from Morag Five. His task group had lost thirty-seven battlecruisers and six dreadnoughts. Altogether the combined fleet had lost ninety battlecruisers and seventeen dreadnoughts. He had sent five battlecruisers to the supply fleet to be repaired.

So now he was left with a combined fleet of 319 battlecruisers, 92 dreadnoughts, and his 32 battlecarriers. As far as the attack interceptors went, the losses were minimal, since Rear Admiral Carrie and Captain Drake had destroyed the weapons of the shipyards before the attack interceptors swooped in to finish the job of disintegrating the shipyards.

Collison stood and let out a deep breath. He was losing ships quickly, and, if they ran into the bigger Morag fleets, they'd be in a world of hurt. Should he keep attacking shipyards, or should he head back to regroup at the supply fleet?

He slowly walked around the holographic display. He was going over the success they had had so far in the destruction of shipyards. They were chipping away at the Morag fleet as a whole. Of course they were losing ships in every star system as well. So far, they had destroyed sixteen Morag shipyards.

Would that be enough to slow down the Morag's warship production so that the Empire and the Solar System could further build up their defenses and their fleets? Maybe he should hit one more star system that held a larger number of shipyards nearby and then hightail it out of here.

He studied the holographic display, his arms crossed and a thoughtful expression on his face. What was nearby that had enough shipyards to be of value? He had to also consider the good possibility that more and bigger Morag fleets would be in the vicinity, so it would need to be a quick hit-and-run, like they had managed at Morag Five.

Or maybe it made more sense to head in the opposite direction and then attack a star system farther away, which would likely put them out of reach of the larger Morag fleets. Collison needed a cup of coffee and a good meal, while he thought over these options. They were safe for now; as long as they were in hyperspace, no one could attack them.

Chapter Twenty-Four

Morag Admiral Voxx was not surprised that his fleet had missed the Humans. The other fleet of Humans would not be so lucky. Plus this fleet had no idea they were being followed. He knew the direction they had headed and couldn't be too far behind. They had no logical reason to change directions. He had their destination narrowed down to three star systems.

Now that the other Human fleet had just taken out all the shipyards in one of the three star systems, the possibilities had narrowed to two. He commanded the fleet that had arrived in the yellow dwarf system to wait there. It was likely the Humans weren't communicating between the two fleets, so there was a possibility this Human fleet could still end up there. If they did, they'd quickly realize they made a grave mistake.

As for Voxx and his part of the fleet, they were about thirty minutes from dropping out of hyperspace in the star system where he had reasoned the Human fleet he followed was headed. Meaning, Voxx estimated his fleet was about twenty-five to thirty minutes behind the Humans. This would not give them enough time to destroy the Morag fleet currently patrolling the system and all four shipyards located in the system.

A smile crossed his face, as he folded his arms across his chest. The time had come to wipe out these Humans trespassing in the Confederation.

—

Rear Admiral Barnes had her fleet at Condition Two. In a few moments, they would move to Condition One and then drop from hyperspace. She knew that the scout ships had observed forty-six Morag battlecruisers in this star system. The holographic display had been updated with the last information the scout ships had discovered.

This star system had four shipyards that she needed to destroy. Two were in orbit around the planet, Morag Seven. Then the two moons that orbited Morag Seven also each had a shipyard. She had planned and planned to decide upon her attack. Since she didn't know where the large Morag fleets were located, she knew she needed to get in and out as quickly as possible. The less time she was there, the less time the Morag had to descend upon her location.

With four targets to hit, her best plan of attack was to split her fleet into task groups. They needed to stay out of range of the defensive grid of the planet. All of the shipyards were heavily armed and protected by energy shields. Barnes knew they would take some losses, but hopefully they would be minimal, considering their superior firepower of the accelerator cannons.

As they neared the hyperspace drop-out point, she moved her fleet to Condition One. Soon after that, they emerged from hyperspace near Morag Seven. Immediately alarms sounded. "How many ships are we up against?" asked Barnes.

"Scans show forty-six Morag battlecruisers," replied Captain Borrel.

"Well, at least they haven't gotten any reinforcements since the scout ships scanned the system. Let's move forward with our original plan. We will take on the fleet, while the other task groups head for their designated targets," said Barnes.

As they approached the Morag fleet, the enemy transitioned into a wedge formation. "Prepare to fire as soon as we're in range," commanded Barnes. "The other task groups should not jump to their targets until we have engaged the enemy fleet."

The time seemed to slowly tick by, as they waited for those words to be said. After what seemed like an eternity had passed, Borrel finally said, "Engagement range, firing all weapons!"

Heavy weapons fire broke out between the two fleets. Antimatter and fusion explosions crawled over energy shields, releasing tremendous amounts of destructive energy. As a few shields were overloaded and failed, more antimatter missiles arrived and blew the ships apart, sending flaming debris in all directions.

The accelerator cannon fire rapidly reached the enemy fleet, smashing into energy shields and shattering them. As the second projectile reached its target, the ships were reduced to bright explosions of light and heat. In massive flashes of light, the enemy ships were destroyed one by one.

Once they had obliterated the enemy ships, Barnes moved on to the first shipyard that surrounded Morag Seven. All her remaining ships in her task force focused all their firepower on the shipyard. The energy shield of the shipyard shattered with the sheer force of the accelerator cannon fire. They then focused their firepower on the weapons that the shipyard possessed.

The shipyards continuously fired all their weapons at Barnes and her fleet. All around her, ships disappeared in brilliant flashes of light. As the accelerator cannon fire found their targets and obliterated them, the battlecarriers sent in the attack interceptors to finish off the now-defenseless shipyard.

Since no threat remained to the battlecarriers or to the attack interceptors, Barnes and the rest of her task group moved on to the second shipyard that orbited Morag Seven.

Captain Elliott on board the battlecarrier *Daneb* was with the task group attacking the shipyard that orbited the second moon of Morag Seven. Elliott watched as the task group focused its fire on the shipyard. Space was lit up with brilliant explosions, as the accelerator cannon fire disintegrated the energy shield that protected the shipyard. They then shifted their focus to the weapons of the shipyard.

The shipyard's massive amount of firepower was directed toward the ships in front of Elliott's. He watched as the heavy weapons fire battered down the energy shields of some of the battlecruisers. The shield started to fail in several areas, and an antimatter missile managed to slip through. The missile blew the ship in two, and a few seconds later, the fusion energy beams finished off the ships, leaving nothing behind but burning pieces of wreckage.

The battlecruisers and dreadnoughts in front of Captain Elliott protected his battlecarrier and the others from the firepower of the shipyard. Within a few minutes, which seemed much longer than it was, the shipyard was rendered defenseless. Elliott immediately then launched the attack interceptors to zoom in and to release their fusion-tipped missiles at the now-vulnerable prey.

Once the interceptors had launched their missiles, they returned to their battlecarriers to rearm for the next target. As they did, alarms sounded.

Captain Elliott shifted his attention from the returning interceptors to his tactical officer. "Report!" Elliott commanded.

"Captain, we have ships dropping from hyperspace. They appear to be Morag battlecruisers and battleships," replied the tactical officer.

"How many?' Elliott asked.

"They are still dropping out of hyperspace, but currently, they have over three hundred and still counting," replied the tactical officer.

"Let Rear Admiral Barnes know we have destroyed our target, but we are waiting for all the attack interceptors to finish docking, before we can jump into hyperspace," said Elliott.

"Message sent," said the communications officer.

Elliott sat back in his command chair. How big a fleet would this be?

Rear Admiral Barnes was in the heat of the battle with the second shipyard that orbited Morag Seven. The accelerator cannons blasted away at the shipyard's energy shield. As they smashed through the energy shield, they shifted their focus to the fusion energy beam cannons and antimatter missile tubes.

The shipyard fired as much as they could, blowing apart battlecruisers and dreadnoughts with their intense weapons fire. Many ships disappeared under the antimatter and fusion energy explosions, leaving little behind. As Barnes's fleet continued to focus their firepower on the shipyard's weapons, they were able to destroy them, leaving them vulnerable to attack.

The battlecarriers then quickly launched their attack interceptors to descend upon the shipyard and pulverize it, leaving only a field of glowing debris in their wake.

As the attack interceptors made their way back to the battlecarriers, an alarm sounded. Sweat broke out on Barnes's brow, and her heartbeat quickened. She took a deep breath to steady herself and said, "What do we have?"

"Ships dropping out of hyperspace," replied Captain Borrel.

"How many? Are they Morag?" asked Barnes.

"Yes, I am afraid they are Morag. Currently over three hundred ships and counting," replied Borrel.

Everyone in the room went silent for what seemed like several minutes. Then Barnes said, "Captain Borrel, find out if our two other task groups are finished destroying the shipyards, and how long until they can be ready to transition into hyperspace."

"Yes, Rear Admiral, right away," replied Captain Borrel.

As everyone waited for the update on the fleets' progress in destroying the shipyards, they all watched the tactical display in front of them that continued to fill with red threat icons.

"Both task groups report that the shipyards have been destroyed, but the attack interceptors are still returning to their battlecarriers," said Borrel.

"I need to know the second those interceptors are back on board. They also need to rearm them as quickly as possible. They might be needed again." Barnes knew that it would take them at least ten minutes to reload the attack interceptors. Hopefully it wouldn't take long for them to get back on board their battlecarriers. They might need to exit this star system sooner rather than later.

"They have stopped exiting hyperspace, Rear Admiral Barnes," said Borrel, as she cleared the lump in her throat. "There are 627 battlecruisers and 179 battleships."

"Let's send out a mayday in the off chance Admiral Collison is nearby. We do have them outnumbered, if we include out attack interceptors. We would take heavy losses if we engage them, but I am afraid that is our only course of action. If we jump into hyperspace, they will just follow us. We must stay and fight this enemy here and now.

"We need those attack interceptors rearmed and ready to obliterate any damaged ships once this battle commences. Inform both task groups to jump to our coordinates immediately to get into battle formation. Have the battlecarriers fall in behind the fleet and have their attack interceptors launched and ready to deploy at my command," ordered Barnes.

On the battlecarrier *Daneb*, Captain Elliott anxiously waited for the last attack interceptors to land in their landing bays, so he could jump in behind Rear Admiral Barnes and the assembling fleet. Their worst fears were coming true. They had run into one of the larger Morag fleets. Thankfully they had an edge on them with their attack interceptors, but he needed his crew to get them reloaded and relaunched as fast as they possibly could.

Captain Elliott gave the command to enter hyperspace as the last attack interceptor landed and was secured into its docking bay. It was just a quick jump to Rear Admiral Barnes's location.

When they arrived at the designated coordinates, Elliott saw on his tactical display that most of the fleet had reassembled, minus about ten battlecarriers. Hopefully they would get here soon. His crews worked hard to reload the attack interceptors, as they all knew the stakes were high. Their very futures could depend on how quickly they could get this job done.

"How far from engagement range is the Morag fleet?" asked Elliott.

"Six minutes, Captain," replied his tactical officer.

"We need to have our interceptors launching as soon as they are rearmed. Get them out there and formed into their squadrons. Their orders are to find and destroy any damaged enemy ships. Go in and finish the job, so the rest of the fleet can focus on the next target. With what we've lost in this star system already, they have us outnumbered in warships. Let's hope they don't have any of their small attack craft that counteracts our interceptors," said Elliott, as he stood and walked closer to the tactical display.

He was going over the numbers in his head and making plans for what the interceptors should do, how they should attack and from which directions. They had to be mindful to stay away from the planet's defensive grid. The Morag fleet would probably try to pin them in between the planet and the fleet. They needed to make sure they didn't lose any ground.

With the planet behind them, that did offer them a small hedge of protection. The enemy fleet wouldn't jump in behind them and attack. Now they could attack from one side or the other, just not from behind. No doubt they would focus their firepower on trying to destroy the battlecarriers, since that's where the attack interceptors would come from. It didn't feel good knowing they would be prime targets for the enemy, especially when that enemy was the Morag.

"Captain, we are launching the interceptors. As they finish reloading, we are getting them out to form into their squadrons. The crews are preparing to reload quickly, when they return for more weapons," said the tactical officer.

"Excellent. I want them to get in there and to find their targets quickly. They need to be mindful of the accelerator cannon fire. They will be in the middle of a battle zone. Weapons will be coming at them from all directions. They will need to fly better than they ever have before, if they want to survive this day and to live to tell their children and grandchildren about this day, the day we defeat the Morag in their own star systems!" Captain Elliott said, with a little more confidence than he actually felt. He swallowed the lump that had formed in his throat. His crew needed him at his finest.

As the interceptors launched and formed into their squadrons, the enemy fleet reached engagement range, and the battle began. Weapons fire between the two fleets became intense quickly. It was hard to say who was winning. Death and destruction were all around. Flaming debris and wreckage floated all around them. His attack interceptors flew in and wove around the wreckage and the weapons fire, as they flew their complicated attack patterns.

They flew back and forth, making them almost impossible for the Morag ships to hit without accidentally striking their own fleet. Captain Elliott smiled at the amazing maneuverability of the attack interceptors, and, so far, the Morag had not launched any countermeasures to the attack interceptors.

Rear Admiral Barnes was relieved that the attack interceptors were reloaded and joining the fight. At the moment, both fleets were slugging it out with heavy losses on both sides. As the accelerator cannon fire slammed into the front line of the advancing Morag fleet, it became a graveyard of dying ships, exploding in bright flashes of light and energy. Soon all that was left of the front line was a field of glowing debris where once a strong front line of enemy battlecruisers had been closing in on Barnes and her fleet.

She knew she had to hold the line. She could not let the Morag push her back up against the planet. If that happened, then the defensive grid of the planet would begin taking aim at the rear of her fleet, where the battlecarriers were staged for rearming the attack interceptors.

Barnes leaned forward in her command chair, as the attack interceptors flew in to destroy any damaged Morag ships. The rest of the fleet focused their firepower on the remainder of the Morag fleet advancing toward them. All across both fleets was widespread damage and destruction. Barnes knew that she would take heavy losses but still thought the battle would likely end in her favor. Unless, of course, another Morag fleet showed up to bolster the one already here.

Morag Admiral Voxx emerged from hyperspace in the star system with Morag Seven. Immediately alarms sounded. He had found them. His cold stare focused on the tactical display in front of him. It appeared that they were almost finished destroying the shipyards. There was no escaping him now though. Even if they entered hyperspace to escape him, he would follow.

Close in on the largest part of the fleet, the one by the planet, Voxx commanded. He would push them up against the defensive grid and annihilate them.

As they closed in on the Human fleet, they got in the attack position. He knew that this fleet had the smaller attack craft, and he had only a small group of the Interceptor Killers with his part of the fleet. He would deploy them once the Humans launched their small attack craft.

If he could pin them up against the planet's defensive grid, it could help them destroy the large battlecarriers that carried the small attack craft. If he could do that, the battle would be his. Without a place to reload, the small attack craft would quickly become useless to the Humans.

He had seen these Earth Humans and their new weapons. The Morag energy shields would be of little protection from them. This would be a fight to the death. Voxx would keep his ship toward the middle of the formation, more protected, and could then command the battle more efficiently, not having to worry about being blown away by the enemy.

These Earth Humans were a formidable foe. Much more intelligent than their counterparts from the Empire. The Morag would have already crushed the Empire, if not for these Earth Humans.

Five minutes to engagement range, Admiral, his tactical officer informed him.

Voxx sat back in his command chair. His cold eyes focused on the enemy in front of him. If he could destroy the ship that the commander of this fleet was in, it might cause enough confusion for the Morag to gain the edge they would need to win this battle. He sent commands to the ships in the front line to focus on the larger ships of the fleet. The commander must be on one of those ships. He would orchestrate the battle from the safety of the back of his formation.

As they closed in on the Human fleet, Voxx felt his blood in his veins pump faster. *It is time to kill some Humans,* he thought to himself, as he smiled a sinister smile. *Focus all fire on those larger Human ships, the dreadnoughts,* he commanded. *We must take down those first.*

The fleets entered the engagement range, and a massive wave of weapons fire was launched from each fleet. Space was alight with giant flashes of light and heat, as energy shields were overloaded and missiles found their vulnerable targets, blowing them into oblivion.

On the battlecarrier *Daneb*, Captain Elliott kept tabs on his attack interceptor squadrons. He knew that this battle would be a fierce one, and he would likely lose a large number of attack interceptors and their crews. His squadrons had already formed and were now in the midst of the Morag fleet taking out any damaged battlecruisers. Many pieces of flaming wreckage floated about that they must be mindful of, not to mention the continued weapons fire from both fleets. It was a dangerous day to be a crew member on an attack interceptor.

As Elliott monitored the ongoing battle, massive fireballs exploded in space, marking destroyed ships on both sides. The accelerator cannon fire ripped the front line of the Morag's fleet to shreds. More and more ships moved forward to fill their positions. The interceptors moved in and finished off any ships that needed a little help getting blown into oblivion.

Captain Elliott winced at the sheer volume of weapons fire hitting their fleet. Massive waves of antimatter missile fire crashed into the energy shields of several ships, quickly overloading them. Once their shields failed, then the ships were riddled with fusion energy beam fire, causing the ships to blow apart, ending the hopes and dreams of those onboard.

Lieutenant Burr was the leader of the Scorpion Squadron, stationed on the Battlecarrier *Daneb*. His squadron was currently headed straight into what looked to Burr like the entrance to hell. Explosions and wreckage were everywhere, and they had to rely on all their training to weave around the dangers and to find the ships they needed to target. He saw small explosions out of the corner of his eye that he knew marked the death of an attack interceptor.

Burr quickly found his first target, a Morag battleship that had been blown into two pieces. He targeted the first large portion of the ship and fired his fusion-tipped missile. Moments later, it exploded in a bright flash of light. As he targeted the other large piece of the ship, multiple threat icons showed up on his tactical display. He turned his interceptor around to follow this new threat and to figure out what it was.

As Burr maneuvered through the glowing wreckage of the once-large Morag fleet, he quickly discovered what the new threat icons were. Interceptor Killers. The Morag's answer to the attack interceptors.

From the looks of it, this Morag fleet had about fifty of them. He sent a message to his squadron to immediately hunt down this new threat. He soon had three squadrons, about sixty attack interceptors, on the hunt for these killers. They weren't hard to find; after all, they were also being hunted by them.

Soon they were using all their piloting skills to outmaneuver the small attack craft. With their superior numbers, it didn't take long to annihilate the new threat, but it did come at a great cost.

They seemed to lose about three attack interceptors to every one Interceptor Killer they destroyed. By the time they had hunted down all fifty, they had lost a little over 150 interceptors. The Scorpion Squadron was down three ships. That was nine of Burr's friends and crew who he would never see again.

Even though he wanted to hunt down some more Morag ships, he now had to head back to the battlecarrier and reload. This battle was moving quickly, and he wanted to get back out there, while he could still make a difference.

Voxx commanded his ships from the safety of the rear of the fleet, placing his commands in the minds of those he needed to. He was losing ships by the hundreds, but the Humans were too. By his estimate, the Humans were destroying more ships than the Morag were, but Voxx had a surprise in motion that these Earth Humans would soon discover. Admiral Ramgen and his fleet would soon be here to lend a hand in the extermination of this nuisance. They would crush them.

His eyes narrowed, as he stared at the display. Ramgen was just a few minutes from dropping out of hyperspace in this system. Voxx need only hold on until then. Ramgen's fleet was larger than the one Voxx had with him currently. His other two task groups were currently converging on this star system, but Ramgen would get here first. Within the next thirty minutes, over three thousand Morag ships would wipe out these Humans.

If they were lucky, the other Human fleet that had been terrorizing the Morag-controlled area of the Confederation would respond to this fleet's call for help. Then they could be done with this much sooner. Bring them all here, and then they wouldn't need to hunt them down.

As ships were dying and the space above Morag Seven turned into a debris field of tangled burning wreckage, alarms sounded. Voxx smiled. Yes, his help had arrived. Voxx reached out to the minds of the commanders who had just emerged from hyperspace but found nothing. He could not reach the minds of any of them. He leaned forward in his chair.

-

As Rear Admiral Barnes evaluated their next tactical move, alarms once again sounded. All gazes turned to the tactical display in front of them. Ships appeared on the display, as they dropped out of hyperspace. Silence filled the room, as they waited for the ships to turn red or green. They all held out hope that it would be Collison and Carrie coming to their aid but knew that, more than likely, it would be another Morag fleet coming to the aid of the one they currently engaged.

They didn't need more enemy ships to contend with.

With great relief and cheering, the icons turned green. Barnes felt a massive wave of relief wash over her. The relief was short-lived as the battlecruiser in front of them was under heavy fire. Its energy shield glowed brighter and brighter; then suddenly the shield failed. The ship blew apart, sending glowing debris in all directions.

Barnes received a message from Collison, "Need a little help?"

"It would be greatly appreciated, Admiral," replied Barnes. Now that the Fourth Fleet and the Eighth Fleet had arrived, the battle would quickly turn in their favor. By the looks of the tactical display, Collison and Carrie had lost a lot of their fleet.

"I am sure more Morag fleets are descending upon this location as we speak. Let's make quick work of this and get out of here," said Collison.

Collison and his fleet began their attack from behind the Morag fleet, smashing into their numbers with massive explosions caused by the accelerator cannon fire. Now ships were dying all across the front and rear lines of the Morag fleet. The fleet was quickly decimated, leaving only a vast field of wreckage and glowing debris. Death and destruction were all around. Both the Humans and the Morag had suffered greatly in this battle.

"Rear Admiral Barnes, I am sending you coordinates to our rendezvous location. Let's get out of here before any more enemy ships arrive," said Collison.

"Sounds like a great plan to me," replied Barnes, as she sat down in exhaustion and relief. They would live to fight another day. As she looked at her tactical display, she knew that this battle had taken a considerable toll in ships and in lives. The ships would be replaced, but the Human loss would be felt for years to come.

As her ship transitioned into hyperspace, she felt that familiar twinge in the pit of her stomach. During moments in that battle, she hadn't been sure she would ever experience transitioning to hyperspace again. Now, with a grateful heart, she closed her eyes and relished the feeling.

Morag Admiral Voxx sat up in his command chair.

Admiral, another Human fleet has just dropped out of hyperspace, said his tactical officer.

How many ships? asked Voxx.

A little more than four hundred, replied the tactical officer.

He was no longer safe at the rear of his fleet. He needed to hold on just a little longer for Ramgen to arrive. They would soon be trapped between the two Human fleets. *Get us to the middle of the formation, where we will be safe,* he commanded.

As the battle intensified, Voxx became more and more anxious that Ramgen wouldn't arrive in time. Human weapons fire now penetrated the area of the fleet where Voxx had his flagship. Maybe he should jump out to the periphery of the star system and follow the Humans when they left. He quickly placed more commands in the minds of his fellow commanders and then said, *Let's move to the periphery of the star system. We will control the battle from there. We must make sure one ship survives to follow them.*

When he made his jump, his fleet continued to bombard the Humans with every weapon they had. Large explosions shook surrounding ships, as neighboring ones disintegrated in bright nova-like explosions. No one seemed to notice his ship was missing on either side of the battle.

He reached out and contacted Admiral Ramgen. *When will you arrive? I don't think we have much time left before all our ships will be destroyed. A second Human fleet arrived to aid the first one.*

Where did these two fleets come from? We've only had one here harassing our shipyards, remarked Ramgen.

We followed the other from the Lamothian and Druin areas of the Confederation. That one initially attacked this star system. The one you've been after is the one that came to assist the first one. So now we know where both of the Human fleets are. They are currently surrounding my fleet, replied Voxx.

We will be there in ten minutes. How far away are your other two task groups? asked Ramgen.

They are twenty minutes out. We will not last that long. By the looks of it, we will not last until your fleet arrives. I have removed my ship from the battle, so we can follow the Humans when they enter hyperspace, said Voxx.

Wise move. Whatever you do, do not at any cost lose those Humans fleets, replied Ramgen.

I will not, said Voxx. He switched his focus back to the battle. He only had a few ships left; they would be destroyed in moments.

Prepare to enter hyperspace and follow these Human fleets, commanded Voxx.

Yes, Admiral, replied his navigation officer.

Admiral Collison was relieved that he had reached Rear Admiral Barnes in time. When they had arrived, the battle seemed to be leaning more to the side of the Morag. Once they jumped in and hit the Morag from the rear, the tide seemed to turn. They then could make quick work of the enemy fleet. Collison was constantly watching the tactical display. He knew that more Morag fleets would be nearby. They needed to finish this and get out of here. Once all the enemy ships had been destroyed and all of the attack interceptors had boarded their battlecarriers, they immediately entered hyperspace, before any other Morag ships had a chance to arrive.

Morag Admiral Voxx watched as the Humans quickly blew apart what was left of his fleet. He slammed his hand on his command chair. They were so close! The other Morag fleets were almost here.

The two Human fleets then quickly entered hyperspace as the battle came to an end. By the looks of it, the Morag had successfully destroyed a large portion of the Human fleets. His sinister smile returned.

Admiral Voxx followed the last Human ship as it entered hyperspace. Then he relayed their coordinates and direction to the fleets imminently due to exit hyperspace in the very system they had just left.

He knew the Humans would see his lone ship following them. They may decide to drop out of hyperspace quickly and destroy his ship. That was the chance he took. His allies were very close behind him though. The Humans most likely wouldn't see them on their tactical displays, as Voxx's ship should be just out of range.

Admiral Collison relaxed in his Command Center. He couldn't believe they had made it out of there, before more of the Morag arrived.

He sighed in relief. "Billingsly, contact Rear Admiral Barnes and Rear Admiral Carrie to figure out where we go from here. We have a couple hours before we drop out of hyperspace in our rendezvous location. Let's get some work done."

"Admiral, there's a small problem," replied Billingsly.

"What's that?" Collison asked, as he sat forward in his chair.

"Scans show one Morag battleship followed us into hyperspace," said Billingsly.

"How did we miss that? How did one ship get by our scans before we left the system?" asked Collison.

"We didn't have the chance to scan the system after the battle. We got out of there as fast as we could. It appeared no Morag ships survived," Billingsly said apologetically.

"This might be the smallest detail that we overlooked that could end up being our gravest mistake. This lone ship has no doubt reported our whereabouts to all the fleets descending upon our location. Which means they're not far behind," said Collison, as he stood and crossed his arms across his chest. "Have the ships at the rear of the fleet take a scan to see if anything's behind this lone ship," said Collison, as he paced back and forth in front of his command chair.

"Couldn't we drop out of hyperspace and destroy this one ship? Then switch directions? It wouldn't take us long to do that," suggested Billingsly.

"Great plan, as long as the fleets that follow this ship are far enough behind," replied Collison.

"Reports are coming in from the scans from the rear of the fleet, Admiral," Billingsly said, as he tried to swallow the lump forming in his throat. "A large Morag fleet is not far behind the one ship that shows up on our scans."

"How large?" asked Collison, as he came to a stop and turned to face Billingsly.

"It looks to be over three thousand ships, Admiral," replied Billingsly.

A hush fell upon the Command Center. Collison took a deep breath. Then said, "If they are that close, then we barely got out of that system before they arrived. If we had scanned the system and went after that lone ship, we would still be in that system, facing a battle that we likely wouldn't have won."

He sat back down in his command chair. "The question now is, what will we do?"

"We could head back to the supply fleet," suggested Billingsly.

"If we do that, we are putting everything at risk—all of our supply ships, our mobile repair yards, not to mention our allies in the Confederation, who I assume haven't reported our location to the enemy," replied Collison.

"What other choice do we have?" asked Billingsly.

"We could go all the way back to the Empire and have a fleet there waiting to destroy the Morag fleet that has followed us," said Collison.

"We could destroy them all then," said Billingsly.

"Let's send an encrypted message to Golan Four. See what they say. They can tell us what fleets are available. I'd rather not take this battle to the Empire though," replied Collison.

Chapter Twenty-Five

Fleet Admiral Derrick Masters had been summoned to the Command Center, beneath the House of Worlds. As he hurried down the halls to get there, he ran into his wife, High Princess Layla.

"There's news from the Confederation. I'm headed to the Command Center now," he told her, as he continued to walk in that direction.

"I'm going with you then," she replied, as she fell into step with him.

Once they arrived, Fleet Admiral Marloo updated them. "Collison, Carrie, and Barnes are being pursued by a large Morag fleet of just over three thousand ships. They need to know where they should go."

"Cleemorl is waiting for them at the supply fleet with his fleet. That would help. Plus the ships that have been repaired to date. It is possible that the Lormallians might aid them as well. They don't want the Morag in their area of space," said Derrick.

"How many ships does Collison, Carrie, and Barnes have left?" asked Layla.

"Not many. They just faced a fleet of eight hundred Morag battlecruisers and battleships in the last system they attacked. Rear Admiral Barnes has 214 battlecruisers, 67 dreadnoughts, 21 battlecarriers left with a little under 2,300 attack interceptors. Collison and Carrie have 171 battlecruisers, 54 dreadnoughts, 32 battlecarriers with about 2,000 attack interceptors left," replied Marloo.

"What about the Morag fleet they faced?" asked Layla.

"All destroyed, except one. Apparently one battleship hid and followed them into hyperspace. According to their scans, the other fleets now following them are close enough behind that they must have been nearby where they had been attacking. They're lucky they got out of there when they did," said Marloo.

"So they only have a fraction of the ships they started with. Not enough to face over three thousand Morag warships. Cleemorl took 30 dreadnoughts, 120 battlecruisers with him when he went, plus Fulmar's portion of First Fleet took 75 dreadnoughts and 600 battlecruisers with 2 battlecarriers. That's still not enough to face down that many enemy ships," said Derrick.

"Inform Collison that First Fleet is waiting at the supply fleet," said Layla. "Without giving away how many ships are there. We don't want the Morag to know they will have us outnumbered."

"What if we can make them believe it is a trap? Have all the ships in the supply fleet and the First Fleet ready to fire when the Morag emerge from hyperspace. If all the attack interceptors are deployed and are ready to fire as well, that would be helpful. If the Morag run a long-range scan before they emerge, they will see a lot of ships on their report, especially if we can get the Lormallians to place their fleet somewhat near ours.

"It would make it appear we have a larger number of ships than we do. Maybe enough to make the Morag second guess emerging from hyperspace in that star system. If we can make them believe that it is a trap, maybe they will intentionally not fall for it. Then there won't even be a battle," said Derrick.

"That's a great plan, Derrick. First, we will tell Collison that First Fleet is awaiting their arrival at the supply fleet, without giving specific numbers. We know that the Morag will intercept this message. Our second step would be to have Admiral Cleemorl meet with Lormallian Councilor Ardon Reull to see if they will change their fleet position to be much closer to ours. If so, or maybe even if not, we will send another message to Collison, saying our allies are awaiting them at the supply fleet too. Hopefully this will make the Morag have a reason to believe that it's a trap—or at least make them question if it's a battle they can win right now," said Marloo.

"Won't the Lormallians be putting a lot at risk if they appear to be helping us?" asked Layla.

"We have already sent transport vessels that way to trade with them. So we've opened up trading possibilities already. What else can we offer right now?" asked Derrick.

"They could tell the Morag, if questioned later, that they were concerned the Human fleet was inbound to attack them next. So they had their fleet positioned to respond to that threat," commented Marloo.

"That would be a plausible explanation. The Lormallians already know that the Morag will come for them. It's just a matter of when," said Derrick.

"Well, let's put this plan in action. We still have a few days before they reach the supply fleet to get all our ducks in a row," said Layla.

Derrick looked at her funny. "Where did you hear that phrase?" he asked, as he chuckled a little under his breath.

"It's a phrase Andrew has used a few times. It just means that we have a few days to get everything figured out and ready," Layla replied.

"Let's set this plan in motion then," said Marloo. "I'm sending Admiral Collison a message that says that First Fleet awaits their arrival at the supply fleet. They are ready and capable of destroying the pursuing Morag fleet when they emerge from hyperspace."

"How do we get word to Admiral Cleemorl without the Morag intercepting that message as well?" asked Derrick.

"What about the trade vessel? It's already headed there. It will arrive before they drop out of hyperspace at the supply fleet. Let's get a message to them that they can deliver once they arrive. That would leave Cleemorl and the Lormallians a little less than twenty-four hours to get everything worked out and in position before Collison and the Morag arrived," said Marloo.

"That's cutting it close, but what other options are there?" asked Derrick.

"I'll send the message to the trading vessel then," said Marloo. "The rest we will just have to wait and see."

Admiral Collison had consulted with Rear Admiral Carrie and Barnes. He had received a message from Fleet Admiral Marloo that Admiral Cleemorl and First Fleet awaited them at the supply fleet. That was very fortunate. The question remained if that would be a large-enough fleet to destroy the Morag fleet chasing them. He knew that Marloo had intentionally left out that information, since the Morag had also likely intercepted their message. If First Fleet was in the Confederation, it made no sense to head back to the Empire. Leave this war in the Confederation; that made the most sense. Maybe things would work out after all.

He sent an encrypted message ahead to the supply fleet to inform them of their situation. They needed to be prepared for the three thousand Morag warships headed their way. He knew they couldn't respond, or they would risk giving up their location as well. So he also put in the message to prepare First Fleet for the arrival of the enemy. That way, they'd know that he knew that First Fleet was coming.

Now, time to rest. They still had a long way to go before they reached the supply fleet.

Admiral Cleemorl had been summoned to the Command Center. As he entered, Colonel Jase Bidwell said, "Admiral, we have received a message from Admiral Collison. They are headed here with a large Morag fleet in pursuit. He has Carrie's and Barnes's fleets with him as well. He reported that a little over three thousand Morag warships are tailing them in hyperspace. Based on his current coordinates, we have about four days to prepare. He also said to prepare First Fleet, so somehow he must know we are here."

Cleemorl slowly sat down in his command chair, as he processed everything he had just been told. "They must have been in communication with Golan Four to know that First Fleet is here."

"Yes, Admiral, and it's safe to assume the Morag also now know we are waiting for them at their destination," replied Colonel Bidwell.

"If they believe a large fleet is waiting to attack them once they exit hyperspace, maybe they won't chance it," said Cleemorl.

"We don't have the numbers to defeat them though, Admiral," said Bidwell.

"No, we don't. We could do some serious damage to their fleet though. Damage that would take considerable time to rectify with fewer shipyards available to them," said Cleemorl. "We need help though. I will speak with Councilor Reull again to inform him that a large Morag fleet is headed in this direction. I'm certain that he doesn't want them here either. Maybe he would be willing to help us. Inform the mobile shipyards to work as fast as possible to get all of these vessels awaiting repair battle-ready. We will need them all."

Lormallian Councilor Ardon Reull was in a briefing with his admirals when a request came in to meet with the Human Empire Admiral Cleemorl. "Something must be developing with the Morag," Ardon said to his assistant, Barlten Aveth.

"He did not give the reason for this requested meeting, just that it was urgent," responded Aveth. "He requested you come to his flagship, *Themis*, as soon as possible."

"Let's find out what he wants. If it's to inform us that the Morag are headed this way, then we have some hard choices to make. While I am gone, set up a meeting with the Ruling Triad and another with our admirals. When I get back, I guess I will need to meet with them both," said Reull.

As he boarded his ship, he wondered what the day had in store for him. His ship quickly took him into space and then on to the Human Empire fleet stationed at the edge of their star system.

Admiral Cleemorl was glad that the Lormallian councilor was prompt in his response for a meeting with him. As his ship docked to the *Themis*, Cleemorl went to the docking bay to meet him. "Thank you for coming today, Councilor Reull," Cleemorl said.

"Yes, I assumed it was imperative, based on your message. What is it that we can do for you?" Reull asked, as he followed Cleemorl to a small conference room.

"Our fleets are headed back from the Morag area of the Confederation. A Morag fleet of a little over three thousand ships are in pursuit," Cleemorl revealed.

"Were your fleets successful in destroying numerous shipyards?" Reull asked, as he considered what Cleemorl had just told him.

"Yes, they destroyed 20 shipyards. Also an estimated 1,400 warships," replied Cleemorl.

"Do your returning fleets have enough ships left, when combined with yours, to destroy this Morag fleet headed here now?" asked Reull. No use in talking around the question. They should just get it out there and figure out what to do.

"Our returning fleets are down in numbers from all the fighting they've already faced. We could face the Morag fleet and would likely win, but at a high cost. I do have something else in mind though, that might turn the tables more in our favor," said Cleemorl.

"I'm intrigued. Tell me more," replied Reull.

"What if we make them believe they're playing right into our hands, right into a trap?" asked Cleemorl.

"Okay, I'm hooked. Go on," said Reull.

"From what we know, the Morag are a very logical thinking race. If we can make it seem illogical to engage in a battle, then maybe they'll choose not to fall for our trap. Then we save ourselves a costly battle," remarked Cleemorl.

"And just how will you do that?" asked Reull.

"We're not. You are," Cleemorl said, as he arched his eyebrows and smiled slyly at Reull.

"How?" Reull asked in complete puzzlement.

"You'll send out a message to the other races of the Confederation that a large Human fleet has just arrived in your star system. A larger Human fleet than you've ever seen," said Cleemorl.

"What if they all send their fleets to engage?" asked Reull.

"You won't send the message, until it's too late to call for reinforcements," replied Cleemorl.

Reull stood, as he contemplated Cleemorl's suggestion. "What if it doesn't work?"

"Then we fight. If it does work, then we live to fight another day. Live to fight for freedom from the oppression of the Morag and their allies. We gain more time to build up our fleets and to protect our worlds from the Morag's reign of death and destruction. We would have hope for a future full of promise and opportunities. If we must fight, we will.

"However, if we could put off this fight, we can continue to weaken the Confederation and the Morag. We could continue to make our hit-and-run attacks on the shipyards. We could destroy the Lamothians and their fleet, further weaken the Druins. We would continue to weaken our enemies, as well as yours. While they focus on us, their focus stays away from you. It gives us more time. And time is a fragile thing. Just imagine what we could do with more time."

As Cleemorl finished, he slowly sat down. "It's all up to you. Are you with us? Will you join us in our fight for freedom? Will you send out the message making the Morag think they're headed right for our trap?"

Reull was quiet, as he considered Cleemorl's proposal. The Humans did have a large fleet positioned in their star system, and more was on the way. If it could stop the Morag from coming near here, it was worth it.

It wasn't as simple as Cleemorl thought it would be though. Reull knew that the Morag would request more information. How many ships, plus the types of ships that were there. The timing would have to be perfect to allow the Morag time to make their decision. While also not enough time to request support from their allies. It would also only be temporary. As soon as reinforcements arrived, they would attack them.

"It does sound like an interesting plan. Only a few flaws in it. First and foremost, the Morag will ask for more information on the number and types of ships. They will base their decision on this. Second, they will send out a request for aid from their allies, and, while it won't come immediately, they will attack, once their allies assemble into a large enough fleet to destroy yours."

"You can include in the message the number of ships we currently have in the system and add that more are still dropping out of hyperspace. This will be true. They are the ones the Morag are following. We will deploy all our attack interceptors, which will add to the total number of ships we have available to fight this battle. If you can put off telling them specifics on the types of ships, it would make our fleet seem that much bigger.

"Second, we intend to leave here as quickly as possible. All capable ships will head to the Lamothian area of the Confederation. The rest will head out of the Confederation to the edge of the Empire. We have some unfinished business with the Lamothians. If the Morag call upon their allies for help, it may leave us an opportunity to more easily destroy the Lamothians."

"Get me the information you want me to send the Morag. I will discuss the plan with our Ruling Triad and will let you know what our decision is. Also note when you think it would be best to send it," replied Reull. "I will also need to report to the Morag that your fleet has left our star system. That way, they do not come here with their fleets, after you've left, and decide to go ahead and attack us while they're here," responded Reull.

"I do not see a problem with that. Being that we will be headed in two different directions, that might help them not follow us

very easily," said Cleemorl. "Thank you for coming here today
and for meeting with us. If this plan works, you will have
demonstrated your willingness to work with us, which will help
future relations between our races," Cleemorl said, as he stood to
walk Reull back to his waiting ship.

—

Over the next few days, First Fleet prepared for battle.
Cleemorl gathered the information he wanted Reull to send to the
Morag. Cleemorl analyzed when would be the best time to send
it. Thankfully Reull had received a positive response from the
Lormallians' Ruling Triad. They would send out the message.

Cleemorl had also asked the Lormallians to position their fleet
nearby, to throw off the Morag as well. The Morag might
question which side they are on and not be willing to take the
chance that the Lormallians are genuinely against them and with
the Humans. This had also been suggested by Marloo from
Golan Four.

The trading vessels had started arriving and had brought news
of the plan that Marloo and Derrick Masters had developed,
including Fulmar coming with another 677 ships from the First
Fleet to destroy the Lamothians. This seemed to be confirmation
that it was a good plan, considering the circumstances before
them.

The Lormallian fleet was now positioned near enough to First
Fleet to make it questionable whether they were there to help
attack the Morag or to help defend their interests. If the Morag
did a long-range scan of the system, which was likely, the
Lormallians would be an unknown variable that could change the
tide on this battle.

Now that everything was set, they had nothing to do but wait.
Soon the Lormallians would send their warning to the Morag.
Cleemorl did have to admit that it caused him a little lost sleep
and uneasiness having the Lormallian fleet positioned so close to
his. Not long ago they were enemies.

Collison, Carrie, and Barnes were now less than forty-eight hours from exiting hyperspace, with over three thousand Morag warships close behind. Fulmar, with more of First Fleet, was due here in just hours. Once they were almost here, Cleemorl would send Collison the coordinates to where they should drop from hyperspace. First Fleet needed to have a clean shot of the Morag when they emerged from hyperspace, if it came to that. The more they could destroy in the first round of fire, the better.

Rear Admiral Barnes evaluated what was left of her fleet. She still needed to destroy the Lamothians for continuing with the feast. The scout ships were headed to the Lamothian star systems to monitor fleet movements. If Collison's combined fleet could make the Morag, Druins, and Lamothians believe the Humans were headed out of the Confederation, maybe they could take the Lamothians by surprise. That was, if, of course, First Fleet could help them destroy this huge Morag fleet that chased them. Or make the Morag believe they were headed into a trap.

Admiral Collison had already moved them to Condition Two and had given out the coordinates of where to exit hyperspace. They had also received a message from Golan Four, saying that their allies were now also in a position to aid in the impending battle. She wondered how the Morag were handling all this information. Hopefully they would decide not to engage in this battle. Then she could take her fleet, with some reinforcements, to destroy the Lamothians.

Cleemorl was relieved when First Fleet and Rear Admiral Fulmar emerged from hyperspace. The tactical display was full of green icons. It was a comforting feeling. When he considered the number of enemy ships in bound to their location, that feeling quickly went away. It would be a hard battle, one they could win with their superior weapons, but it would come with a great cost.

Cleemorl met with Rear Admiral Fulmar to update him on the latest information. He knew that the portion of First Fleet that had arrived with Fulmar would need some time to make some repairs on their ships from their long hyperspace jump. Fulmar had pushed them to the limits to make sure they arrived as quickly as possible.

As Cleemorl thought back to his conversation with Fulmar, he chuckled to himself. Fulmar had left the Empire with First Fleet to come here and destroy the rest of the Lamothian planets. Now, he would have to face down a large Morag fleet first.

Morag Admiral Voxx paced back and forth in front of his holographic display. The Lormallians had just informed him that the Humans had a large fleet positioning themselves on the periphery of their system. Not only that but more ships were still dropping out of hyperspace. At the current count, there were over 1,600 ships setting up in their system in an offensive formation, plus more still emerging from hyperspace.

Voxx closed his eyes and took a deep breath. With the fleet already there, plus the ones they were pursuing, they'd have over two thousand ships, plus whatever small attack craft they had left. Also, a point they could not overlook, from the data coming in from their long-range scans, was that the Lormallians were also positioned on the periphery of the system. Were they there to keep the Humans away from their planets? Or were they there to aid the Humans against the Morag? If the latter were true, they would be outnumbered.

If the first were true, maybe, just maybe, they'd help the Morag destroy the Humans. Voxx must consult with Morag Councilor Damora as to the likelihood of the Lormallians being with them or against them. Voxx had gotten the impression that the Lormallians were no longer a part of this war, but, if the war was brought to them, how would they react? They were an unknown element that could be the deciding factor in this battle.

Then Voxx knew precisely what he had to do. They needed to see where the Lormallians stood. Whose side were they on? The

Morag also had to make sure the Humans did not return to destroy more of their shipyards. There was only one way to do that.

When he informed Admiral Ramgen of his intentions, Ramgen said, *What if it's a trap? What if they have enough ships and firepower to destroy us?*

Once the battle turns from our favor, we jump out and assemble with our allies. Once we have enough reinforcements, we return and wipe them out of the Confederation, once and for all. Leave no ship intact. Make them regret ever sending fleets here in the first place, responded Voxx.

Then we continue to fight a war against the Humans of the Empire and those of the Solar System, commented Ramgen.

We have no other choice. It's us or them. They help each other, as well as gain more and more allies every day. We must destroy them now, while we still can, said Voxx. *Let's inform our allies of the location of the Human fleet. The Druins and Lamothians are close enough to send reinforcements if we need them.*

Lamothian Admiral Zahn had received the coordinates of the Human fleets' location from Morag Admiral Voxx. The Humans would pay for destroying their Lamothian homeworld. No Human would leave the Confederation. Those who survived the battle would be consumed in their celebration feasts.

Zahn quickly assembled his fleet, leaving only a small contingent of ships behind to protect Xanther and their other star systems. They knew where the enemy was. Now all they had left to do was annihilate them.

Druin Admiral Falorr had received Morag Admiral Voxx's request for help in defeating the Human fleets that had been terrorizing the Confederation. He would send a group of ships to aid Voxx but would also keep a large number of ships in their own star systems, in case the Humans had something else planned. He would not leave his star systems under-protected.

Captain Laine on scout ship 125 had been monitoring the Lamothian fleet patrolling Xanther, taking Captain Hadley's place, as she sought where the Humans were sourced from.

"Captain, it looks like the fleet is assembling," said Lieutenant Henley.

"I wonder what they are doing?" replied Laine.

"Captain, the fleet is entering hyperspace," said Henley.

Laine smiled. It looked like this fleet was headed to supplement the Morag fleet tailing Admiral Collison. They would not have time to get there before the battle occurred. "Let's see how many ships they leave behind," said Laine. "This might leave us a golden opportunity to easily destroy Xanther."

"It looks like they had left behind the 57 battleships that had been patrolling this system before the larger Lamothian fleet arrived," said Henley.

"Let's scan the space stations and the planet for Human life. See if any are left alive," said Laine. As he waited for the results of the scan, he imagined what it would be like to be captured by the Lamothian race. Laine quickly shook off that train of thought and hoped that some Humans were still alive that they could rescue.

"Captain, I detect no Humans on the surface of the planet. Also none on the space stations," said Henley.

"According to Captain Hadley's previous scan, numerous Humans were on the planet and space stations," Laine said, as he took a deep breath. They all knew what that meant. They were too late to rescue the Humans, but they could still punish the Lamothians for what they had done. "Let's send this information on to Admiral Cleemorl. If he's going to attack Xanther, now is the time."

-

Cleemorl had the mobile shipyards and the supply ships jump out of the system before Collison and the Morag arrived. Cleemorl wanted the supply fleet safe, and they would fall back to the other side of the Lormallian-controlled area of the Confederation. If the Morag didn't emerge from hyperspace to destroy the fleet, then Cleemorl could call them back. If the Morag did appear, the supply fleet's new location would be the Humans' fallback position.

"Admiral, we have received an encrypted message from Captain Laine on scout ship 125. He says that the Lamothian fleet entered hyperspace, only leaving behind fifty-seven battleships to patrol the star system where Xanther is located," said Bidwell.

Cleemorl took a deep breath. This was their chance to destroy Xanther. The Lamothians were obviously headed here to destroy the fleet that had destroyed their homeworld. They would not make it in time to join the Morag fleet trailing Collison, but maybe the Morag had intentions of waiting for their allies to rendezvous with them before they attacked. He slowly walked around the Command Center, as he considered the possibilities.

"Contact Rear Admiral Fulmar. I want him to attack and to destroy Xanther, taking the part of First Fleet that I originally brought here—120 battlecruisers and 30 dreadnoughts. He can take 2 battlecarriers full of attack interceptors to help him destroy Xanther. That will give him 320 attack interceptors. If they all launch their four fusion-tipped missiles at the surface of the planet, that will be 1,280 missiles. That should do the job. If not, they would have time to reload and to launch a second batch. Our portion of First Fleet will easily destroy the small Lamothian fleet left to patrol the system. The Lamothians will learn to heed the warnings of High Princess Layla," said Cleemorl.

"Will that weaken our position here too much?" asked Bidwell.

"No, we'll take on Fulmar's portion of First Fleet that he brings here, so we may lose 152 warships, but we gain 677. I feel confident we can still get the job done," replied Cleemorl.

Shortly after that, Rear Admiral Fulmar and his task group jumped out of the system. Cleemorl smiled. The Lamothians would be utterly unprepared for the attack headed their way.

Chapter Twenty-Six

Collison moved his fleet and those with him to Condition One. In five minutes, they would be dropping out of hyperspace in the periphery of the Lormallian star system where First Fleet and the supply fleet awaited.

So much hung in the balance. What would the Morag do? Would they fight? He had his fleet ready, and everyone knew what to do and when. They had a great battle plan. It all hinged on the Morag.

Collison tried to relax, knowing this situation was out of his control. He had already planned and threw that plan out the window and planned again and again. He had finally settled on a plan of attack. Hopefully it fell in line with what Cleemorl had planned.

Collison once again checked the tactical display in front of him. "Billingsly, run our long-range scan of the system. I'd like to have an idea of what we have and where they are positioned."

Billingsly ran the scan and had everything on the tactical display. It looked like a large number of ships in the system. The long-range scanner was not able to determine the types of ships, only the number of ships. Maybe, when the Morag ran their long-range scan, the number of ships present will make them think twice about exiting hyperspace behind them.

Collison's fleets would only have a few minutes to get in position, once they exited hyperspace, before the Morag started to exit as well. Then the battle would begin.

-

Any moment now, Admiral Collison and the rest of the fleets would emerge from hyperspace. Cleemorl closed his eyes and hoped that their plan would work. He didn't want to face the Morag in a fleet battle just yet. He wanted to use their fleets to destroy all the Lamothians. If they battled the Morag, they might not have enough ships left afterward to go after the Lamothians fleet and the rest of their planets, like they had planned. This plan just had to work.

Cleemorl reviewed his fleet numbers as he anxiously waited for Collison to exit hyperspace. First Fleet now had 600 battlecruisers and 75 dreadnoughts in the system, all of the ships that had been sent back for repairs had at least been returned to battle capability, and all of the ships that normally would have protected the supply fleet had stayed to help defeat the Morag. When he added in the ships that Collison, Carrie, and Barnes had left as already reported, that would give them a sizeable fleet. When the Morag ran their long range scan, they should see over 6,000 ships. Most of this number would be the attack interceptors, but the scans wouldn't be able to discern that information until they were closer.

As he sat down in his command chair, alarms sounded. He thought to himself, *Here we go.* He slid to the front of his chair and had his gaze glued to the tactical display in front of him.

"Admiral Collison and the fleets with him have begun to exit hyperspace," reported Colonel Bidwell. "The Morag will be following shortly behind them."

"Have First Fleet prepared to fire as soon as they have a target locked on. If we can manage to destroy enough Morag ships in the first round, maybe they'll leave," commanded Collison.

As they all anxiously awaited the arrival of the Morag, they hoped against hope that maybe they would not show up. Maybe the Humans' bluff would work. They were prepared for the plan not to work, but everyone hoped it would not come to that. They would soon find out.

Collison, Carrie, and Barnes and their fleets had all finished exiting hyperspace. Their fleets quickly got into position. Then they waited.

-

Morag Admiral Voxx had finished running his long-range scan. The Humans had managed to get a sizeable fleet to the Confederation. They wouldn't have had time to come all the way from Golan Four. So, either they were closer by, or they were already here. If they were already here, why? Were they planning more attacks?

He decided to drop out of hyperspace farther away from the assembled Human fleets. This would give him time to prepare for battle. Maybe enough time to access the Lormallians and their intentions in this battle. The Lormallians had a large fleet in the system as well. Much larger than the Morag had known about.

As they emerged from hyperspace farther away from the assembled Humans, alarms immediately sounded. *What do we have?* he asked his tactical officer.

They have 1,088 battlecruisers, 226 dreadnoughts, 56 battlecarriers, and just over 4,700 of the small attack craft, responded his tactical officer.

What about the Lormallians? Voxx asked.

They have 967 battlecruisers and 87 battleships, responded the tactical officer.

Contact the Lormallians and see if they will help us destroy the Humans, ordered Voxx.

After a few tense moments, the communications officer responded, *They have replied that they are not a part of this war. They are positioned to protect their star system and planets from any aggression against them.*

So they are not on our side. However, I'm willing to bet that they will join the Humans before the day is done, if it looks like the Humans will end up on top. We have the larger fleet, but the Humans have superior weapons— unless this fleet stationed here does not possess the new weapons like the Earth Humans have. We must test them. This is something we need to know. Prepare the fleet for battle. Have them target the fleet in the center of the formation, commanded Voxx.

He sent his commands to the various ship commanders. They at least needed more information before they left. If this fleet did not possess the new weapons, they had an even greater chance of coming out on top.

My fleet will target the Human fleet in the center, while Admiral Ramgen and his fleet should focus on the ones we chased out of our area of the Confederation. It's time to kill some Humans, Voxx said, with a cold smile on his face. *No one comes to our part of the Confederation and gets away with it.*

Five minutes to engagement range, Admiral, said the tactical officer.

Admiral Cleemorl had consulted with Collison, Carrie, and Barnes and had taken the lead of the fleets. They would follow his guidance, as the senior ranking officer of the fleets. Cleemorl and First Fleet would focus on fighting the Morag head-on, while Barnes took her fleet and jumped to the right flank of the Morag formation. There they would fire a round of accelerator cannon fire, then move to the rear of the fleet. She would keep jumping from one side to another, until the Morag counteracted this attack. Once that happened, she would rejoin the rest of the fleet and continue bombardment of the front line of the Morag fleet.

Collison and Carrie would focus their accelerator cannon fire on the larger Morag battleships. Especially the eight Conqueror battleships. Cleemorl knew that the Lormallians would not join this fight if they believed the Morag might use these ships to destroy any of their planets.

The attack interceptors would focus their firepower on any damaged ships. Cleemorl knew they would lose a large number of them, but they were vital to the success of this battle. Their battlecarriers would be stationed at the rear of the Human fleet, so that the interceptors could reload. Part of the fleet that had been left to protect the supply fleet would be defending the battlecarriers here.

It did appear that the Morag had a few of the carriers that held their small attack craft, the Interceptor Killers. So the attack interceptors would need to hunt them down and destroy them as well.

"Three minutes to engagement range, Admiral," said Colonel Bidwell.

As the fleets closed the distance between them, tensions in the Command Center increased. Cleemorl knew this battle would be a hard one, one they might not survive. However, sometimes in war, great sacrifices must be made.

Once they reached the engagement range, weapons fire quickly lit up the space around them. Thousands of explosions and flashes of light marked the death of ships on both sides of the battle. The battle was brutal.

"Send a message to Golan Four, updating them that the fleet battle with the Morag has begun," commanded Cleemorl. He knew they would be anxiously awaiting news of what was happening.

His ship shook underneath him. He gazed at the displays and saw that their shield held steady. The battlecruiser to his left had their shield knocked down with a massive hail of missiles. Cleemorl winced as the antimatter missile arrived and blew it apart.

The entire forward section of the advancing Morag fleet became a furnace of dying ships from the tremendous number of accelerator cannon fire focused at them. Not all of his fleet possessed these weapons yet, but a vast majority of them had already been outfitted with them. All of the new ships had them, so more of them possessed this superior firepower than not.

All of his dreadnoughts did have the particle beam cannons, which accelerated a large number of small particles into a beam and the resulting kinetic energy, where the beam strikes, tore a hole in the energy shield, and then the beam would strike the ship.

He winced as he saw another of his battlecruisers blown apart, as its shield was overloaded and then struck by a pair of antimatter missiles.

The enemy fleet continued to advance, as their front line was time and time again pulverized by the accelerator cannons. His ships that did not possess them focused their firepower on the damaged ships. Every ship had its targets and knew its part in the plan of attack. It would take them all to come out on top of this.

He closed his eyes and shook his head. When he opened them again, he saw two of the Morag Conqueror battleships blown into oblivion.

-

Lormallian Admiral Garr watched intently, as both the Morag and the Humans battled it out. It was impossible to tell which race would come out on the other side of this battle. He hoped it would be the Humans. He had been instructed to hold off, until they couldn't hold off anymore, before joining the attack on the Morag. It would be better for them to stay out of it. It would also be better for them if the Humans won this battle. They were stuck in a tough position. Damned if they do, damned if they don't.

Currently the tide of the battle seemed to favor the Humans. They definitely possessed greater weapons power.

Part of the Human fleet disappeared and then reappeared on the right flank of the Morag's fleet. They released a couple rounds of accelerator cannon fire and then jumped to another side, only to launch two more rounds and disappear again. They were able to do this a couple times, before the Morag counteracted their attack.

Garr was relieved to see the Humans focusing some of their firepower on the large Conqueror battleships. Those ships would be capable of destroying a planet reasonably quickly. He felt even greater relief when one by one they were destroyed in bright nova-like explosions.

The attack interceptors flew in and found damaged ships to launch their fusion-tipped missiles at, finishing off numerous Morag battlecruisers and a few battleships. Smaller bright explosions marked the death of some of them, as they wove back and forth throughout the fleets to find their targets.

-

Morag Admiral Voxx watched intently as the ships in his fleet assaulted the front line of the Human fleet. Unfortunately it did appear that most of the Human ships did possess the accelerator cannons. Only about 25 percent of them did not. He constantly watched the tactical display. The Morag were doing damage to this Human fleet, but Voxx was losing ships faster than the Humans.

Let's have part of the fleet jump to the rear of the Human fleet and see if we can take out some of those battlecarriers. If the attack interceptors have nowhere to reload, they become ineffective, Voxx commanded, as he placed the orders into the minds of some of the commanders. Soon a large number of his fleet disappeared and then reappeared behind the Human fleet. The Humans quickly responded and shifted numerous ships back to protect the battlecarriers. Not before the Morag destroyed four of them though.

-

As Captain Elliott, on board the battlecarrier *Daneb,* monitored the battle unfolding before him, he noticed a large number of the Morag fleet disappear. He had a sinking feeling in the pit of his stomach. Soon the Morag fleet appeared behind the battlecarriers and began their assault. Thankfully Cleemorl had foreseen this possibility and had placed a small task group in the rear to protect them, until other ships could be repositioned to help protect them.

In the confusion of the battle, four of the battlecarriers were destroyed, as their energy shields were battered down, and massive explosions of pure energy shattered them into glowing pieces of wreckage.

As more of the fleet repositioned to protect the battlecarriers, the Morag ships once again disappeared. Elliott hoped they wouldn't return.

-

Admiral Collison focused his firepower on the eight Conqueror battleships. The battle continued to grow in intensity. Ships on both sides were dying in brilliant explosions. Space was littered with glowing debris and wreckage. At this moment, no way to tell who might win.

As the accelerator cannon fire found its target, it overwhelmed the Morag energy shield, smashing through it and then rendering the vessel vulnerable to the second projectile that pulverized its target on impact.

Collison smiled as, one by one, he destroyed the Conqueror battleships. His fleet was taking heavy losses as well. If they survived this battle, their time here in the Confederation was most likely finished for now.

Suddenly Collison's ship shook violently, throwing him to the ground. He stood and glanced at the damage control console and the several red lights now flashing. He shifted his gaze over to the energy shield; it was still holding at 70 percent. A few more direct hits though, and it wouldn't be.

Rear Admiral Carrie was focused on helping Collison destroy the Conqueror battleships. Once that was done, she focused the firepower of her fleet on the still advancing line of the Morag. They just kept coming and coming. Flaming debris was all around. The number of green icons on the tactical display grew less and less. The red ones were disappearing as well, but, at this rate, they would simply destroy each other.

How much longer they would last, she couldn't tell. When part of the Morag fleet disappeared, it didn't take long for her to figure out where they were headed. She had already instructed her portion of the fleet to jump back to where the battlecarriers were. The Morag arrived first and were already bombarding the small supply fleet stationed there to protect the battlecarriers.

By the time they had destroyed enough of the Morag ships to make them flee back to their main fleet, the Morag had successfully destroyed four battlecarriers. It was a loss that would be felt, but, for now, their priority had to stay on surviving this battle themselves. She was also aware that, more than likely, they had already lost enough attack interceptors to consolidate what was left into the remaining battlecarriers.

She left part of her fleet behind to help protect the battlecarriers, and the rest jumped back to continue the ongoing bombardment of the front line of the still advancing Morag fleet.

As the Morag continued to fire their fusion energy beams and antimatter missiles, more and more ships found their shields knocked down. More antimatter missiles arrived, and those ships all died in bright explosions.

Carrie noticed one of the battleships in the center of the Morag formation. "Let's focus our fire on that ship. Maybe it has one of the Morag admirals on it. If we can destroy it, then maybe that will cause enough confusion to have them abandon this battle."

-

Morag Admiral Ramgen found himself and his ship had become a primary target of the Human fleet. Admiral Voxx and his flagship were positioned a little farther back in the formation.

Ramgen's battleship shook violently, and various alarms sounded. The smell of smoke filled the air. Lights in the Command Center dimmed and then came back on.

Admiral, our shield has taken a direct hit. It's barely functioning. I've diverted all the power to the energy shield, said the systems officer.

The sound of tearing and stressed metal filled the air. Other than that, the Command Center was eerily quiet as they all held their breaths, hoping against hope that they'd survive to fight another day.

Suddenly a loud tearing noise was heard. The lights went out completely, and a sudden rush of coldness filled the room. Then in a searing blast of heat and light, Admiral Ramgen and his crew died.

-

Cheering filled the Command Center on Carrie's flagship, *Exeter*. They did it! They had destroyed the Morag battleship that likely held one of the admirals on board!

The celebration was short-lived, as the Morag continued their onslaught.

"Let's find another battleship that another admiral might be on. Focus our firepower on another battleship. Let's end this!" Carrie commanded.

Morag Admiral Voxx was disgusted at what he witnessed. The Human fleet had destroyed his eight Conqueror battleships and were now focusing their firepower on the battleships. He had just witnessed Admiral Ramgen's flagship get incinerated right before his very eyes. Ramgen was an up-and-coming admiral who had a strong and successful future in front of him.

They were losing too many ships. They were destroying numerous Human ships as well but at a slower rate. If this kept up, they'd all end up dead. Today would not be his last. He would live to fight another day. He would live to see these Humans face their destruction, and it would be a violent and vicious demise. He would enjoy every moment of it. Today was not that day, however.

He needed to salvage what was left of his and Ramgen's fleet. Just before exiting the star system, he sent out a message to the Humans. "Leave the Confederation, or face imminent death. Do not return, or you will be annihilated."

After it was sent, he commanded his fleets to enter hyperspace and to return to the Morag area of the Confederation. He would call upon the Druins and the Lamothians to make sure the Humans left. Voxx had done his part. The rest was up to them. He needed to focus on rebuilding his fleet and preparing for the next attack. He knew the Humans would be back. Most likely sooner than later. The Confederation needed to be ready.

Epilogue

When the Morag entered hyperspace, cheers erupted across the Human fleet. They had done it! They would live to fight another day! They had lost a lot of ships and a lot of friends who could never be replaced. The Lormallian star system was littered with debris from the thousands of destroyed ships. It was a graveyard of death and destruction.

The Lormallians had stayed out of the battle, which is what Cleemorl and the other Human admirals had expected. If they had joined in, they likely would soon be at the receiving end of the Morag's revenge.

Cleemorl knew that more Confederation fleets could be headed their way, so they needed to fall back to their rendezvous location and access their situation. He knew that the Lamothians were still inbound to their location; however, they'd have another day before they arrived. Cleemorl smiled as he thought about the surprise they had in store for the Lamothians. By the time they arrived here, the Human fleet would be gone.

However, the bigger surprise for the Lamothians would be when they soon realized what a grave mistake they had made in coming here, when they learn that their planets are under attack.

Rescue efforts began immediately after the enemy fleet exited the star system. Many attack interceptor crews had been able to eject before their ships were blown apart. The ships that were still partially intact were also searched for any surviving crew members.

He sent a message to the Lormallians, thanking them for being willing to help them, if the situation had warranted it. He also mentioned that the Empire was looking forward to continuing its trade agreements and continuing its peace agreement with the Lormallians and their allies.

As the fleets began to enter hyperspace, Cleemorl sat down and relaxed in his command chair. This trip hadn't gone exactly as planned, but they did just destroy a majority of a Morag fleet. So now the Morag had even fewer ships with which they could attack the Empire with. On the other hand, the Humans had lost a lot of ships too. The reports were still coming in. Once they dropped from hyperspace at their rendezvous location, they would regroup and decide where to go from here.

For now, it was time for some long-awaited sleep. As he walked to his quarters, his mind traveled to the Empire and to Cheryl. He couldn't wait to see her when he returned. When would he return? That question remained unanswered for now.

-

As Charles Wright landed on Golan Four, he couldn't wait to see his daughter. The last time he had been here had been for his daughter's wedding to Andrew, Prince Andrew. That was still a little odd to think about.

When he stepped from the ship, his daughter Kala ran into his arms and gave him a big hug. "I've missed you so much, Kala!" he said.

"I've missed you too, Dad. How was your trip? And what mystery has you traveling all the way to the Empire to solve? Ever since you mentioned it, I haven't been able to get my mind off it," said Kala.

"Well, you will never believe it, but I've found some amazing things on my most recent dig. I found artifacts from a spaceship that lead me to believe it came from here. The planet Falton Two was referenced in a couple places. I wanted to search the archives here and see what I could dig up," replied Charles.

"I'm sure High Princess Layla will allow you to use the archives to find out all that you can," replied Kala.

"The maps I could access do not show a planet called Falton Two. I am hoping the maps here will have its location noted," said Charles.

The two slowly walked inside the palace doors and ran into Fleet Admiral Derrick Masters. After briefing him on Charles's discovery, Derrick said, "I have not heard of Falton Two either. Let's look at the maps we have in the Command Center, beneath the House of Worlds. The most up-to-date maps are housed there."

After a quick walk to the House of Worlds and a short journey underground, they reached the Command Center. Derrick pulled up the holographic display and searched for Falton Two. "It's not here. I don't see it anywhere. At least it's not in the Empire. I guess there's a chance it could be in the Confederation. We do not have a fully accurate map of all parts of the Confederation. If this planet still exists, it must be there."

"I will do some research here at the archives. If I cannot find the answers I seek, are there archives located somewhere in the Confederation? One that I could possibly access?" asked Charles.

"We will need to speak with Layla, but there are archives located on the Lormallian planet of Bator Prime. It is possible— now that we have an alliance with the Lormallians—that you might get permission to visit there. We may find the information you seek by asking Lormallian Councilor Ardon Reull. I believe his brother is in charge of the archives on Bator Prime," said Derrick.

"That would be great if he had the information I seek, but hopefully I can find the information here," said Charles.

As the three of them emerged from the House of Worlds, Derrick headed to talk to Layla, and Charles and Kala headed to find Andrew. "Thank you for your help, Derrick," Charles said, as they parted ways.

-

High Princess Layla was rehearsing her message she had for Lormallian Councilor Reull. She paced back and forth, when Derrick arrived. He caught her up to speed on what Charles was looking for. "I have never heard of this planet that he searches for. Hopefully he will find the information he seeks in our archives. If not, I am confident that we will be welcome to use the archives on Bator Prime. We will deal with that when we need to. For now, I need to prepare my message for Ardon Reull. The next trading vessels that head to Lormallia will be delivering my message."

"Are you ready to record your message?" asked Derrick.

She turned and smiled at him. "Let's do it."

Admiral Cleemorl was meeting with Admiral Collison, Rear Admiral Carrie, and Rear Admiral Barnes on Cleemorl's flagship, *Themis.* "We were sent to the Confederation to aid your fleets in case this situation occurred. We also had a second mission, to destroy the Lamothians and their planets. They still did not heed High Princess Layla's warning, so they must be dealt with. I sent Rear Admiral Fulmar to destroy Xanther. He may destroy the other planets in that same star system. We need to evaluate what ships we have left and determine if we have enough to carry out our objective. The Lamothians will still have a sizeable fleet, as well as possibly two more inhabited planets left."

Admiral Collison cleared his throat. "My fleet, combined with Rear Admiral Carrie's, only has 53 battlecruisers, 21 dreadnoughts, 30 battlecarriers, and just about 1,254 attack interceptors left. We plan to send 22 battlecarriers back to the Empire for repair and resupply. We do not have enough attack interceptors in our supply fleet to refill more than we already have. So we will keep eight battlecarriers here for whatever our next objective is."

Rear Admiral Barnes took a deep breath and said, "I lost a majority of Third Fleet as well. I have 76 battlecruisers, 33 dreadnoughts, 19 battlecarriers, with approximately 943 attack interceptors left. I will send 13 battlecarriers back to the Empire for repairs and resupply. Six battlecarriers will stay here for whatever comes next. For the record, I would be more than happy to help you destroy the Lamothians, Admiral Cleemorl."

Cleemorl then addressed the room. "First Fleet has 230 battlecruisers, 25 dreadnoughts. I sent 120 battlecruisers and 30 dreadnoughts with Rear Admiral Fulmar to Xanther, plus 2 battlecarriers full of attack interceptors. They should be arriving within the next sixteen hours."

Carrie then said, "From what we had staged with the supply fleet, those that have been repaired, and the ships that had been resupplied, we have 44 battlecruisers, 18 dreadnoughts, 3 battlecarriers, with 264 attack interceptors. We will send 1 of those battlecarriers back to the Empire for repairs and resupply."

Cleemorl had been busy scribbling down the information shared by the others. "So here is what we have left, not including what Fulmar has with him. A total of 403 battlecruisers, 97 dreadnoughts, 17 battlecarriers, and 2,461 attack interceptors. We know the Lamothians have a fleet of over 1,000 ships. I am not sure we have enough ships left to attain our objective of destroying the Lamothian fleet. We would have enough ships to destroy the other two planets that the Lamothians inhabit, assuming Fulmar destroyed the two in the star system where Xanther is located. According to the scout ships, one system only has 23 battleships on patrol. The other system only has 39 battleships on patrol."

The room went silent as they all considered their options. "Do we know the current location of the large Lamothian fleet?" asked Barnes.

"Yes, we had Captain Malachi on scout ship 255 follow them into hyperspace. He reports that they are still headed to our last known location. He estimates that they will exit hyperspace in approximately twelve hours. Once they discover we are gone, we can assume they will head back to Lamothian star systems," reported Cleemorl.

"So, if we destroy the rest of their planets, we need to leave immediately," said Collison.

"Yes," responded Cleemorl. "Let's vote. All in favor of heading to the Lamothian-controlled star systems to finish destroying their planets, raise your hand."

Every one of their hands were raised.

"Well, I guess that settles it then. Let's get prepared to enter hyperspace in two hours. The more we can get ahead of the Lamothian fleet, the better," said Cleemorl. "We will avoid the large Lamothian fleet for now. I am sure we will get the chance to annihilate the fleet sometime in the near future."

-

Lormallian Councilor Reull had received a message from the Empire. As he watched, he saw the image of the High Princess Layla Starguard. Then she said, "Thank you so much for allowing the Human fleets to station safely in your star system. We are looking forward to a long and fruitful alliance between our races. The future is looking bright. Trading has started and will multiply as time goes on. Please let us know if there's any way we can help or can aid your people. Thank you again for your assistance."

Ardon was satisfied that the Humans were not angry with them for not joining the battle against the Morag. He had been concerned about it, but the Lormallians were stuck in a difficult position. If they had helped the Humans, the Morag would have quickly come back and destroyed a planet or two for aiding the Humans. For now, the Lormallians could continue to remain neutral. He knew there would come a day, a day fast approaching, where the Lormallians would have to step into the fire and reveal their alliance with the Humans. The longer they could put that off, the better. However, they did not want to jeopardize their alliance with the Humans either.

For now, they would continue to build up their fleets and to add to their planetary defenses. The big battle was yet to come. He hoped they could stay out of it but knew the chances of that were very remote.

-

Captain Hadley, on board scout ship 368, still followed the transport vessel from the Lamothian star system, when it finally dropped from hyperspace.

"Lieutenant Maddox, scan the system," Hadley said.

"It appears there is one inhabited planet in this system, no defenses. There are no battleships or defensive grid. No space stations or shipyards," replied Maddox.

"Where exactly are we?" asked Hadley.

"We are not in any star system that's on the map. We are closest to the Morag area of the Confederation," replied Maddox.

"Let's move in closer and scan the planet," commanded Hadley.

After a tense few minutes, the scan was complete. "Captain, you're not going to believe this, but this planet is full of Humans," said Maddox.

"What? How can this be? Watch that transport vessel. See where it goes. Are these our people? Is this where they bring them?" asked Hadley.

They sent their location in an encrypted message back to Golan Four with the information they had gathered to date. So far, they had a lot of questions but very few answers.

They were a long way from the Empire. They watched the transport vessel land on the planet. "Let's find out everything we can about this planet."

"Are we picking up any communication from the planet?" asked Hadley.

"Yes, quite a bit of communication is going on. Through that, I have discovered the name of this planet, Captain. It's called Falton Two. It appears to be a core world and part of the Confederation," said Maddox.

They all looked at each other in surprise and confusion. "What in the world have we just found?" asked Captain Hadley.

Back on Morag Prime, the Morag High Council was in an emergency session. Councilor Brant seethed in anger. *These Earth Humans will regret this day, the day they dared to enter the Morag-controlled part of the Confederation. How dare they destroy our shipyards. Yes, they may be celebrating this small victory, but they will never win the war. They just made themselves a bigger target. They must be dealt with. If we destroy Earth and the Solar System, we will significantly weaken the Empire. They won't have them to fall back on. The Earth Humans are the ones who have developed all these new weapons. We must cut off the head of the snake. We must destroy the Earth Humans. They have become our primary threat, our primary target.*

That is all true, Lead Councilor Addonis agreed, *but, if we send a large-enough fleet to destroy Earth, then we leave our star systems in the Confederation vulnerable to attack from the Empire. The Empire grows every day, in the number of planets, in defenses, and in fleet size. They must be dealt with first, as the closest enemy, and then we will move on to the Earth Humans,* said Lead Councilor Addonis.

What about the Lormallians? asked Councilor Delann. *When will we deal with them?*

According to Admiral Voxx, the Lormallians informed him of the Humans' location as they were following the Human fleet out of our area of the Confederation. They let him know how many ships were there. The Lormallians had a fleet staged nearby but did not engage either fleet. They said they would remain neutral, unless they felt their planets were threatened in any way. I do not think they would be foolish enough to attack us. We can deal with them at a later date. Our first priority must be the Humans, said Addonis.

It will take us more time to build up our fleets to a large enough number to protect our home star systems and to attack the Human Empire. Plus we have to defend against that new weapon the Earth Humans have. Admiral Voxx informed us that a majority of the Empire fleet also possessed this new weapon. We should assume that, by the time we are ready to attack, they all will have it, said Councilor Hiram.

We are still another month or two away from finishing the development of the particle beam cannons and the accelerator cannons. Then we must outfit all the ships with the new weapons. We are a good four to five months or more from being ready to attack the Human Empire, plus they destroyed 20 of our shipyards, so our shipbuilding will slow down as well, said Addonis.

That gives them time to build up their fleets and defenses as well, said Hiram.

We must make sure we are the superior fleet. In number, in weapons, and in tactics. We will rebuild our fleets, and then we will crush the Human Empire. Once they have been brought back to submission, we will deal with the Earth Humans, said Addonis.

High Princess Layla was meeting with the Visth and the United Worlds Alliance. They had supplied them with a few ODPs to protect their core worlds, with the promise of more as they became available.

She briefed them on the progress the fleets had made in the Confederation, destroying approximately 3,800 of the Morag fleet and twenty of their shipyards, as well as destroying planets Druin Nine and Lamothia.

They were very pleased with the progress that had been made. "The Morag will come back to exact their revenge, High Princess Layla," Stralon Karn, the Visth representative, commented.

"Yes, and we will be ready for them. With our Empire growing daily and our alliances strengthening as well, they will find it very difficult to destroy us," replied Layla.

"Thank you for your hospitality and for allowing us to observe the meetings of the House of Worlds. We have learned a lot and have a lot to do. We look forward to working with you more in the future," said Karn.

As Layla watched them get onto their ship, she couldn't help but feel hope for the future. They just had to find a way to make the future of the Empire a bright and peaceful one. She placed her hand protectively over her stomach. Now she had even more reason to hope for an end to this war with the Confederation. She wanted her child to grow up without fearing what the next day might bring.

She would do everything in her power to make sure that happened.

The Forgotten Empire: The Confederation and The Empire at War

Other Books by Raymond L. Weil
Available on Amazon

Moon Wreck (The Slaver Wars Book 1)
The Slaver Wars: Alien Contact (The Slaver Wars Book 2)
Moon Wreck: Fleet Academy (The Slaver Wars Book 3)
The Slaver Wars: First Strike (The Slaver Wars Book 4)
The Slaver Wars: Retaliation (The Slaver Wars Book 5)
The Slaver Wars: Galactic Conflict (The Slaver Wars Book 6)
The Slaver Wars: Endgame (The Slaver Wars Book 7)
The Slaver Wars: Books 1-3
-

Dragon Dreams: Dragon Wars
Dragon Dreams: Gilmreth the Awakening
Dragon Dreams: Snowden the White Dragon
Dragon Dreams: Firestorm Mountain
-

Star One: Tycho City: Survival
Star One: Neutron Star
Star One: Dark Star
Star One
-

Galactic Empire Wars: Destruction (Book 1)
Galactic Empire Wars: Emergence (Book 2)
Galactic Empire Wars: Rebellion (Book 3)
Galactic Empire Wars: The Alliance (Book 4)
Galactic Empire Wars: Insurrection (Book 5)
Galactic Empire Wars: Final Conflict (Book 6)
Galactic Empire Wars: The Beginning (Books 1-3)
-

The Lost Fleet: Galactic Search (Book 1)
The Lost Fleet: Into the Darkness (Book 2)
The Lost Fleet: Oblivion's Light (Book 3)
The Lost Fleet: Genesis (Book 4)
The Lost Fleet: Search for the Originators (Book 5)
The Lost Fleet (Books 1-5)
-

Raymond L. Weil

The Star Cross (Book 1)
The Star Cross: The Dark Invaders (Book 2)
The Star Cross: Galaxy in Peril (Book 3)
The Star Cross: The Forever War (Book 4)
The Star Cross: The Vorn! (Book 5)
-

The Originator Wars: Universe in Danger (Book 1)
The Originator Wars: Search for the Lost (Book 2)
The Originator Wars: Conflict Unending (Book 3)
The Originator Wars: Explorations (Book 4)
The Originator Wars Explorations: The Multiverse (Book 5)
The Originator Wars Explorations: The Lost (Book 6)
-

Earth Fall: Invasion (Book 1)
Earth Fall: To the Stars (Book 2)
Earth Fall: Empires at War (Book 3)

The Forgotten Empire: Banishment (Book 1)
The Forgotten Empire: Earth Ascendant (Book 2)
The Forgotten Empire: The Battle for Earth (Book 3)
The Forgotten Empire: War for the Empire (Book 4)
The Forgotten Empire: The Confederation and The Empire at War (Book 5)

All Dates are Tentative
The Forgotten Empire: War in the Confederation (Book 6)
(January 2022)
The Forgotten Empire: The Fall of the Confederation (Book 7)
(Late Spring 2022)

ABOUT THE AUTHORS

Raymond Weil lived in Clinton, OK with his wife, Debra, of 47 years and their beloved cats. He attended college at SWOSU in Weatherford, Oklahoma, majoring in Math with minors in Creative Writing and History.

His hobbies included watching soccer, reading, camping, and of course writing. He also enjoyed playing with his six grandchildren. He had a very vivid imagination, writing more than 47 science fiction novels over his writing career.

He was an avid reader and has a huge collection of science fiction/ fantasy books. He always enjoyed reading science fiction and fantasy because of the awesome worlds the authors would create. He was always amazed that he was creating these worlds too.

Julie Weil Thomas lives in Tulsa, OK with her husband Barrett and two boys. She attended university at the University of Oklahoma in Norman, OK where she received a degree in Finance with a minor in Accounting.

Her hobbies include watching her boys play numerous sports, reading, camping, and scuba diving. She got her imagination from her dad. She grew up listening to Raymond's many imaginative stories and watching anything and everything science fiction.

Julie is honored to carry on her dad's stories as best as she can. For as long as the fans are interested in reading the stories, Julie will continue to write in the worlds that her dad created.